Lin Oliver and Theo Baker

THE SHADOW MASK

THE SEQUEL TO *SOUND BENDER*

SCHOLASTIC PRESS ▤ NEW YORK

IN MEMORY OF DOC WATSON,
WHOSE MUSIC HAS GIVEN
ME SO MUCH JOY.
— L.O.

FOR ANARRES.
— T.B.

Copyright © 2013 by Lin Oliver and Theo Baker. All rights reserved. Published by Scholastic Press, an imprint of Scholastic Inc., *Publishers since 1920*. SCHOLASTIC, SCHOLASTIC PRESS, and associated logos are trademarks and/or registered trademarks of Scholastic Inc.

Library of Congress Cataloging-in-Publication Data

Oliver, Lin.
The shadow mask : the sequel to Sound bender / Lin Oliver & Theo Baker.
p. cm.
Summary: Leo's cruel and greedy Uncle Crane is forcing him to use his ability to hear sounds from the past to find and steal the other half of the mysterious Siamese twin mask that was once owned by Leo's father — or be separated from his younger brother forever.
ISBN 978-0-545-19694-9 (hardcover) — ISBN 978-0-545-51031-8 (ebook)
1. Extrasensory perception — Juvenile fiction. 2. Masks — Juvenile fiction. 3. Brothers — Juvenile fiction. 4. Orphans — Juvenile fiction. 5. Uncles — Juvenile fiction. [1. Extrasensory perception — Fiction. 2. Masks — Fiction. 3. Brothers — Fiction. 4. Orphans — Fiction. 5. Uncles — Fiction.] I. Baker, Theo. II. Title.
PZ7.O476Sh 2013
813.6 — dc23
2012022680

10 9 8 7 6 5 4 3 2 1   13 14 15 16 17/0

Printed in the U.S.A.   23
First printing, January 2013

The display type was set in Agency Thin.
The text type was set in Alisal.
Book design by Whitney Lyle.

The authors once again wish to thank our editors, Abigail McAden and Zachary Clark. Your insight and guidance have been extrasensory. Thanks also to David Saylor and Debra Dorfman for your creative vision and leadership, and to Ellen Goldsmith-Vein and Eddie Gamarra of the Gotham Group for their unwavering support.

While *The Shadow Mask* is a work of fiction, the records mentioned within this book are very real and can be found with a little effort. However, the authors do not necessarily urge our readers to look for them this time around.

Finally, the authors would like to thank all of our beloved readers, and especially those who took the time to send us a note about *Sound Bender*. Without their near-daily support, the authors probably couldn't have gotten out of bed.

PROLOGUE

My hands are trembling as I reach out to touch the ancient Japanese sword. Its curved silver blade glistens under my fingers. I am careful to avoid the razor-sharp edge. I close my eyes and prepare for what comes next. The jolt of electricity through my body. The surge of sounds in my head. The contact with a time long ago.

My heart beats fast. What will I hear? The shriek of a fifteenth-century samurai warrior as he charges the battle-field? Or the *whoosh* of the sword being drawn from its wooden sheath? Perhaps a cry of pain as the samurai plunges the blade into his opponent's flesh?

I wait. But I hear nothing.

"I'll thank you to keep your chubby paws off my precious possessions, Leo. That sword is six hundred years old and worth a small fortune."

It's Uncle Crane standing behind me. I don't know how

he crept into the Sword Room without my hearing him. Usually, the clicking of his expensive Italian loafers on the polished wooden floor announces his presence.

"Sorry, Uncle Crane, I was just . . ."

But he doesn't wait for my answer, just turns on his heel and leaves. That's how it is these days. It's been exactly one month since my parents vanished in a plane crash in Antarctica and my brother and I moved in with him. He swore to take care of us as our father entrusted him to do. But now, we don't speak except in anger. There is nothing between us but dead air. And my power, my newfound ability to touch objects and hear their past, is also dead.

It's been three weeks since we returned from the island, but it feels like forever. Three weeks since my defiance cost Crane the business deal of the century. And in those three weeks, my power to sound bend has all but disappeared.

Yet somehow, I feel it still lives inside me.

Waking up in the middle of the night, I can hear a faint echo in my ears. Dream sounds from within my head. A distant drumbeat. A wailing cry. A voice speaking in some ancient language. But then I come fully awake, and the silence returns. When I touch the gleaming Japanese sword or the prehistoric raptor fossil or the rare Martian meteorite, I hear nothing. Just three weeks ago, touching them would have produced a rich soundscape in my mind — the past, alive and calling to me. Now there is nothing.

Where is my power? Where has it gone?

I stand in the Sword Room and wonder, surrounded by silence.

CHAPTER 1

heard the door to my room click open and slam against the wall.

"Wake up, Leo! You're about to be famous." The voice belonged to my brother, Hollis, and he was sprinting right for me. "The guy on the news said they'd run the story after the commercial. Sit up, bro, and check it out."

I rubbed my eyes and rolled over. Things were pretty hazy. It took me a moment to comprehend that I was in my room in Uncle Crane's penthouse, staring up Hollis's nostrils as he worked the control panel above my bed like a video game. I knew it was incredibly early because I couldn't even hear the guys at the salami factory across the street loading up the trucks, and they're up earlier than roosters.

"Hollis, what the—"

Suddenly, the TV came on, the sound of the morning news blaring.

"Got it," Hollis said, and jammed himself into my bed, pushing me until I was crammed against the wall. "Pay attention, Leo, or you're going to miss it."

"Miss what?" I asked, but then I recognized the voice on-screen, and suddenly wide awake, I sat straight up. The voice belonged to Dr. Cabot — Becky — from the Center for Human/Dolphin Relations. From the moonlight shining on the deserted beach around her, I could see she was on the South Pacific island of Makuna, where I had helped her find a lost pod of dolphins.

An ultracaffeinated reporter named Jillian Scotto was shoving a microphone in Becky's face, grinning into the camera and trying to keep her sculptured hairdo from standing straight up in the tropical winds. Becky was in her usual cut-off jean shorts and golden bikini top, her blond hair blowing free in the breeze.

"If you're just joining us," Jillian said in her smiley voice, "I've been talking with Dr. Rebecca Caroll, a researcher at the Center for Human/Dolphin Relations, run by the eccentric Dr. Jay Lylo —"

"Hey," Becky cut in. "He's not eccentric . . . and that's Dr. Cabot."

"Right. So, Dr. Cabot has been investigating a mysterious pod of dolphins living off this remote island atoll, which, as you can see, still bears the scars of extensive military experiments. These dolphins appear to be related to several dolphins that were used here in a secret Russian military experiment in the 1980s."

"They are *definitely* related," Becky said firmly. "The dolphins living here are the direct descendants of the dolphins originally used in this experiment. We are trying to rehabilitate them and eventually return them to the open seas. Their parents should have *never* been used as soldiers."

"Dolphin soldiers?" Jillian asked Becky. "Did they carry special dolphin guns?"

"*Come on*, Jillian," Hollis shouted at the TV. "How stupid are you?"

Becky ignored Jillian's lame question and continued with her point.

"As part of this military experiment, the dolphins were forced to wear cybernetic helmets to help detect underwater mines and jam enemy sonar. After the military program ended, they were left here to die. And their descendants, malnourished and orphaned, have been living here ever since. We at the Center for Human/Dolphin Relations are firmly opposed to any nation using or experimenting on dolphins for military purposes."

"She did it," I said, and pumped my fist. "Becky said she was going to get cameras there to show the world what happened to those dolphins, and she really did it. How awesome is that, Hollis?"

"Very. And you were there, too, bro. You started the whole thing."

On-screen, a strong wind came gusting up and blew Jillian's scarf into her face.

"Well, it's certainly a . . . a . . . fascinating story, Dr. Cabot," she said, desperately fighting with the scarf and trying to keep her hairdo together. "At least it's . . . *different*. And let me give you a 'you go, girl,' for rocking that bikini!" she added.

Becky smiled and leaned into the microphone to say thanks, but the story quickly cut to stock footage of dolphins jumping through hoops and splashing around in a theme-park pool. Becky would have *hated* that.

"See, Leo?" Hollis said, clearly impressed. "You're a star. Too bad you can't take any credit for it. You'd be an instant legend at school."

"Yeah," I said weakly, suddenly aware of this sinking feeling in my chest.

A close-up of Jillian reappeared on the screen. She had apparently won the battle with her scarf, because now it was fastened neatly around her neck and tied off in a bow.

"This story actually has its origin in New York City," she said, pressing her earpiece, "and now we go live to our on-the-scene reporter Mike Hazel, who's standing by with his eye-witness report."

"Thanks, Jillian," Mike Hazel said. "I'm reporting to you from this dreary industrial waterfront in north Brooklyn."

"Look, Leo!" Hollis screamed, jumping to his feet on my bed and pointing at the TV. "That's Finkelstein's salami factory across the street. I bet they're right outside."

"Oh no," I muttered to myself, and hugged my chest.

"What do dolphins, Cold War experiments, and Russian spies have in common?" Mike Hazel asked the camera.

"This warehouse in Brooklyn for one, where the evidence of a Cold War experiment gone wrong was first uncovered. We're talking here about a strange, futuristic device, some sort of anti-sonar helmet meant to be worn by dolphins. It was found in one of the crates of the international import-export firm, Crane's Mysteries, a firm one of my sources has characterized as operating, quote, 'on the edge of the law.'"

"Yikes," Hollis whispered, and squinted at the screen.

"This is really bad," I said, my throat tightening.

I was the one who had discovered that dolphin helmet in Uncle Crane's warehouse. It was one of my first sound-bending experiences, and when I touched it, I heard the tortured cry of the dolphins. After that, there was no going back. I went all the way across the world to Makuna to uncover its secret. I had to. But I didn't stop there — I tossed that terrible helmet off a cliff and watched it shatter into a thousand pieces so it would never harm another dolphin again.

The problem was, I had stolen it from our Uncle Crane, and that little act of bravery had cost him a half-a-million-dollar sale to some of his Russian clients — and started the deep freeze between us.

"We tried to talk to the firm's owner, Crane Rathbone, earlier," Mike said.

Oh no. This was getting worse. The TV cut to shaky footage from earlier that morning of Mike Hazel pounding on the door to Crane's Mysteries — the run-down brick warehouse in Brooklyn with its slick and swanky penthouse apartment on the seventh floor. The same penthouse apartment where Hollis and I live, where we were now sitting together in my bed.

"Mr. Rathbone," Mike hollered, "this is Mike Hazel from Fox Five news. We just want to get your side of the story. Please open up, Mr. Rathbone."

The door opened a crack, and Klevko poked his head out, looking confused and tough. He's our uncle Crane's right-hand man who handles all his business, takes all his abuse, and, every now and then, provides a little muscle for Crane's shady operation.

"Mr. Rathbone," Mike said, "would you care to tell us how you happened to get a piece of classified Russian military equipment in your inventory?"

"Who is Mr. Rathbone?" Klevko said as he stepped outside and noticed the camera. "No Mr. Rathbone here."

"Well, then, sir, could you tell us how —"

Klevko just slid his finger across his neck and grabbed Mike by the collar with one of his beefy hands, while the other reached for the camera, his outstretched palm filling the shot. The camera shook, the footage blacked out, and they cut back to Mike.

"Wow!" Jillian said, cutting in all the way from her outpost in Makuna. "Looks like they're not talking. Do we know who first uncovered that dolphin helmet, Mike?"

"We're working on that, Jillian. My sources indicate that the helmet may have been found by a thirteen-year-old boy, a native New Yorker by the name of . . . Leon Loman. We've been unable to find this . . . Leon, yet."

I shut off the TV with a shudder. The room was silent for a long moment.

"Did that just happen?" Hollis asked. "You should at least call and tell them your name is Leo Lomax."

"I'm a dead man," I said, and held my head.

My phone buzzed on my nightstand. Hollis grabbed it.

"It's from Trevor," he said, reading the text. "He wants to know if you saw the story. What should I tell him?"

"Nothing. Just turn it off, chief." I grabbed the phone from him and threw it in my closet.

I rubbed my eyes and tugged at my hair, but what I really wanted to do was dive under the bed and start tunneling my way out. That story was bad news for me. Crane's business involved buying and selling rare and ancient artifacts, usually smuggled. He operated in deep secrecy. That's why we lived in this abandoned part of Brooklyn in this run-down warehouse—so no one would suspect that it housed six floors of priceless goods. Crane was going to explode when he found out that his company had been exposed on the local news.

And I knew he was going to blame me. He'd been looking for any excuse to nail me. That story gave him more than he needed, even though I'd had nothing to do with it. I had to think of something to tell him, some sort of story, but my brain was like Jell-O. I needed to talk to Trevor, who is not only my best friend, but also has more brain cells than there are stars in the sky. But there was no time. At any moment, Crane would be coming.

"He's going to be furious," Hollis said.

"No kidding."

"What are you going to do, Leo?"

"Find a spoon and start tunneling out of here."

"Wait . . . you know about the tunnel?" Hollis asked in a whisper.

I'd meant it as joke, but Hollis wasn't laughing.

"You don't know, do you?" he said. "Listen, Leo, I know a secret way out of here. Get dressed, and I'll meet you in the hall in thirty seconds. And dress warm, there's a north-eastern storm coming today — you know, one of those mini ice-crystal storms."

He'd meant *nor'easter,* but I didn't correct him. I could tell he was worried, and I knew what he was worried about. Crane had been threatening to split up Hollis and me, to send me to some terrible tough-love military academy. As long as Hollis and I were together, I could handle tough love.

But if Crane split us up, we'd both be sunk. We're all the family we have.

"I'll figure this out, Hollis," I called after him as he left my room. "I won't let Crane send me away. You and me, chief, we're stuck together like glue, like Chang and Eng."

Hollis glanced back at me briefly, nodded his head, and smiled. "The conjoined twins? Weird, Leo."

I got dressed in record time and met Hollis in the hall. We sprinted down the long white corridor that led from our bedrooms into the main rooms of the penthouse, jogging across the glass bridge into the Sword Room, which is actually filled with hundreds of antique swords. When we thought we heard Crane's footsteps, we ducked behind some cast-iron armor from the Middle Ages, but it was just Klevko's wife, Olga, already busy waxing the floors. Uncle Crane is obsessively neat, and so poor Olga has to obsessively clean.

"Hullo, boys," she said in her thick Polish accent when she saw us creeping by. "I left sweet buns in breakfast room. You go eat. Dmitri, he is there eating buns, too."

There was no time for sweets, and Dmitri was the second-to-last person in the world that I wanted to encounter. He's Klevko and Olga's son, a strange, sneaky kid the same age as Hollis. Dmitri also works for Crane, and I'm pretty certain that one of his main jobs is spying on me. I don't trust him one bit.

We smiled at Olga and scurried across the next glass bridge leading into the Mask Room, which contained totem poles, a full-size dugout canoe suspended with invisible wires from the ceiling, and walls and walls of terrifying masks.

"Watch this," Hollis said as we entered the semidark room. He walked up to a particularly monstrous wooden mask, half-human and half-monkey, with a giant dragon tongue snaking out from its menacing face. Clearing his throat, he spoke directly into its open, horrible mouth.

"My beloved mother, Marie," he said.

"You've officially lost it, chief," I whispered.

"You mean I found it, Leo. Look."

He pointed to the white stone wall near the ground. A three-foot-by-three-foot section of it was sliding back to reveal a small dark opening into a tunnel. Hollis pointed to a tiny electronic sensor behind the mask's mouth, blinking red.

"Voice activated," he said. "Dmitri told me the password. The kid will do anything for five bucks."

"Does it—"

"Yup. Leads to a secret stairwell. I wonder how Crane can even fit through it."

"I don't," I answered. "Like all rats, he has a collapsible skeleton."

Hollis scrunched up his face and made rat noises. But then I heard footsteps approaching, and I dove for the hole, grabbing Hollis by the collar on the way down.

As soon as we were both inside, huddling on the dusty floor, the secret opening shut automatically, and we were in total darkness.

"Motion sensors?" Hollis whispered.

"Must be," I answered, and searched my pockets for my phone to use as a flashlight, but in my haste to get out of there, I'd forgotten it in my closet.

More footsteps approached. They were clicking off the floors, walking slowly toward us. I knew it was Crane in his expensive Italian shoes. No one else's heels clicked like that. He was probably heading for our rooms.

"Follow me," Hollis said, turning on his phone to light up the tunnel.

I could barely make out Hollis's shoes in front of me, let alone my surroundings, but we appeared to be in a thin tunnel between the walls. I let my hand slide along the foamy insulation to see if I could channel anything, but no luck. My powers were still dead. I wondered if sound bending was a thing of the past for me. But there was no time to dwell on that—we needed to get to the ground. Stump would be waiting for us in Crane's black limo, just like every morning. If we could get there before Crane found us, I'd be home free.

"Here's the stairs to the ground," Hollis said.

A narrow metal stairwell was in front of us, disappearing down into the darkness. I could see a few old footprints on the first steps, surrounded by inches of dust. It might have been years ago, but Crane had used this escape route at least once.

"They look pretty rickety, Leo. We should go slow."

"No time," I said. "Crane's on our trail, I know it. Gimme your phone for a light."

Hollis chucked it to me, and I led us down the narrow stairwell. The stairs were metal and shaky—they seemed to be just an old fire escape built into the building. After the first few creaky flights, I went faster and faster until I was taking three at a time, this terrible dread growing in my chest.

My only thought: Get to the car, Leo, and everything will be fine.

I could figure everything else out later.

Finally, we reached the ground floor, just a small concrete landing with oily corners and a giant door with a push bar wrapped in chains. I cracked it open and felt a blast of freezing February air. We were around the corner from the front of the building, and I just barely saw the trunk of Stump's limo.

"I'll go first," Hollis said. "See if it's clear. Oh, and give me my phone back."

"Here. Thanks, Hollis, really. We'll be all right."

"No sweat, bro. Wish me luck."

Hollis strutted out into the gray morning and walked over to Stump's limo with perfect nonchalance. When he was halfway there, I couldn't wait any longer, so I slipped out of the darkness and crept toward the waiting limo, hiding in the shadows and behind garbage cans as I went. Stump was standing by the car, the door open, waiting patiently in his driving cap, his usual red plastic straw hanging from his mouth. Once Hollis was in, I broke my cover and walked with a fake confidence toward the open door of the limo.

I was within thirty steps. I could see inside it, the velvet upholstery glowing in the purple neon light. My adrenaline was pumping like crazy. I was going to make it! Crane wouldn't be able to touch me. I saw Hollis's legs inside, and I broke into a run.

Hearing me, Stump turned to face me, and I smiled at him from ear to ear. But he didn't smile back. He just chomped on his red straw frantically, looked at something behind me, then looked away. I stopped dead in my tracks.

I felt a hand on my shoulder.

"Not so fast, Leon."

Crane.

I didn't answer. I couldn't even move.

"Stump," Crane said from behind me. "Hollis is late for school."

Stump nodded, then looked me right in the eyes. His arm twitched, and he seemed to search for something in his pocket. He looked back at me again and opened his mouth, letting the straw fall from it.

"But what about—" he started.

"Go on, Stump," Dmitri said, suddenly emerging from the lobby and taking his place right next to Crane.

"Now, Stump," Crane said. Sharply.

Stump shrugged at me and adjusted his cap. Slamming the door, he ran around to the driver's seat, with Hollis pounding on the tinted windows and trying to open the locked door. The car sped off as Hollis popped his head out of the sunroof. I broke free and ran after him.

"Leo!" he shouted as the car disappeared around the corner.

All I could do was watch him go.

CHAPTER 2

After the car turned the corner and disappeared, I kind of lost it. I think I flailed my arms or something ridiculous like that, but I'm not really sure. I remember this sinking feeling, as if the ground was melting away beneath my feet. When I snapped back to myself, I realized I was staring into the darkness of a storm drain, and I had an eerie feeling that a very small part of me, like a miniature version of my body, had split off and fled down the sewer. I was missing something, something important, almost like I'd tossed my keys or my wallet down the drain.

Then I heard someone pick up my backpack and felt a hand on my shoulder. From the way the touch made me shudder, I knew it was Dmitri.

"Come on, Leo," he said, and pushed me back to where Crane was waiting.

Crane was standing in the middle of our desolate street, looking tremendously out of place in his expensive clothes amidst the crumbling buildings. I couldn't see his face, just the top of his shiny bald head as his fingers moved across the keyboard of his phone. He didn't even give me the courtesy of looking up, just had Dmitri guide me to him.

Don't show him any emotions, I told myself. Don't feel anything. I briefly considered jumping Dmitri, wrestling him to the ground, and then taking off. But where would I go?

"I didn't do anything, Uncle Crane," I said as Dmitri pushed me in front of him.

Crane ignored me as if I were completely invisible. Just kept typing on his phone.

"I had nothing to do with that thing on TV," I tried again.

"Oh, Leo," he said, still not even glancing my way. "I'm touched that you believe you hurt me and my business, but you think too much of yourself. You're a pesky mosquito at best. And I have trained myself to ignore itches."

"Are you going to send me to some boot camp? You promised you wouldn't split Hollis and me up if . . . if . . ."

Crane looked up from his phone. "Go on."

"If I helped you locate the other half of that Siamese twin mask."

"You remember. Good," he said, and returned his gaze to his phone. "Dmitri, go fetch your bag for school."

"Yes, Mr. Crane."

"Do you have your MetroCard, Leo?" Crane asked when Dmitri had trotted away.

"Yeah, I've got it," I said, and took out my wallet. "I can take the subway to school, no problem. I'll be late, but that's okay. So I better get started. Got a long walk to the subway station, but I could use the exercise. Glad we had this talk, Uncle Crane."

Crane threw his head back and laughed.

"Leon," he chuckled. "You're no longer enrolled at your old school. I've been so busy with my paperwork that it seems I forgot to send in your out-of-borough waiver. How foolish of me."

"I'm ready, Mr. Crane," Dmitri said as he walked up to us and put his hand on my shoulder. His grip was tight.

"You'll be going to school with Dmitri for the time being, Leo. No more of that lah-di-dah Academy of Science and Arts for you. No, now you'll get a chance to see what it's like when the world isn't handed to you. The way I was raised: fighting and clawing for every scrap I could get. Just like Dmitri here. Maybe then, you'll understand that you shouldn't bite the hand that feeds you, little Leon."

"You can't take me out of my school!"

"Really? I believe I already have."

"But—" I stood there with my mouth open.

"Don't worry, Leo. Dmitri will make certain that no school-yard toughs harass you for your milk money."

"Milk money?" I said blankly, repeating Crane as if I were dreaming.

Crane reached into his pocket, fished out a fifty-cent piece, and put it in my coat pocket, patting it twice.

"But, Uncle Crane," I stammered. "I said I would help you."

"That you did, Leo. Now I can be certain you will. I'll see you shortly at school for our meeting with the assistant principal. Until then, I have a lawsuit to prepare against your good friend Mike Hazel."

"Crane, I swear, I had nothing to do with that!"

"Enjoy your subway ride, little Leon," he said.

"Wait. Can't we ride with you?"

"Sorry, my dear nephew. My limo isn't available to boys who feel compelled to blab family secrets to the media."

Flashing me a crooked grin, he slithered off into the dank lobby of the building, hollering, "Klevko!"

"It's okay," Dmitri said to me. "I have a business at school, so I can buy you lunch today. After today, you'll have to work."

"What subway do we take to school?" I asked, removing Dmitri's hand from my shoulder. Even though I was being forced to ride with him, I wasn't going to let him shove me around.

"Crane is wrong. No subway. We take the bus. Two buses. But first, we run." Dmitri tossed my bag at me. "Follow me." He put on his beanie, then gave me a "friendly" sock to the gut. When I looked up, he was halfway down the block.

We took two buses to school, but all I could think about the whole time was how I could call Hollis. He had probably assumed the worst — that I was already on a plane, shipped off to Sergeant Hammerfist's Tough Love Academy for Troubled Youths somewhere in uncharted Alaska. The best I could hope for was that Stump had been in on Crane's plan and had let Hollis know I was okay. But I couldn't rely on Stump to be a decent human being anymore, not after he'd turned on me. No, I needed to talk to Hollis, to tell him personally that I was okay.

Dmitri was no help. He pretended to sleep on both bus rides, but I knew he was really watching and listening to everything I did because every now and then, when he thought I wasn't looking, he would crack open an eyelid. Don't show him anything, I told myself. Feel nothing.

Our bus arrived at Satellite North Middle School at 8:45 and pulled up behind Crane's waiting limo. We were so late that all the kids were already inside. When Dmitri and I approached the limo, the back door opened, and Crane got out. Dmitri scurried past him, ran up the steps, and through the front doors. Crane looked me up and down disapprovingly, then smoothed out my clothes with his hand.

"Your personal grooming leaves much to be desired," he said.

"You have to tell me, Crane," I said, rejecting his attempt to plaster down my unruly hair. "What are you going to do to me?"

"Leo, I've done nothing but fail to turn in some paper-work. A problem that can be easily fixed, if you have the right attitude. This isn't a punishment, but a chance for you to build some character, eh? Now let's get to our meeting."

We had to pass a security checkpoint and go through a metal detector to get inside the building. I only saw a few kids in the hallways, but they seemed much bigger and tougher than me. And although the halls were mostly deserted, they were ringing with echoes of walkie-talkie communications and distant voices and laughter that somehow seemed in a different key.

While we waited to see the assistant principal, Crane ducked out to take a number of phone calls, while I listened to Ms. Confalone, the school secretary, answer the phone in her no-nonsense Brooklyn accent. I tried to remain inconspicuous to the row of kids waiting on the "bad kid" bench, but that would have required a Romulan cloaking device. I knew they were watching me like hawks, and every now and then, one of them would say something in another language and gesture at me, and then they'd all laugh. When Ms. Confalone told me I could go into Mr. Dickerson's office, I was more than ready to go alone.

"Welcome to Satellite North, Leo," Mr. Dickerson said from his desk, hardly even glancing up from the file of papers in his hands. He had hairy hands, and he was a hulking man, seemingly much too big for his beige suit and small desk. He had a big round head, a forehead filled with worry lines and bushy eyebrows, a comb-over, and a giant veiny neck that made his collar button seem about to pop. I sat down.

"Just going over your permanent record, Leo. You've missed quite a lot of school lately."

"Yeah, um, my parents died a month ago. . . ."

"Oh yes, I see," he mumbled, and scribbled a few notes on the paper. "My condolences. And who is Crane Rathbone?"

"My uncle."

"And he's your guardian?"

I told him yes. Mr. Dickerson grunted, scratched his giant neck, and made more notes, while I just sat there twirling my shoelaces and looking at his collection of old model cars.

"You're almost half a semester behind, Leo. Think you can get caught up?"

"Definitely. But I'm not supposed to be here," I sputtered. "I go to the Academy of Science and Arts."

"Went to," he said. "Let's see. You've got a 72 average in Spanish and a 67 average in Math. . . ."

"But I have great scores in Music and Science."

He furrowed his brow and squinted at the paper, making a clicking sound with his tongue as he shuffled through more pages and scratched some more neck hair.

"Those are electives," he answered. "And I'm seeing lots of disciplinary write-ups, Leo. Care to explain?"

"Disciplinary write-ups? Let me see that file. I told you I'm not supposed to be here."

The office door opened and I heard the tail end of an argument outside, then Crane slid into the room.

"Forgive me, Mr. Dickerson," he said, patting me stiffly on my arm as he sat down. "Business. Yet I hope my absence gave you a chance to get to know my nephew."

"Indeed, Mr. Rathbone," he said, not even looking up. "Indeed. A mixed file, I would say. Slightly above average state test scores, some areas of proficiency, some areas that need much improvement, and an overarching disciplinary problem." He took out a calculator from a desk drawer and punched numbers into it for a really long time. "For a 75 percent overall average . . ."

"Average," Crane echoed him, and winked at me.

"But what about Science and Music?" I tried again.

"They don't factor in. Leo does show some promise, Mr. Rathbone, but he has a poor work ethic and a history of behavior problems."

"I've noticed the same problems myself, Mr. Dickerson. My nephew, here, needs discipline. I hope you can straighten him out."

"Well, we'll certainly try," he said, scribbling more notes.

"And please feel free to contact me directly if Leo acts up, especially any unexplained absences," Crane said, handing him a card. "Leo's education is my top priority."

The walkie-talkie on Mr. Dickerson's desk jumped with static, and a muffled woman's voice said something about a fight in the boys' bathroom. "On my way," he grumbled into it, and somehow managed to squeeze into his tiny sport coat. Then he closed up my file, shoved it at me, and told me to get my schedule printout from Ms. Confalone.

Mr. Dickerson hurried out in a huff, and I followed him, handing my permanent record to Ms. Confalone. I felt like some sort of criminal being admitted to a prison. As I waited for her to print out my schedule, Crane pinched my cheek and said, "Study hard, little Leon." This sent all the kids on the bench into hysterics. The damage done, Crane left without a good-bye. The kids continued to snicker, and one of them said, "Be a good boy, little Leon," in a high-pitched voice.

Ms. Confalone gave them a stern look. "Hey, you guys, knock it off. There's nothing funny here. You could try saying hello to the new kid."

No one did. Just more snickering. I pulled out my beanie from my coat pocket, put it on, and pulled it down low.

"Here you go, Leo Lomax," Ms. Confalone said, handing me my schedule and giving me a much-needed smile. I let myself smile back. "And swing by if you got questions. A new school can be tough. But you'll catch on. I got confidence."

"Thanks, Ms. Confalone," I said, scanning my schedule. I had English, Math, History, and Spanish, with Music and Science only once a week. And next to my name, it said "basic track."

"Ms. Confalone," I said, taking off my hat.

"That's me, Leo."

I got really close to her and showed her the paper. "It says basic track here, but I've always been in honors track."

"You think you're supposed to be in honors track?" she repeated, much too loud. All the kids on the bench cracked up and started saying things in another language. "Sorry, Leo, the paper says basic track. You'll have to talk to Mr. Dickerson about making the switch. Do you want an appointment?"

"Nah, don't bother," I said, putting my hat back on and pulling it down so low it practically covered my eyes. "Bye, Ms. Confalone," I said, and walked out.

"Bye-bye, honors boy," one of the kids teased.

"Look, there goes Leon the gifted child," another said.

A third said something in what sounded like Polish or Russian, and they all cracked up, their hyenalike echoes following me into the deserted hallway.

CHAPTER 3

had already missed most of my first-period math class. I had ten minutes before I was supposed to be in second-period History, which left me no time to waste. I had to get to a phone . . . urgently. I needed to talk to Hollis, to let him know I was okay — well, not okay, but at least alive and in New York. Funny, when our parents were taking care of us, I never worried about Hollis one bit. Never really gave him a second thought. He was just my pain-in-the-neck kid brother. Now that they were gone, my only thought was to get to a phone and hear the little punk's voice.

I raced up and down the main hall, its flickering fluorescent lights making the musty walls seem a sickly shade of yellow-green. I remembered seeing a pay phone in one of the hallways, but I couldn't recall where. Even if I found it, I'd still have to break that ridiculous fifty-cent piece to make the call. I thought maybe the cafeteria was open and would have change. I stopped and listened, my hearing particularly sharp like it sometimes was just before a sound-bending experience. Over the buzzing of the fluorescent lights, I heard the faraway clanging of dishes rattling against one another. I turned down a hall and followed the sound, which led me to double doors with a sign that read CAFETERIA. Peering through the small pane of glass, I saw a guy stacking dishes next to the food line.

I pounded on the window, and he looked up, then shook his head no. He didn't even know what I wanted, and the answer was automatically no. I thought of Kay, the cafeteria lady at the Academy of Science and Arts, who always let me in early to get a hot chocolate before first period. Already, after not even an hour in this dreary cave of a school, Kay and her cheerful smile seemed like a dim, unreal memory.

I wandered back to the main hall where I spotted a sheepish-looking kid with glasses, digging into his locker. He was smaller than me, so I approached him.

"Hey, do you have some change?"

He spun around from his locker and scanned the hallway, then looked me up and down, seemingly not understanding my question.

"Do you have two quarters for fifty cents?" I tried again.

"What?"

"I'm Leo. I need to break this fifty-cent piece to make a phone call."

"Oh," he said, closing his locker. "You're new here, right? Let me see that fifty-cent piece."

"Here," I said as I ground my teeth and reached into my pocket.

As soon as my hand opened my pocket, I felt a strange force. My muscles tightened and my fingers became claw-like, and as I thought of Crane putting that fifty-cent piece in my pocket to teach me a lesson, I felt a giant surge of anger course through me. As my fingers touched the metal, the ground beneath my feet seemed to lose its solidness, and in a flash, I saw myself in a kind of alternate version of Satellite North, like a secret underground version. Everything around me had lost its color and shape until all I saw was a series of hazy brownish hallways, looming over me, Crane's voice echoing through them. Just little fragments, one on top of the other, his voice filled with rage.

"Up the river, past the rapids . . ." his voice shouted inside my head. "No, no, it's a blind alleyway. . . . Those liars, those terrible liars . . . I'll find the other half, Mother, I'll find it and prove them all wrong. They're following me, I know it. They're out to get me. . . ."

"Let me see that," I heard the kid in the hall say. He snatched the half-dollar from my hand and took off down the hall. I snapped back to reality just in time to see him run past a bank of lockers and disappear around a corner. All I could do was stand there, dazed, trying to get my mind around the realization that my sound-bending power had returned.

"You jerk," I finally sputtered. I didn't chase him, though, just stared at my empty hand, in shock. My power had returned, but with an unfamiliar feeling to it. I'd never had a sound-bending trance like that one before. I'd never gone to that underground space.

As I looked around, trying to focus on where I was, I was suddenly overcome with all the sounds of my new school — blasts of walkie-talkie static, sneakers squeaking on the linoleum floors, snatches of distant laughter echoing through the deserted halls. It was as if my ears had opened up. Smiling, I leaned up against some lockers and took out my digital recorder from my backpack. Throwing on the headphones, I pushed *record* and listened to the symphony of sounds — the garbage truck backing up in the alley, the phones ringing in Ms. Confalone's office, the Jamaican school nurse talking in her lilting accent to a sick girl, a fire-truck siren wailing several blocks away, a Chihuahua yapping from an apartment window. It was so cool, a true combination of the sounds all around us that we never notice. I knew Hollis would love it, too — he was writing a new song for his band, and I had promised to record some city sounds for him to weave into the piece. This was perfect.

I was so immersed in the soundscape that I nearly jumped out of my skin when I heard a deafening blast of walkie-talkie static and felt someone taking off my headphones.

"Where's your hall pass?" a voice said.

I looked up at a bearded man in a security guard's uniform. He was almost as hulking as Mr. Dickerson.

"I didn't get one."

"Of course not, young man. Let's go."

"Where?" I asked as I tried to keep up with his officious pace.

"Where you always go for cutting: the assistant principal's office."

As we marched back into the school office, I pulled my beanie down.

"Got another one for you, Ms. Confalone. Found him in the hallway with some sort of electronic equipment."

"Already, Leo!?" she said, shaking her head. All the same kids were still on the bench, but they weren't laughing at me anymore.

"I just needed to make a phone call," I said, wrenching myself from the security guard's grip. "Listen, Ms. Confalone, I didn't know the rules, honestly. I just need to make a quick phone call. It's incredibly important. Can I use your phone?"

"Does my phone say, 'Help yourself, kids?'" she answered. "I don't think so, Leo."

"It'll just be one second, I swear. I need to let my kid brother know where I am. My parents died, and we're all we have. It'll take one second, I swear."

"Hmm . . . if it's short, okay," she said, bringing the phone to the desk. "Dial nine to get out."

"You're a lifesaver, Ms. Confalone. Real quick."

I stared at the numbers with a sinking feeling. Hollis's phone was brand-new, and I didn't know his number. Crane had just given him a fancy top-of-the-line model as a reward for being so . . . so . . . not like me. Hollis has a taste for expensive things, and much as I hate to say it, the kid has been known to be won over by the latest gadget. Crane knew that and used this weakness to try to win Hollis's loyalty. It didn't work all the time, but it didn't fail all the time, either. I kicked myself for never memorizing his new number.

So that left Trevor. And although I'd called him every day for the past four years, I kept his number on speed dial and rarely had to actually dial it. I remembered that there were some twos in it, and a nine, and a four-five-seven — or was it a seven-five-four? Ms. Confalone was eyeing me suspiciously, so I just trusted my fingers and punched the keys.

"Trev, it's me. I'm at a school in Brooklyn. You have to give Hollis a message. Tell him I'm okay, that I'm not at some military academy. Let's all meet up at Jeremy's after school. I might be late, but just wait for me, okay?"

"Who is this?" a man's voice said.

Blocking Ms. Confalone's view with my body, I discretely hung up and dialed again, repeating my speech as soon as the call was answered.

"¿Qué?" The reception was bad, so maybe I'd misheard.

"It's me, Leo. Trev, can you hear me? It's Leo. Can you hear me, Trevor?"

I saw Ms. Confalone look at me suspiciously, so I went on. "It's Leo, you hear me, Trevor?"

"Give me that phone," Ms. Confalone said, and snatched the receiver.

"Hello," she said into the receiver, glaring at me. "This is Satellite North Middle School. Do you know a young man named Leo Lomax? No? He just called you talking a bunch of nonsense? I'm sorry, sir," she said, hanging up the phone.

"Leo, you gave me a long story, and I did you a favor, and then you make prank phone calls and bother a nice old man?"

"I didn't mean to—"

"What's the problem here?" Mr. Dickerson's voice rang out from behind me.

"Mr. Lawrence caught Leo here cutting class. And then Leo had the nerve to beg me to use the phone to make prank calls."

"Off to a fine start, Leo," Mr. Dickerson said. He picked up my file from Ms. Confalone's desk and scribbled more notes into it. All the tough kids were watching me like predators, taking everything in. I knew that what I did next would cement my reputation.

"And I'm just getting started, Dickerson," I said, pulling my beanie down low. "That's a promise."

"Then you can start tomorrow at 6:30 a.m., Mr. Lomax," he said, ripping out a piece of paper and handing it to me. "Detention."

"What's your problem anyway?" I said, and snatched the paper. "You think you know me or something. I never had any problems till I met you. I'm just trying to be a person, but you guys are all over me. You don't know me. You don't know the first thing about me. You don't know what I'm capable of."

Mr. Dickerson furrowed his bushy eyebrows, scratched his gigantic neck, and, for the first time, looked me up and down. "What's that in your pocket?" he asked, referring to my digital recorder.

"Nothing."

"Take it out, Leo."

I pulled out my recorder and held it in my hand, and at the exact same moment, both our eyes were drawn to the steady red light. Oh no.

"You're not recording, are you, Mr. Lomax?"

"No," I said, my heart beating fast, but I controlled myself. Feel nothing, I told myself. *Feel nothing.* "No, red means standby mode; the green light means record."

As Dickerson paused to consider my lie, I smirked at the kids waiting on the bench.

"Because in the state of New York, Leo, it is illegal to record anybody without their knowledge."

"I know. It's not—"

"If I see that thing again, it's mine. Got it?"

Just then, the bell rang, and I heard all the doors open and the sounds of kids hollering and laughing and brushing up against one another and banging their locker doors.

"Got it. See you tomorrow, Mr. Dickerson," I said, and bolted for the office door. All the kids on the bench also left with me, and as I merged into the stream of rushing students and screams, one of the bad kids grabbed my arm.

"Nice one, Leo. Or is it Leon? That recorder was on, right?"

"You bet," I said. "Someone has to keep an ear on those jerks."

"Cool, man. I'm Pieter. We're going to cut third, too. Come find us by the basement stairwell, and bring that recorder. Later." They disappeared into the crowd.

"Those are bad kids, the sons of Ukrainian gangsters," I heard Dmitri say as he came up behind me and put his hand on my shoulder. I was actually kind of glad to hear his voice. He grabbed my schedule and examined it as we walked.

"I'll show you to class, follow me."

"Okay, dude. But first, show me to the library. I need to e-mail Hollis."

"No time. But I'll text him for you," Dmitri said, and pulled out a slick touch-screen phone.

"You didn't tell me you had a phone!"

"You didn't ask. What do you want to say?"

"Here, let me see that. I'll text him."

"No. Do not touch my phone."

"Fine. Just say that I'm alive and still in New York. And to get in touch with Trevor, and that we should all meet up at Jeremy's store after school. I might be late, but tell them to wait."

"Okay, Leo," he said, punching in the message. "That's what friends do. Who is Jeremy?"

"Jeremy Sebold. He was a student of my dad's. He owns a record store in Brooklyn, and I go there after school for tutoring."

"You get tutored in a record store? That's weird."

"My dad asked him to be in charge of my music education. See, my dad studied world music and taught at . . . never mind, Dmitri, it's a long story. . . . So, can you just hurry up and press send?"

"Sure. I'd like to meet Jeremy after school. We can talk about music from Poland. I will teach him all about polka."

"I think that's a pass, dude," I said as we turned a corner. "You don't have to go."

"We're going," he said. I didn't like the way he assumed he was in charge of me. "Here's your class. I'll be outside when it's over, then I'll buy you lunch and you can watch me run my business, so you learn how it works. Bye, Leo." Then he shoved me into the classroom.

Class was loud and boring. Mostly loud. Nobody even quieted down when I had to introduce myself and talk about my hobbies and interests. It was English class, and they were in the middle of discussing some book about a boy's dead dog, a book that clearly only one or two kids had actually read. I pretended to take notes, but really I was trying to plot a way out of this school, and maybe, to get Hollis and me out of Crane's clutches . . . possibly for good. Maybe we could stow away on a freighter to Panama. Or we could disguise ourselves as MTA workers, find one of those abandoned subway stations, and live underground for a while. I heard stories that tons of people live in those old stations. Bums and lunatics mostly, but maybe they'd look after us until it was safe on the surface.

After class, I was heading for the door when a girl with long, dark brown hair came up to me. She was one of the two kids who had read the book. I didn't have time to notice too much about her, except that she was pretty and wearing a strange necklace that looked like animal teeth hanging from a leather cord. It was the kind of thing my dad would always bring back from one of his music trips to some remote island. Behind the fangs, she also wore a tiny little heart locket on a silver chain.

"Hey, Leo," she said.

I was surprised she knew my name. I didn't think anyone in class was listening when I said my hobbies were setting world sports records and moth collecting. I wasn't about to give those kids any real info about me.

"You're not Leon Loman, the kid from the news, are you?" she said.

"They got my name wrong," I said, taking her into my confidence because she was the first friendly face I'd seen all morning, and besides, how could you not like someone wearing a necklace made of teeth? "But I'm the same guy. But don't tell anyone, okay?"

"I thought that was you. I'm Diana."

"I like your necklace, Diana. Are those real teeth?"

"Yeah," she smiled. "Canine teeth from Borneo. I live there."

"Really??"

"Well, sometimes. Beats this place, that's for sure." She laughed, then stopped herself short and looked at me curiously. "This might sound weird, Leo, but I swear I know you from somewhere. Where do I know you from?"

"Beats me. I don't know anyone here. Except for him," I said, and pointed to Dmitri, who was squatting against the wall outside of class.

"Ew. You hang out with him?"

"Hey, babe," Dmitri said, standing up and giving my new friend Diana the creepy eyes. "Feel my muscles."

"Gross," she said with a shudder, and got out of there fast. Dmitri seemed pleased. I just shook my head at him. You have to be pretty disgusting to gross out someone wearing a dog-tooth necklace.

Dmitri bought me a chicken sandwich from the cafeteria. I wolfed it down standing up as I watched him run his business. I'd been afraid that Dmitri would be selling cigarettes or something really bad to the eighth graders, but he mostly sold kids' stuff: candy, sodas, snap'n pops, pushpin slingshots, stuff like that. He kept everything behind a fake panel that he'd installed at the back of his locker. He also had old tests and homework worksheets back there, as well as two teachers' edition books, which I presumed were for sale, too. All told, Dmitri made $14 during lunch, which he slapped on top of a hefty bankroll hidden in his pocket.

I made it through the rest of the day without incident, just trying not to get noticed. After every class, Dmitri was always waiting outside to put his hand on my shoulder and guide me to my next class.

By the end of the day, it almost seemed normal for me to be attending Satellite North. Hadn't it been just yesterday that I was a student at the Academy of Science and Arts, hanging out with Trevor, watching Hollis play around with all the synthesizers in the sound lab, checking out books from the well-stocked library? It was just yesterday, but yesterday, I was a different person.

CHAPTER 4

By the time school let out, the nor'easter storm was moving in. It was almost dark out, but it was a strange darkness. The dry air was swirling with a frozen mist that made millions of little rattling sounds on the pavement. It was almost like the sun was blocked out, and the only light left was what was trapped beneath the clouds before they covered Brooklyn. The storm was just starting, but I could only see fifty or so feet in front of me.

"Seriously, Dmitri, you don't have to come all the way uptown with me," I said as we trudged down the school steps. "You probably have lots of work at the warehouse, right?"

"I'm not working at the warehouse today," he said to me with a half smile.

"So your work is to follow me around?"

"I'm just being friendly, Leo. Haven't I been a good friend today, buying you lunch, showing you to your classes?"

"Friendly, got it," I said, and walked faster, my boots crunching the thin layer of ice crystals on the sidewalk. I saw a blind alley a few feet ahead of me, and with the low visibility and the crowds of students piling out of school, I thought now might be a good time to make a run for it.

"Hey, Leon! Wait up!"

I turned to see the murky outlines of Pieter and his friends jogging up to us.

"Hey," Pieter said again. "Is that . . . is that *Dmitri* with you?! You're mine, Dmitri! And you, too, Leon!"

"Run," Dmitri said.

"Huh?"

"Just run. Follow me to the subway."

I didn't have time to try another plan because Pieter and his friends were racing toward us. Even though they were shouting at us in a language I couldn't understand, their voices were cracking in anger. We sprinted through the frozen mist, sliding on the concrete at times, weaving in and out of the Brooklyn blocks, all with half-seen gray figures on our trail and their bodiless voices all around us.

"Unhappy customers?" I panted as we slid into an alleyway and began to scale a chain-link fence.

"Just jerks. Their parents are Ukrainian gangsters, so I screwed them."

"Faster," I cried as we left the alley for an avenue, this somewhat fun chase through the ice mist becoming a little scary. But then my feet and calves tickled, and under my shoes I felt the reverberations of a subway train rumbling under the ground. "Look! There's the entrance."

We dashed for the glowing green light by the stairwell to the subway, cutting across the traffic, hydroplaning down the stairs, and nearly knocking over everyone on our descent underground. It was warmer down there, and as we reached the bottom of the stairs, I heard the ferocious drumming from a subway musician echoing through the tunnels. In one swift movement, I pulled out my wallet, got out my card, slid it through the reader, and went through the turnstile. Dmitri just hopped over it.

"Think we lost them?" I asked as we broke into a jog, and sweat poured out of me because of the stifling heat underground.

"I don't think so."

"Yeah, I hear them, too. Follow me, we'll take the 5 all the way uptown."

Even though I'd never been in that particular station, I know the subway system like the back of my hand.

"Just try not to run," I said, "or the cops will stop us."

I led Dmitri on a wild and crazy path to the 5 train, going through tunnels under the tracks just to take another tunnel back to the other side, running up stairwells and taking the escalators down, zigzagging throughout the subway station until I was dizzy. We passed three guys playing plastic-bucket drums and a dazed-looking dude playing the bongos, no doubt accompanying some frenzied voice in his head. As we ran, the drumming from the subway musicians played like a theme song over the chase, sometimes distant and far away, sometimes deafening and right on top of us.

We got to our platform just as the train lights showed in the tunnel. The brakes screeched, drowning out the bucket drummers as we jumped on board and blended into the crowd of straphangers. Outside the train window, I could see Pieter and his friends running up and down the subway platform, looking for us. I put my hood on, pulled my beanie low, and hunched down, staying that way until we were clear of the station and deep underground. We'd made it. We were free, and I felt amazing.

So did Dmitri. He stood up, stretched, and puffed out his chest, staring at his reflection in the dark window the whole time. Even though he was definitely not what you'd call a good-looking kid, with his greasy hair and crooked teeth, he seemed pleased with what he saw. He smiled and grabbed my arm, squeezing my muscles.

"Not bad," he said. "You're pretty fast for being so chubby. We'll make a good partnership."

"Yeah, Dmitri, but we won't last long if those guys chase us every day. What'd you do to them anyway?"

"I sold those Ukraine dogs fake tests. So they all got Fs and got caught for cheating, too."

"Dmitri, why are you conning the princes of the Ukrainian Mafia?"

"Because they killed my grandfather. They shot him in the back like cowards. That's why my family had to leave Yugoslavia."

"I thought you were Polish?"

For the entire hour-and-twenty-minute ride, Dmitri opened up to me like the Grand Canyon. How his family had defected from Poland before the Berlin Wall came down, how they lived in Yugoslavia, but then had to escape from the civil war, the spies, the Mafia entanglements, his grandfather's murder. His parents fled to South Africa, to Greece, to Turkey, just trying to find work and a little peace. It was in Turkey where Klevko met Crane, who was on an expedition to the underground city of Derinkuyu. Dmitri wasn't alive for most of that—Crane brought them over to the States when he was three—but I was starting to get him. He had a lot of anger and mistrust, and he admired Crane more than anyone else. I guess that was natural. After all, Crane had taken them in and given them a place to call home.

Even though it appeared that I was giving Dmitri my full attention, I was also planning a way to ditch him before we reached Jeremy's store. I needed a window alone with my friends and Hollis, so we could figure out how this whole news story broke, how to get Hollis and me back together, and maybe how to get us away from Crane for good. I wasn't crazy about double-crossing Dmitri, but I knew that he was playing the same game as I was, and that he would double-cross me first chance he got.

It was almost completely dark when we got out. The frozen mist was thick and chaotic in the howling wind with ice crystals several inches thick in some places. Cars streamed by on the streets, nearly invisible except for their muted yellow and red lights. It was strangely quiet out, too, muffled. The nor'easter storm made everything sound far away and indistinct.

"It's only a couple blocks from here, Dmitri."

"No problem," he shrugged, putting on his beanie.

"Let's play a game," I said, and then as swift as a kung fu master, I pulled his hat over his eyes and socked him a "friendly" punch to the gut.

"Oooh," he grunted, and hunched over, but I was already a ghost.

I dashed down the sidewalk, cutting across intersections, weaving through the blocks so Dmitri couldn't sniff out my trail. Miniature ice crystals stung my face. I felt great running, and felt even better when I spotted Jeremy's shop and the orange light illuminating the crummy hand-painted sign, RPM RECORDS. Someone was home.

The door jingled when I threw it open. There wasn't any music playing in Jeremy's shop today, but the voices of Hollis and Trevor were better than music. They shouted my name, smiling ear to ear, and came rushing over to me. Jeremy followed, his ponytail all twisted into a gnarly knot. He always wound it around his finger when he was nervous. One look at him and I knew that he had been worried about me.

"W-we only h-have a l-l-little time," I stammered, freezing. "I d-ditched Dmitri, he thinks I'm p-p-playing a game. . . ."

"Here, Leo, wear my jacket," Trevor said, and wrapped his puffy jacket around me. Trevor was at least a head taller than me, and his jacket came down to my knees, but I was grateful for the extra coverage. Hollis gave me a huge hug, crushing my hands against my chest so that I couldn't even hug him back.

"D-d-dmitri will find us, soon —"

"Leo, just relax and warm up," Jeremy said. "Hollis filled me in as much as he could."

"But, I have to get it out before Dmitri —"

"We're already working on it, Leo," Jeremy said. "I've been calling your old school since noon."

"Can you get me back in there?" I asked.

"Yes . . . well, maybe . . . eventually."

"Even if he can, we still have Crane to worry about," Trevor said. "We've been looking at your parents' will for the past hour. Your dad left a copy here with Jeremy."

"So far," Jeremy continued, "we haven't found anything that would let us change his decisions for your school."

"Maybe we need to get out of Crane's place altogether," I said. "What do you think, Hollis?"

"That wasn't cool what he did this morning," he said, not entirely convinced that we should pick up and go. As I searched his face, I realized how traumatic the whole day must have felt for him. First, our parents' disappearance in a horrible plane crash, then a wrenching move to our step-uncle's strange home, and now an abrupt separation from me, the only real family he had left.

"I agree with you, Leo," Jeremy said. "Crane's is not the place for you guys. But we haven't found anything your uncle —"

"Stepuncle," I corrected.

"Got it. Crane hasn't done anything illegal or that violates the will. But if we find something, or if Crane gives up his custody of you guys —"

"Then they're going to send us to a foster home," Hollis said, his voice tight as if there were rubber bands around his vocal chords. "And probably not the same one."

"No one's going to a foster home," Jeremy said firmly. "You guys hear me? I won't let that happen. Hollis, forget I ever mentioned it. And you guys can stay with me for as long as it takes."

"And you can stay with us, too," Trevor said. "I know my mom and dad will say it's okay."

"Thanks, Trev," I said as I slapped him five, and held on for a moment longer than usual. "I still don't get it. I mean, we don't have a lot of family, but why in the world did our parents pick Crane?"

"Money?" Hollis guessed.

"That can't be right," I said.

"I knew your dad as well as anyone did," Jeremy said, stroking his beard, "and I can tell you money didn't mean much to him. He and your mom, they valued experiences more than anything else. But this will is so strange — it seems like they only made it up six months ago."

"Well, I don't care what the stupid will says," I proclaimed. "Hollis and I aren't going to Crane's tonight. Not after what he put me through today."

"Cool, I'll call my dad right now," Trevor said.

"Slow down, guys," Jeremy said. "It's not going to be that easy. You're going to have to hang on a little longer. Crane is your legal guardian, and he knows his rights. And since he won't return my calls, I have to assume he still wants you guys in his care. He'll definitely make life impossible for all of us if we don't play this whole thing exactly right. It's going to take patience, and there'll be lawyers involved, and —"

The bells on the door jingled.

"That's Dmitri! He found me," I cried, and bolted past Jeremy's desk for the back room where Jeremy stored all his special records. "Tell him I'm not here."

"Don't get my records wet," Jeremy called out to me as I kicked the door closed behind me. It was pitch-black in the back room, and I hadn't gone more than two feet before I crashed into a wall of invisible records, so I crouched by the door and listened.

"Am I late for work, boss?" a muffled voice asked. I recognized it as belonging to Jeremy's one and only employee, a guy we affectionately refer to as Stinky Steve. As Crane would say, his personal grooming leaves something to be desired.

"Steve!" Jeremy hollered. "It's five o'clock! I'm about to close. And are you really wearing shorts?"

"The day I wear pants is the day I die. Want me to wear a suit and tie, too? Never! You're just a secret yuppie, Jeremy. Admit it."

Jeremy knocked on the door and told me that it was safe to come out. I poked my head out and immediately the

Stinky-Steve Scent wafted across the room and up my nostrils.

"Leo!" he shouted. "How goes it, big guy? You're famous, man, all over the news. Can you believe it, the famous Leon Loman in our store?"

"You saw the story?" I asked.

"You bet. Saw it at 7 a.m. and then the repeat at noon. Mike Hazel told me it'd be on today. Yeah, that's right. I spent all yesterday afternoon with him. Not to brag, of course."

"What?!" I bellowed.

"Yeah, I had him over at my house. I've known him for years. He's always at the WFMU record fair — he's the weirdo always wearing the jacket that says 'Rafferty' on the back."

"You're kidding. Mike Hazel is the mysterious Rafferty Man!" Jeremy cut in, shocked. "Man, you'd never know it to look at him on the news."

"He acts like such a tough guy, beating down people's doors and stuff. But the guy's obsessed with Gerri Rafferty, the wimpy king of the soft-rock ballad. Man, you just never know — there's no accounting for taste."

"What did you tell him, Steve?" I demanded, although I already knew. Stinky Steve and his runaway mouth.

"Oh, just about how you found that helmet in Crane's warehouse. He knew the rest. I was so proud of you for helping save those dolphins that I thought, 'Hey, my man Leo deserves a little credit.' But I made sure to give Mike a fake name to protect your privacy."

48

"And 'Leon Loman' was the best you could come up with?" Jeremy said, slapping his forehead.

"This is awful," I groaned. I held my head and tried to breathe deeply, but Steve's stench had spread itself thickly around the shop.

"What's the prob?" Steve asked. "I thought you'd like the attention. Besides, Mike promised to mention RPM Records on the air for the info I gave him. You know, quip pro qualm."

"That's quid pro quo," Trevor said. "It means 'this for that' in Latin, in case you were wondering. And by the way, he didn't mention the shop."

"I guess Mike's not such a stand-up guy after all," Steve said.

I shivered violently, from the cold or the deep mess Steve had gotten me into, I couldn't say. Jeremy tossed me his wool scarf from the chair.

"Steve, make yourself useful," he said, and handed him five bucks from the register, "and get Leo some soup from the diner. And don't say anything else to anyone."

"Sure thing, boss. I don't know the soup special today, but they usually have lentil and creamed corn chowder and on Tuesdays they have that Mexican meatball soup, *albondigas*. I love that word. *Albondigas*."

"It doesn't matter, Steve," I snapped at him. I had about twenty meaner things I wanted to say, but I held them in.

"Just go," Jeremy told him. "And hustle for a change."

"I don't know why you're so tense," Steve said to him. "I just came by to tell you I found this note in a record you traded me last week. It was a Hungarian record, kind of garage pop with some prog leanings, the one where all the guys in the band are in a cave or some such. . . ."

"I know the record," Jeremy said flatly.

"Yeah, so I found this note in the jacket. It was made out to you. Here," he said, handing it to Jeremy, his stench rising every time he moved. "Okay, I'm off." The door jingled.

Jeremy tossed the note on his desk, while I glared at the door, seething with anger at the thought of Stinky Steve. He had caused all of this. Made Crane turn on me and ruin my life. I hated Crane so much. And I hated my parents for leaving us with him. I hated my parents for leaving us at all.

"Hey, look at this," I heard Hollis saying as he picked up the note from Jeremy's desk. "That's Dad's handwriting."

As he handed it to Jeremy, I caught a glimpse of my dad's distinctive handwriting and the green ink he always used. My thoughts froze and my eyes bore down on the note in Jeremy's hand.

"You're right, Hollis. It's a note from Kirk . . . I mean, your father."

"Let me see that." I snatched the card from Jeremy.

As soon as I touched it, everything changed. My head spun and the ground felt as if it were opening up. I had the sensation of slipping underground . . . into an underground record store where and all I could make out were hazy stacks of records piled as high as the ceiling and all arranged like a complex maze. The whole shop seemed to fill with the howling frozen mist from the storm outside, gray and frigid. From some of the mazelike rows of records, a black inky substance began to pour into the mist, carrying with it the voices of my parents, distorted and fragmented, little snatches of conversation playing on top of one another, with no rhyme or reason.

"I just have this feeling. . . ." my mom said.

"They're insisting. . . . Bertie says we have no choice. . . ." my dad answered. "We'll hide underground . . . in the interior. . . . Little pockets of life exist there, with vegetation and moss and lichen. . . . You read what Bertie sent. . . ."

". . . It could be years. . . ." my mom said, her voice crying now. "They'll have enough to last years if we're stuck. . . ."

". . . That's the plan." My dad's voice was firm. ". . . catch a plane . . . over the icebergs . . ."

". . . What'll we do in Antarctica all that time?"

The last voice I heard was my dad's. "It could be years . . . or never. . . . The plane is rigged to . . ."

The room started to spin, and their two voices merged into one until I could no longer make out what they were saying. It was too much. My hands shook, and as if driven by some deep self-protective reflex, I dropped the note, my knees going wobbly.

CHAPTER 5

When I came out of the trance, I was staring right into Hollis's green eyes. His nose was less than five inches from mine. I knew I had only been gone for a few seconds, but from the expression on Hollis's face, it seemed like he didn't recognize me.

"Leo," he whispered. "What's going on?"

I blinked my eyes hard and rolled my neck. "Nothing, bro. I just didn't feel well for a second. Lousy school-cafeteria food, probably."

Hollis didn't buy it. He stared right at me, and I felt him searching my face for clues.

"You didn't look sick. You looked . . . I don't know . . . like you had gone away. Like you weren't here."

I had my reasons why I hadn't told Hollis yet about my sound-bending power. I told myself I had to wait until I fully understood the power myself. I thought Trevor with his great science brain and I would work on figuring it out, test its limits — then I would tell Hollis in a clear and scientific manner. But the truth was — is — that the real reason I didn't tell him was that I didn't want to scare him. I couldn't have him believing that I was something different than he thought I was, not when I was all he had to cling to these days. That just wasn't fair.

"What's the note say?" Trevor asked, and I shot him a thankful look.

He took the card from my hand and read it aloud, Hollis looking over his shoulder at the words.

"'Jeremy,'" he read. "'Thought of you when I found this, because I know you're collecting Hungarian records right now. I think you'll enjoy it. Kirk. And P.S., you still owe me that Spiricom record.'"

"That's it?" Hollis asked.

"That's it," Trevor answered, and handed him the card. Hollis held on to it, his eyes welling up with tears as he looked at our dad's handwriting. I knew the feeling; I had to fight back tears myself. It's like you're hoping for a message, a word, a sign, a clue, any communication from the person who is gone.

Hollis turned the card over and examined it carefully.

"Look," he said. "This is a business card. It says, 'Bertrand Veirhelst: Belgian diplomat. Dad didn't know any Belgian diplomats, did he, Jeremy?"

"Beats me," Jeremy answered. "Your dad knew a lot of people, some of them were bound to be Belgian diplomats."

I had been listening to the conversation, but half of my

mind was also replaying what I could remember of those fragments of my parents' voices. I was trying to arrange them into a real conversation that made sense, and when I heard the word *diplomat,* suddenly it started to click. Was the "Bertie" my dad mentioned really "Bertrand"? Maybe he wasn't really a diplomat? I'd seen a ton of spy movies where the diplomats were actually spies. What if my parents were involved in some sort of international plot? Nah, that was crazy. But then so was the way their plane disappeared, an innocent flight to Antarctica for a musical performance and then nothing, no trace of them or the plane. No radio signals. No SOS or calls of Mayday from the plane. Just radio silence, complete radio silence, and my parents were gone forever. The official story of their disappearance never made sense to me. How could a whole plane just vanish like that? Maybe there was more to it. Maybe they were still alive. . . .

"So what's that Spiricom record, Jeremy?" I cut in.

Jeremy tugged at his beard and seemed to fumble for words. "It's nothing, just this stupid record I was always promising to give him. Did he ever mention it to you, Leo? Because he was always bugging me for it. It's really not that . . ."

"Did you ever give it to him?"

"Uh — uh — I'm not sure, Leo. He gave me that cave album six months ago, or so. . . ." Six months! I thought, exactly when he wrote his will.

"Where is the record?" I asked.

"Maybe I still have it, I don't know."

Jeremy looked down and nervously fidgeted with the handmade silver ring he always wore. He'd been our tutor for over a year, and he always answered our questions truthfully, no matter what we asked. It wasn't like him to avoid a subject.

"Will you look for it, Jeremy? I mean, if it was that important to my dad, I'd like to hear it."

"Leo, there's twenty thousand records in my back room."

"It's really important to me."

And it was, suddenly. Maybe that record would tell me something about the trip to Antarctica, about the crash, maybe give me a clue to their secret life, if they had one. Jeremy could tell I wasn't going to let the subject go.

"Okay, Leo. I guess I could take a peek," he muttered nervously, and scurried off into the back room.

"He's lying to us," I said as soon as he'd left.

"And you're lying to me," Hollis said, looking at me with eyes that said, "Who are you?"

"I'm not exactly lying," I said to him. "Just leaving a few things out."

"Whatever is going on here, Leo, you should tell me," Hollis said, his voice cracking with anger. "Everything that's happening to you is happening to me, too. I have a right to know. I'm not just your stupid baby brother."

I looked over at Trevor. He was nodding.

"He's a smart kid," he said. "He'll handle it."

"Handle *what*?" Hollis was yelling now.

"Okay," I said, taking a deep breath. I'd practiced this speech a hundred times, trying to figure out the best way to tell him, so he would believe me, so he wouldn't be hurt or confused, so he could believe that I was the same brother he'd always known. I'd had it all worked out in my mind, but when I was face-to-face with him, I couldn't remember where to start.

"We don't have a lot of time, and I'll talk to you more about this later, but you know how I found that dolphin helmet in one of Crane's crates?" I began.

"Yeah," he said sarcastically, rolling his eyes.

"Well . . . I didn't just find it by luck. I have this . . . this ability, or power."

"Power? Oh, great. Meet my brother, Spider-Man."

"Hollis, just listen. I can hear sounds from the past. When I touch certain things. It's this type of psychic ability. I know this sounds weird, but you have to trust me that it's true. Remember that package I got that first day we moved into Crane's?"

Hollis didn't answer. He looked at me as if I was a stranger and he was a lost child.

"You remember," I continued. "It was from Dad. He'd sent it years ago. . . ."

"Shut up, Leo," Hollis snapped. "Just shut up."

"Hollis, listen. Inside the package was a letter about how I was actually born on an island in the South Pacific, and how their holy man initiated me into the island's tribe and gave me a new name. Dad included a strange blue disc, which had a recording of my naming ceremony, and after I listened to it, suddenly I had this new power. This ability.

I can hear the past, just by touching things. I know it's hard to believe, and I'm sorry I kept you —"

"Trevor," Hollis said, deliberately looking away from me. "What's wrong with Leo?"

"Nothing, as far as I know," Trevor said. "He's telling the truth. I don't believe in magic, and I think he should be examined in a lab, but I've seen him sound bend with my own eyes. He's not lying to you, and I'm pretty sure he's not sick or crazy."

"Hollis, think it over," I said. "Think about everything that happened right when we moved in. You'll know I'm telling the truth. I had to lie to you, because this ability is powerful and we don't understand it yet. I'll prove it to you. I'll show you the letter and the blue disc with my ancestral name. But you have to promise not to tell anyone. Not a single soul."

"Don't worry, Leo, I won't tell." He laughed uncomfortably. "I don't want to brag about the fact that my brother is a total mental case."

"I'll tell you everything about it, I swear. You have to believe me."

The door jingled, and a howling wisp of ice crystals swirled into the warm store, followed shortly by the stench of old water and eggs.

"*Albondigas* time!" Steve shouted, holding the take-out bag triumphantly over his head. The soup smelled pretty rotten. Or maybe it was Stinky Steve. Or maybe both.

Hollis walked over to Steve to take the soup — probably

just to get away from my gaze. He hadn't gone three feet when he stopped dead in his tracks.

"*Oh*, hey, Dmitri," he said, and my heart stopped beating. "When'd you get here?"

My eyes flicked all over the store, and finally I saw Dmitri's head poking above a rack of records. He was sitting on a ledge by the door. I only saw his face, his pulled-down beanie, and his beady eyes, black like shards of obsidian. He wasn't covered in ice crystals like Steve, and he didn't seem to be cold. How long had he been hiding there? Had he heard everything? Would that little spy take everything he knew directly to Crane? Feel nothing, I chanted to myself. Feel nothing.

"What took you so long, Dmitri?" I tested.

"I called Stump to come get us," he said, ignoring my question. "He wants us in the car right now. The storm is getting worse, and he still has to drive home one of Crane's associates."

"Dmitri, do us a big favor and tell him they'll be right out," Trevor said in his deepest voice, one that almost sounded like his puberty voice.

"Hey, what about the *albondigas*?" Steve said.

"I'll drink it," Dmitri said, and snatched the bag, looked around the store in quick suspicious glances, then headed outside to the parked limo.

"How much did he hear?" I whispered to Trevor as soon as he was out of earshot.

"Keep it together, Leezer," Trevor answered. "Dmitri probably just came in with Steve. We would have heard him. Just keep cool. Even if he heard something, I doubt he could put it all together."

"Yeah," I said, but I didn't believe him. "Hollis, not a word to Dmitri."

Hollis pursed his lips and shrugged.

"Hey, what's up, guys?" Steve said, confused by our nervous huddling, and suddenly without the soup. "And where's Jeremy?"

"Right here," Jeremy said. For a brief moment before the door closed, I could see into the back room, and not a record was out of place. I don't think he had looked through them at all.

"You find the record?" I said, half asking, half accusing.

"No, but don't worry about it, Leo. It's just this stupid record. Guys, keep your heads down, stay out of Crane's way, and come here after school every day until we figure this out. You guys gonna be okay till then?"

"I am," Hollis snapped. "Leo's the one you have to worry about."

Dmitri stuck his head in the door.

"Stump's about to lose it," he called.

"You guys better go," Trevor said.

"Come on, Trev," I said. "I'll get Stump to drop you off, he owes me one after driving off without me this morning."

We left the shop for the cold, dry icy air. The ice crystals were a foot thick in places, and the way the wind tossed them it was impossible to tell whether the ice was falling from the sky or being picked up from the ground. It sort of reminded me of footage I'd seen of inland glaciers, where the air is so dry there's no weather systems, only frozen ice being blown around. We ran for the open door of the limo, glowing purple inside, and slammed it. Dmitri was sitting up front with Stump, drinking his soup straight from the container. In the back, there were three cups of steaming hot chocolate in the drink holders.

Just as I took my first sip, Stump lurched the limo forward, and I burned my mouth.

"Stump, you're killing me," I said after swallowing a mouthful of scalding hot chocolate. He didn't say anything, but he kept glancing at me in the rearview. "And thanks for this morning, too," I added. "That was a real gutsy move, buddy."

"Sorry about that, kid. I've been feeling rotten about that all—" But then he stopped, and I noticed Dmitri giving him a strange stare. His tone of voice changed immediately. "Just doing my job," he added quickly. "You understand. I gotta eat, right?" He looked at Dmitri who had just fished a meatball out of the container and was gorging on it.

"Guess so."

We drove at a snail's pace. Through the tinted windows, everything was dark smoke and ice and the occasional dim light blinking or swirling by like some sort of energy creature. Stump kept trying to gun it, but then the tires would spin and the engine would make a grinding sound. From what I could see, the city seemed deserted. And it was so quiet. The only sounds were the ice crystals hitting the windshield, the engine revving every now and then, the howling but muffled wind outside that seemed almost half alive, the tires crunching, and our slurping sounds and "ah's" as we drank. I recorded it all until we dropped Trevor off.

"See you tomorrow, Leez. Text me back this time."

All the bridges were closed, so Stump took the Midtown Tunnel to Brooklyn, but so had everyone else still on the road. I'd never been sure about the tunnel, whether it went underneath the riverbed altogether, went along the floor of the riverbed, or was just a tube going through the water. Whatever the case, we were stuck forever. Stump kept muttering and cursing under his breath, but Hollis and I were silent. We couldn't talk with Dmitri around, even though he was pretending to be asleep. Maybe it was better that way. We both had a lot to think about. Hollis, I'm sure, was trying to figure out how he could rely on me when I turned out to be a completely different person than he'd imagined, someone completely unfamiliar.

But this was feeling familiar to me. I had a fleeting sensation that all these events outside of my control were connecting, starting to line up, in a way I couldn't yet explain. I felt like even though I was sitting in Stump's limo, a different part of me was somewhere else. I didn't know where my life was leading, just that I felt a strong pull in an unknown direction.

When we finally made it out of the Midtown Tunnel, it was a complete whiteout.

CHAPTER 6

As the limo rolled at a tank's pace into our neighborhood, the scene outside the window reminded me of an Antarctic outpost in the dead of a polar night. I didn't let myself imagine that for long. We pulled up in front of Crane's Mysteries, and before we had even come to a full stop, Klevko came running out of the building in a short-sleeve T-shirt. When he reached out to grab my shoulder, I flinched like a frightened puppy, remembering his rough handling of Mike Hazel. But Klevko was just being affectionate, and anyway, maybe Mike Hazel deserved Klevko's rough handling for digging around in other people's lives.

"Beautiful weather, beautiful," Klevko sighed, and stared off dreamily. "Reminds me of my childhood in Poland. Cold weather warms the soul, no?" It must have warmed his, because he was dripping sweat. He led us into the tiny lobby with its old-fashioned metal elevator. He opened the small door to the basement apartment where Klevko, Dmitri, and Olga lived.

"Matka made you delicious soup with ground meat, Dmitri. Go eat," he said, tousling Dmitri's crew cut as he disappeared through the little door into their dingy basement apartment. But as soon as Dmitri was inside, Olga came rushing up to the little door, hollering at Klevko in Polish. Klevko bent down and hollered back at her, and they began a tremendous argument, all in Polish. At one point, Olga even stuck her wooden spoon through the little door and shook it threateningly. They argued and wrestled over the spoon until Klevko was able to jam both it and Olga's voice back inside. He closed the door.

"That woman never leaves me alone. I have such a pleasant evening. I see you boys come home, and enjoy the nice weather, and as soon as I go inside, *whack*." He smacked his hands together to illustrate.

Hollis and I just watched in amazement. Our parents rarely argued, and when they did, it was usually over what music to put on during dinner. And·there was certainly never any wooden spoon involved.

Klevko checked his watch, then hurriedly shooed us into the elevator, pulled the metal gate closed, and engaged the *up* lever with such force that I slammed against Hollis when we took off.

"Get off me!" he snapped.

"Sorry," I mumbled. Hollis was clearly in a bad mood, and I couldn't blame him.

Even though our apartment is on the penthouse floor, the elevator screeched to a stop on the fourth floor. Somehow I knew that only I was getting out.

"Leo . . ." Klevko started.

"I know, I know. Crane waits."

"Yes. Boss wants to see you now. He waits."

I turned to Hollis. "Wait up for me, okay?" I asked him. "I'll try to explain everything."

He didn't answer. I reached into my backpack, pulled out my digital recorder, and gave it to him.

"Here, take a listen. I recorded some stuff for you today . . . for the piece you're writing."

"Are these real sounds, or . . . you know . . . Leo's special sounds?" he whispered.

"They're real, bro. From school. You'll like them. Maybe when I'm done with Crane, we could just hang out, listen to them, and make some music or something."

I saw Hollis's face soften. This was the Leo he knew.

"Yeah," he said. "Okay. That would be cool."

Then I felt Klevko's hand give me a friendly shove out the elevator, and I was alone on the fourth floor.

I stepped out and waited for the elevator to lurch upward, then looked around to take in my surroundings. Aside from our penthouse, all the floors of Crane's warehouse looked alike, and the fourth floor was no different. It was a vast open room lined with rows and rows of wooden crates, each crate labeled with a number written in black ink. Ever since I took the dolphin helmet, I hadn't been allowed to go into the warehouse on my own, but I had seen enough from my earlier explorations to know that each of those crates contained something amazing — rare dinosaur fossils, ancient Greek urns, clay tablets from Egypt, jewelry from the kings and queens of Europe, lost paintings by dead masters. No one was permitted to ask Crane how he acquired these rare treasures. Maybe that's why he called his business Crane's Mysteries.

I heard Crane's lizardy voice echoing up and down the maze of aisles. He was laughing, and I knew he had turned up the charm. I could hear that there was a woman with him, and she had a booming, almost operatic laugh that made the whole floor seem slightly less menacing.

I followed the voices until I found him. Crane was wearing a black suit, black shirt, and black tie, the only splotch of color coming from his red silk pocket handkerchief. Even in the dim light, I could see his diamond pinkie ring flashing as he waved his hands in animated conversation. With him was a stylish middle-aged woman with long black hair, wearing lots of flowing scarves, dangly earrings, and several necklaces with what seemed to be wooden carvings hanging from them. They had paused in front of a smallish crate, from which Crane was carefully lifting out a mud-encrusted burlap bag.

I recognized it right away as the bag that contained the one half of the twin mask my father had brought back from Borneo, the one I had told Crane I knew all about. Oh yeah, I had also promised to help him find the other half, too. Crane suspected the mask might be a rare find, half of a legendary Siamese twin mask. If it was the real thing, and if he could find its matching half, it would be worth a fortune. Naturally, that was music to his ears.

"You wanted to see me, Uncle Crane?" I asked.

Crane put the burlap bag down on top of the crate and wheeled around as if he were thrilled to see me.

"Leo!" he cried. "There's my nephew! Come say hello to an old friend of mine and yours, Dr. Margaret Reed."

The woman turned toward me, gasped, put her hand over her mouth, and shook her head in mock surprise as if she couldn't believe what she were seeing.

"My, how you've grown up!" she said.

"Indeed he has," Crane agreed. "He's got my brother Kirk's face." Then he reached out and pinched my cheek. "But with more robust cheeks, wouldn't you say? He's got room to put two weeks of acorns in there."

He let out a belly laugh, and I was glad to see Dr. Reed didn't join in.

"Leo's just home from his tutor," Crane said to her, switching tracks. "His education is my highest priority, just as my dearly departed brother, Kirk, and his beloved wife, Yolanda, would have wanted."

Dr. Reed smiled at me. "I doubt you remember me, Leo, but when you were about four years old, our families spent a summer together in Madagascar. Your father and I were collaborating on a field study of native instruments. He was fascinated by the bamboo tube zither."

"Ah yes, the bamboo tube zither, that sounds like Kirk," Crane said, smirking.

"Are you a professor, too?" I asked her.

"I'm an anthropologist," she said. "I teach here in New York, but my true love is to do field research. I specialize in the tribal life of Borneo." Dr. Reed came closer so I could see her face clearly. "Now do you remember me, Leo?"

"Sort of," I lied as she took my hand, pressed it, and rubbed my shoulder.

But at her touch, I started to see hazy images in my mind, and I heard the croak of a bullfrog as clearly as if it was sitting on a lily pad in front of me. Other sounds cropped up, too, the buzz of dragonfly wings, the rustle of palm trees in the wind. Quickly, I let go of her hand.

"Was that the trip where we were by the pond with all those orange and yellow frogs?" I asked her.

"Yes!"

"And I found an orange frog that we named Jessie. I caught it with your daughter. She had long brown hair, right?"

"Diana! Yes, Leo. She had a huge crush on you, you little rascal," she said, and laughed with her opera voice.

"Diana," I said, remembering the girl at school. "Does she wear a dog-tooth necklace these days?"

"Why, yes, Leo," she said, surprised. "As a matter of fact she does. It was made for her by a tribesman in Borneo. But how would you know that?"

"I think I met her in school today. Does she go to Satellite North Middle School?"

"She does, but only while I'm teaching here in New York. The rest of the year, we live in Borneo. But tell me, Leo, why are you at Satellite North? I thought you were at the Academy of—"

"Yes," Crane butted in, stepping in front of me and speaking only to Dr. Reed. "We're doing everything we can to get him back into the Academy of Science and Arts. Those worthless bureaucrats at the school district switched up his file and dropped him from his classes. I've been on the phone with those blindworms all day, but all they know how to do is push a pencil and shuffle papers. I'd have more luck navigating Daedalus's labyrinth blindfolded than getting them to fix this ridiculous clerical error." And after that web of lies poured out of him as smoothly as spider's silk, Crane asked me if I'd enjoyed my first day.

"It was great," I played along. "I met a ton of smart kids, and all my teachers made me feel at home. Mr. Dickerson's a really nice guy, too."

"Wonderful, Leo," Crane said, patting my shoulder awkwardly. "And as much as I'd love to discuss your schooling and listen to you and Dr. Reed wax on about the old days, I'm afraid Dr. Reed has to be leaving shortly, and I wanted to bring you into our conversation about this mask here."

Crane picked up the burlap sack, clumps of dried red mud falling to the concrete floor, and carefully removed the mask.

"Dr. Reed has spent so much time in Borneo, she's practically an Indonesian citizen," he said. "And a little birdie told me that the Sultan of Brunei has offered her marriage no less than three times."

"But what about Diana's dad?" I blurted out, remembering a fuzzy image of a bearded man who was always tinkering around with a sailboat.

"Claudio," Dr. Reed said, bringing her hand to her mouth. I noticed she wasn't wearing a wedding ring. "Yes, Leo. That trip was just before Claudio and I parted ways. My life in Borneo didn't interest him, and we were spending so much time apart. . . ."

Her voice trailed off, and I was sorry I had asked the question.

"So do you like it in Borneo?" I asked quickly, not wanting to make her any more uncomfortable.

"Oh yes," she smiled. "So much that I'm heading back in only a few days for a six-month assignment."

"Well, I can assure you, Dr. Reed, you'll not find any artifacts half as remarkable as this mask," Crane said.

"I agree, Crane. It is quite remarkable. Have you been able to date it?" she asked him.

"I've had the wood carbon-dated. I just got the results, and they indicate that it is approximately three thousand years old."

"That old? Hmm . . . Well, that date does correspond to when we believe the island was first settled."

"But there's more, Dr. Reed," Crane said. "The teeth are made of alexandrite, a stone native to Brazil and Sri Lanka, but not Borneo. And though I have only managed to get a rough estimate, argon dating suggests that these stones were quarried more than ten thousand years ago, possibly much earlier. . . ."

"That can't be right, Crane. Have you repeated the argon dating?"

While they discussed argon dating, I studied the mask.

It was the size of a human head. The face was made of a golden wood covered in a thick layer of black goop. But despite the goop, the wood almost glowed underneath it. It had only a smooth bump for a nose and giant batlike ears. The sharp teeth were made of stones that seemed to change from red to green, colors that almost seemed imaginary, which changed depending on how you looked at them. By its chin, there was a rough edge, probably where the other half of the mask, the twin side, had once been before it was snapped off.

But what grabbed me and wouldn't let go were its giant hollow eye sockets. They were so eerie, almost like it had once had eyes, but they had been scooped out. The wood in the eye sockets became darker and darker until at their very centers, they were completely black. I kept trying to avoid looking into the depths of its hollow eyes, fearing that if I looked closely enough, I might see some ancient chunks of flesh. But those eyes seemed to follow me and draw my sight toward their black centers. I had the urge to reach out and touch the inner eye sockets with my fingers. The thing gave me the creeps.

"Leo," I heard Crane say. "Stop daydreaming and pay attention. I asked you a question."

"Sorry, I didn't hear it."

"I asked you to tell Dr. Reed how your father acquired this mask."

The truth was that I had almost no idea how or where he got it, but I had made up an elaborate lie when Crane had first asked me about it. He was so desperate to know the facts that I made them up and traded that information, all false, for Crane's permission to let me go to the dolphin island on his private jet. But now I was stuck in the lie, and I had no choice but to live with it.

"He was traveling up a river in Borneo for days on end," I began, "through rapids and jungles until he finally reached a small village where the shaman gave him the mask. He said it was a Kayan village."

Dr. Reed gave me a questioning glance.

"He said that?"

"Yes," I lied.

"But the Kayan don't make masks of this type."

"Leo's description perfectly matches the topography of the area near a fork in the Kayan River," Crane said, "where it splits into the Kayan and the Bahau. I plan to go there and see if I can find the other half, its twin."

"I just don't know why a mask with these characteristics would be from that region," Dr. Reed said. "It's far more similar to Dayak work, but even then, it's not typical of the region. And the alexandrite stones . . . I've never heard of them being used in any Bornean works. You said it yourself, Crane, the closest place they could have come from is Sri Lanka, an entire sea and almost three thousand miles from Borneo."

"But are you aware, Dr. Reed," Crane said softly, "that Dr. Eugène Dubois, discoverer of the Java man skull, was also given a Siamese twin mask, similar in all respects to this half here, by a village elder on Java? That mask also traveled great distances."

"That story about Dubois is a legend, Crane. I know he made sketches of the mask and loaded it onto his ship, but the mask disappeared en route to France. Those sketches have always been viewed with suspicion."

"Yet I'm sure you know, Dr. Reed," he went on, his voice suddenly getting tight and agitated, "that many other explorers have also described being given masks such as this one? Explorers to Burma, to India, and even the Nepalese Himalayas. All of them conjoined-twin masks. All of them containing elements not native to the areas where they were found. And all of these masks mysteriously disappeared en route — none ever made the journey back, but simply disappeared like ghosts. And what's more, Dr. Reed, every one of those adventurers who happened to discover such a twin mask, would find himself the victim of plots: sabotage, blackmail, even murder."

"Legends, Crane, legends."

"But, Dr. Reed, surely you know that there is an element of truth in every legend. Wasn't the great walled city of Troy just one of your 'legends,' until Calvert and Schliemann dug it up? And wasn't Atlantis a just a 'legend,' until Evans discovered the lost Minoan civilization on Crete? And what of the ruins found beneath the surface of Hera?"

I couldn't take my eyes off Crane. He was spouting facts and names like he had just swallowed a history textbook. His calm, deliberate businesslike manner was completely gone, replaced by a speedy almost hysterical tone. His hands were flailing so fast his diamond ring practically made streaks in the air.

"All right, Crane," Dr. Reed said, not too impressed with his flood of historical facts. "Let's say your legends are true. I still don't know what you're hoping to prove by finding the other half of this mask."

I wanted to say, "Aside from earning a fortune from it?" but I resisted the temptation.

"That there is much we don't know about the ancient world," Crane said with absolute authority. "These conjoined masks that have cropped up all over might be relics of an ancient civilization, one that existed when there was a solid land mass between India and Australia. When ancient people could travel by land."

Dr. Reed laughed, her operatic guffaw sounding not as kind as it had at first. Crane turned as red as the silk handkerchief in his suit pocket. He wasn't someone who was fond of being laughed at, and I admired Dr. Reed for not caring.

"Come on, now, Crane," she said. "You honestly think you know more than all the professors who have studied the ancient world their whole lives? That you, an amateur, are going to discover evidence of an entire ancient culture we know nothing about? That takes a lot of nerve."

"You call it nerve, I call it passion," Crane said, using his silk handkerchief to wipe his brow. "History fills me with passion."

Dr. Reed shook her head.

"I know you, Crane. Your passion is money."

"If there is a dollar to be made from the study of history, why not?" he said, neatly folding his handkerchief and placing it back in his pocket. In that single gesture, he completely regained his business voice and cool composure.

"A leopard doesn't change its spots," she mused. "So when do you intend to go on your expedition?"

"As soon as Leo here can help me pin down the exact location of the village," he answered.

"Ah, the one near the Kayan," she said, looking at me with a raised eyebrow. "I'll be interested to see what you find, Leo."

"Leo has remembered much of what his father told him about the location," Crane said, "but I'm hoping that if I bring him along as a kind of guide, more details will emerge from his rather imprecise brain."

I stared at Crane in disbelief. He had never mentioned taking me to Borneo, or anywhere else for that matter, other than to that crummy middle school in North Brooklyn.

"It's a shame you cannot join me on my expedition, Dr. Reed," Crane said. "Your expertise would be invaluable."

"I'm flying to Samarinda in only three days, and there is much to do before then," she answered. "Leo, I'm sorry you won't get more time to reconnect with Diana. Perhaps we'll all meet again soon."

"*Enchanté*, mademoiselle," Crane said, and kissed her hand. "Your intoxicating presence is welcome here anytime."

"Stop it, you old mule," she said, laughing. "And would you mind terribly if Leo walked me down? We have years to catch up on, and I'll have to steal whatever little parts of him I can."

"You may," Crane said, and when she picked up her purse, Crane looked at me and discretely put his finger to his lips. *"Au revoir."*

Dr. Reed took my arm as if I were some sort of English gentleman as we headed to the elevator. Klevko was waiting for us. Before we got in, she leaned in close to me and whispered in my ear.

"We have to talk," she said.

"We do?"

"You may be able to lie to your uncle, but you can't fool me. I know a lie when I hear one."

And without another word, she dropped my arm, took Klevko's, and strode into the elevator.

CHAPTER 7

Klevko took us down to the street level, but he didn't give Dr. Reed much time to catch up with me. He kept touching her dangling earrings and carved necklaces as if he intended to sell them at some point.

"You are very beautiful woman," he said. "I have a gentleman's — how do you say? — eh . . . eh crush. You have a husband?"

"Thank you, Klevko. But a gentleman should keep his hands to himself."

"You are a handsome woman for being so old. You remind me of Leo's mother, Yolanda. Two beautiful *matkas*. Not like my wife, Olga. She says you have the evil eye."

"I'm sorry she feels that way," Dr. Reed said as Klevko let us out of the elevator into the lobby.

"Stump, he waits for you outside," he said. Before he had

finished his sentence, we heard Olga screaming at him from inside their basement apartment.

"Klevko," she hollered. "Get in here now. Your sausages, they get cold. I didn't cook them for you so they could get cold."

"Olga, she is mean old woman, but she makes kielbasa like my own *matka* made," he said sheepishly, then turned and disappeared into his basement apartment.

Dr. Reed grabbed my arm, looked over both shoulders, and pulled me close to her, talking in a nervous stage whisper over the howling wind outside.

"Okay, Leo, I don't know why you've told Crane that tall tale, but you're in over your head. It's not going to hold up."

"So you knew that what I told Crane was a lie?"

"Of course. I was your dad's contact in Borneo and set him up with the Kayan villages he visited."

"Oh, then he actually was on the Kayan River? Wow, I just made a bunch of stuff up and fed it to Crane."

"Leo, lies have a way of coming true if they're repeated enough times. But your uncle isn't going to let this go. He's obsessed with that mask. *Obsessed.* I can see it in his eyes and the way his hands tremble when he touches it. He's going to do everything in his power to find the other half, which is why I don't want him coming anywhere near the Kayan villages, or even Borneo at all."

"I don't get it. My dad didn't seem to think that mask was anything *that* great. I know Crane, and he only cares about money."

"Obsession is about more than money, Leo," she said, shivering from the icy air that was penetrating through the cracks in the floorboard. "Crane is working with some wild ideas, and I believe he wants to prove his theory right. He actually believes that mask and all the other mysterious masks were made before the end of the last ice age, before the glaciers melted, when the continent of Asia stretched all the way to Australia. He believes he's going to uncover proof of a civilization that has never been documented."

"Weird. Can you get rich from that?"

"You can get famous. You can get respect. Your uncle has a lot to prove that has nothing to do with money. You know about his mother, right?"

"His beloved mother, Marie?"

"Yes, Leo. What do you know about her?"

"Only that saying her name opens a secret panel. And that she married my grandfather Tiberius when Crane was eleven and my dad was six. They were stepbrothers. My dad loved Tiberius but didn't like to talk about his step-mother much."

A car honked twice outside over the wind. It was Stump, waiting to leave.

"I don't have much time, Leo," Dr. Reed said, "so you're going to have to fill in the blanks yourself. It will help you understand Crane. What I can tell you is that Marie Rathbone was a famous medium, you know, a psychic. She led a number of spiritualist circles and séances."

"Like talking to the dead?" I asked.

"Yes. But of course, she was a fraud, like most medi-
ums—using slight-of-hand tricks and preying on people's
desire to believe. After she married your grandfather
Tiberius, she accompanied him on all his archeological
expeditions around the world. And soon, she began pub-
lishing her own 'archeological' books, all of them phony
Hollow Earth fantasies—"

"Hollow Earth?"

"Yes, a bogus theory that was immediately disproven
when we began peering beneath the Earth's surface
with—"

"With sound waves, right?" I said. "Sort of like radar, or
echolocation." I'd read about that when I was learning about
dolphin echolocation. Scientists would shoot high-energy
sound waves through the Earth, and based on the way that
they bounced around, they could tell what the interior of
the Earth was like.

"Splendid, Leo," she said. "Before we were able to examine the Earth's interior scientifically, there were hundreds
of books claiming the Earth was hollow inside. Some even
claimed that the hollow Earth was populated by a species
of humans far more advanced than us, possessing magical technologies, who had to retreat underground for
reasons unknown. Of course, most of those ideas actually
came from science-fiction novels. Marie's books represent
the very worst of the Hollow Earth field. Just dreadful
gibberish."

Dr. Reed eyed the door. "I have to go," she said. "Crane's
driver is waiting."

"Just tell me a few more things," I said. "Stump can wait one more minute."

Dr. Reed sighed, tapped her lips, and looked at the door. "Marie claimed she was in telepathic contact with these beings under the Earth, and that they led her to artifacts to prove their existence. Metal discs inscribed with bizarre symbols from Brazil, deformed skeletons, crystalline stones from lost cities of the Maya, the list goes on and on. Of course, every object she produced was quickly determined to be either completely ordinary or a total fake, and her reputation became a joke. I'm sure as a young teenager, this hurt Crane deeply. He was very attached to her."

"So you think that's why he wants to show the world how smart he is?" I asked. "To prove something?"

"Just my theory," she said, "but I know a thing or two about human psychology."

The lobby door swung open, and Stump stepped inside letting in the swirling wind, covered in white ice like a ghost.

"Lady, come on!" he hollered. "This ain't a hotel."

"One moment, sir," she said politely to him, then got even closer to me, whispering, "Find out more about Marie Rathbone, Leo. It will help you understand your uncle."

"I will," I said. "One last thing, Dr. Reed. Do you know someone named Bertrand Veirhelst?"

"Bertie? I never met him in the flesh, but he was a legend among all us globe-trotters like your father and me. He was a diplomat from Belgium, but his true love was the study of other cultures. He helped countless anthropologists acquire visas to study cultures abroad, your father as well, I believe."

"You said 'was.'"

"Yes, Bertie passed on not more than three months ago. A tragic fall from his apartment balcony."

"Lady, you can't sleep here!" Stump said, holding the door open. "We gotta beat it before we're snowed in completely."

Dr. Reed kissed me on the cheek and slid her business card in my pocket, telling me to call her soon if I needed some motherly attention, then disappeared into the storm. The door shut.

My head was spinning as I walked to the elevator. I had a lot of disconnected information swimming in my head. Old Marie Rathbone and her otherworldly artifacts. That twin mask with its hypnotic eyes. A mysterious Belgian diplomat who died falling off his balcony. My parents' voices and the fragments of their conversation I had heard in Jeremy's shop. Could it be that they were all connected? Was Bertie a secret spymaster, and my parents his spies? They were always traveling all over the world. And of course, with these thoughts came the familiar hope, the desperate, crazy hope that somehow my parents were still alive.

As I made for the elevator, I found that the metal doors were halfway open. I looked through the opening and the brass bars and saw Crane on one knee. He was whispering into the dark little doorway of one of the basement bedrooms. I got the distinct feeling that I was seeing something not meant for my eyes, because when Klevko spotted me, he immediately closed the apartment door. Hastily, he pulled Crane up as he slid open the gate.

"I can get up myself, you clod. I'm not an invalid," Crane snapped. "And hello there, Leo. Dmitri was just telling me an intriguing story about your adventures today."

"R-really?" I stammered, my heart beating fast. Had Dmitri heard my conversation with Hollis? Had he already told Crane everything? Think fast, feel nothing, I repeated to myself. "Dmitri makes up tons of great stories," I said with a nervous laugh.

"He was telling me, Leo, how well you're doing at your new school," Crane said, looking at me hard. I tried to determine if he was just toying with me, trying to get me to spill the truth, or if he and Dmitri really were talking about school. As always, Crane's face was a mystery.

"Dmitri thinks so highly of you he wants to take you on as a partner in his business," Crane said. "Klevko, why are we standing still? Seventh floor, you donkey."

"Yeah, I'm just trying to blend in," I said as the elevator lurched upward.

"Well, I hope your partnership with Dmitri won't interfere with our partnership. I'm depending on you, Leo. You're making excellent strides, excellent strides, and perhaps soon your paperwork will go through and you can go back to your old school. . . ."

"Really? That's great."

"Soon, Leo, very soon. But first I want you to do something for me tomorrow. I'd consider it a personal favor."

He pulled out his keychain and handed me one of the keys. It had a tag on it with an address in Staten Island.

"I want you to go to your parents' storage locker in Staten Island tomorrow."

"Tomorrow?" I said, remembering my plan to go Jeremy's.

"I hope it's not a problem. I'm at a dead end and need more clues. Bring back anything you can find about that mask and your father's trip to Borneo."

As we got off the elevator, it occurred to me that Crane and I had never gotten off the elevator at the same time, just the two of us. I'd never learned where he slept. I was curious to finally see where it was that Crane retired to, so I stood by the elevator and waited for him to make a move, but apparently he was doing the same thing.

"Well . . . uh, good night, Leo."

"Hey, Crane," I said. "This might seem random, but do you know anything about diplomats?"

"A man in my position must know an exceedingly large amount about diplomats," he said. "Most are worthless slugs with massive debt — they can be easily bribed. The other half are spies. They, too, can be bribed or black-mailed once you have penetrated their cover. Why do you ask, Leo?"

"There's just this kid at school who was giving me a hard time today named Pieter, and he said there was nothing I could do about it because his dad was a big deal diplomat. His name is Pieter Veirhelst, and I think his dad's name is Bertrand."

"Pieter is surely lying," Crane said. "Diplomats send their kids to diplomatic schools — but the boy's father might be connected to his embassy. Tell you what, Leo. Bring back something useful tomorrow, and I'll give you information on this supposed diplomat. Deal?"

"Deal," I said.

"Very well, one of my men will pick you up from school. Now is there anything else?"

"Um, not really," I said.

"Then go to bed, Leo. Go on."

As I left, I snuck a peek over my shoulder and saw Crane, still standing by the elevator, watching me. By the time I crossed the glass bridge for the Mask Room, the lights were no longer on, and the room glowed dimly with an eerie white light from the storm outside. The entire floor-to-ceiling window was like a giant flat-screen TV, broadcasting a white and orange picture, making the masks on the walls seem like fun-house shadows, with their four hundred blind eyes staring at me. I broke into a run and ran the rest of the way to my dark room.

I pushed open my door and sprinted for the control panel, turning on the lights as bright as they'd go. When the room was lit up, I turned to my desk only to discover that my computer had been removed.

Crane. He was everywhere.

But Crane hadn't gotten my phone. It was in my closet. And it had eleven new messages.

I listened to nine messages from Hollis, Trevor, and Jeremy, each one a different shade of nervousness depending on the time. They had been so worried about me, especially Hollis. He'd left five messages before Dmitri's text—he must have had a rotten morning. After a message from Jeremy, there was a message filled with eerie static that rolled like waves. The sounds sent shivers up and down my spine, and when the tingles moved to the back of my neck, I could have sworn I heard a voice in the static, just a whisper, a tinny little voice trying to break through. It sounded flat, inhuman. And just when I thought I could hear something understandable, the message cut off abruptly.

"Next message, 8:44 p.m.," the robot voice-mail voice said.

It was a message from Mike Hazel. Luckily, and my first stroke of good luck in a day, I'd never bothered to record a voice-mail greeting, so it was one of those automated replies that just said my phone number.

"Hi, this is Mike Hazel from Fox Five news. I'm trying to contact a boy named Leon Loman, and one my sources gave me this number, saying you might know him. I'm looking for some background information regarding a story I'm working on. Give me a call back before midnight tonight, my deadline."

It was 10:30. I turned off my phone and made for Hollis's room.

He was asleep in his bed, still in his clothes with his arm around the neck of his acoustic guitar. I decided not to wake him, and sat down at his computer to do some research. I had a lot to look into.

I tried Bertrand Veirhelst first. His obituary on the *New York Times* site said he was a Belgian diplomat, but there was much about him that they didn't know. He was born in Rwanda and lived there until he was a teenager, and resurfaced next in Belgium where he was running a sort of immigration business with his wife until it was discovered that he also had another family in Turkish Cyprus. He then disappeared for seven years, until he resurfaced in Kiev, Ukraine, just after the fall of the Soviet Union, working for a giant natural gas company. His whole life was like that—he'd appear in some strange place, disappear for a number of years, then reappear several years later in another strange place. If he wasn't a spy, then he did everything he could to make his life read as if he were one.

Next I tried Spiricom, that record my Dad was so eager to get hold of. There were no direct hits, but after a long and winding search, somehow I found myself on a webpage about a guy named Konstantin Raudive. He was a scientist from Latvia, and he had made all these recordings of white noise and static, which, he claimed, contained the voices of dead people. He claimed that if you listened very carefully, you could hear the flat, nonmelodic voices of the dead trying to communicate with the living. I couldn't find any of the recordings online, but I looked through tons of different pages about those voices, called electronic voice phenomena, or EVP, and just followed all the links wherever they took me. Nothing was connecting . . . yet.

I remembered that strange voice-mail message. Even though just thinking of it gave me a nervous sinking feeling, I knew there was a voice in it. I wanted to listen to it, but I didn't want to chance turning on my phone only to have Mike Hazel call me.

It was almost midnight by the time I started my search of Marie Rathbone. My head was swimming with hundreds of fragmentary thoughts about spies and kooky scientists, twin masks and hollow Earths, voices from the dead and snatches of my parents' voices that I'd channeled from my dad's note. *That card!* Maybe if I listened again, I would be able to hear more this time.

Hollis was still wearing his jacket, so I kneeled on his bed and very carefully reached my hand into his pocket. He mumbled something and turned, half waking up.

"Hey," he said softly.

"Hey. You sleep. I'm just getting this card."

"Leo," he yawned and rolled over. "Can you really do that sound thing?"

His voice had lost its suspicious edge. Things always make a different kind of sense when you've been asleep and just wake up. Maybe that had happened to him.

"Yeah, I can," I told him. "I'm going to Mom and Dad's storage locker tomorrow after school. You should come with me, and I'll show you how my power works."

"Okay. Wait, we're going to Jeremy's tomorrow."

"I know, but I have to go to the storage locker. I'll explain tomorrow morning. You should go back to sleep."

"Make sure you tell Trevor." He yawned and rolled over. "Oh, and don't forget to show me that blue disc, and that letter from Dad."

"I will tomorrow," I promised. But as I sat by his side, watching him fall back asleep, I realized I hadn't seen the disc since I got back from Palmira. I dimly remembered that when I got back, I had to put it somewhere really safe, a place where Crane or any of his minions would never find it. In my mind, I went through my room to remember where I might have stashed it, but never got that "aha" feeling. And that gave me a terrible heavy pressing feeling in my chest. After all, Crane had been in there to take my computer. There was no telling what else he'd found.

I went back to my room and laid my head back on the pillow, just staring up at the ceiling. Reaching into my pocket, I pulled out the card with my dad's handwriting and held it in my hand. This time, I heard nothing. I waited for what seemed like a long time, half closing my eyes and catching myself falling asleep now and then. I awoke suddenly when I heard a rattling boom from overhead — the sound of something big on the roof crashing. Then the power went out. Completely. In the total darkness, the sound of the howling wind outside was deafening.

I turned my phone on. It was 1:45. There were two new messages on it, both probably from Mike Hazel, who had missed his deadline. I left it on as a night-light, laid my head back on the pillow. I didn't even remember closing my eyes.

CHAPTER 8

awoke feeling as if no time had passed. Someone was pounding on my door. Without waiting for me to answer, Dmitri barged right in.

I sat up and shot him an icy stare. "If you're just going to come in, Dmitri, why even knock?"

"Why do you sleep in your clothes, Leo? If you don't have pajamas, I can ask my *matka* to get you some." He marched to my bedside, forced me aside, and, from the control panel, turned on the lights in the room.

"What are you doing, Dmitri? Just get out of here and let me sleep. It's the middle of the night."

"Stupid Leo, you think it's the middle of the night!" He exploded in a snorting laugh, splashing me with some spittle. "It's seven thirty. The power in the building went out, so none of the clocks are working. The buses will be crowded. We have to leave right away."

It all came rushing back, the misery of my previous day at Satellite North. I didn't know how much more I could take of those dingy halls filled with tough guys who were just dying to beat me up and a principal who seemed out to punish me. Mr. Dickerson, who was probably waiting for me at detention. For my detention at six thirty . . .

"Oh no," I gasped, and held my head, digging my fingers almost into my brain. "Dmitri, I had detention today. Can we get Stump to drive us to—"

"Stump drives Hollis, not you and me."

"Okay, I'll be ready in five minutes," I told Dmitri, but he just stood there, not leaving. "Uh, Dmitri, a little privacy, please."

"I am supposed to stay with you, Leo. Your uncle wants me to protect you."

"And you do everything he tells you to?"

"No," he said sharply. "I make my own decisions. It is my decision to give you some breakfast." He dug into his pocket and handed me an off-brand granola bar that was all soft and out of shape.

"Thanks, Dmitri. Now give me some space. We're partners, right? So believe me when I tell you that you don't have to protect me in here. Come on," I said, pushing him step-by-step to the door.

"Okay, partner. I'll come back in five minutes."

I waited until I saw him disappear down the hall, and actually followed him to make sure he wasn't hanging around spying on me. He wasn't, or at least, not that I could see. I went into Hollis's room. There was a hot chocolate and blueberry muffin on a black lacquer tray next to his bed.

"Hey, where'd that come from?" I asked him.

"Klevko brought it up. He said it was from Crane. Didn't you get the same thing?"

"Nah, Dmitri made me breakfast," I said, and held up the granola bar.

Hollis tore the muffin in half, then held out the cup to offer me a sip.

"Thanks, chief," I said, washing the delicious muffin down with a huge swig of chocolate. "I have to run. I just want to remind you about the storage locker. Meet me there after school. Herc." I gave him a scrap of paper with the address.

"How am I supposed to get there?" he asked. "It's all the way in Staten Island."

"You'll figure it out," I said. "Not hard to do when you have a personal limo and driver."

Dmitri came back exactly five minutes later, and together we raced to the bus stop. The nor'easter had dumped several feet of ice crystals during the night, and though it was just misting now, Dmitri said it would be back later. The buses were slow due to the horrible weather, and packed. Dmitri elbowed his way into the last seat on the bus and immediately pretended to fall asleep just like he'd done the day before. The traffic was terrible due to the storm, and by the time we arrived at Satellite North, it was nearly nine thirty. I'd missed my detention by a whopping three hours.

"Can you find your classes okay?" Dmitri asked as we stomped the snow off our boots just outside the entrance. I nodded. "Fine, I will come get you at the beginning of lunch. Today you will begin working for me."

I wanted to tell him no, but because I didn't have any lunch money and I'd already eaten that disgusting granola bar, I was in no position to turn him down. We went in together — Dmitri headed for the stairs while I raced to my English class. And that's when I crashed into a huge, hulking mountain of a man.

"Well, well, well, Mr. Lomax." It was Mr. Dickerson, in a tiny parka with an elastic bottom that rode up around his stomach. "I looked for you in detention this morning, but all I saw was an empty seat. Your empty seat, however, was quite well behaved."

"Listen, about that, Mr. Dickerson, the power went out in our neighborhood, and it took me forever to get here."

"I'm sorry to hear that, Leo. That means it will take you forever to get out of detention after school."

"Oh, sorry, Mr. Dickerson, but I can't do it today. I have . . . um . . . previous plans."

"You're starting to annoy me, Leo," he said, a blood vessel on his neck twitching. The walkie-talkie on his belt blasted something I couldn't understand, and he mumbled a few incomprehensible words back into it. "We'll have to postpone this chat for now," he said, "but you can be sure I'll be discussing your truancy with your uncle."

Then he lumbered off in the direction of his next victim.

I made a dash for my English classroom, and as I entered, I pretended to be breathing hard and winded. With a little ceremonial bow, I made my way to the only remaining desk, the last seat in the last row. My teacher wasn't amused, but a few kids laughed. Diana was one of them, and as I settled into my desk while giving her a cocky smile, I realized my desk was right next to the crown prince of the Ukrainian Mafia, my good friend Pieter.

"How you doing, honors boy?" he whispered. "Missed you in detention this morning. But we'll find you and Dmitri after school."

I wished he had lowered his voice when he said the word *detention*. I'm sure Diana heard it, and after eight years without seeing each other, it wasn't exactly the first impression I wanted to make on her. As the teacher put the homework reading on the board, I stole a few glances over at her. I could see how she was her mother's daughter. The long dark hair, the native jewelry, the way she was tuned in to everything around her. But her eyes seemed sad, somehow. I wondered how she had survived at this school.

After class, I was surprised when she joined me as we walked out into the hall.

"So I hear we're old friends," she said. "I knew I had seen you somewhere before. You still like frogs?"

"I can take them or leave them," I said. Pieter and two of his buddies were following us down the hall. One of them made smooching sounds with his lips. "Check out lover boy," he said in a high-pitched voice. I whipped around to confront him and noticed that the speaker was the squirrelly little kid who had stolen my fifty cents.

"You got something caught in your teeth?" I said in my toughest voice.

"No, do you?" he retorted weakly.

"You got my fifty-cent piece?" I said, and took a step toward him.

"Yeah, I got it," he said, bracing for a showdown as Pieter put his hand on his shoulder, providing backup. "Come and get it."

"Don't pay attention to them," Diana said, pulling me away. "You'll only make it worse."

"Yeah, you're right," I said, to laughter behind me. "I'll bet you'll be glad to go back to Borneo. No one harassing you in the halls there."

Diana laughed, and I noticed she had that opera laugh just like her mom. "There are no halls there," she said. "Just orangutans and jungle. I kind of like the orangutans but other than that, it gets pretty boring. I miss the city."

"Your friends?"

"Not so much. I don't have all that many friends—I-I mean I have some friends, but I'm always going back and forth, so it's tough. But I miss all the other city stuff the most. The subways, the streets, the hot-dog carts—New York. And my dad—he lives in Manhattan with his new wife. Your parents live here?"

"They did. They died."

She stopped walking and looked at me, and her face got

very soft and concerned. I can't stand it when people give me that look. It makes me feel so pitiful.

"I'm so sorry, Leo. My mom said you were living with your uncle, but she didn't tell — I should have realized. . . ."

"It's okay," I told her. I didn't really want to talk about it, especially with any chance that Pieter and his idiot friends were following us. I didn't know much about surviving in a tough school, but I knew you don't ever want to show weakness to guys like that.

True to his word, Dmitri was waiting for me outside of class just as the lunch bell rang. He grabbed my arm and hurried me to his locker, which was at the very end of the corridor near the cafeteria.

"This is the best place for business," he said. "I catch the kids on the way in and on the way out. Your uncle, the boss, has taught me it's all about location."

He opened up his locker and gave me a tour.

"Top shelf, cans of soda," he said. "Three dollars."

"Three dollars? That's a very high price."

"They don't sell them in the cafeteria," he said. "People want a soft drink, they have to pay my price — for a 300 percent profit."

I could hear my uncle Crane's influence.

"Next shelf, candy. Red Vines are popular with the girls. Sixth graders want anything weird like skeleton pops or gummy bacon. Charge them as much as you can. They're stupid."

"What's in back of the panel?" I asked him.

"Stink bombs. Whoopee cushions. Fart spray. You know, all the prank stuff. You stick to the little stuff, I'll handle anything big, like tests or homework answers."

With that, Dmitri took a folder of papers from behind the panel, tucked it into his backpack, and headed down the hall.

"Hey, where you going?" I called after him.

"Business meeting in stall three of the boys bathroom," he said. "Be right back. You mind the store."

With Dmitri gone, I closed the locker and slouched up against the wall. Lots of kids streamed by on their way into the cafeteria. No one stopped, and I was beginning to think this business was all in Dmitri's imagination. Then a sixth-grade girl in a green parka with a furry hood came up to me.

"You with Dmitri?" she asked.

I nodded.

"One red licorice," she whispered, and took two dollars out of her pocket and slipped it into my hand. I opened the locker and handed her a package of red licorice, which she slipped under her parka. The whole deal took less than ten seconds. I folded the money up and tucked it deep in my pocket. I liked the feel of having cash and found myself thinking that with a little more business, I could accumulate a money wad like Dmitri's.

I started making contact with each kid as they passed, sending a message with my eyes that I was open for business.

"Cream soda," a boy said to me, pausing by the locker. It was the kid who had made off with my half-dollar. I thought to continue our showdown from earlier, but this was business, not personal, and he was a paying customer. I handed him the can of soda, and he handed me his money, which I was glad to see included the fifty-cent piece he had stolen from me. It was a nice circle.

"Three stink bombs," one of Pieter's friends said, pulling up to the locker and striking a cool pose.

"Jelly beans, and none of those purple ones," said another kid.

Within ten minutes, I had sold out of all the soft drinks and red licorice and had what I estimated was twenty-five dollars in my pocket.

"Hey, I'm Anton," a tall guy in a hooded New York Rangers sweatshirt said, stopping by the locker. "Give me a root beer."

"Sorry, man, I'm sold out," I told him.

"Maybe you didn't hear me," Anton said, standing up to his full height. "I want a root beer."

"I heard you, buddy," I said. "Did *you* hear me? I'm sold out. Now keep it moving."

But he just moved in close, getting right up in my face and speaking in what any normal person could call an angry tone. His face was so near to mine that I could smell the cafeteria ravioli on his breath.

"Dmitri always saves me one," he said. "We have an understanding."

I felt a rush of anger well up in me. I hate to be shoved around. Probably it comes from always being shorter than most guys my age, but whenever I feel like I'm being bullied, I just want to scream and yell. So before I could even think about it, I took my hand and pushed Anton back, not to be aggressive because he was much bigger than me, but just to get him out of my face. As soon as I touched his sweatshirt, the hall started to spin, the locker faded from my sight, and I heard something wooden smacking against concrete.

"One minute left on the clock, and the Rangers are down by one," I heard the disembodied voice of an announcer say. "Looks like the Blackhawks are going to take this one." Then I heard Anton's voice, screaming, "You suck, Rangers. I want my flippin' money back." Then silence. Just as quickly as they had come, the voices in my head disappeared.

"Don't touch me, punk," Anton was saying, prying my hand off his sweatshirt. I looked around and realized where I was and what had happened. It took me a moment to understand that it was a sound-bending trance, because it was so short, but there was no other explanation for what I had heard.

"Listen, Anton, I'm sorry you had a bad time at the Rangers game," I said to him. "But a real fan wouldn't tell his team they sucked. You better learn some loyalty."

Anton looked at me suspiciously.

"How'd you know I said that?"

"I have my ways," I said.

"What are you, some kind of mind reader?" he asked.

"Maybe I am."

One of his other big hockey-playing friends had come over to see what was going on. He was wearing a Rangers hoodie, too, and had a scar next to his eye that looked like it was from a recent injury.

"Hey, Moe, this guy says he can read minds," Anton said to him.

"Okay, read my mind," Moe said. "And don't tell me I'm thinking about what a little punk you are, because you don't need to read my mind to know that."

"I have to touch something of yours," I said. "You know, to pick up your psychic vibrations. And I charge two dollars a reading."

"I'll pay you after you read my mind," he said, tossing his backpack at me with such force I nearly fell down. I felt around the bag, touching various objects, but no sounds came into my head.

"I'm waiting, big shot," Moe said. "What's in my mind?"

I clutched the bag tighter and frantically ran my hands over it. I couldn't channel a thing. Trevor and I had thought that my power worked best when I was feeling something intense, but the intimidation I was feeling from this guy produced nothing. I thought to fake it and tell him he had gotten that scar from a hockey game, but that was pretty weak.

"He's lying," Anton said. "What a freak."

"A liar and a punk, how pathetic can you get?" Moe said. He grabbed me suddenly by my shirt and pushed. I wasn't ready for it and went slamming into the lockers. They laughed, and at the sound of ringing metal, a crowd quickly gathered.

I clenched my jaw and felt a surge of anger that actually made my shoulders tremble. That seemed to do it, because immediately, my hands locked on the backpack, and for a brief flash, my power activated.

"Hey, Alicia, it's uh . . . uh . . . me. It's Moe, from Math class. I got your number from Courtney. Uh, do you maybe, uh . . . ? Agh, never mind."

Beep. The call ended, and I was back, smirking at Moe.

"Moe, you're thinking about Alicia," I said, pressing my fingers on a spot above my right eye. "Next time you call her, don't just leave a wimpy message. Be bold, Moe, and she will say yes."

"Alicia?" Anton said to Moe. "The cross-country girl? I thought you said you didn't—"

"Butt out, Anton," Moe said, his face turning red. "So, kid, give me my bag back."

I rubbed my thumb and index together—the international signal for pay me.

"You got it, kid," Moe said, and put two bucks in my hand. "What's your name anyway?"

"You can call me Leon. Leon, the gifted child," I said to a rapidly growing crowd. "And for just two dollars, I will tell your fortune." Suddenly, I felt great, powerful—the same way I'd felt after outrunning Pieter and his friends yesterday. Maybe the same way that Marie Rathbone felt when she was conducting her séances.

By the time Dmitri returned from his business deal in the bathroom, I had a small crowd of kids gathered around me wanting their fortunes read. Surprisingly, I was able to sound bend most of the time. The crowd was exhilarating, and I used their energy to power my trances. When that didn't work, I would just think about Crane and Dickerson and a silent rage would seem to trigger my power. And when my power didn't activate at all, I'd tell the person what they wanted to hear. It's amazing what you can figure out just by watching someone — like the girl wearing the purple tights. She'd been in my Spanish class and had spent the whole class drawing pictures of horses.

"You've always wanted a horse of your own," I said, and watched the sad look form on her face, and let her expression guide my reading. "As a little girl, you always wanted a pony. You asked for one every year. You never got one, but someday soon, you'll be riding your very own horse. That'll be two dollars, please."

Dmitri watched me carefully. When lunch was over and we headed back to class, he wanted to know more about how I was able to read minds, but I told him it was just a trick and distracted him by counting the wad of money I had earned. Thirty-seven dollars. His all-time record for a day was forty, so he was extremely impressed. As we walked up the stairs, he talked a mile a minute about our partnership and the bright future we had together. I don't know whether he was thinking about the conversation in Jeremy's record shop — I still wasn't even sure if he had heard anything. But whatever he thought of my powers, it was totally overshadowed by his greedy little money scheme.

During seventh period, I got a summons to go to Mr. Dickerson's office.

"Go right in, Leo," Ms. Confalone said when I arrived at her desk. "And beware, he's in a foul mood."

Mr. Dickerson was jammed behind his little desk, looking especially puffy and red in the face. He didn't ask me to sit down, nor did he look up from his file.

"I've just had a conversation with your uncle," he began. "Apparently, I was mistaken."

"Oh?" I said, and pressed my finger above my right eye.

"I thought he wanted this school to teach you some discipline, but it appears I'm a bit mistaken." I noticed that Mr. Dickerson's large hairy hands were trembling. "So, uh, you don't need to come to detention today, Leo. And I'll forget about your absence this morning. How does that sound? Good?"

"What did Crane say to you?" I couldn't help but ask.

"We just chatted," Dickerson said, "and he mentioned that you have an errand to do for him after school. So I told him that family comes first. And you'll be sure to mention to him that I said that. And tell him, you know, that there's really no need to talk to his associates on the school board. Really, no need. Make sure you mention that, okay, Leo? You may return to class now. That's all."

Good old Uncle Crane, I thought. I recognized his work. He wanted me at the storage locker, looking for clues about the mask. And no way was he going to let a flabby hard-nosed bureaucrat like Dickerson get in the way. But that was fine with me. Just fine.

I felt light on my feet as I headed back to class, almost breaking into a happy dance. I had a wad of money in my pocket, an influential uncle telling off the vice principal for me, and a bunch of new kind-of friends who thought I was cool.

Trevor, who loves science, is always telling me amazing stories about how animals survive by adapting to their environment. Take camels. They've developed the ability to close their nostrils to stop desert sand from blowing into them. Or polar bears. They've developed white coats to camouflage them in the snow so their enemies won't find them. Or my favorite, the blind cave tetras. They're this weird fish that live in such deep, dark underwater caves that they actually no longer have any eyes at all. Trevor says the ability to adapt is the key to survival.

As I headed back to class after my second day at Satellite North Middle School, I thought, Yes, Leo Lomax. You are a survivor. Those blind cave tetras have nothing on you.

CHAPTER 9

ook for the man with the glass eye," Dmitri said as we
stepped out of school.

"I think he's already spotted us," I said.

There was a man across the street in a black suit with
black sneakers and a top hat, leaning against a leafless tree.
Everything about his body language said that he was staring off at the sky and thinking of something far away,
except there also was an unmoving brown eye staring at
me. That was the glass eye.

We crossed the street, and when we were a few feet
from him, the man bowed and extended his hand.

"Pleased to meet you, Leo," he said. "I ask you not to
be afraid of my injury. My name is Kyu-ho Hu. I am a
courier for Crane's Mysteries, and as such, I am at your
service." He had an accent and spoke slowly and carefully,
but deliberately.

"Nice to meet you, too," I said, somewhat surprised by how nice it was to meet him.

"This way to my car, Leo," he said with a stately sweep of the hand. "Hello, Dmitri," he also grumbled, almost out of the side of his mouth. "Take Leo's backpack."

Dmitri did as he was told. I was starting to see some of the benefits of getting on Crane's good side—first Dickerson groveling to me, and now this nice man with a glass eye treating me like royalty.

His car was a beat-up looking blue cargo van from circa 1985 covered with dents and a bumper hanging by a screw. TWIN DRAGON COURIERS was painted on the side in white letters.

"Please sit up front, Leo," Kyu-ho said, while Dmitri had to jam into the back, which was filled with stacks of cardboard boxes. I swear some of those boxes were moving. The backseats had been torn out for more cargo room, so Dmitri had to wedge himself into a tiny sliver between three irregularly shaped boxes, his hands pinned to his chest, and his legs in wildly different directions.

"I apologize in advance for any traffic," Kyu-ho said as he backed up and immediately slammed into something metallic. The van scraped against the metal, doing what sounded like considerable damage. Finally, we were clear of it. In his side-view mirror, I saw a rusted yellow pole sticking up from the sidewalk.

"That pole came out of nowhere," I said.

Kyu-ho laughed nervously. "Yes, I believe it did."

As he plunged into traffic, cutting off a huge truck whose

driver leaned on the horn, I looked in my rearview to say, "So long, suckers," to Satellite North. I never wanted to go back there. I wondered how they'd remember me, this shadowy kid named Leo who appeared out of nowhere for a few days, worked for Dmitri's shady operation, dueled and bested Dickerson, told people's fortunes, and disappeared just as suddenly as he'd come. If all went well, I could go back to my old school soon, with Trevor. But just thinking of Trevor made me uneasy. He wouldn't have approved of anything I'd done today.

"Does my driving make you nervous, Leo?" Kyu-ho asked, motioning with his good right eye to my hands, which were grasping the seat belt with white knuckles. I wanted to tell him that it did when he didn't keep his eye on the road.

"No, Kyu-ho. I just have some things on my mind. So tell me, how do you even drive with only one eye? I thought you needed two to see how far away things are."

"Simple, Leo. I fill in what I cannot see with what I have seen before. And since I see that you are uneasy, I will save my story of how I lost my eye for a time when you have found more peace."

We drove the rest of the way in silence, over the Verrazano Bridge, into Staten Island, and to an abandoned-looking mini-mall, with all the stores long boarded-up, except for the public storage facility.

Dmitri and Kyu-ho followed me into the building, Kyu-ho dragging a hand dolly for all the heavy gear he assumed I'd gather. I asked them to wait in the lobby for me and went to the fourth floor to locker 429. The hallway was unbelievably clean, strange because I knew that behind all those metal sliding doors were the messy and cluttered belongings from people who had moved on from their old lives.

I undid the lock and slid the door open. It was pitch-dark inside. I smelled first—the air was stale and cold, a faint odor of soggy cardboard mixed with the unmistakable but trace smell of home. And it was quiet in there, still and silent, almost like opening up a lost tomb that had been sealed for thousands of years. I turned on the lights and closed the door behind me.

The room was filled with stacks of boxes piled all the way to the ceiling. Metal racks and shelves by the side of the wall housed smaller boxes and items, while bigger items on top of the boxes were covered in blue tarps and old sheets, a familiar grain of wood or a corner to an old piece of furniture peeking out here and there.

There was so much of my parents' stuff that I was overwhelmed. I thought I would feel sad, but oddly, I felt more angry than sad—angry with them for abandoning us. I dashed through the room, taking down boxes at random, ripping them open and dumping their contents on the ground, until the whole storage locker looked like a piñata warehouse attacked by rats.

The door slid open, and I turned to see Hollis come in.

"You made it!" I said.

"Yeah. Who's that guy with the weird eye? He asked me if you needed any help."

"That's Kyu-ho. He works for Crane."

"I figured. Everyone who works for Crane is missing some hunk of their body."

"Kyu-ho's really nice, Hollis, and he's helping me —"

"Leo, you never called Trevor last night," he said, picking up some of Mom's purses and sunglasses.

"Ah, man, I forgot. Was he pissed?"

"You know Trevor, he was puzzled about why you had to cancel Jeremy. I think that's about as close to pissed as he gets. So are you going to show me your power or what?"

I could tell from his tone of voice that some of his suspicion had returned. But I was going to fix that.

"Pick anything in this room, Hollis, and I'll tell you what I hear."

"All right," he said, slowly walking the aisles, picking up random scraps of our old life and putting them back down. He stopped at a pair of our mom's sunglasses with red frames and pink lenses. He was quiet, and from the little smile on his face, I knew he was remembering that day she wore them to take us on the Cyclone roller coaster at Coney Island. He held them for a minute, and when he looked up at me, I could see him batting back the tears.

"It's kind of creepy in here," he said, putting the sunglasses back in the box. "I still don't get it, Leo. What are we doing here?"

"I'm trying to find some old info of Dad's to help Crane. You know that."

"But why?"

"So things can go back to normal, like before."

"Before what, Leo? Things won't ever be normal again."

While Hollis walked through the stuff, I searched as well. I needed to find the mask information for Crane, but I had my own mysteries to investigate. I wanted to find that Spiricom record and any information I could dig up about Bertrand Veirhelst, as well. Most of all, I was hoping to find something about our parents' trip to Antarctica, something that might help us discover what really happened on that plane. It was a desperate hope, I knew, but maybe there was something in there, some little clue that might indicate that there was still a chance for them. Maybe they really were part of a plot or something; maybe they were still alive, hiding out, counting the minutes until they could come back. And just like one of those mummified Egyptian pharaohs, all their things would be waiting.

I had opened up a box that had a bunch of my old art projects. I saw one drawing I had made for Father's Day when I was in kindergarten. A small stick figure meant to be me was on one side of the picture, while on the other side, separated by a blue river, were three other stick figures. Typical of my art style, in the middle of the picture I had also drawn a Venus flytrap getting zapped by lightning. One of the stick figures was wearing headphones, and the other two were wearing giant feather headdresses.

As I held the picture, my head filled with voices from the past.

"Is that your father?" I heard my kindergarten teacher, Ms. Elise, say in my inner ear.

"Yeah," I squeaked in a five-year-old's voice. "He's away on a music trip."

"Your picture would be much better, Leo, if you learned to color inside the lines."

As soon as I put the picture down, the voices faded, but not the feeling. I remembered why I had drawn that Venus flytrap—that was Ms. Elise. She was always telling me not to make noises and to color in the lines, and she used to make me feel so bad about myself that once I wrote, "I hate Ms. Elise," on a scrap of paper, and because I felt so bad about writing that, I hid the scrap of paper deep in my desk.

"Okay, Leo," Hollis said. "I've made my choice. Try this."

Hanging from his hand was a silver necklace with a beautiful stone of green and red, almost like a watermelon. My mom wore that necklace every day. Her violin teacher gave it to her after her first recital. He had told her that her hard work and her gift had made music as beautiful as that crystal, and that there was a whole world of other precious stones out there for her to find if she worked hard and fulfilled her potential.

Hollis put the necklace in my hand. I held it but I didn't hear anything. I closed my eyes and concentrated hard. Still nothing. I opened my eyes to tell Hollis that it wasn't working and that he should pick something else. His face looked so hopeful.

"Can you hear her?" he whispered. "Tell me you can."

Hollis had always had a special connection with our mom. Maybe it was because they shared a musical gift.

Or maybe it was because he was the baby of the family. Or maybe because Dad and I were always such a team, they formed their own bond. I could feel how much he missed her, and I felt how unfair it was that she'd left him alone without anyone to understand him. I trembled—with anger, with sadness, I couldn't say—and for a brief moment, I clutched the necklace tight and snapped into a sound from the past.

Momentarily, the aisles of the storage locker hummed with her cello, playing something sweet, moving, sad.

"What do you hear, Leo?" Hollis's voice snapped me back to reality.

I opened my eyes and saw his green eyes, hopeful and sad at the same time. I broke the connection with Hollis and looked down at the green and red jewel in my hand, my knuckles white.

"I heard Mom," I said. "She was playing, I think." And then without thinking, I added, "She said that she was going to give this to you one day." I dropped the necklace into his hand.

"Really? She wanted me to have it?"

I nodded. I had lied, but I was sure what I said was true, or at least it would have been true.

"But what song was she playing? Or did you hear her first recital, or what Mr. Yatzik told her when he gave it to her?"

"No, it doesn't work that way."

"So how does it work?" he asked, putting the necklace back into its red satin drawstring bag and then into his jacket pocket. "What's it like? Does it work on everything? Why do you only hear some parts, and not others?"

"I don't know how it works, it just does. Each time is different. Trevor and I have been trying to figure it out, but we haven't made much progress. Most things that I touch, I get nothing. I have to be in the right mood, I guess. Or the object has to be tied to something important, or emotional. It's hard to explain."

"But what's it like when you do hear something?"

"Sometimes, if it's not a serious trance, it's almost like normal life. I touch something, and I just know—like when you know the answer before the question."

"That's happened to me," Hollis said, nodding his head. "I get that feeling in music—especially when I'm just jamming with other kids. I can sense what they're going to play next."

"I bet that's true, Hollis. I can sound bend, but you and Mom have the power to make music. My power is complicated. Some objects, Hollis, are almost like magnets. Like that dolphin helmet—it grabbed me, called out to me, and when I touched it, I was in this other world for what felt like hours. I call it the space. I can see things in that other world, the space, but it's—"

"Hold on, bro. You see things?"

"Yeah. What I'm seeing are sounds, I think. Like I'm seeing sounds with my ears. Almost like what you see when you listen to music with headphones on and close your eyes. It's exactly like that. But it's been changing lately. It seems to work best when I'm angry or let myself feel . . ."

I was going to go on, but I noticed Hollis had stopped listening and started to sort through another box. He does that when the conversation gets too intense for him, just kind of checks out. I watched him dig into a box marked toys, take off the lid, and dump its contents onto the floor. Out came almost every single old toy that we'd had since I could remember. Toy cars, action figures, stuffed animals, Frankenstein LEGO contraptions superglued together — I never followed the directions.

"Hey, look!" he cried. "There's Ghosty!" His eyes lit up, and we both huddled close to the little toy car.

Ghosty was Hollis's Matchbox car. It was all black and had the words *ghost rider* written on it. We used to play this game with our toy cars and a plastic parking-garage set. The parking garage had a little elevator that could fit two model cars, and when you spun the crank, it would raise the elevator up to the top of the garage, it would ding, and the elevator would open up onto this curly slide. The cars would go streaming down the curly slide for three levels. Hollis and I spent hours racing our cars on that thing. Ghosty was Hollis's car, and something about it — I think it was because it had a broken wheel — made it unbeatable. It would make a grinding noise and edge the other car into the side of the slide and then go flying right past it.

Ghosty. That car used to drive me nuts. No matter which car I used, I never beat it. And Hollis would always squirrel it away, and wait for just the right moment to use it and break my heart.

"Let me see that," I said, and grabbed it. My head filled with sounds from the past.

"Ghosty's like magic," I heard a younger Hollis say in my secret ear. "It can't be beat."

"It's not fair that you have Ghosty," I heard myself whine. "Let me use it this time." And I heard skin slapping skin.

"Give it back, Leo, it's mine!"

Within my trance, I remembered this moment, could see it as clear as life. Hollis and I were in suits and had snuck off to our room to play. But I knew this wasn't a good memory, because I remembered what I said next to Hollis, the lie I told to get even and break *his* heart.

"Fine. You can have Ghosty, Hollis. But guess what, Mom told me you're adopted. And that means you're not their real kid."

Suddenly, I was back in the storage locker in the present, holding Ghosty and hearing myself say, "I'm sorry, Hollis. So sorry." Even though the trance had ended, I could still see Hollis's face that day, how it was first flat and confused, and then how his forehead scrunched up, his eyes squinted, and his lips trembled. I saw him blink out tears that rolled down his suddenly red face. I knew I'd done a terrible thing. That was the first time I ever felt awful, like maybe I was a bad person, but I didn't say sorry, I just opened the door to our room to leave. Outside, everybody was wearing black and sitting on couches and mumbling with these masklike half smiles on their faces. My mom's mom had just died, I think.

"What'd you hear this time, Leo?" Hollis said, taking the car back and putting it in his pocket. "And what are you so sorry about?"

"I just heard you beating me with Ghosty for the millionth time. I'm sorry you always won, you little punk."

The kid had gone through enough already, I figured I didn't need to lay on another emotional apology. Besides, the good news was that at least Hollis wasn't resisting the idea that I had this power. That was progress.

"I'm going to look for this stuff for Crane," I told him. "You should look around, too, and find me anything that seems interesting."

"Um . . . okay." Then he paused. "Actually, I think I'm just going to find a few things from our old room, and then have Stump take me home. I don't like it in here — it's too quiet. All this stuff . . . it just keeps reminding me that they're never coming back."

"Maybe . . ." I said. "Hey, look, there's my old Fisher-Price record player! Think there's an outlet in here?"

"I don't know, Leo," Hollis said, and I recognized the expression on his face — the scrunched-up forehead, the squinty eyes, the red color seeping into his cheeks, the lower lip starting to tremble.

"Hollis, I'll only be a few minutes more. If you just wait for me, we can go home together. Okay?"

But he didn't answer. He had turned his head from mine, but I knew he was starting to cry as he opened the door and let himself out of our parents' tomb.

I felt terrible for Hollis, and part of me knew that I

should get out of there and go home with him, be there for him. But I still had a lot of work to do for Crane, and a few things to find for myself. And then maybe, if I were lucky, Hollis wouldn't have to feel so sad all the time.

I decided to find the Spiricom record first. The whole back wall of the storage locker was filled with boxes of my dad's records. I can't possibly estimate how many records he had, but his collection took up our whole living room and eventually snaked its way into the hall.

As I looked at the wall of boxes, I imagined a map of the world overlaying the boxes and tried to match up my world map with how they were arranged back at home. But where in the world was Spiricom from? It could be anywhere. I paced the aisles, saying, "Spiricom, Spiricom, Spiricom," under my breath until I was carrying on an imaginary conversation with my dad.

Dad, if you'd just talk to me, tell me, it'd be so much easier. I know you're trying to leave me a message. I know there's something I'm supposed to find. Just talk to me, communicate. Communicate.

I'm not saying there was any connection, but in the next second, I suddenly knew what I was looking for. Spiricom. It meant "spirit communication." It had to. I looked at the wall of boxes again and saw my old living room in my mind. I saw the whole wall of records on their shelves — I even saw all the pencil marks on the measuring wall next to the shelves, where my dad used to mark our heights.

And I remembered! Way at the top of the shelves, near the highest window, he had a tiny section that was labeled

EXTRATERRESTRIAL. I tore through about seven or eight boxes until I found one with about fifty really weird records in it—recordings of séances and freaky psychology experiments, records about rockets and space travel, UFOs and the moon landing, a record called *Starbody*, Star Trek records, Space: 1999 records. He had several of this weirdo named Sun Ra—this jazz guy with freaky eyes and a distant stare, always dressed in robes and Egyptian jewelry. And then I was holding it: Spiricom!

The Spiricom record had a white cover with blue writing. There were two records inside of the jacket, and a pamphlet called "The Magic of Living Forever." It was a deluxe and complicated record, a special record, and not one that Jeremy would have forgotten giving to my dad. Jeremy didn't forget records. But I could see why he didn't want to talk about it. Even though everything on it seemed friendly and inviting, the record gave me the creeps.

I stayed perfectly still, holding it in my lap. Shivers crept up and down my spine and to the back of my neck. I knew I should put the Spiricom record away—but I couldn't. I had to hear what was on there. I plugged in my Fisher-Price record player and put on the record, preparing myself to be really terrified.

Like I had thought, the Spiricom record was about communicating with spirits. It started with this old geezer talking, explaining the history of electronic voice phenomena, or EVP, and talking about the scientist named Raudive, who had made all those white-noise recordings of people from beyond the grave. Finally, he played some of the recordings Raudive made. Frankly, they didn't sound much more interesting than walkie-talkie static. But he played one recording several times, and when he slowed it way down, I did hear a voice in there. It was distorted and flat and speaking in another language, but it was a voice of some kind.

Then the old geezer started claiming that he had recorded actual two-way conversations between living and dead people. He had spent years inventing a piece of equipment called a Spiricom device, which a voice from the dead had told him how to build. The idea sounded completely nuts, but then, my power was nuts, too. And the speaker didn't sound nuts — he sounded like a milkman on an old black-and-white TV show.

Still half hoping to be terrified, I flipped the record over to the other side. As I played it, I began to get really sleepy and leaned against the wall, half closing my eyes. I listened as if in a dream. One guy would talk in a normal voice, ask a question, and then there would be a response in this distant mechanical voice, distorted, muffled, and impossible to understand — the voice surrounded with these piercing tones of sound — almost like those artificial voice boxes in all those antismoking commercials — the voice of the dead man, Dr. Bill they called him. He spoke slowly and unintelligibly in his mechanical voice — I kept listening with the hope that maybe Dr. Bill might say something that was unquestionably real, something that really proved the possibility of communicating with the dead, and that maybe there was more to death than we thought. I was incredibly tired but fought off my exhaustion with the thought that real proof for life after death was just around the corner, just a few more rotations of the record away, but my body was inching sideways and down toward the floor with each turn of the record, until I was lying in a pile of my oldest stuffed animals and I was catapulted into my earliest memories.

My mom's voice surrounded me. These were early times, happy times, when there was nothing in the world that couldn't be cured by her hug, her laugh, her voice singing to me. Half asleep and dimly aware of the record playing the ghostly electronic voice, I let my hands explore the stuffed animals and the old blankets around me, taking in all the sweetness and warmth I could from each old soft thing. I heard my toddler voice mixing with their laughter, music and love surrounding me like a warm hug. I felt no anger toward them, only longing. I missed them so much.

But gradually, the music and the laughter faded, and in the corners of my inner vision, I began to see that black mist. It was the same black mist I saw in Jeremy's record store. And it brought with it the voices of friends I no longer knew, memories of disappointment and pain. The black mist spread and extended its inky tentacles deep into my thoughts, corrupting and rotting my power from the inside. I heard memories of death, the deaths of people my parents knew, the deaths of grandparents, until I was in complete blackness and I heard myself weeping in my old room, that dreadful day I learned my parents were never coming back.

I knew then I was asleep, stuck within a nightmare, and it was unfair. And just when it felt like I would never escape this darkness, I felt a hand on my shoulder.

There, standing before me, was the figure I saw when I first listened to that blue disc from my dad, the shaman from the island of my birth, the being of light who gave me my sound-bender powers. He was decked out in a feathered headdress and he shined golden against the blackness.

"You are trapped in darkness," he said without moving his lips. *"You mustn't be afraid. Remember that in the darkness there is more than enough light, but it is hidden deep within Mother Night. Will you remember my words, Sound Bender?"*

"I will," I said.

"Then awaken!"

CHAPTER 10

opened my eyes to a deafening metallic clamor. Someone was pounding on the sliding aluminum door of the storage locker.

"Leo, open up!" Dmitri shouted.

"Beat it, Dmitri," I said without thinking, finding that my Fisher-Price record player had turned itself off and the record was over. What had just happened?

"Leo, the nor'easter is back. Kyu-ho said we need to leave in thirty minutes."

"Then come get me in thirty," I said, trying to shake off this uneasy feeling. Something wrong had just happened, something half sound bending, and half nightmare. But I was back, and there was a lot to do. "I'm in the middle of important work. Bring the hand dolly when you come back."

"Okay, Mr. Leo," he said. Then after a pause, he said what I knew he would say. "Can I come in?"

"Absolutely not."

For the next thirty minutes, I tore through all the boxes I could open, setting aside anything remotely related to Borneo, Antarctica, and Belgian diplomats. Of Borneo, I found a ton, including CDs of my dad's field recordings and his travel journal detailing his month-long trip almost hour by hour. I also found some stuff about their trip to Antarctica, but not as much as I'd hoped. And of Belgian diplomats, I found nothing. But I did find a musty old book by Marie Rathbone, titled *The Immortal Underground*. It was a clothbound hardback with thin yellow pages, and someone had underlined, with a ruler, a bunch of stuff in a red pencil.

I sorted my finds into two sets of boxes. One I would keep for myself, which included my old Fisher-Price record player, some toys from my old room, a few of my dad's records that seemed really cool, including the Spiricom one, the files from Antarctica, and my father's personal travel journal from Borneo. The second set was for Crane, and it contained all of my dad's planning notes for his trip to Borneo, his sketchbook of native instruments, and his attempt at musical notation of their tribal melodies. By the time I was finished, I had gathered a stack of boxes taller than my head. After they were loaded into the car, there was even less room for Dmitri, and he literally had to play a game of 3-D Twister in the back.

The nor'easter was returning in full force, and by the time we crossed the Verrazano Bridge, we were swallowed up by a dizzying moonless cloud of ice. Every now and then, I would get a flash of that terrible feeling from my dream, an echo of something dark accompanied by the electronic voice of Dr. Bill from the Spiricom record. Both the record itself and the Spiricom device seemed somewhat fake, and didn't make me believe that communicating with the dead was possible. But I also found it hard to believe that that man who made the record, the one who sounded like a friendly milkman, had spent years working on that record and his Spiricom device only for a hoax. He must have believed that it was all true, just like when I first told Trevor about my power; how could he doubt something that was so clearly true to me, something I had lived and experienced? Maybe there was something to communicating with the dead?

Nothing was clear in my thoughts. I needed Trevor to help me separate fact from fiction. But what I *wanted* was my parents. I would have given anything, *anything*, just to talk with them again. I felt like crying, but with Dmitri in the back watching my every move, I forced myself to keep it all inside. Feel nothing.

"You are more uneasy than before, Leo," Kyu-Ho said to me.

"Do you believe in life after death, Kyu-Ho?" I asked.

"Confucius, the great philosopher, taught that there is a heaven, but we should not seek it in this life, for it is beyond our understanding. We must build our society as if it were heaven. Confucius teaches us to remember the past, mourn our ancestors, and thank them for what they have given us to help us on our way."

"But what do you really believe, Kyu-Ho?"

"In my dreams, Leo, I have traveled to the land of my ancestors. I have seen the Land of the Dead with my missing eye, and it haunts me. I search for peace, but I fear I will never find it."

That was deep, and I had no answer. Any reassurance that everything was going to work out fine would just be insulting—he hadn't tried to sugarcoat it, and neither would I. So I remained quiet on the moonless trip across the bridge, and for the rest of the ride.

We got off the Brooklyn-Queens Expressway, and when we turned off the avenue for the waterfront, I realized that the whole area was still without power. Some power lines were still on the ground, half buried in ice crystals. None of the streetlights were on, not even the traffic lights.

All of the windows of Crane's Mysteries were black—from the second to the seventh floor. Klevko came out, carrying two electric lanterns, to help with the cargo as I said good-bye to Kyu-Ho. He bowed and told me he hoped that I could find peace. I did the same. Then he drove off, taking off the rest of his bumper on a fire hydrant not thirty feet from me.

"These boxes are for Crane, Klevko," I said, pointing to the ones I had put together especially for him.

"I will deliver them now," Klevko answered. "He is waiting."

"And these two are for me." I indicated the boxes with my toys, the Antarctica information, and my dad's journal.

Klevko gave me one of the lanterns. "Still no power in the building," he said. "I call the power man all day, but they tell me there's not enough people in our area to fix the power. Maybe they come tomorrow. For now, we have backup generator for elevator and security. Dmitri will help you with personal boxes."

We rode the elevator to the seventh floor, Klevko quickly disappearing into a hallway with Crane's boxes, while Dmitri trailed behind me with the hand dolly. He loaded the boxes into my dark room, then left down the hallway without a light.

Hollis was in his room, but he wasn't doing great. He was curled up in his bed, hugging his knees, and didn't even flinch when I entered. I knew he was reeling, because when he's really sad he tries to stay as perfectly still as possible. When he was young and sulking, he would disappear for hours on end, making my mom both furious and terrified that she had lost him. She'd always find him somewhere, in a closet under a pile of clothes or some crawl space, not talking, as motionless as a hibernating squirrel. He was clutching Ghosty in his hand.

"You all right?" I said, kneeling by his bed.

He shook his head, just slightly. His eyes were open, but he didn't look at me.

"Are you mad at me?"

He shook his head no.

"Just not feeling so good?"

He nodded, and I heard him grunt softly. I noticed that

above his bed, he had hung our mom's watermelon crystal necklace on a nail.

"I'm right next door, chief. I'll check on you in a little while, but come get me if you need anything or want to sleep in my room. Okay? I'm going to take care of everything."

Back in my room, I set the lantern on my nightstand and got into bed with all the papers I had gathered about Antarctica. I read through their itinerary, a schedule for my mom's string quartet, information about the colony they were staying at, maps of the continent and the icebergs, packing recommendations, and other papers. But nothing that had anything to do with who organized their trip, the plane they took down to explore the icebergs of Antarctica, or who flew it. Or even the plane's route. I needed more information. Much more information. To get to the bottom of their disappearance, I was going to have to call the rest of my mom's quartet, dig through her old e-mails, even go down to Antarctica myself and get whatever I could from the base. But that would take time, lots of time, and even more money.

I moved on to my dad's travel journal instead. For every music trip he took, he kept a careful and thorough journal of almost everything he did, everyone he met, and every thought he had — in case he ever needed to go back. All of it written in green ink. The trip to Borneo lasted over a month, and the whole journal was filled with green ink. I flipped through the pages, trying to find any mention of that mask he brought back, but soon I was reading more and more of each entry, until I was caught up in his adventure, traveling up the Kayan River in a longboat through murky green waters, the jungle on every side of him, stopping at river villages where the people lived in long row houses. I could visualize them, covered in elaborate tattoos, their stretched earlobes carrying dozens of heavy wooden rings. According to his journal, he visited over twenty villages, some of them somewhat modernized and near plantations, some of them down murky backwaters of the river where the villagers lived as they had for thousands of years. Some of the villages represented all that was left of their tribe, with their language, their customs, and their culture shared by only thirty people.

Someone knocked on the door.

"Hollis, is that you? Just come in, chief."

When nobody answered, I opened the door, but no one was there. I checked in Hollis's room, and he hadn't moved a muscle.

Returning to my bed, I picked up where I left off, reading strange tales by the lantern light. One visit to a town called Byong Ku got my attention.

11/5, 6:30 p.m.: Arrived at village of Byong Ku earlier today after a four-hour trek over a mountain ridge. Very eerie and deserted. Two guides from my party went ahead to make contact with the villagers and ask permission for me to visit. They approved, and at 4:30 p.m., I entered their village. My main guide, Lapsing, says these villagers do not mix with the rest of the villages in the area, that they have isolated themselves for unknown reasons.

The villagers greeted me warmly. They have seen a few other Westerners, missionaries mostly, but live in a completely traditional mode. Approximately 60 villagers present. Lapsing reports that their language is unique to their village. One of the scout guides, Trogo, shares some words with them, but only a few, and much is lost in translation. The villagers accepted the trinkets and food we offered, and have invited us to stay with them and sleep in their row house. I am intrigued by them, but in what way, I cannot yet say.

11/6, 4:45 p.m.: Have spent the day observing and inquiring about their music traditions, but am having difficulty communicating this idea. They seem unaware of music. I have seen no musical instruments, nor do they seem to make music in their daily lives. They have allowed me to observe a medicine woman tending to a dying man. She performed a "soul-catching" ritual on him, using an engraved pole and smoke. The old man shows no improvement and will surely die within the day.

11/7, 10:30 a.m.: Old man died last night.

11/8, 3:50 a.m.: Have just returned from old man's death ceremony. The villagers do make music but only during death ceremonies. The villagers deny they are making music at all, and now back at the row house, they claim to have no memory of the elaborate ceremony just performed. Death ceremony was as follows. The dead man's wooden coffin was placed on ceremonial rocks at dusk, and laid with flowers and plants by all villagers. At nightfall, a fire was lit, and all adult men and women donned ancient masks, some comforting, some grotesque like the particularly haunting twin mask. They quickly entered profound trance states. The men played different pitched hollow rocks and lithophones with mallets, while the women danced. Children assisted. No singing. Trogo explains that while in trance, the villagers transport themselves to the Land of the Dead, said to be over another mountain ridge and across a river. During the death ceremony, they guide the dead man's spirit into the Land of the Dead, playing music so he will follow and not stay back to haunt the village and the surface world. When the dead man's spirit reaches the Land of the Dead, the music stops, and the ceremony is over. Made several high-quality recordings to be examined later. Now to bed.

I shut my eyes as well, imagining this horrific ritual half a world away—seeing the tribespeople in their masks dancing around the fire to ghostly drums, their leader wearing the grotesquely haunting twin mask. It was such a disturbing vision that I was actually relieved when I heard an insistent knocking at my door. It wasn't a friendly knock and it seemed to rattle my very bones.

"Who's there?" I croaked. I shoved the diary under my mattress just as the door opened and Klevko barged in, looking sweaty and agitated.

"Leo! Get up right now. Crane wants you."

"Tell him not now, that I'm sleeping," I said. Crane. Everything single thing he did seemed planned to catch me off guard.

"No. Crane demands to see you. You follow me, yes? You must. I cannot leave the room without you," he said, and twitched his pec muscle.

There was no arguing, so I followed Klevko as he headed swiftly down the hall. I jogged after him to the Sword Room. Outside the window, it was completely white. Klevko walked to the armored knight figure and looked at it suspiciously.

"I know about the secret panel, Klevko. Go ahead."

I had discovered that secret passageway shortly after moving in.

He nodded and pushed the knight's pinkie, opening a tunnel entrance next to the giant-screen TV. We went in and got into the tiny elevator. He slid a key into a socket by the D.N.D. button, and it lit up green. We were going to the Do Not Disturb Room, Crane's room so secret I'd never been in there.

"The D.N.D. Room," I said. "I'm moving up in the world."

"Not up, Leo," he said. "We go sideways, then down."

The dark elevator trembled quickly, then the whole car shot away with a grinding jerk. I went slamming into Klevko.

"You are sweaty, Leo."

"So are you, big guy."

The elevator seemed to pivot on a dime and shot downward. It was getting difficult to breathe in that little coffin of a space.

"We are far below street level," Klevko whispered. The elevator lurched. "And now we are here."

Klevko opened the elevator, which led into a completely dark hallway, except for a small blinking red light. In that reddish glow, I could barely make out a giant metal door at the end of the hall. It looked like a bank vault, with a wheel and everything. Klevko guided me down the hall, and when we reached the door, he put his finger on the blinking red light until it turned steady red, then spun the huge wheel until it clicked into place. The door swung open and banged against the metal hallway, the noise reverberating in my ears.

"I stay here, Leo. You go in."

Klevko gave me a friendly shove and slammed the door behind me. I groped around in the darkness, feeling the polished metal walls on either side. I knocked my knuckles against them and heard only a muffled thud — that meant the walls were several feet thick. Sweat was beading along my forehead and dripping down my cheeks, and I could hear the sound of my own breathing. Ahead, the air felt cooler.

"Right this way," Crane's voice slithered out of the darkness.

"I can't see anything," I called out.

"Yes, Leo, but I can see you on my surveillance camera. I will guide you. Just follow my voice."

I fumbled toward the sound and turned a corner, then saw a sliver of light at the end of the passageway. I followed it until I reached a metallic door. I pushed it open, and there he was, sitting at a polished black desk, the lantern on it shimmering off his pale white hands and shiny smooth head. Behind him, the wall was lined with old military muskets and rifles. To his right, a giant safelike contraption took up half the room. On the wall to his left, hung a life-size painting of an old balding woman with a face just like Crane's.

"Have a seat, Leo." He motioned to a carved wooden chair in front of his desk.

"No," I said. "Not until you tell me what this is all about. I spent this afternoon doing you a favor, but you're still messing with me."

Slowly, as he rocked back and forth in his chair, a smile spread across his face. "I see you're beginning to speak up for yourself. Good. Very good, Leo." He reached into a drawer, pulled out a folder, and tossed it on the desk.

"What's that?"

"My return favor, Leo. I always honor a business transaction. Information about your Belgian diplomat."

I sat down and opened the folder on the desk. Inside was only a blank sheet of white paper.

"There's nothing here," I snapped.

"Exactly. There is no Bertrand Veirhelst in the flesh. Your Belgian diplomat only exists on paper. I'm afraid this Pieter, your little school-yard tough, was having a bit of fun with you. Bertrand Veirhelst is a straw man, as hollow as a drum."

"I don't understand, a straw man?"

"A straw man is a manufactured agent, an invented fiction meant to confuse the enemy. Governments will spend years inventing their straw man, then leak his information to the enemy so they'll chase a ghost and ignore the real spies in their midst. Bertrand Veirhelst is such a straw man, a man who appeared to move in the world and talk with people, but who only existed on paper."

I could hardly believe it, but I checked my astonishment in front of Crane. "I guess that's okay because I won't be at Satellite North much longer, right?"

"Not so fast, Leo," he said, pulling out that familiar burlap bag and placing it on the desk. "The information you gave me from the Borneo expedition, while voluminous, failed to illuminate. I have been poring over it. Your father visited almost thirty villages, none of which match your description. And nowhere in his files is there anything about a mask, just rubbish about music."

"I told you everything I know about that mask," I lied.

With a suddenly violent movement, Crane pounded his fist on the desk so hard that the lantern trembled. His face had turned red. "Half-truths and lies, and nothing more, Leo. I am frustrated beyond belief, and as you know, I do not enjoy frustration." He removed the mask from the burlap bag and slid it across the desk, its hollow eyes staring at me. "I am convinced that somewhere in that empty skull of yours, you know more. Perhaps your dull memory will sharpen with touch. Now take the mask in your hands and tell me what comes to mind."

I just shook my head. Feel nothing, I told myself. Feel nothing.

Crane leaned back in his chair, his head out of the lantern light, and rocked for a long time. "You and I have not always seen eye to eye," he said in a different tone of voice. He had switched tracks. "We've quarreled and argued and plotted, just like two brothers. Just as I used to quarrel with my dear brother."

"You mean 'stepbrother.'"

"No, Leo, we were brothers in every sense but one. I loved your father, and he loved me. Why else would he leave you to me? No, we understood each other. More than you can imagine. I have always followed his work, you see. And in his memory, I have continued his work, just as you have. Now let us continue his work . . . together."

"You're nothing like my father," I said through clenched teeth. "Nothing."

"That's right!" he boomed, lurching forward into the light. "Your father wasted his life chasing music. Music?!" He laughed savagely. "A worthless trifle for the stupid and weak. While I . . . I . . ." He paused to laugh. "While I have uncovered real treasures . . . real objects only spoken of in legend, the real objects that history would rather forget. And what has that gotten me? They call me a gray-market dealer, a shady businessman on the fringes of the law. But no matter. I'll prove them wrong. My work is exactly like your father's, only he was too cowardly to search for real truth."

"I hate you!" I screamed.

"Good. Now take it!" he growled from his throat, shoving the mask into my hands.

I grasped the mask, my hands like claws, my thumbs digging into the hollow eye sockets with all their savage force. The world melted away in a flash of inner lightning, and I went down. I felt myself disappearing into that storm drain from the day before when Crane split Hollis and me apart, dropping down fast as a bullet into the sewers, drumming sounds all around me, pulsing and beating. My being seemed to race underground as fast as thoughts through murky tunnels and mazes, zigzagging but always going down, always down, traveling through the entire Earth itself into another underground maze, going faster and faster, drawn by a terrible black hole until I reached a cavernous wall, and there saw the other half of the shadowy mask gazing across its underground domain, eyes black as death. All around me the hypnotic beat of otherworldly drums.

Summoning all my powers of concentration, I pried my hands off the mask and snapped back to myself. My fingers were stinging with pain. My right thumb was bleeding, caught on a sharp edge.

Crane was watching me carefully. Did he know that I had traveled through time and space? I honestly couldn't tell, and he certainly wasn't saying.

"I'm starting to remember more," I said.

"I thought you might, Leo. Now tell me everything."

"Not yet. I want something from you," I said, and wiped the blood on my thumb onto the white sheet of paper. "I don't ever want to go back to Satellite North. I want to go back to my old school immediately."

"I will see to it as soon as —"

"I'm not done, Crane. I want you to fund a fact-finding mission to Antarctica. I want to know everything that happened to my parents. Everything."

"Hmm . . ." he said, taking the white piece of paper and scribbling on it. "If you lead me to the other half of the mask, which I believe you can, I will allot one hundred thousand dollars for the mission," he said.

"I want a hundred and fifty thousand."

"We'll see how much I can sell the mask for. If it's complete, it should raise a pretty penny. But first, you must guide me to it."

"You're going to sell the mask? I thought this was about history, about truth."

"Of course it is. The mask will be photographed and documented, then I will sell it to the highest bidder. Perhaps that will be a museum. It matters little to me. Come now, Leo, we understand each other. You know I have only two loves, Leo, money and my dear mother. Now sign this document."

He slid the paper across to me. In black ink, he had written:

I, Crane Rathbone, on the date of February 17, do hereby swear to fund a fact-finding mission to Antarctica totaling no less than $100,000, if Leo Lomax will guide me and my expedition and prove instrumental in recovering the missing half of the Long Pulling Conjoined-Twin Mask, to match the half in my possession, inventory #8367-99909-76187-33. Additionally, I, Crane Rathbone, also pledge to reinstate Leo

*Lomax into the Academy of Science and Arts effective imme-
diately upon successful execution of this contract.*

There was a dotted line for my signature, right next to
Crane's signature, just above my bloodstain. I took the pen
in my hand and signed.

"The mask is underground, in a cave or a tunnel," I said
to him. "I believe it's in the village of Byong Ku."

"And you believe this why?"

"My dad said the villagers there wore it during some
weird death ceremony."

"Excellent, Leo. That wasn't so hard was it? A little
unpleasant, but that's behind us now. If you continue to
be helpful, you will find that your future will be much
brighter. Now pack a bag, and pack one for Hollis as well.
Tomorrow night, we leave for the jungle."

CHAPTER 11

'm not sure how someone is supposed to feel after signing a shady midnight deal with Crane Rathbone — in blood, no less — but I felt great.

When I got back to my room, I had no idea what time it was because all the power was still off, but it felt late. I poked my head into Hollis's room and was relieved to see he had fallen asleep. As I looked at him clutching Ghosty, I wished with all my power that I could bring our parents back . . . for him, and for me.

As I reviewed what I needed to do to get ready for the trip, the only thing nagging at me was Trevor. My phone was dead, but I didn't want to call him anyway. What I had to tell him was complicated, and you don't always hear everything you're supposed to on the phone. An e-mail was out of the question for obvious reasons, so after pacing the room for a while thinking about my friendship with him, I decided to put my thoughts down on paper. If I couldn't get in touch with him tomorrow through electronic means, I could always drop a letter in the mailbox.

FEB 17

Dear Trevor,

I hope you'll believe me when I say that I've tried to call you a million times over the last few days, but for various reasons, I've never been able to get through. And although I've needed you more than ever, maybe it's better that we didn't actually connect.

Tomorrow, I'm leaving with Crane and Hollis for Borneo, for a trip lasting anywhere from a week to a month. I've agreed to help Crane locate the other half of that Siamese twin mask. You remember it, right? It's worth a fortune, and he is obsessed with finding it.

Now I know you probably don't understand why I'm doing this, or you probably think that Crane has black-mailed me in some way. But it was my decision, and you're the only person in the world who I can be totally honest with about why I made that decision.

I believe there is a chance my parents are still alive. Maybe I just hope there's a chance. In any case, I can't rest until I know for sure. Remember that note I channeled in Jeremy's store? Well, I heard something on it, a conversation between my dad and a shadowy Belgian diplomat, who turned out to be a spy, which makes me wonder if my parents' death might have been faked, for reasons I don't know yet. Even if they really are dead, I've got to know what happened to them. And even if it turns out they simply died in a plane crash like everyone says they did, I'm starting to believe that maybe there's more to death than we think. And maybe I can use my power to know for sure.

I hope you understand. I know Crane is a bad guy, but I made the deal with him in the hopes that good will come from it. I would have asked him to bring you on the trip, but I don't think he likes you much after our last trip, and I think that whatever it is I'm searching for, I'll have to find it alone.

Please understand.

Your best friend,

Leo

I read it over once, and though I didn't get everything down the way I wanted, it was close enough.

I unpacked one of the boxes with a few of my old toys and the records I brought home from the storage locker as well as the CDs my dad had made from his Borneo trip. I set up my Fisher-Price turntable, which gave me a little feeling of home. It was certainly the lowest-tech thing in my superautomated, supersleek, supermodern room at Uncle Crane's. Before going to bed, I reread the contract just to make sure Crane hadn't put in anything sneaky, but he hadn't. I wanted to stash that somewhere safe while I was gone. As I was looking for a good hiding place, I did double duty and also searched for the package from my dad, the one with his letter and my blue disc. I looked in every drawer, in between books on my bookshelf, even stood on a chair to check way back in the top shelf of my closet. When I still couldn't find the disc, I considered the very real possibility that Crane had swiped it like he swiped my computer. I wanted to make sure to find a perfect hiding place for my contract so he couldn't ever claim that it had disappeared, too.

I folded up the contract into a tiny square and crept out into the Mask Room. It was still white outside, but the whiteness was less thick and I could almost swear I saw the moon reflecting off the ocean in the distance. I scanned all the ghostly masks, and when I found one with a large gaping serpent mouth, I stashed the contract in the hollow cavity inside of it. Then I went to bed.

I slept like a baby. No weird dreams, just relaxing, restful sleep. When I woke up, the sheets and my pillow even felt soft. Maybe my bed had just needed to be worked in a little. When I finally glanced at my bedside clock, it said 9:15. The power was back on!

I took a deep breath, smiled, then ordered some breakfast from Olga on the control panel. Bacon and eggs, with a side of French toast. So long, stale granola bars. I noticed that there was a stack of adventure clothes that had miraculously appeared in the corner of my room. Before my food came, I took a long, luxurious hot shower. Just like that weird record, *Fresh Metzger*, I'd found in Jeremy's store a few weeks back, I felt fresh. Today was going to be a good day. Today was a fresh start.

After I'd gotten dressed in some of my new adventure gear, waterproof khaki pants and a shirt that felt made out of Windbreaker material, Dmitri arrived with my breakfast, carrying it all on a black lacquer platter. I was starving, and it smelled delicious.

"Here is your breakfast, Mr. Leo," he said. "Matka made the bacon extra crispy for you and squeezed fresh orange juice."

"Put in on my desk, Dmitri. Thanks."

I sat down and got busy, making a French-toast-with-eggs-and-bacon sandwich. Just as I was about to dig in, I heard Klevko's voice on the intercom in my room.

"You have a visitor downstairs, Leo," he said. "The man who has a ponytail like a woman."

"His name is Jeremy, Klevko. Can you just send him up?"

"No. That would make the boss very unhappy."

"He's a friend of mine, Klevko. It's not like he's going to steal anything."

"I will have to search him. If he is clean, I will escort him to your room."

"Be sure to fingerprint him, too, Klevko."

"But I don't have fingerprinting equipment here," he said, sounding slightly panicked.

"It was a joke, Klevko. I didn't mean it."

"Security is no joke," he said without laughing. Just before the intercom clicked off, I heard him say to Jeremy, "You, with the hair longer than my grandmother's, put your hands out to the side. . . ."

I had just enough time to wolf down the rest of my breakfast sandwich before I heard footsteps in the hall. I ran out of my room to see Jeremy walking toward me with Klevko trailing close on his heels like he was a criminal about to bolt.

"Tell your buddy here that next time he can skip the pat-down," Jeremy said. "I don't appreciate the physical contact."

"You can go now, Klevko," I said. "We're fine."

As Klevko turned to go, Jeremy called after him. "By the way, there's another visitor on the way. He's a skinny thirteen-year-old, pretty scary, so you'll want to beef up your security measures. Call a code red or code orange or something."

"Trevor's coming?" I asked Jeremy excitedly. "How's he getting here?"

"A hundred or so years ago, they invented something called the subway. . . . "

"No, I mean, how'd he get off school?"

"It's a snow day. He texted me to say he was stopping by. He texted you, too, but I guess you didn't answer him. Speaking of which, I've been calling you nonstop, but your phone's been going straight to voice mail. You've got to stay in touch, my man."

"Sorry, Jeremy," I said as we walked into my room. "I'm all right. Things have been quiet here, and dark. We lost power for a while, that's why you couldn't get through, but it's back now. You didn't have to come all the way over here."

"No problem. It's good to see you. And I get a chance to check out your room. So this is it, huh?"

Jeremy glanced around, silently checking out all my deluxe accessories — the control panel above the bed with its intercom and TV remotes, the Swedish-designed bed with its chrome headboard, the mini-refrigerator built into the wall, the modular closet organizer with built-in shoe racks and wire baskets.

"Not bad. It's a little spare, but not bad. Not like your old room, that's for sure."

"Yeah, that was so crowded with stuff, Hollis and I had to jump over piles to get to our beds," I said. "That was fun."

"Oh, I see you got some records here!" Jeremy said, and walked over to the boxes on the floor. Just like it was a reflex, he started flipping through them.

"I got them from my dad's storage locker. Maybe we can go sometime and you can pick out some of the good ones."

"Sure, Leo. But it looks like you're doing okay without me. Not bad," he said, flipping through each one. "Oh, you got the Sun Ra album, *Space Is the Place*! Did you know the cover folds out, and you can see Sun Ra from head to toe? Check it out."

He opened up the cover. It was a gatefold cover, one of those ones that open like a book. Along one whole side was a continuous image of Sun Ra, wearing a robe and a wild Egyptian headdress.

Jeremy put it back and flipped through more records.

"*Oh,*" he said, his voice tightening. "I see you found that Spiricom record, too?"

"Yup. No thanks to you. Why'd you lie about it?"

"What do you mean?"

"Come on, Jeremy. You never forget a record. Especially not one as weird as that."

"I-I didn't mean to, Leo. I thought it might scare you, I guess. In fact, I think I'm going to take this from you. I'll hold it for you—"

"No, it's mine. Besides, I listened to some of it already, and it's no big deal."

Jeremy walked over to my bed and flopped down, leaning back on his elbows so he could get a good look at me.

"You guys have had a big shock," he said. "A trauma like that can make people believe strange things."

"Like that you can communicate with the dead."

"Yup, like that."

I sat back down in my desk chair and rolled it over to Jeremy, so we could talk face-to-face. I respected his intelligence. So did my dad, which is why his will placed Jeremy in charge of overseeing our education. Maybe this was a conversation I could have with him, man-to-man.

"Do you ever think, Jeremy, that maybe there's something to it? I mean, the guy on the record seemed to think there was. And so did Raudive and Jürgenson and about a million other scientists. Are they all nuts? Maybe there's more to death than we think."

"Leo," he sighed, twirling his ponytail around his fingers until they were white. "This is exactly why you shouldn't have that record, and exactly what I was scared of."

"Why? You don't know everything."

"Yeah, Leo, but talking with dead people? Come on, use your head."

"I have. And you always say listen to your feelings. Have you ever died? No, you haven't, so you don't know what it's like. Maybe we can actually talk with them. Maybe the dead are still around. Don't a lot of people believe that after you die, that you're born again into a new body? Maybe the dead are all around us. And if they are, shouldn't we try to find them, to talk to them? Shouldn't we try to know what happens when you die? What about those voices Raudive recorded? I heard them."

Jeremy took a moment before he answered me. I could tell he was planning his answer carefully.

"Listen, Leo," he said at last, looking directly at me. "I think it's possible that maybe parts of people stay around after they die, like scattered fragments, just stray parts of their minds. And a lot of people do believe in things like heaven and reincarnation, and maybe they're not wrong. There are as many opinions about death as there are people, and the truth is, they're all just opinions, beliefs. No one knows for certain. But to think you can communicate with the spirit world is just . . ."

"You want to say crazy, I know it."

"I don't think you're crazy. I think you want to believe something that will make you feel better. I get that."

I didn't answer. Jeremy wasn't giving me enough credit.

"Okay, try to think of it this way," he said. "Imagine there's a guy alone in a room. And in this room, they play a steady tone that he just barely hears. It's called a subliminal sound, and it's so quiet that he only hears it about half the time. Now some scientists outside the room ask the guy to write down whenever the tone gets louder or softer. Even though the volume of that tone never actually changes, it seems to get louder and softer to him."

Jeremy was sounding like Trevor, who always explained everything with a scientific experiment and ended with a question.

"So why did the sound change for him?" Jeremy asked, and without waiting for my answer, went right on. "Because his unconscious mind, the part of our self that we aren't aware of when we're awake, the part that dreams and makes us do all the things we can't account for, it ebbs and flows like the tide throughout the day. When he's more alert and focusing on something, he doesn't hear it. And when his unconscious is in charge, he does. He lets it in."

"I don't get your story, Jeremy," I snapped at him. "Are you telling me that I shouldn't listen? That I should tune everything out?"

"No, Leo. It means that our minds can deceive us. We can hear things that aren't there. Make connections between fragments where there are no connections. Hear voices in static."

This was so frustrating. I hate it when people make a really good argument that goes against everything that you want to believe. Like that there aren't mermaids under-neath the sea or that aliens aren't right here on Earth living among us. You can put up all the great arguments you want, but in the end, who's to say it's not true?

"Jeremy," I said, standing up from my chair to let him know I was done with the conversation. "All I know is that you're not supposed to lie to me. You're my tutor and you're supposed to teach me, to tell me the truth. But you lied to me. My dad was interested in that Spiricom record, but you wanted to keep that from me, and that's not fair."

"Leo, I'm sorry. I was treating you like a kid, and I shouldn't have. Listen, I'm the one who first told your dad about this record, and I can tell you, none of this leads anywhere. You just go in circles, chasing ghosts and grasping at straws. There's never enough information. Every little piece you find seems connected and intriguing, but it's all just fragments."

I walked to my closet and got out my duffel bag. It was time to start packing.

"So listen, Hollis and I are leaving with Crane tonight. We're going to Borneo, and I'm going to help him recover part of a lost artifact. A Siamese twin mask. My dad brought back half, and we're going to find the other half. Maybe after I get back, we can make a fresh start."

"*What?* You're going to Borneo? Tonight? And you're helping Crane? Is he making you, or is he up to something tricky?"

"No, it was my decision."

"I don't get it, Leo. Three weeks ago you called him a crook and destroyed that horrible dolphin helmet of his. You stood your ground, man. And now you want to go off with this . . . this grave robber?"

"People change, Jeremy. I can handle Crane. And is what he does really so different from what you do?"

"Like night and day."

Jeremy, always so laid back and cool, was standing up and yelling at me. Well, yelling for Jeremy, which is just talking really slowly and with extra calm. It was driving me nuts. He was so sure of himself, and so sure of what I should do, but what did he know about my life? I wanted him to see my side—that making a deal with Crane was good for me. Good for Hollis.

"You travel around the world looking for records," I said as if someone else was in control of my mouth. "You find them, their owners don't know their real value, you buy them for cheap, bring them back to your store, and sell them for the highest price. You're always telling me that records are artifacts, right? What's the difference?"

He opened his mouth and slapped his leg. "Everything. I mean, I'm just buying records. They're just toys, you know? They're just records."

"Just records?" I asked, raising my eyebrows, and took the Spiricom record from him and put it back in my pile.

"Listen, Leo. I'm going to talk to Crane. If he lets me come on the trip with you, do you want me to? I'd like to because I feel like you're on shaky ground here."

"I don't know where he is," I answered, "but do whatever you want. I have a lot of stuff to do before tonight, and I have to pack, so . . ."

"Okay," he said, defeated. "I'm going to go find Crane. I'll be back."

I buzzed for Klevko, who brought the elevator up. As Jeremy got in, I heard him ask to be taken to see Crane. I was glad I wasn't going to be present at that meeting. Jeremy wasn't exactly popular with my uncle. In fact, Jeremy and Crane Rathbone were about as opposite as two men can get.

I went to rouse Hollis. It was after ten but he was still sound asleep. I knew he'd had a rough night but he'd made it through okay, at least well enough to get under the covers. I dangled a little piece of string I had over his face, and his lips made these chimplike movements until finally he cracked an eyelid.

"Hey, Hollis," I whispered. "How'd you like to fly on a private jet tonight?"

He sat straight up, eyes wide.

"And then once we get where we're going, we'll go on a yacht."

"Whoa . . . really?"

"Well, it'll be a boat in any event."

"Wait, what's going on, Leo?"

"Crane wants me to come with him to Borneo, to help him find the lost half of that mask he's crazy about, and I said I'd only go if you went, too."

"*Really?*" But then he thought twice. "Borneo? I don't know, Leo. That sounds weird. How long? And who else is going?"

"Just you and me and Crane, maybe Klevko and Dmitri, too. I don't know how long, a week, maybe more."

"What about school?"

"Crane's going to take care of it. And once we get back, we'll be going to the same school again. What do you say? It'll be a chance for us to get out of Brooklyn, cruise down the river, do some adventuring, and then we can come back here and start fresh. Come on, chief. Are you in?"

"Let me think about it," he said, but I knew he was just playing his cards close. He would come around soon.

"All right, but don't think too long. Trust me, you don't want to miss a chance to fly on a private jet. There's nothing like it."

"Are you forgetting, I took the private jet back from Palmira with you guys?"

"Yeah, but that was a flight in anger. This one will be different. More fun."

"And the yacht?"

"The yacht might just be a long motorboat, but who cares? It'll be like when we used to go on those crazy trips with Dad, only we'll be going with Crane, and you know him, he travels in style. Come on, just say yes." And I bounced around the room like a boxer, throwing soft punches on his arm. "Come on, come on, come on, Hollis."

"*All right.*"

"Hooray!" I cried, and grabbing a pillow from his bed, danced around the room like Muhammad Ali, then launched myself at him with a flying guillotine attack. But he was ready for it, and he got in a couple of good blows with his other pillow. We laughed and wrestled until we were giddy and winded.

"What's with you, Leo? You're so hyper," he said, chucking a pillow at me, which I dodged.

"You missed me again! I just feel good, chief. The power's back on, and I feel powerful!" I pulled the front of my shirt over my head, so that my belly was exposed. When we used to wrestle when we were younger, that was the way I turned into Jessie the Frog, my superpowerful alter ego. "I am transforming into Jessie the Frog. The frog is out. The frog is back!"

"Noooooo!" Hollis screamed.

As he raced for me and pounced, I heard footsteps in the hall, then the door opened, and Trevor and Klevko stepped in.

Without missing a beat, Trevor took two long strides on his spidery legs and literally flew halfway across the room, landing a perfect body tackle on me.

"The New Guy saves the day!" he shouted.

"Not the New Guy!" I screamed from the ground.

The New Guy was Trevor's alter ego. When Hollis and I used to wrestle, he would mostly just watch, but every now and then, just to mix it up, he would say, "And then the New Guy saves the day," then attack one of us at random and play the wild card.

"You boys wrestle like little birds," Klevko snorted, pushing up his sweater sleeves to show his massive arms. "If you want, I show you how men in my country spar."

"That's okay, Klevko," I said, knowing that one attack move from him would have any of us twisted up like the little pretzel shards at the bottom of the bag.

He looked Trevor up and down disapprovingly.

"You are skinny like one of Olga's string beans," he said. "You could never wrestle a bear, like I do."

"That's disappointing, man, because bear wrestling is my favorite sport," Trevor said.

Klevko ignored Trevor's sarcasm and turned to me. "Leo, I go find your uncle and see if he has crushed your other friend yet. And unless you want this one to be crushed, too, you must keep this visit short."

When Klevko was gone, I crawled to my feet and got us each a bottle of water from the mini-fridge in the wall.

"So, I hear it's a snow day for you," I said to Trevor.

"Yup. And since you don't ever feel like answering your phone, I thought I'd come by and see if you were all right."

"Cool," I said. "Let's go hang out in my room for a bit. Hollis, get ready, all right?"

"Yeah, all right," he said, and flipped on his TV.

I hadn't been back in my room with Trevor for ten seconds when Hollis hollered for me. As I was leaving, Trevor asked, "Hey, your bathroom doesn't have like a futuristic levitating toilet or something, does it? I think I just peed my pants laughing."

"Normal toilet, man. I'll be right back. Let me just see what the boy wants. Oh, and if you have time, there's a letter on the desk for you."

I walked out and stuck my head into Hollis's room.

"Check it out, bro," he said, motioning to his TV screen.

Mike Hazel was on, but all of his cocky confidence and door-busting bluster were gone.

"And as I sign off," he said, looking earnestly into the camera, "I'd like to repeat my apology to Crane's Mysteries. On behalf of myself and the Fox Five news team, we had no right to insinuate that Crane's Mysteries had anything to do with that Russian dolphin helmet, and we apologize once again for characterizing Crane's Mysteries as operating 'on the edge of the law.' In the news business, we're only as good as our sources, and we were misled. But we take full responsibility. Ernie, back to you."

Hollis shut it off.

"That didn't take long," Hollis said. "The man got Craned."

"Yeah, how's that crow taste, Mike Hazel?" I taunted the blank TV screen. "What a stupid fake name anyway."

As I walked back to my room, it was clearer to me than ever before that my uncle Crane was no one to mess with. He always got his way.

CHAPTER 12

Trevor was sitting at my desk, reading my letter and stroking his chin. I waited for him to finish it.

"What do you think, Trev?"

He scrunched up his face and shook his head.

"Boy, I don't know, Leezer. I don't even know where to begin. Does Crane know about your . . ." He lowered his voice. ". . . power?"

"I'm not sure. I don't think so, unless Dmitri heard everything when we were in the record store, which I don't think he did . . . unless he's managed to get his hands on the blue disc."

"Is that a possibility?" Trevor asked, alarm in his voice.

I just shrugged. I knew I had been sloppy with the disc, and I didn't want to confess that to Trevor. I sat quietly, watching him assess the situation. You could almost see his amazing brain working.

"You've used your power already to help Crane, right? And you'll use it on the trip, right? Even though we both know the man's a crook."

As always, Trevor didn't miss much.

"I admit it's not great to be helping him," I said. "But I have to do what I have to do."

"Do you?"

"Yeah, I do. For Hollis and me, I do."

"I can't really put myself in your place," Trevor said, shaking his head. "I don't know what it's like to lose your parents. I can't imagine my life without my mom and dad. So maybe you do have to do what you have to do."

One of the things I like best about Trevor Davis — have always liked ever since that first day I met him in kindergarten at PS 78 — is that he can put himself in another guy's place and really get what he's going through.

"I just think you need to look at this from all sides, Leo," Trevor was saying. "Use some critical thinking." That was the scientist in him speaking.

"I have. Trev, look at me. Do I seem nutty or off my rocker? Or am I sobbing uncontrollably?"

"You seem fine, Leo. I mean, you seem really good but . . ."

"But what?"

"This is today. How will you be tomorrow, or the day after that? Two days ago you were ready to run away, you wanted out of here immediately. And now . . . I can't stop you, Leo. I know you've made up your mind, but I think it's really dangerous. Dangerous for a lot of reasons, not the least of which is Crane."

"You and Jeremy," I sighed. "You guys think everything I'm doing is so dangerous."

"Maybe because it's true, buddy."

"Listen, Trev, even though you're not going, I need you with me on this. And I want you to help me when I get back. . . . I've been thinking that maybe I should use my power to see what's beyond the grave."

"Oh boy, now you're talking crazy, man, even for you. But tell you what, I want you to promise that when you get back, you'll let me take you to a lab or a hospital or something and do some serious tests. If your power is for real, then it belongs to science."

"So you're not going to hold this trip against me?"

"Just until we're thirty. Then I'll let it go."

We slapped each other five. As we hugged it out, I heard Crane's raised voice from the next room.

"*You.* Why are you still here, you filthy beatnik? I asked you to leave minutes ago. I ought to chop off your ponytail for trespassing."

Trevor and I dashed down the hall where Crane was pointing angrily at Jeremy, who was sitting in a chair in the Sword Room.

"It's okay, Uncle Crane. Jeremy was just here to visit me," I hollered.

"Ah, Leo, hello, my boy!" Crane said. "I was just on my way to your room when I encountered this disheveled hepcat perched on my furniture."

"I'm just waiting for the elevator," Jeremy said. "Trust me, man, I don't want to be here, either."

Crane walked to the intercom and pressed the speaker button.

"Klevko!" he boomed into it. "What's taking so long, you slow donkey? I need you to show this bum out, and make it the hard way."

"Coming right up, boss." Klevko's voice sounded frantic, and I thought I heard Olga yelling in Polish in the background. The poor guy couldn't catch a break—he was getting it from all sides.

Crane turned to me and got what appeared to be an actual smile on his face. "In the meantime, Leo, I've brought you a gift for the trip, the Rolls-Royce of digital recorders, the Zoom H4n."

"The Zoom H4n! No way."

"Think about the price you're paying for it, Leo," Jeremy whispered, his eyes practically boring a hole into mine.

Crane was holding a box for the H4n in his hands. My dad had bought me the Zoom H1, and it was my trusty tool, but the H4n, that thing was legendary.

"Wow," Trevor said. "Those things cost a small fortune." His comment made Crane take notice of him standing behind me.

"What's this, Leo? Is that your gangly friend, Trevor the traitor? What is this, Leo, some kind of setup? Are you trying to double-cross me?"

"No, no, no, Uncle Crane. It's cool."

"Ice storms are cool."

"I mean, everything's fine, Uncle Crane. They both

stopped by on their own, because they couldn't reach me by phone. They just wanted to see if I was all right."

"Why wouldn't you be all right? You're in my care." Then, turning to Jeremy and Trevor, he dismissed them both with a wave of hand. "Now that you've seen that Leo is fine, please leave at once. Leo, you may ride with them down the elevator, and after you've said your good-byes, you can pick up your new toy from me. I'll be in the Cloud Room."

Crane sat down on a black leather couch in front of the giant-screen TV and flipped it to the news.

"You just missed it, Uncle Crane," I said. "Mike Hazel apologized."

"Of course he did," he said. "I have half a dozen slobbering tearful apologies from him in my voice mail. It might be too late for the poor fellow, though. I hear that his job is in jeopardy. Now show your associates out, Leo."

"Guys, I'm sorry," I whispered. "We gotta go."

Crane never gave them a second look as I walked Jeremy and Trevor to the elevator.

"I'm so sorry, guys," I kept repeating to them as we waited for the elevator to come. But they didn't say anything. It was Dmitri, not Klevko, who was working the elevator, and he took us to the street level. I walked them outside. There was still a ton of ice on the ground, but the sun was also shining.

"You need a ride home, Trevor?" Jeremy asked. "I've got my car."

"Yeah, thanks, Jeremy," Trevor said, then turned to me. "Leo, do what you have to do, but come home quick, and come back to us."

"Be safe," Jeremy said.

"I will," I said as they walked away from me. I stayed outside and watched them until they turned the corner and were gone. Walking back into the building, I noticed that the faded words on the front that had formerly said CRANE'S MYSTERIES, had been repainted, and now read, LEGENDARY RATHBONE.

I picked up my hard-won Zoom H4n from Crane, then went back to my room and shut the door. I concentrated on packing, trying to stay as busy as possible, telling myself every now and then that I would "start fresh" as soon I got back. I used Hollis's computer to get my dad's recordings of the Byong Ku villagers onto my iPod and took a phony dust jacket from one of my English books from school and put it over Marie Rathbone's book, *The Immortal Underground*, and slipped it into my backpack, along with my dad's travel journal. I packed a blank spiral notebook for me to use as a journal, in case I had thoughts or observations to record.

Hollis and I both had packed only a small duffel bag and a backpack each, but Crane had so much luggage that he had to hire a deluxe van to take us to the airport. Dmitri and Klevko were coming along for the trip, too, but the thought of traveling in the same car as them was distasteful to Crane, so he made them take a cab.

It was late afternoon when we left the warehouse and

drove along the BQE, right next to the East River, across from Manhattan. I decided to distract myself with conversation.

"So what's the plan, Uncle Crane?" I asked him. He was in the back row and had it all to himself.

"Please be more specific, Leo."

"You know, this all happened fast. What happens when we get to, what's that city called again, in Borneo?"

"Samarinda. Fear not, Leo. I have every detail exquisitely planned. First we'll make a stop in Mumbai to fetch an associate of mine who will be helping us on our expedition. We'll go through customs in Samarinda, then fly up to Tanjung Selor. All told, the flight should last just over twenty-five hours. Hope you boys brought a book."

"And when do we go on the yachts?" Hollis asked.

"Very funny, Hollis. There'll be no yachts. We'll be traveling by long motorboats."

"Leo said there'd be yachts," Hollis said, shooting me a critical look.

"You're like me, Hollis," Crane said. "We require luxury. But don't worry, we'll be traveling in style. In Tanjung Selor, we'll rendezvous with our entourage. I've arranged for a crew of more than twelve porters and valets to wait on us hand and foot. My rule: If you have to rough it, don't."

He let out a big laugh, obviously appreciating his own humor. To my surprise, Hollis nodded and laughed, too.

"From Tanjung Selor," Crane went on, "we'll travel up the Kayan River, through dense rain forests for several days. At night, my porters will set up camp with heated tents and real beds, and prepare a fresh meal."

"Not bad," Hollis said.

"I'm glad you approve, Hollis. Now if that's all, I have many more preparations to make before we board," he said, then returned his attention to his phone. For the rest of the ride, I played around with my new H4n, making weirdo voices into it and distorting them with one of the recorder's million different effects. Of course, I had to listen with my headphones on because Crane didn't appreciate my noises.

We drove into a special gate at the airport where the private jet hangars were located, and drove up to a small jet waiting on the runway. It was a different jet than the one we took to Palmira, and I wondered how many planes Crane had in his stable.

"You boys go ahead and board while they finish deicing the plane," Crane said. "I have a few details to sort out with Klevko and Dmitri."

Hollis and I bounded from the van and dashed for the passenger boarding stairs. Hollis was hopping up and down at the prospect of a flight on our own luxury jet. Before we could board, one of the flight crew stopped us.

"You may not enter the Sultan's plane in such a hyperactive state," he said in an accent I didn't recognize.

"The Sultan of Brunei?" Hollis asked. "You mean the richest man in the world?"

"Yes. Now run around the tarmac and burn off your extra energy."

I looked back and saw Crane huddling with Klevko and Dmitri, while the flight crew was loading all of his two dozen bags onto a trolley.

"We'll be calm," I said to the stern attendant. "Can we go on now?"

He nodded.

Hollis and I took the first half of the stairs at a brisk walk, but we ran the second half. Inside, it was nice, but not Sultan of Brunei nice. There were comfortable-looking leather seats, each with a little TV and plenty of legroom, but not as great as the plane we took last time.

"I bet that's where the deluxe part is," Hollis said, pointing to a set of satin and gold double doors up the aisle. A man, dressed different than the rest of the crew, was standing by the doors.

"Open sesame," I said when we got to him. Then I noticed that he wore a sword under his coat.

"This is the Sultan's private domicile," he said. "Please help yourself to any of the seats you see in servant's class."

"Servant's class?" Hollis said, eyeing me.

"Oh well," I said. "You have to admit, it's still pretty nice."

As we found a couple of seats across the aisle from each other, Crane strode onto the plane, Dmitri and Klevko in tow.

"Uncle Crane, do you actually know the Sultan of Brunei?" Hollis asked. "What's he like? Does he really have 290 golden toilets?"

"Indeed, he has 291, if you count the toilet on the plane," Crane half answered Hollis, and handed me a giant pile of books and maps about Borneo. "Some light reading for your flight, Leo. I expect you to have this material mastered by the time we arrive. Now I'm off to my quarters."

He walked to the double doors, and the man with the sword bowed and let him through. I only got a fleeting glance in there, but I was nearly blinded by the gold chandelier and all the other gold stuff in there.

"Did you see that?!" Hollis shouted. "We have to get back there."

But before I could answer him, good old Dmitri plopped himself down in the seat right next to me, cutting off my view of Hollis.

"Are you serious, Dmitri? There's a whole plane to choose from."

"I thought we could talk more on the plane, like friends."

"For twenty-five hours?"

"I can help you with your research, Leo. The boss wants me to be your assistant on the trip."

I understood. After everything I'd done for him, Crane still didn't trust me. "Dmitri, you can assist me when we get there. For now, man, just give me some space so I can stretch out."

"Okay, I'll sit behind you."

Klevko sat behind Hollis, and Hollis gave me a look that said, "These guys are sticking to us like gum on a shoe."

But his apprehension was checked when one of the flight attendants passed by to give us our bags of goodies, with special socks, a grooming kit with a gold-plated comb and toothbrush, sleeping masks, and a golden coin with the Sultan's face on it. I'm not sure which Hollis liked more, the grooming kit or the gold coin. He's crazy for grooming kits and anything made of real gold.

As we taxied for takeoff, I took a peek between the seats and found Dmitri staring right at me with those beady little eyes.

"Did you bring something to read, Dmitri?"

"No."

"Want something?"

"No."

"Suit yourself. But do me a favor, will you? Don't just stare at the back of my seat the whole time. It bothers me."

He didn't answer. I dug through my bag for a long time, stealthily replacing my fake cover for Marie Rathbone's book, *The Immortal Underground*, with a cover from *Borneo: Her Customs and People*. Hollis settled in to watch a movie, complaining that it had Malay subtitles. Klevko closed his eyes, and from his heavy breathing I could tell it wasn't long before he'd be asleep. Dmitri continued to stare at me, taking his spying responsibilities much too seriously for my taste.

And as the engines revved up and we took off into the sky above New York, I opened that weird old book and, in no time, was lost in the strange, twisted world of Marie Rathbone.

CHAPTER 13

The pages of the book were yellow, the corners worn and folded down from many years of use. It had obviously been read over and over, I assumed by Crane, but maybe by my dad, too. After all, the lady was his step-mother and he was probably curious about her ideas. The entire first page was underlined in red.

I, Marie Rathbone, will now tell you a story of a fair and noble race of humans, the noblest that ever lived. My story is the result of many years of research and exploration, aided by my immortal and honorable guides, Castillo and Pontor.

We are not the first civilization. Though we believe our-selves to be the highest and most wise civilization in all of recorded history, we are in fact a mere shadow of the glori-ous civilization that once lived on our Earth. This civilization was called the Boskops, and in their arts, culture, technology, and beauty, they surpassed even the wildest dreams of our wildest dreamers.

The skeptic among you now asks: Where is the evidence? Surely such a great civilization would leave a mark? Yet, we already possess evidence for civilizations far older than "history" admits. Can we ignore Plato, the Greek philosopher who, in painstaking detail, described Atlantis, that ten-thousand-year-old city of wonder? Or the Indian epic, the Mahabharata, which describes seventy-thousand-year-old airplane battles?

Oh, dear skeptic, I was once like you: blind to the truth.

This very book that you hold in your hands documents my long journey from ardent skeptic to true believer. In it, I will lay out the true history of our planet. Of the Boskops who lived on a vast continent that has since sunk below the Indian and Pacific oceans. They lived and flourished from before the melting of the last ice age, from 40,000 BC, until 11,000 BC. At that time, half of this wondrous civilization left the planet Earth and ventured to the stars. The other half stayed behind and moved underground, into the Hollow Center of the Earth, where over thousands of years, they mastered their minds, and eventually developed perfect immortality.

It is of this underground half of whom I now write. . . .

I looked up from Marie Rathbone's book and rubbed my eyes. I had tried to keep reading, but from there she started mentioning words like *ectoplasm* and *magic trumpets* and *spirit guides*, and I couldn't take it anymore. What kind of nut had my grandfather married?

Thankfully, one of the flight attendants was serving dinner. I put the book down, grateful for the interruption.

"You hungry, Hollis? Smells good, huh?"

"Yeah, I'm starved. I can't follow this movie. It's all dubbed in Malay."

The flight attendant brought two steaming dishes of food and placed them on the tray tables in front of us.

"What's that?" Hollis asked her, picking up one of the plates to sniff it. His habit of smelling food before he tasted it used to drive our mom crazy.

"Kolo mee," the attendant said. "Very tasty. Noodles and pork."

Hollis grimaced. "You don't happen to have any cheeseburgers up there, do you?"

"If you'd like, sir, I'll ask Chef to make you one right away," she said. When she left, Hollis beamed at me.

"Did you see that, Leo? They'll make anything you want. Is this the life or what?"

"I'll eat Hollis's if he doesn't want it," Dmitri said from behind me. "I will tell you what it is like in Crane's room if you give me your food."

"Eat your own food, Dmitri. Don't be such a pig," I said.

"My boy has a big appetite," Klevko muttered, opening his eyes from his nap. "He cannot help himself."

After dinner, which was delicious, I tried to return to Marie Rathbone's weird book, but every time I'd read a sentence my brain would fog up and I'd forget what I'd just read. We'd been in the air for a few hours, and I was getting sleepy. I reclined my seat all the way until it was practically flat, dimmed the lights, put on my headphones, and listened to my dad's recording of the Byong Ku death dance.

Like all my dad's recordings, it started with an introduction. He was whispering over the crackle of fire and what sounded like a chorus of frogs.

Kirk Lomax, November 7, the time is 8:45 p.m. I am seated by the fire outside of the longhouse. The village is mourning the death of an old man, whose name I've been unable to gather. His body has been placed in a traditional wooden coffin. Many young men wearing masks have begun to play a steady beat on various rocks and lithophones. I have heard enough music to know that they are preparing to begin a ritual ceremony. So, I've decided to shut up and let the recorder do the work.

My dad was whispering in the same way he always did when he'd tell us a fantastic story at night. And with the main cabin lights off, his voice was so soothing that I fell asleep before the ceremony, hearing only the sound of distant drums in half-remembered dreams.

We landed at one point, and in the shadows of the night, I saw a slim man get on the plane and head for the back. And, oh yeah, both Dmitri and Klevko wore sleeping caps the whole night.

When I woke up the next time, I could tell it was daylight behind the windows, even though they were still closed. Hollis was up and pacing the aisles. He kept looking at the sliver of light below the Sultan's private quarters.

"I gotta get out of here!" he said. "I feel so cooped up."

"Calm yourself, bro," I said. "We still have seven hours to go."

"Then I have to at least get in there," he said, pointing behind the golden double doors.

We walked up to the guard. I was feeling pretty caged in, too, and a little punchy.

"Hey can we see your sword? What's your name? Is it a special kind of sword?"

"Can we just take a peek back there?" Hollis asked him, perfecting our overwhelm-with-questions strategy, but it was a no go.

"You cannot see my sword. My name is Laclac. My sword is quite normal, yet it is exquisitely crafted. And neither of you may even glance in the private domicile."

"What about the guy I saw go in there in the middle of the night? Or was that a dream?" I asked.

"Perhaps you dreamed something similar, boy. But yes, a man entered a few hours ago. A Mr. Singh, the gentleman from Mumbai."

We never did get a look back in Crane's private quarters, but we bothered Laclac for the rest of the flight. I made sure to always keep one eye on Dmitri. I would never put it past him to dig through my bag. I caught him watching me a few times. Once he was straight-out looking at me.

After a delicious breakfast of different sweet cakes and something called roti, a pancakelike concoction, we began our descent. I caught my first glimpse of land. It was green, really green, and cloudy. I'd read the first three pages of

Borneo: Her Cultures and People, and it said that Borneo was primarily rain forest, one that was 130 million years old.

"No skyscrapers," Hollis said. "I bet there aren't any ice-skating rinks, either."

We'd been cooped up so long that neither one of us was making much sense by then.

Our runway, which was right next to the ocean, was surrounded by green grass. As we landed, I saw that there was a crowd of people waiting on the runway, and the moment we came to a stop, they gathered around the plane.

The flight attendant explained that this was Samarinda, and not our final destination. All of us had to pile out, haul our bags through customs, get our passports stamped, and then get back onto the plane. I caught a glimpse of Mr. Singh, a tall Indian man who looked distant and bored, but no one introduced us.

Piling back onto the plane, we were told that it would be another hour flight to our final destination, Tanjung Selor. Once we were in flight, Hollis and I stared out the window. We saw no cities, no signs of civilization, just the vast green of the jungle, the brown earth, and the winding muddy rivers that crisscrossed it all.

I had never felt farther away from home in my whole life.

CHAPTER 14

O ur guide was there to meet us when we landed at the tiny strip of an airport in Tanjung Selor, a man named Dr. A. Haga. He spoke English and seemed nice enough, but Crane completely ignored him, telling him he should speak only to Klevko. Dr. A. Haga had arranged for another large van to take us to the port where we would pick up our boats and set out on our journey upriver. Our driver gunned it through the narrow, palm-tree-lined streets filled with motor scooters, as Klevko and Dr. Haga sat in front, arguing about money, and Crane and Mr. Singh pored over maps in the last row. Hollis and I still had not been officially introduced to Mr. Singh, and he showed no particular interest in making our acquaintance.

The port was bustling. Steam was rising from the murky brown river crammed with small wooden boats. I had no idea what time it was, and as we climbed from the van, we

172

were immediately surrounded by people selling wagon rides or freshly caught fish or private tours on one of the hundreds of small wooden boats in the brown water. All around the port, there were dozens and dozens of stalls selling artifacts, souvenirs, and even monkeys. The porters got busy taking our bags, mostly Crane's, down to the waterfront.

"Look, *there are* some yachts!" Hollis said, pointing to a few covered boats.

"They stay close to the city," Crane said. "Where we're going, we need a more maneuverable craft."

Klevko got out of the van and waddled over to us, dabbing his pouring sweat with an equally sweaty handkerchief.

"There is problem, boss. Dr. Haga does not like your new terms. He says, 'No, we do it for the money you promised us.' I say, 'No, you do it for the money we pay you.' But he refuses."

Crane smiled ear to ear.

"It will be my pleasure to take care of this, Klevko. Boys, take these rupiahs and buy yourselves a souvenir. This might get ugly." He handed us a wad of brightly colored money. "Dr. Haga!" he boomed, strutting up to the van where the frustrated-looking man was just climbing out. "We had a deal, Dr. Haga!"

"Yes, we had a deal, Mr. Rathbone," he yelled back. "And you broke the deal."

"I am merely modifying the deal. Come now, this is how business is done, Dr. Haga. . . ."

"Let's go check out the port," I whispered to Hollis. "Maybe Crane will get Dr. Haga to throw in a yacht for a day."

"Wait for me," Dmitri said, jogging after us. He was unshakeable.

We walked along the rows of stalls and small shops lining the port, refusing offers of meat on a stick, bundles of live snakes, or key chains and trinkets made from mountain rocks. The air was humid and close, with steam rising all around us, partially obscuring the turquoise and brightly colored old buildings in the distance. Hollis stopped at one of the stalls selling what looked like shrunken heads on leather cords.

"Leo," he said, an uneasy quiver in his voice. "Those couldn't be real, could they? I mean, I saw on TV that some tribes in Borneo are headhunters."

"Hollis, you can't get all spooked at everything you see," I explained to him. "We're going to see a lot of stuff, and you have to let it run off you."

"But we're talking a real human head here, Leo. Without a skull. That's major."

I could see the fear growing in his eyes.

"Dmitri, I'm horribly thirsty," I said. "Would you please go buy me a bottle of water?"

Dmitri didn't like the request one bit, but now that I was the favored nephew, he understood he didn't have the right to say no to me. When he trotted off to find water, I turned to the man in the stall.

"Can I see that for a minute?" I asked him, pointing to a particularly gross little head.

"This real," he said. "Very scary."

He reached up with a hook and took down one of the

shrunken heads. I held it in my hands, closed my eyes and concentrated. At first nothing happened, but then I focused on the fear I'd seen in Hollis's eyes, and I felt so angry at this merchant for trying to scare my little brother that gradually the sounds faded away, and the marketplace, which was once so alive with random life, suddenly looked like a giant nightmarish machine, with everyone on a track. I heard the sounds of conveyer belts and assembly lines and people muttering to one another in Mandarin, or some sort of Chinese dialect. In the background, I heard a bell ring and the dull drone of drills and a mass of feet shuffling in a large space.

"Leo?" I heard Hollis saying, a note of panic in his voice as he snatched the shrunken head out of my hands. Instantly, I was back to myself, fully present in the marketplace.

"No worries, bro," I said to him. "That thing is a fake, made in China."

"You sure?" Hollis asked.

"Heard it being made in the factory with my very own ears." Then I turned to the merchant.

"And what's the big idea?" I said. "You're selling fake garbage."

"No fake!" he said, grabbing the head from Hollis and putting it back, then he threw up his hands and let loose a stream of angry incomprehensible words, shooing us away. "You go, you go."

"Wow," Hollis said. "You really can do this sound thing. Your face looked weird, too."

"It's not pretty, but it works," I said, giving him a playful punch in the arm. "Hey, check it out," I said, pointing to a stall selling weird instruments, just as Dmitri returned with our waters.

"Cool. I want to check it out," Hollis said.

"We can all go see the instruments together," Dmitri told him, flexing his little man muscles.

"You two go," I snapped at Dmitri, just to show him he couldn't push me around. "I've had enough of your evil eye, man."

I gave Hollis a wad of rupiahs and watched them hurry off down a row of stalls. Exhausted and in a daze, I looked around the port trying to take it all in, and spotted Mr. Singh up the street. Tall and slim, he was standing with his arms crossed and wore a serious look on his face. I got the feeling Mr. Singh didn't do a lot of laughing. He was watching a transparent white screen, which was filled with shadows of dancing figures flickering from the light of a candle behind the screen.

As I approached, I heard a man behind it speaking, and I knew he was telling a story by the way his voice would rise or fall, or inject terror or sympathy into the moving shadow puppets. I got up next to Mr. Singh.

"It is a Wayang Kulit," he said. "A living play. A tourist attraction, for certain, as the Wayang Kulit is native to Bali and Java, but very entertaining."

"Do you know the story?" I asked as a bevy of little shadow characters burst onto the screen with a flurry of cymbals.

"Very well," he said, still with his arms folded. "This is a scene from the Hindu epic, the *Ramayana*."

"But aren't we in Borneo?"

"Indeed. Borneo is home to Hindus, Buddhists, Muslims, and a host of other religions."

"What are all the little guys doing?"

"Those are magical monkeys. The hero of the epic is Rama, who is the earthly form of Vishnu, the supreme god. Evil demons have absconded with Rama's beloved, Sita. These monkeys who live in the forest have offered Rama their help to rescue his princess. But Rama is hesitant to follow his dharma."

"Dharma?"

"A complicated concept, young Leo, which requires many days of subtle conversation to understand."

"You know a lot about Indian history, right, Mr. Singh?" He didn't answer, but I continued anyway. "Is it true that Indian history goes back seventy thousand years?"

"Vedic tradition says that the *Ramayana* epic was composed almost a million years ago."

"A million years? Can that be true?"

"It is a matter of interpretation," Mr. Singh said, not offering the interpretation.

"What about reincarnation?" I asked, trying a different track. "About how you're born into a new body after you die. Do you believe in that?"

"Again, it is a matter of interpretation. These are difficult concepts, Leo, and require extensive conversation. A busy port is no place for these meditations."

"What about on the river?" I asked. "We'll have lots of time. Can we talk then?"

"There will not be enough time."

"But we could be on the river for weeks," I said. "How much time do you need?"

"Many lifetimes," Mr. Singh said, and raised his eyebrows. Then he put his finger to his mouth and returned his gaze to the shadow play.

"Leo? Leo?" I heard a female voice call my name from far away, but I thought I was just tired, so I ignored it. "Leo? Is that you?" Then someone tapped my shoulder. "Leo, it is you!"

I turned and nearly jumped back. I shook my head but Diana Reed really was standing right next to me. She seemed perfectly at home in the port of Tanjung Selor, wearing sandals and shorts, a colorful shirt, her dog-tooth necklace, and light green flowers the color of her eyes pinned in her hair. I was shocked to see her, but happy, too. She gave me a big hug as if we were long-lost friends.

"Diana?" I sputtered. "W-what are you doing here?" I turned to introduce her to Mr. Singh, but he had disappeared.

"I'm supposed to be here, Leo! The question is what are *you* doing here?"

I looked across the port and saw Crane and Dr. Haga, still arguing nose to nose. "I'm, uh, just here with my family. Your mom knows about it, I think. Hey," I said, taking the huge wad of rupiahs out of my pocket, "I've got plenty of rupiahs. Do you want to buy a souvenir?"

"Oh, that's sweet, Leo. But I've already bought most of this junk at one time or another. Are you in the city for long? I'm not, but then maybe I might be stuck here for a while. I could show you around. We're supposed to go upriver today, but I'd rather hang out in the city for a little while. There's not much to do in the jungle."

"We're supposed to leave today and take a boat up the Kayan. Where's your mom?"

"She's just over at the port trying to find a boat. Some rich American jerk booked up ten longboats all for himself."

"That stinks," I said. "But, listen, are you guys going up the Kayan River, too?"

"Yeah. Almost all the way until it forks into the Bahau."

"Let's find your mom," I said. "We're going the same way. That's my stepuncle over there," I said, and pointed to Crane, who, it appeared, was nearing a deal with Dr. Haga. "He's the rich American jerk. But I'll get him to take you guys, too. There should be plenty of room."

"Really? You could do that?"

"It's no problem," I said. "Come with me."

It didn't take long to find Dr. Reed. She had spotted Crane as well and was waiting for him to finish up his deal with Dr. Haga.

"Now that wasn't so difficult was it, Dr. Haga?" Crane said as we approached. "A little unpleasant, but the hard part is over. Yes?"

"Yes, Mr. Rathbone. I see it your way now," Dr. Haga said, wiping his brow.

Crane smiled with power. Dr. Haga reached out to shake Crane's hand, but the gesture was ignored. Crane was busy looking around, his eyes drawn to Dr. Reed, who was waiting to talk with him nearby. They made eye contact, and at once, both Dr. Reed and Crane spotted me and Diana.

"Leo!" Dr. Reed cried.

"And this must be your lovely daughter, Diana," Crane said. "Charmed, my dear."

"Yes, she is lovely, isn't she?" Dr. Reed said, and smoothed Diana's hair with her hands.

"*Mom!* You're so annoying!"

Dr. Reed smiled at Diana. "No matter what culture I study, teenage girls always find their mothers annoying."

"That's because they are!" Diane said.

Then both she and her mom laughed, and I felt my throat tighten a little watching the obvious love they had for each other. Dr. Reed turned to Crane.

"So you've come after all, Crane? Tell me, have you found any promising leads for that twin mask?"

"Alas, I have not, but I thought an exploratory mission might yield some seeds for further missions. This is primarily a pleasure cruise for us," he lied, "and I thought it might be a good opportunity for my nephews to see how real archeology is done."

"Uncle Crane," I said, "Diana was telling me she and her mom can't find a boat to take them upriver. I told Diana we could take them. Since it's just a pleasure cruise, the more the merrier, right?"

Crane laughed dryly.

"No, we wouldn't want to impose," Dr. Reed said, but I gave her a look that said, "Let me handle this."

"I agree," Crane said. "We've got little room to spare as it is, Leo, and I doubt we are heading in the same direction."

"But we're both heading to the fork in the Kayan," I protested. "We'll just drop them off. Besides, if Dr. Reed and Diana come, they can tell me all about the countryside. It'd be great for my education."

Crane cracked his knuckles and ground his teeth. "Well, if Dr. Reed agrees . . ." he managed to choke out.

"Say yes, Mom," Diana said. "I hardly ever get a chance to show anyone where we live most of the time."

"Splendid," Dr. Reed agreed, and laughed in her opera voice. "Let me inform our porter to bring our bags here. I'll just be a moment," she said, and ran off down a row of stalls.

"Splendid, indeed," Crane said, giving me his most unpleasant look. "Quite a large company, Leo. And where are Dmitri and Hollis?"

"There they are!" I said, noticing them running up to us, both of their arms filled with instruments.

"Check it out, Leo!" Hollis cried. "I got everything they had. I got a sape, a rain-forest guitar. And two different nose flutes." He put one in his nose and made a shrill squeaking sound.

"Cool!" Diana said, and then she noticed Dmitri hovering in back of Hollis. "Oh, hi, Dmitri," she mumbled, turning a shade of green. He looked at her and flexed his muscles. I don't know who told him that was an appealing thing to do, but whoever it was couldn't have been more wrong.

"And look at this Kwai horn." Hollis was rattling on. "It's over four feet long. Show them the drums, Dmitri. I got a gedang and these bronze klon gongs. And the guy called this a frog drum, even if it's just a gong. Here, Leo, I got it for you. Give it a smash!"

He gave me a mallet, and I smashed the life out of it. Everyone in the marketplace stopped for a moment and stared at the kid with the gong. "The frog is back!" I screamed.

"I'll go round up Mr. Singh while you young people make a horrible racket," Crane said. "As soon as Dr. Reed returns, we set off. Now where is Klevko?"

Hollis handed Diana one of the drums while he strummed the rain-forest guitar and I let loose on the frog gong. For a minute, I felt free and happy, like I was exactly where I was meant to be, playing in a trio on the banks of the Kayan River.

But of course, that feeling was not to last.

CHAPTER 15

At high noon, we set off on the Kayan River, traveling in ten longboats. Including our twelve porters, there were more than twenty people in our expedition. We were split up into groups of two, with each boat being driven by one of the porters from Tajung Selor. Crane and Mr. Singh led the expedition in the front boat, Diana and Dr. Reed were next, Hollis and I followed them. Klevko and Dmitri brought up the rear. The remaining longboats were jammed with Crane's luggage, our gear, food, and supplies. Mostly Crane's luggage.

Before we left, Crane complained bitterly about having to leave three of his suitcases behind to make room for Dr. Reed and Diana. Since landing that morning, he had already changed outfits twice, finally settling on head-to-toe safari gear complete with a khaki tie. Klevko stuck with his black elastic skintight T-shirt, and Dmitri favored a tank top, making it a point to parade around Diana lifting up his arms so she could admire his twelve armpit hairs.

The driver of our boat was Tamon Dong, which Dr. Reed told us meant something like "stepfather." He drove the boat like a maniac in the fast currents, steering within inches of sandbars and jutting rocks. Hollis and I were both nervous at first, but we could tell he knew the river well. Since I sat up front, it was my job to raise my hand whenever I saw snags or obstructions, which could capsize the boat. I took my job very seriously. Hollis sat in the back near Tamon Dong and the deafening motor.

After only half an hour on the river, we left behind the modern houses and roads and rice fields lining the banks and entered a primitive, wild landscape. Thick jungle surrounded us on every side, with the green trees and vines rising into the haze and steam. As we plowed deeper and deeper into the jungle, Hollis took out his gedang hand drum and started to play, supplying a rhythmic sound track to our journey up the river.

"So where is this big deal mask supposed to be?" he asked during one of his less ferocious drumming patterns.

"Byong Ku."

"Thanks. Pardon my ignorance, bro, but what is a Byong Ku?"

"It's a village that's supposed to be about twenty miles beyond where the Kayan River forks into the Bahau."

"Oh good, that clears everything up."

"It's hard to say exactly, Hollis, because Crane told me he can't find Byong Ku on any maps."

"Really?"

The drumming stopped completely, and I heard the fear in his voice, so I changed the subject. "So, your drumming is sounding good."

"Yeah," he said, picking it back up. "It is. Now I just have to work on the nose flute. By the time we reach that Bahau fork, I want to be able to play both at the same time."

"Hey, I'd pay to see that."

He didn't answer. It was so hot and muggy on the river that it was difficult to breathe. And besides, the kid talks with his drums.

We didn't stop to eat because Crane wanted to get as far upriver as possible the first day. Tamon Dong gave us a snack of sticky rice wrapped in green palm leaves and a banana, which we ate in the boat. The plan was to forge quickly ahead to the fork, which was about an eighty-mile journey as the crow flies — but almost twice that long because of all the twists and turns. Then we'd drop off Diana and Dr. Reed and continue along, and try to sniff out the exact location of Byong Ku. From my dad's travel journal, I knew that he had visited a village called Polon Man the day before arriving in Byong Ku and another one called Tryong Loa the day after he left. Both of those villages were on the map, and there was about thirty miles of river between them. That meant that Byong Ku must be hidden somewhere between the two villages. Of course, I never told Crane about my dad's travel journal — I just told him I remembered Dad telling me Byong Ku was between those two villages. He bought it without hesitation.

As darkness fell, we pulled to the bank to set up camp. In the twilight, thousands of frogs were croaking. It was an amazing noise, almost like a thousand different people all making their phoniest zombie groans at the same time. Hollis and I were exhausted from all that sun and the jet lag, so while the porters were setting up our deluxe tents, all we could do was lean against the boat and listen to the hypnotic frogs.

Several of the porters walked downriver to a nearby village to acquire a pig for our dinner. Dr. Reed and Diana left with them. Apparently, they knew several people in the village and were going to stay with them in their longhouse. The rest of us ate our dinner of fresh pork and sticky rice around the fire, getting eaten alive by insects, while Dr. Haga rambled on about all the flora and fauna in the rain forest, even taking out a little field notebook now and then and holding it up triumphantly to drive home a point. But with the shrieking night insects, and Dr. Reed far away, Crane shut him up relatively quickly.

As I sat there on the ground, thousands of miles away from any reality I knew, I became overwhelmed with anxiety. What if my sound-bending power shut down again and I couldn't locate the mask? What would Crane do to me down here in the jungle in the middle of nowhere? I didn't have Trevor or Jeremy to help me. I didn't have anyone I could really be honest with . . . not even Hollis. I wished I could tell him that I had Dad's travel journal, that we were really here so Crane would fund a fact-finding mission to Antarctica. I wanted to tell him that I hoped our parents were still alive somewhere, maybe involved in some complicated plot, just hiding out and counting the moments until they could come back and make everything okay again. But I couldn't say any of that. The last thing I would ever do was set Hollis up for another disappointment.

I'd told Trevor in my letter that I'd have to find that mask alone, but as I sat around the campfire with that awkward group, it finally occurred to me how alone I actually was.

"You don't look well, Leo," Crane noticed. "I'm surprised, a robust boy like yourself. Apparently the outdoors doesn't agree with you."

"I'm just really tired," I lied. "Must be the jet lag. I think I'm going to turn in. You coming, Hollis?"

We left the campfire and went to our tent. Inside, it was definitely deluxe, with two foam beds complete with soft blankets and mosquito nets. There were filled water bottles by the beds, an emergency air horn that I almost couldn't resist trying out, toilet paper for late night excursions into the jungle, and even flip-flops. But our tent was nothing compared to Crane's — his was twice the size of everyone else's, and I bet Hollis dreamed of all the adventure luxuries he believed were inside.

We flopped down, and I listened to Hollis try to learn the sape, his rain-forest guitar, while I picked up *Borneo: Her Customs and People*, to read myself to sleep. Of course it was really Marie Rathbone's book, *The Immortal Underground*, and it was boring beyond belief—lots of complicated theories about erratic boulder layers and ice ages, lots more about methane burps and carbonization, magnetic fields and sunspots, which the person who had underlined it all seemed especially interested in. I fell asleep holding the book in my hands.

We broke camp and were on the river before sunrise. Hollis had woken up at some insane hour to pee, and sleepwalking outside without his flip-flops, he noticed a ticklish sensation on his leg and looked down to see a humongous centipede had made its way up his shin almost all the way to his knee. He came back shaken and agitated, and spent the rest of the night tossing and turning, scratching itches, swatting bugs, and generally freaking himself out. When Tamon Dong woke us up an hour before sunrise, Hollis was rotten to him and snappy at me.

"I should never have let you talk me into this crazy trip," he said, and glared at me as we got ready for the day.

Crane was also the worse for wear. His eyes were bloodshot and he even sported some patchy stubble. Seeing him less than perfectly groomed made me incredibly uncomfortable. After screaming at one of the porters and blaming him for stubbing his toe, Crane pulled me aside to a bluff overlooking the river.

"That was a clever trick you pulled yesterday, Leo. Very clever."

"I wasn't trying to trick anyone."

"Oh really? It was just accidental that you invited the saintly Dr. Reed and her lovely daughter along? I can be quite accommodating, Leo. I'm a man who knows how to do a favor if asked. But this is *my* expedition, and therefore *my* approval is needed before even the slightest deviation from *my* mission is considered."

"I didn't mean anything by it, Crane. Diana's a friend from school, and I just wanted to do her a favor."

"You'd do well, Leo, to keep your mind off girls and your eye on the prize. We have a partnership, and there isn't room for anyone else in this deal. Understood?"

I nodded.

"I've got my eye on you, Leo. Now I hope you won't mention anything to anyone about our true mission. I don't trust that Reed woman. For all I know, she's after the same mask we are."

"She's an anthropologist, Crane. She doesn't sell that stuff, she studies it."

"First rule of business, Leo. Trust nobody."

Back on the boats after breakfast, we continued up the river, sometimes going hours without spotting any signs of human life. By midday, we entered a more mountainous stretch, the jungle on either side of us rising high and steep into the steam and the clouds, little green patches peeking out here and there. I spent my time making recordings of Hollis's drumming, but when I listened back to it, found that the engine grinding swallowed up most of his music. Sometimes I'd watch the other boats to see if anyone was watching me. I caught Dmitri four times, Mr. Singh twice, and I think I also caught Diana once, though I can't be certain.

"Hey, Leo, look at this," Hollis said to me in midafternoon. He stuck his leg out and pointed to a swollen red lump just below his knee. "What do you think that is?"

"I don't know," I shrugged. "Looks like a mosquito bite."

"But it itches like crazy. I've been putting river water on it all morning to try to get it to stop itching."

"Why would you do that, chief?" I asked, frowning at the brownish murky water. "There could be parasites in the river."

"Parasites?"

"Forget it, Hollis. Listen, I'm sure it's just a mosquito bite, but if it's still bothering you, we can get Dr. Reed to look at it when we pull in."

"She's not that kind of doctor, Leo. Even I know that."

"It'll be fine, chief. Why don't you work on your nose-fluting. Your drumming is starting to put me in a trance."

"This trip sucks, Leo," he said with a worried tone, then started squeaking out some nose flute. I was just trying to get his mind off that bite — honestly, it didn't look too great.

When we pulled in for the night, the bite had gotten even more red and swollen, and Hollis claimed he was feeling nauseous. Between the chorus of croaking frogs and Hollis's worried face, I was feeling pretty nauseous, too. Just short of a full panic, I raced around the camp until I found Dr. Reed, rocking leisurely in her hammock and reading.

"Um . . . Dr. Reed?"

Before the nervous words were even out of my mouth, Dr. Reed sat up, took off her glasses, and hunched toward me, the way that all moms seem to do automatically when a kid needs help. "Leo, what's wrong, honey?"

"I don't want to bother you, but Hollis has this weird bite, and I was wondering if you could—"

"Of course, Leo. Bring him right over."

I brought Hollis to her. Dr. Reed smiled at him, rubbed his shoulder, and sat him up in the hammock. "Now let's take a look, shall we?"

"I think this centipede bit me last night," he explained while she looked at his leg. "It crawled all over me. It was as long as my leg. They're not poisonous, are they? Leo doesn't think so, but I'm not so sure because my stomach is feeling really twitchy and sick."

"All centipedes are venomous, Hollis," she said as she pressed the areas around the bump. "But unless you have bad allergies, their bites aren't usually dangerous."

"It itches like crazy, and I was putting river water on it all morning until Leo told me to stop because there are parasites in the water, so maybe I've got a weird jungle disease or something."

"Nope," she said, patting his leg and standing up. "It's just a mosquito bite. It's swollen and inflamed because you've been scratching it. And your stomach hurts because you've been worrying about it all day!"

"So it's not dangerous?" Hollis asked.

"Not as long as you're taking your malaria medication. Malaria is carried by mosquitoes," she said, slapping one on her neck. "And they love the warm water here, and sweet boys. That's why we take the pills."

Hollis and I looked at each other blankly.

"Your uncle didn't get you the antimalarial pills," she said, more of a statement than a question. Dr. Reed could tell we knew nothing about any pills. "And I assume he didn't take you to a travel doctor, either. Outrageous."

In a huff, she marched across camp to Crane, who was lounging in a chair while Klevko fanned him with palm leaves. He wore a large sun hat, with a thick mosquito net covering his face. She got right in his business, the volume of her voice causing all the porters to momentarily stop their work and watch the scene.

"What makes you think you can care for these children?" she yelled. "How does a responsible adult bring them into the jungle without antimalarial tablets? Please explain, Crane."

"We left in a hurry," Crane said quietly. "There wasn't enough time. No need for an inquisition, Margaret. I've traveled in countless remote places, and I am malaria free."

"Then you're lucky," she huffed, her hands on her hips. "What if they're not so lucky? I'd ask you if you want that on your conscience, but you haven't any conscience."

"No?" Crane said, shooing Klevko away and baring his teeth ever so slightly.

"You're exposing them to undue risk, Crane. Foreigners die from malaria out here. Do you know that? Do you?"

I glanced back at Hollis, all alone and unmoving in the middle of the bustling campsite, watching the whole thing from a distance. He had his hand on his belly and a look of sheer terror on his face, as if he'd just eaten some tainted meat.

"No need to get hysterical, Margaret," Crane hissed from behind his mosquito-net hat. "The boys are under my care. I'll see to their health and safety, thank you very much. Now why don't you go back to your hammock and do some deep breathing. You're clearly unhinged."

Dr. Reed shook her finger at him and opened her mouth, but then thought better of it. Instead she took both me and Hollis back to her area and rummaged around in her duffel bag until she produced a bottle of pills.

"Take one of these every day," she said. "They might make you feel a little weird or give you nightmares, but that's perfectly normal. Most importantly, they'll protect you both in case you're bitten by an infected mosquito."

"Don't you and Diana need them?" I asked, suddenly aware that I hadn't seen Diana since we'd pulled ashore.

"Oh no, Leo. I always bring two bottles in case I lose one."

"But what if it's t-too late?" Hollis stammered. "What if I already have it?"

"It's very unlikely, Hollis," she said, pushing the hair out of his eyes. "So stay positive, drink lots of fluids, and make sure you apply bug spray generously."

He nodded, but we cold both see his lower lip trembling. Dr. Reed tousled his hair again, reached out, and pulled him in tight. He nuzzled his face into her shirt like a little puppy.

"You poor thing," she said softly, rocking him. "I know this all seems so scary. The big bad jungle. But everything's going to be just fine."

"Want me to get your nose flute, chief?" I asked him. "I'll bring them both and we can play them. A concerto for four nostrils."

"This isn't funny, Leo," he said.

He was right. Malaria wasn't funny. Getting sick deep in the jungle, miles from anywhere, wasn't funny. Risking my brother's life for a stupid deal with Crane wasn't funny. Not at all.

Seeing Hollis in such a sorry state, I slunk away. I didn't want to see any more of this. And I didn't want to be there when Dr. Reed turned her attention to me, and asked what we were *really* doing in Borneo. I wanted to just get inside my tent and bury my head in the pillow.

"Hey, Leo," I heard as I crossed the campsite. I looked around and saw Diana trotting over to me with a few wild-flowers in her hand. "I think I lost him."

"You mean the small creepy one?"

She laughed. "Yeah, Dmitri keeps following me around, flexing his muscles and staring at me with his beady little eyes. It's the grossest thing ever."

"Stick with me," I said, trying to match her energy. "I'll protect you."

"Hey, some of the porters were telling me about Hollis," she said. "Don't worry. I've been coming here for years, and I've only seen two people get malaria."

"Yeah, but he's pretty freaked."

"Maybe I'll go cheer him up."

Diana was doing a pretty good job cheering *me* up. I smiled at her and we made eye contact, but almost immediately, a shudder flashed across her face and she sighed loudly, dropping the flowers.

"Hey, babe."

I spun around and there he was in his tank top, showing off his arm muscles.

"Dmitri, stop following Diana around everywhere. She doesn't like it."

"That's what she says," he smirked. Then his expression changed, and he was dead serious. "But I didn't come just so she could admire my six-pack. Crane sent me to get you."

"Why? What does he want?"

"He wants you to come to his tent."

"Okay, Dmitri," I said, glancing at Diana. "Tell him I'll be there in a few minutes."

Dmitri looked down at the Swiss Army knife on his belt and shook his head.

"Now, Leo. Mr. Crane said now."

And before I could argue with him, he had his hand clasped firmly on my shoulder and was pushing me in the direction of Crane's tent.

CHAPTER 16

rane's tent was huge. Inside, it was uncomfortably warm, with a plush red rug on the floor, a double bed to one side, and two chairs to the other. Mr. Singh sat in a canvas folding chair, his chin in his hands and his legs crossed. Crane was in the other chair, wrapped in a bathrobe, with Klevko applying a thick mint-colored cream to his face and head. From what I could see, Crane's skin was all splotchy, and his gray stubble made my skin crawl. The cream didn't smell too fresh, either. I looked away from him and noticed the Siamese twin mask hanging from a piece of twine from the ceiling.

Crane must have noticed my disgust, because he quickly adjusted his bathrobe and ordered Klevko to put the greenish cream away.

"I apologize for my ghastly appearance," he said. "I have very sensitive skin. Too much exposure to the elements is painful and causes me to break out in these hideous rashes. The chums at school used to mock me mercilessly. Thank goodness I had Mother to help me understand that they were fools and simpletons. I'm sure you did not know about my condition, Leo?"

Before I could answer, he continued.

"Of course you didn't. It's a deeply private matter, certainly not one that Dr. Reed needs to know about. That bombastic woman puts her nose where it doesn't belong. There are too many opinions here, and too many eyes. I'm unhappy about it. I must be in a position to dictate what happens on this expedition."

Mr. Singh leaned over and whispered something in Crane's ear. "Yes, I'm getting to that, Mr. Singh. Now, Leo, we are nearing the point of no return in our expedition. I hope, for your sake, that you are still firmly committed to our partnership. You know what will happen if you break my trust, right?"

"All bets are off," I said.

"Indeed. I doubt whether Hollis would like his dear brother shipped off to Luxemburg to continue his schooling. No, I assure you, he wouldn't. Nor would you like to lose your fact-finding mission to Antarctica, which I believe will prove most illuminating."

"What do you know, Crane?" I demanded. "If you know something about my parents, you have to tell me."

"I know nothing definite, Leo, only what I hear from my contacts. Rumors and speculation, certainly, but even I am beginning to doubt the official story. Rumors often harbor a seed of truth, like this mask here." He gazed up at the dangling twin mask with a faraway look in his eyes. "I believe there is more to it than meets the eye. Much, much more."

As he gazed dreamily up at the mask and stroked his smooth chest, it dawned on me that Crane couldn't split up Hollis and me — I had a signed contract saying so. But now Crane was modifying the contract. He was so sneaky about it that my neck got hot with anger, and my hands tightened into fists.

"Crane," I growled through closed teeth. "You promised that I could go back to school with Hollis!"

"I keep my promises, Leo. As long as you keep yours. Keep the thought of Luxemburg very close to your heart. Now leave me to recover, and find the source of that ear-splitting racket outside. Tell whoever is making it to cease and desist immediately."

Crane leaned back in his chair, staring up at the dangling mask, its eyes as dark as night, its teeth as sharp as fear.

As I left the tent, I heard Crane barking, "Klevko, my ointment!"

Outside, night had fallen, and most everyone was gathered around the fire. Music filled the air. Crane's driver, Lim Sum, was playing a perfect groove on the gedang drum while Hollis played his nose flute. Most of the worry had disappeared from his face, and he was absorbed in his music. Like always, making music had soothed him.

The porters were grilling river fish over the open fire, stamping their feet and clapping along to the beat. Diana and Dr. Reed were reclining on the ground, smiling and urging Hollis on. It all sounded so good that I joined them, pulled out my H4n, and played some of my recorded frog noises under the music. It sounded awesome.

"The frog is back!" Hollis said, then pulled off some crazy trilling runs on the nose flute. It was just a tiny little toy, but he made that thing sing.

Egged on by my success, I grabbed the frog gong and the mallet, held it up high, and smashed the life out of it. The metallic clash boomed like thunder and drowned out the rest of the music. When the clash faded away, no one was playing anymore.

"Guess I killed the music," I said to everyone's stares. "Sorry."

"That's cool, bro," Hollis said. "First rule of performing: Always keep them wanting more. Where were you?"

"With Crane. He wanted to tell me that we'll be camping here tonight, so we should settle in."

"Like we couldn't have figured that out," Hollis said, giving me a suspicious look.

"Boys, Diana and I are having dinner with some of our old friends tonight. In Balong Lum, a traditional village just up the river," Dr. Reed said. "I know they'd be happy to have you. We're going to discuss how to keep the palm-oil plantations from slashing and burning the rain forest and encroaching on their native lands."

"Yeah, just another fun evening in Borneo," Diana said.

"Your mother is doing important work," Dr. Haga said. "You shouldn't make fun."

"Boys, would you care to join us?" Dr. Reed persisted.

"No, Dr. Reed. They'll be staying at the campsite tonight," Crane's voice slithered out of the darkness. He emerged into the firelight in a fresh khaki suit, his splotches healed, his cheeks smooth and shining. "Dr. Haga has prepared an extensive lecture on the tree shrews of Borneo for them. A fine bit of education. But by all means, feel free to join your friends at any time. . . . Now, is one of those times."

Klevko brought Crane's plush chair from the tent and set it down right next to the fire. Mr. Singh joined him. With a deep sigh, Dr. Reed rose and beckoned for Diana to follow her. Nodding good-bye to Hollis and me, she took Diana's hand and they headed off on the trail upriver.

As the food was being handed out, Dr. Haga stood up, cleaned his glasses on his shirt, and pulled out his field notebook. "So, we begin tonight with the rare and skittish greater slow loris. A nocturnal beast, the greater slow loris is not a shrew at all, but is actually a member of the lemur family —"

"Knock it off, Haga," Crane barked as soon as Dr. Reed and Diana were out of sight. "The sound of your voice makes me want to retch."

The minute Hollis and I were done with our dinner, I grabbed him and escaped to our tent for the night, once again claiming jet lag. Crane and Mr. Singh stayed behind to pore over the maps.

"So, Leo, when you were in Crane's tent," Hollis said as we walked by flashlight through the campsite to our tent, "were you sound bending in there?"

"No, Crane can't ever know about my power. I don't want to be out of control in front of him. Or pretty much anywhere out here in the middle of nowhere."

Something rustled in the bushes near us, and we picked up our pace.

"I know the feeling," Hollis said. "But you have to admit it's pretty weird, Leo. Suddenly, you're all buddy-buddy with Crane. I bet you're using your power to help him find the mask. Am I right or am I right?"

I grabbed him by the arm, pulling him close. I looked over both shoulders as some sort of creature wailed from deep within the jungle. "Don't say *anything* about that, okay?"

"About what?"

"My power," I whispered. "Listen, Hollis, I'm helping Crane because I want to make sure he never splits us up again."

"I heard you the first time," he said too loudly, pulling his arm away. "But what am I doing here? What am I supposed to do?"

"Nothing, just take it easy and enjoy the ride."

"But I just want to go home. I missed band practice. I hate the thought of getting sick here. I hate Borneo."

"But you're feeling okay, now?" I asked.

"So far," he said, and scratched his leg.

"Don't itch it, bro. And stay positive."

That's when some sort of giant moth the size of a small bird fluttered out of the darkness and made right for Hollis's flashlight. At least we hoped it was a moth. We ran the rest of the way. Zipped up in our tent, we took our antimalarial tablets and settled in. As Hollis played his sape rain-forest guitar, I picked up crazy Marie's book and read for a while, hoping to find somewhere in that huge formless book the real reason why Crane wanted that mask so badly. I tried to concentrate, but I found my thoughts drifting with the sound of the river and Hollis's sape, and every now and then, my thoughts would wander to Diana, wondering what she was doing and even what her favorite thing to do in New York was.

"What'd you think of that, Leo?" Hollis said, taking a break from his sape.

"It sounded awesome. It didn't sound like any of the new music you usually play. What was it?"

"I don't know," he said, strumming a few passages from the song. "I just followed my fingers, you know? It came so easily, I didn't even have to try."

"You made that up? Whoa, you should write it down. Or I can record it for you so you don't forget it."

"I won't forget it," he said. "You reading that Borneo book again?"

I considered telling him that the book resting on my chest was written by Crane's beloved mother, Marie, but then I'd have to explain her complicated theory about the weird race of people living in the hollow center of the Earth, and I knew that would creep him out so completely he probably would forget the song he'd just invented and start worrying about malaria again.

"It's called *Borneo: Her Customs and People*," I said. "I'm reading about the island's first settlers. It's getting pretty good, actually."

"Have fun, bro," he said, yawning, and started playing his song again, more softly.

Now that I'd lied to Hollis about enjoying it, I had to make a good show of being super fascinated with Marie's book. But as I read on, I actually did start enjoying it. Crazy Marie had moved on from methane burps and was now talking about ancient civilizations, about how every old civilization made up stories about how they were created. A great many of those creation myths told of a foreign visitor or visitors arriving from the sea, claiming to be from far away. Most of those visitors were described as having beards, and some of them as having feathered arms. But they all did the same thing—they traveled the lands spreading new knowledge and teaching: how to farm, how to read and write, how to keep a calendar, and how to build monuments. And when they had taught everything they knew, they returned to the sea, always promising that one day in the future, they would return.

According to Marie, most of those ancient civilizations turned their foreign visitors into gods, believing them to possess great and magical powers. But perhaps, Marie argued, those myths were really factual accounts. Not just stories, but history. Maybe those visitors were real people. Then she started getting all weird and went into how half the Boskops retreated into the hollow Earth while the other half blew their spirit trumpets and blasted off for the star Sirius. It was at that point that I realized Hollis had stopped playing his sape and was fast asleep. Listening to his breathing and the strange jungle ambience outside our tent, I got so scared and lonely that I almost went outside to find Dmitri, who was surely lurking somewhere nearby. But then I heard female voices echoing through the night.

I poked an eye through a sliver of our tent and watched Dr. Reed and Diana walking along the jungle trail to our campsite.

"That wasn't so bad, was it, Diana?" Dr. Reed said, laughing. "The chief and all your old friends were happy to see you."

"You mean they were happy to see you," Diana said. "You could at least include me, and not just sit me with the kids. I don't know what to talk to them about."

"Anything at all."

"Like subways and pizza and skyscrapers? Don't you get it, Mom? I don't like it here. There's no one to talk to."

They were nearing the camp, and not wanting to seem like a spy or vampire, I shut off the lantern and dove into my bed, listening to them continuing the same argument they'd been having for years. I felt for Diana. Like me, her parents had made a lot of unusual decisions in their lives, never realizing that their decisions affected her life. Those decisions made Diana weird, strange, alone. But at least she had a mom to argue with.

When everything was quiet outside, I poked my eye through the tent again. Dr. Reed was on her hammock, rocking back and forth. But Diana had made her bed on the ground, in a clearing away from the trees. She was on her back with her hands folded neatly on her chest, her face pointing up at the night sky. I watched her for a long time, but she didn't move a muscle. I kind of wanted to go talk to her, but she looked so peaceful I was afraid I'd be bothering her.

"What are you staring at?" Hollis said, sitting up.

"Nothing," I said quickly, jumping into bed. "Go back to sleep."

With Hollis tossing and snapping at bugs, and my mind racing through images of old fossils and Boskops beings and twin masks dangling from the ceiling, I was wide-awake. I poked an eye through the tent again and surveyed the site. Diana was still lying on her back, in the same position as before. It was impossible to tell if she was awake or asleep. Dmitri and Klevko were definitely asleep because I heard them snoring. Crane was definitely awake; the light in his humongous tent was on. I also saw a tall shadowy figure lurching around the campsite, then lurch into the jungle and disappear. It had to be Mr. Singh.

Plenty spooked, I read Marie's book with my flashlight until the night faded into the gray-blue of morning.

CHAPTER 17

Wat makes you ugly are the dark circles under your eyes," Dmitri said to me the next morning as I zombie-shuffled out of my tent for some breakfast. I'd hardly slept at all, an hour at best.

"Thanks, Dmitri," I said, noticing Crane dragging himself out of his tent. He also sported dark greenish-brown circles under his bloodshot eyes. Yet the campsite was humming with Hollis's sape guitar, and I found him giving a recital of his new song to Diana and Dr. Reed by her hammock. I zombie-shuffled over.

"That was wonderful, Hollis," Dr. Reed said, touching her chest. "Just wonderful."

He pretended like he didn't care and tuned his strings, but I knew he was thrilled.

"I didn't realize you knew classical music so well," Dr.

Reed continued. "But being Yolanda's son, it shouldn't be surprising that you can play Brahms so beautifully."

"Huh?" Hollis asked.

"Oh yes, what I remember most of our summer in Madagascar was listening to your mom practicing Brahms, his String Quartet in C Minor. The house was alive with that wonderful piece, even when she wasn't playing! It was so soothing and beautiful, we'd all nod off. But you were just two or three and probably don't remember that."

Before Hollis could respond, Crane came bounding over, full of manic energy, telling everyone we had to get on the river in five minutes. Mr. Singh trailed after him. Apparently he'd developed a mysterious injury, because he was limping around on a crooked old cane. Had he injured himself on his midnight stroll into the jungle?

"Let's get moving, gents," Crane said, pointing specifically at Hollis and me. "Five minutes, everyone. Lim Sum, stop dawdling."

We set off into the dark steaming water like a ghost ship armada, the sun behind us and shadows in front of us. We didn't see another soul on the river all morning, just the steamy jungle surrounding us, getting thicker and denser with every turn. I could barely keep my eyes open. All morning, I drifted in and out of consciousness, riding the currents of Hollis's gedang drum. After a lunch of sticky rice, we passed through some light rapids and then a hot drizzle. It was scorching out, the air as thick as syrup. So hot I could barely breathe.

In the trees, there were hundreds of little gray blurs darting around. It took me a second to finally recognize they were animals. Others were also sitting by the riverbanks, mamas holding babies, and smaller ones were playing or cracking rocks on little pellet-size fruit.

"Monkeys!" I screamed.

"Hey monkeys! Over here!" Hollis shouted, and took out his nose flute. "Maybe I can get their attention," he said, and tried out a few different tunes. One of the little gray blurs glanced up briefly, then resumed rummaging around for brown pellet fruit. I heard Diana's mini-operatic laugh from upriver.

"I didn't know you spoke monkey," I said.

"I don't, but maybe that guy speaks nose flute."

Even Tamon Dong, our driver, laughed at that. But the monkeys didn't hold Hollis's attention for long. Almost immediately, he was back to scratching at the red lump on his leg. "So, chief, your nose flute is impressive," I said, trying to distract him. "And your drumming is insanely good. When are you going to combine them?"

"I don't know," he said, focused on his mosquito bite.

"'Cause I bet you could do it," I said. "You're an unbelievable musician. That thing you played last night —"

"Yeah, but I was just copying Brahms. Dr. Reed said so."

"So what? You're just a kid. You can write your masterpieces when you're older."

"Mozart wrote his first symphony when he was five."

"Come on, Hollis, you write tons of music. All those

songs you wrote last month for the Freight Elevators were amazing."

"We're called Secret Stairwell now, and those songs were just okay." He paused for a long moment. "When we get back, I want to rededicate myself to music," he declared.

"*Rededicate?* Hollis, you're in like five bands."

"But we're just screwing around. It's pretty simple music, actually."

"It doesn't sound simple to me. I'd give anything to play even half as well. You can play every instrument ever made."

"But I want to *really* learn an instrument. When we get back, maybe I'll call Arturo or Gabor from Mom's old string quartet and see if they can teach me. Unless I'm too old already."

"You're eleven!"

"Those classical musicians can do stuff normal people can't. And they never mess up, not once. They're like superheroes. It takes years to get that good. You think I could be that good, Leo?"

"Sure, chief, but classical music? Seems pretty boring."

"It isn't boring, Leo. Maybe I should be more like Mom. I wish I could just ask her what to do."

Hollis puffed away some of the sweaty black hair that was hanging over his eyes and wiped his brow. He was pouring sweat, and his skin had a grayish pallor, except for that bump on his leg. That thing was red as an apple.

"Leo, I don't feel good," he said, rocking back and forth. "My stomach's twitchy again."

"We've just been on the river too long. Once you get on solid ground, you'll—"

"But I feel all hot, too," he said, suddenly shivering.

I waddled to the back of the boat and felt his forehead. "You don't feel hot. And besides, you can't get malaria. We're taking the pills."

"But that thing bit me before we took the pills. And what about all the water I was rubbing on it? Dmitri was telling me this morning about all the different parasites and bacteria in the water, and all the weird jungle diseases you can get. Some of them, Leo, nothing happens for years. But then one day you wake up and your eyes are all clouded over, and then you go blind."

"Stop listening to Dmitri," I said, wrapping one of our rain ponchos around him.

"Don't touch me, Leo. You can't make it better. I need Mom."

I did, too. She could make it better; she could make anything better. No matter how sick you felt, she knew just exactly what you needed, just what food to make for you or how to touch you to make it all okay. I'm not saying she was a doctor or anything, but she could always make it better.

Clouds had moved overhead, and it started drizzling. When the drizzle turned to raindrops, we gathered all the boats together in the middle of the river. It was decided that the armada would pull in for the night just upriver, near the Pomantong Cave.

As soon as we were ashore, I took Hollis by the hand and raced him over to Dr. Reed, weaving between all the porters who were scrambling to set up the rain tarps and Crane's deluxe tent.

"He's got a slight fever," she whispered to me, touching his forehead with the back of her hand. "Let's get you somewhere out of the rain, sweetie," she said to Hollis. "How about Crane's tent?"

"Okay," Hollis said meekly.

I was sick with worry. I was such an idiot to bring Hollis to this dangerous place. An idiot to take a chance with his life. All of my worst fears swarmed in my mind like a hornet's nest, and the only thing I could do was walk. I just kept walking along the riverbank, away from everyone, until my heartbeat started slowing. Finally, I was able to tell myself that it would all be okay. It had to be.

I found a spot alone under some trees, overlooking the river. I sat down and stared into the clouds and mist, and listened to the raindrops plopping into the water, just trying to breathe. Eventually, the rain faded into a light drizzle, and together with the breeze rustling the leaves, it all sounded like someone saying *shhhhh*. But soothing, like a mom calming a toddler. The sun began to set, and the frogs began their chorus of croaks. For a moment, I found a little peace.

"There you are!"

I turned to see Diana trotting up to me. Her hair was wet and shining, but her green and yellow eyes were warm and soft.

"You're so dark and mysterious, Leo. Going off by yourself to think deep thoughts in the rain," she said.

"I'm just so worried about Hollis."

"My mom thinks he just has a virus," she said. "She knows a lot about this stuff. Come on. Let's get your mind off this."

"And do what?"

"Catch a frog, what else?"

I jogged after her as she skipped ahead of me, stopping at times to touch an orchid or to search for monkeys up in the jungle canopy. Occasionally, she'd turn around to see if I was still there and chuck a pebble at me. She laughed and teased me the whole time, and I began to feel a little more at ease. It was almost like we were still little kids back on that path to the pond in Madagascar, surrounded by plants and animals so colorful and astonishing they seemed out of a dream.

Sometimes Diana would get down really low and cat-like, crouch close to the ground looking for a frog.

"Look!" she gasped, approaching a bizarre green and red spotted thing near the ground. "This is very special. Come here."

It was a plant of some sort, at least ten inches tall, shaped like a cylinder with an opening at its top. It looked like a jug—except for the spikes running along its back. Inside it was filled with a reddish liquid.

"A Venus flytrap!" I said.

"Not quite. It eats bugs like a Venus flytrap, but it's a pitcher plant. A *Nepenthes*. If we're really lucky . . ."

She trailed off and picked up a long leaf from the ground, carefully lowering it into the mouth of the *Nepenthes*, her mouth open in concentration. Her eyes lit up. "Yes," she whispered, and brought the leaf out, slowly raising it to her face. "Look, Leo. Come closer."

I leaned over to her, almost cheek to cheek, so close I could feel the warmth of her skin. I looked down into the leaf, and there I saw a tiny shape, a green speck no bigger than a pencil tip. I looked even closer, and I saw an eye.

"You see it? It's a tiny frog," she whispered. "They spend their lives inside the pitcher plants — from eggs to tadpoles to full-grown, like this little guy."

I put out my finger and hovered it over the frog, unsure of what to do.

"Here," she said, and grabbed my hand, guiding my finger to the leaf. I let my finger slide down toward the tiny green speck with eyes. When it was within an inch or so, the little guy jumped, seemed to disappear for a moment, then I saw it just below my fingernail.

It croaked.

"It's beautiful," I said, feeling my heart beat fast after I said it. She smiled at me, a full fantastic smile, and when she looked at me, I felt myself drift dreamily into her eyes.

We put the tiny frog back, watched him settle down into the safety of the *Nepenthes* flower, and felt the warmth of the sun breaking through the clouds. I felt like I could stay in that spot forever, but I knew I couldn't.

"We better get back to camp," I said after a while, and she nodded.

Hollis was lying in bed in our tent, with Dr. Reed watching him. She explained that he might be reacting to the malaria tablets, or have a minor flu bug. Diana gave him wildflowers, and I offered to stay with him so the girls could get ready for dinner.

"Hey, buddy," I said to Hollis after they'd left. "They say you're A-OK."

He stared at me with his dead animal eyes, all wrapped in blankets. "I feel hot."

"Keep the covers off if you're hot."

"Then the mosquitoes will bite me."

I knew what he was feeling. When you get stuck in a worry mode, everything seems bleak. To distract him, I told him about the tiny frog Diana and I had seen. Just describing it made me smile. But not Hollis.

At dinnertime, I brought him some sticky rice and river fish, but he didn't touch it.

"Try to sleep," I said to him, but his eyes remained open. I thought about singing him Brahms's Lullaby, but I can't sing a lick. Poor Hollis, he just tossed and turned and scratched at his bite. It took hours, but eventually he fell asleep, and I guess, so did I.

I woke up on my own just before sunrise, yawned, and rolled over to check on him.

"Hey, chief," I whispered. "You feeling better?"

But there was nothing in his bed except a pile of sheets. My brother was gone.

CHAPTER 18

bolted from our tent. The minute I stepped outside everything felt wrong. The camp was entirely silent. The porters
were gone — no one going about their morning chores or
cooking breakfast or loading up the longboats like usual.
The campsite felt abandoned. Even Diana was gone — her
sleeping bag was all rolled up like she'd never slept in it. It
was just like that morning back in Brooklyn when Crane
had split us up, that eerie feeling that I'd just chucked my
wallet down a storm drain and lost something important.
And what was more important than Hollis?

"Hollis," I called out. "Where are you?"

I made for Dr. Reed's hammock, breaking into a run
halfway there.

"Oh, you're up early, Leo." She yawned and fumbled for
her glasses.

"Have you seen Hollis?" I asked, trying to control the panic in my voice.

"No, Leo," she said. "He's not with you?"

"No. Where are all the porters?"

"I assume at the Pomantong Cave. It's about a mile inland. It's a small cave that houses the bones and relics from many of their ancestors and legendary chiefs. They likely went to pay their respects."

"I bet Hollis went there."

"Oh no, Leo, they would never allow that. It's a very sacred tribal place. No outsiders would ever be allowed." She sat up and rested her bare feet on the ground. "So Hollis really isn't with you?"

"Maybe he's with Diana, then."

"I don't think so. She just left to take a bath and wash her hair in the river. Give me a second and I'll —"

"Is she up this way?" I said, pointing upriver and starting to run.

"No, no, no, Leo. *I'll* check on Diana. Let me get my shoes on and I'll help you."

But I couldn't wait any longer. The panic had set in. I dashed around camp like a crazy man, calling Hollis's name louder and louder. Crane stuck his head out of his tent, his eyes bloodshot and his expression furious.

"Modulate your voice, Leo."

"Hollis is missing."

"I'm well aware of that now," he said bitterly. "He may be a child, but he's not deaf. You boys cannot seem to follow directions. You were both told not to leave the campsite for any reason. Now I'll have to organize the porters into a search party. That should set us back several hours."

"They're all gone," I shrieked. "They're visiting some cave."

"I'll send Klevko, then. And Dmitri. Really, Leo, you must lower your voice."

"They're also gone," a voice said from inside a nearby tent. It was Mr. Singh.

"Somebody has to do *something*," I said, stomping my foot. "For all we know, Hollis could be lost in the jungle. Or attacked by an orangutan. Or collapsed somewhere, burning up with malaria."

"Such drama, Leo," Crane sighed, stepping outside, somehow fully dressed. "Someone wake that lazy ox, Haga. It's time he stopped spouting off about shrews and did something useful."

"He is gone as well, Mr. Rathbone," Mr. Singh said, stepping out of his tent with a yellowed book he'd obviously been studying tucked under his arm. He leaned on his knobby old cane.

"Now where the devil has he disappeared to?" Crane was bright red with frustration.

"He told me last night he was going to the sacred cave with the others," Dr. Reed said, rushing over in her hiking boots and rain poncho. "It's bad luck to pass here and not bring gifts to the spirits of the elders."

"Superstitious nonsense," Crane fumed. "I pay these fools to work for me, not to run off to caves for voodoo rituals."

Dr. Reed waved her finger at Crane.

"You have no right to make fun of their traditions," she yelled at him. "They believe their gifts will help a beloved ancestor live more happily in the afterlife. And who are you to mock that?"

"Dr. Reed," I interrupted. "Does Hollis know about the cave, the traditions?"

"Why, yes," she answered. "I told him all about the Pomantong Cave while you were chasing frogs with Diana. He seemed especially interested in the sacred jars."

"Sacred jars?" Crane snorted. "I believe I've heard more than enough."

"Yes, Leo," she said, ignoring Crane. "People in Borneo have special jars, family heirlooms passed down for centuries. Some legends say that if you put your ear right next to one of those jars, you can hear the dead ancestors talking in soft, low voices."

"How do I get to the cave?" I asked her, my feet burning to take off running.

"That trail leads to it," she said, pointing to a small trail that snaked into the jungle canopy. "But as I told you, Leo, you shouldn't—"

I didn't wait for the rest of her answer, just grabbed her by the sleeve and pulled her onto the path leading from camp.

"Leo, I forbid you to go there," Crane said. "I can't risk you—"

But by the time he'd finished his sentence, I was too far away to hear it.

After our parents' deaths, Hollis had asked a lot of questions about what happens to you after you die. Jeremy tried to suggest answers. The counselors at school gave him pamphlets to read. But the questions persisted—and why wouldn't they? Our parents had never been found. Where were they? It was a haunting, horrible thought. I knew if Hollis thought there was even a remote chance that a visit to Pomantong Cave might give our parents a happier time in the afterlife, he'd give it a try.

Dr. Reed trailed after me as I raced down the path, pushing away spiky branches and leaves. I had no idea where it led, only that I was moving deeper and deeper into the rain forest. The fear I felt for Hollis pumped me full of so much adrenaline, I was practically flying. My breath came short and shallow. My calves burned. I let my hands touch everything I passed, hoping to sound bend Hollis's voice. But I heard nothing, just my blood pumping in my ears.

After I had run for about ten minutes, I heard footsteps coming my way. It was Dr. Haga, accompanied by Tamon Dong and four other porters. Each of them had a patch of black soot on their foreheads. One had tears streaming down his face, and the others looked visibly shaken. My heart skipped a beat. Had something horrible happened to Hollis?

"Dr. Haga, where's Hollis?" I panted. "Is he with you?"

He shook his head. "We have come from Pomantong, Leo. A terrible thing has happened there. The cave has been looted and the sacred jars are broken. Only shards are left . . . and bones."

Dr. Reed had caught up to us, and I looked to her for an explanation of those black sooty marks.

Dr. Haga spoke in a trembling voice, his usual detached teacherlike manner all but gone. "With the disruption of the funeral site, the ghosts of the dead have scattered. They are now *toh*, free-floating nature spirits. The *toh* care little for humans. The porters wear the black marks to disguise themselves from the *toh*."

"When was the cave broken into?" Dr. Reed asked.

"Within the last two months, but we did not stay to examine it," Dr. Haga answered. "It is a very bad omen. We must hurry away."

"Can you show us the way?" I asked Dr. Haga. "I think Hollis may be there."

"We did not see him, Leo. And I suggest you keep away. But if you must go, follow the path until you dead-end at the giant stone ridge, then go right. The cave is not far from there."

Dr. Reed and I raced down the path for another five minutes, the longest five minutes of my life. The jungle was thick around me, but I could see the stone cliff just ahead of us.

"Leo, stop," Dr. Reed whispered sharply. "Listen."

From deep inside the thicket, I heard a wailing that sounded like a human baby.

"Orangutan," Dr. Reed whispered. "Sounds like a juvenile. We have to be very careful, Leo. You don't ever want to get between a baby and its mother."

"But what if Hollis did? What if . . ."

I couldn't bring myself to finish the sentence or wait any longer. In a panic, I tore away from Dr. Reed toward the stone wall ahead, with no other thought than to find my brother. How I wished I could hear his voice. What good did it do to have a power if I couldn't use it to protect Hollis?

I reached the stone wall towering above me, trees overhanging and clinging to the cliffs, and ran along it until I saw two rows of poles stuck into the ground. Each pole was topped with a carved wooden head. Some were painted, others decorated in feathers. The two rows framed the entrance to the cave, a small dark opening about fifteen feet up the rock face. I climbed, my hands scraping and tearing until I could poke my head into the darkness.

"Hollis," I called in a loud whisper. "Are you in there?"

There was no answer and my heart sank.

"Bro?" My voice trembled.

"Leo? Is that you?" His voice sounded so small coming from inside the cavern.

I pulled myself all the way up and into the opening, just in time to see Hollis step out of the shadows, his face streaked with tears. On his forehead, he wore a patch of soot, just like the porters, and in his hand, he held a shard of one of the old sacred jars. Inside the cave, I could just barely make out scattered bones.

"I brought them instruments," he said, running to me and bursting into tears. "I brought Dad a drum and Mom a flute. I thought they'd like that."

I held on to him as he cried on my shoulder. I didn't say anything, just held on to him while his body shook with tight little sobs.

"I wanted to talk with Mom," he said between gasps. "But the jars were already broken. And there were bones all over. The porters were screaming and crying."

"That sounds really scary," I said. "But you're safe now."

"I thought maybe I could hear her voice," he sobbed. "One last time."

I held him tight. Dr. Reed joined us and tried to comfort Hollis, but she sensed we needed to be alone, the two of us, so she left to wait for us on the path. I don't know how long we stood there at the entrance to the cave. After a while, Hollis's sobs subsided, and I reached into my pocket and pulled out a slightly used tissue. It was all I had.

"No thanks," he said, half laughing and half crying. He wiped his face with the back of his hand, and as he did, the shard of pottery dropped to the ground. I bent down to pick it up. As soon as I touched it, a shock ran through my body and my powers activated with full force. I went into a sound trance — not the peaceful kind with the lapping waves, but the black, inky wormhole one, dark and threatening. My ears filled with sound — wailing cries of mourners followed by shattering sounds of objects being smashed to smithereens. Then came the voices.

"No, don't bother with the beads, Dmitri. They are worth nothing."

"Look, Ojciec. A gold one!"

"Yes, take that one."

"Are we going to tell the boss?" I heard Dmitri's voice say.

"No! This is for us. Tell no one. Not even Matka."

I think I screamed and dropped the shard in the dirt, and as I did, the voices disappeared.

"What was it, Leo?" Hollis asked. "What did you hear?"

"Grave robbers," I said, coming to my senses.

"Were they evil spirits, Leo?"

"No, just people," I said. "Regular, selfish people."

CHAPTER 19

When we got back to camp, I wasn't surprised to see Klevko and Dmitri already there, seamlessly blending in with everyone else — but I knew better. I didn't have to wonder why Dmitri always kept two hands on his duffel bag, guarding it closely until his boat had pushed off into the water. From what I could tell, Klevko and Dmitri hadn't been the first ones to loot the grave site, but they'd felt no shame in scavenging for scraps. Maybe if they'd heard what I heard, they might have felt differently.

Hollis had heard it all. He'd woken up early and followed the porters to the site, desperate for some sort of closure, hoping to hear any sort of message, any sort of scrap of Mom and Dad. And when the porters entered the cave, Hollis heard them screaming and sobbing in pain — he just thought they were mourning, so he went up afterward. That's when he saw the smashed jars, the over-turned coffins, the bones.

As he boarded the boat for our day on the river, he still wore that black sooty mark on his forehead, and kept that awful squinty look on his face all day. The porters were morose and silent. The mood was dark — Hollis didn't even play his drums. I felt terrible for him. The worst thing about grief is that any little thing can trigger it, anything at all, and once it's back in the open, it's like you have to go through the whole thing all over again — the disbelief, the anger, the loss, until you're left with an empty feeling so immense that you can't imagine how you'd kept all that grief inside you.

As we motored rapidly up the Kayan, I tried to cheer Hollis up by pointing out the amazing natural sights we were seeing. Old trees that looked like bent human forms. River snakes that slithered in the muddy ooze. Birds of all sizes and shapes, in every vivid color of the rainbow. And every now and then, I'd catch a glance of Diana and remember the little frog and how I said, "It's beautiful," and stared dreamily into her eyes. My brain told me to feel really embarrassed about feeling all mushy inside, but I wasn't embarrassed.

The fork was only a day and a half away — Crane hoped to reach it by noon the next day. That's when Diana would go her way, and I'd go mine. And who knew when we'd see each other next, if ever?

All day long, we motored up the river until the sun began to set to the west of us. As we pulled to the embankment and climbed off the boat, Tamon Dong stopped us and held up a thin silver necklace with a tiny heart-shaped locket. I recognized it was Diana's and said I'd give it back to her. As I took it, my hands felt drawn to the locket and I heard the pre-echoes of a deep sound-bender trance. But before I succumbed to its spell, I was able to slip the necklace into my pocket. After all, it's not nice to pry open someone's locket.

Diana and Dr. Reed stayed by the fire with Hollis as the porters fished out our dinner and set up camp. We had camped near a giant cave, and at twilight, about a million bats flew over the campsite, so many of them the sky went completely dark. They were fruit bats, Dr. Haga explained, and it was dinnertime for them, too.

Dr. Reed felt Hollis's forehead and said she thought his fever was gone, but he still wasn't hungry. Before he got in bed, he fished around in his duffel and pulled out the watermelon crystal necklace that had belonged to our mom. Holding it in his hand, he flopped down on the bed and stayed silent for a long time. I just lay on my bed next to him.

"Today sucked," he said after about an hour of silence.

"At least you're not feeling sick anymore, right? It must help to know that you don't have malaria."

"Guess so," he muttered, opening his hand to look at the crystal. "They say some crystals have healing powers. Do you believe that, Leo?"

"I don't know what I believe anymore," I answered truthfully. "Anything's possible."

"Thanks for that," he said.

"For what?"

"For not talking to me like a kid."

I stayed with him for a long time until he closed his eyes and seemed to doze off. Then I remembered Diana's necklace in my pocket and peeked an eye through the tent. Diana was stretched out on her sleeping bag, lying down with both arms folded under her head. I crept over to her.

"Lose something?" I said, and with my pen I dangled the locket over her face. "Tamon Dong found it."

With a gasp, she grabbed the necklace and held it against her chest.

"Thank you so much," she said as she took her necklace back and clasped it around her neck. "I didn't even know I'd lost it."

"Yeah, losing things without realizing it is the worst."

"I would have died if I lost it," she said. "My dad gave it to me. Do you remember him?"

"Sort of. I remember a dad, with a beard maybe. He was nice to me, I think."

"He gave this to me right before he left us."

"I'm so sorry—"

"No, he didn't leave us," she corrected herself. "My mom drove him away. She was so obsessed with Borneo he had no choice."

"Do you get to see him? He's not in Mongolia or something, is he?"

"He's in New York with his new wife and their two girls. He tries to arrange special time for us, but . . ."

"It's not the same," I said.

"Yeah. It's just been me and my mom for eight years, which can get rough."

"Wanna trade? Crane's not so great, either."

"Hmm . . . no," she said, and I knew that she'd realized she was being insensitive, since I didn't have a mom. All I had was Crane.

"It's tough for all of us," I said. "No one ever asks a kid what they want."

We were silent for a minute.

"All right, I should get to bed. Good night, Diana."

"Don't go yet, Leo. I'm not even tired at all."

"Okay," I said, wanting to check up on Hollis, but I sat down on the wet grass. "I'll stay for a bit if I can ask you one question."

"Sure, ask away."

"So, I'm just curious. You always sleep outside, on your back. What are you thinking of before you fall asleep? You seem so peaceful."

"See for yourself," she said, rolling out some of her tarp for me. "It's a new moon tonight and no clouds. Just lie back and look up, Leo."

I did. The night sky was unlike anything I'd ever seen in New York or anywhere else. I could see thousands of stars, millions of them. Diana was a stargazer!

"Whoa, there's so many—"

"Don't talk, Leo. Just let your eyes adjust and drift."

I folded my arms behind my head, just like she was doing. The stars weren't just little white specks here. There were blue ones and red ones, shiny ones and dim ones, whole lustrous shapes seemed made entirely of yellow, orange, and golden flecks. The night sky above us was like a giant dome, and it felt endless and infinite. The view was so pristine and vivid that I really could sense the vast distances. There were different-colored clouds pouring through the sky like creamy dyes, all flecked with the glittering jewels of stars. And I even saw the Milky Way, a giant purplish cloud near the horizon. My mom always tried to get me to see the Milky Way whenever we were out at night. She'd point at this faint hazy wisp and ask me if I saw it. I never really did. But tonight there was no denying it.

After a long time, Diana pointed her finger up and toward the horizon. I positioned my head under my arm and followed it.

"Since we're in the south," she said, "all the constellations are different. "But you see that one, near the horizon? That's you. Leo the Lion. Most of your constellation won't come out for a few weeks, but that faint star, Regulus, is part of Leo. That's your star."

"Do you have a star?"

"Just the moon." She laughed. "Diana was the Roman version of Artemis, the moon goddess."

"She's the hunter goddess, too, right? I love all that old Greek stuff."

"You know there was a Greek philosopher named Plato," she said, her voice soft and serious. "And he believed that human beings came from the stars, that we filtered down from them into our selves. He didn't have any telescopes and didn't know the science behind astronomy, but he was absolutely right. Everything in us is made of star stuff. Everything that makes life possible was formed millions of years ago when nearby stars exploded and went supernova."

"Isn't that how black holes are formed, too?"

"You're so dark, Leo. But you're right, whatever's left of the star becomes a black hole. How'd you know that?"

"My friend Trevor is obsessed with black holes. But I don't really understand them."

"No one does. They're completely mysterious. There's no way to ever find out what's inside them, because nothing can escape from them, not even light." We were silent for a moment.

"Ever seen any UFOs out here?" I asked. When she laughed, I got a little embarrassed by my own question.

"If you look closely, you can see tons of shooting stars and satellites. But no UFOs, not yet anyway."

She laughed again, mysteriously. "Sometimes — now don't make fun of me, because I've never told this to anyone. Promise you won't."

"Promise."

"I'm alone so much out here that my only friends are the stars. And sometimes, when I'm wishing I were anywhere but here, I imagine that I can travel throughout the universe and visit all the countless stars and their civilizations. They teach me about their way of life, and they're happy someone is finally visiting them because they're all so far away from each other, so they're all lonely, too."

"Sounds like fun," I said.

"You don't think it's weird?"

"No, I think it's awesome," I said, but what I meant was that Diana was awesome. "And I think we're all pretty weird, but I don't think we're alone. I have this . . . figure . . . that shows up in my dreams sometimes. He's sort of my guide. The last time he showed up, I was trapped in this awful nightmare, this pitch-black space so dark it didn't even have shadows. I tried to yell inside my dream just to wake myself up, but I couldn't escape. And then that figure appeared, and he gave off this intense golden light. I just remembered what he told me: 'In the darkness there is more than enough light, but it is hidden deep within Mother Night.'"

"What do you think he meant by that?"

"I don't know. Maybe one day I'll be smart enough to figure it out. So now I bet you think I'm really weird."

"Weirder than me," she said. "But I don't mind."

She reached her arms up over her head, and I felt her hand softly graze my hair. I felt crystal clear. Everything I looked at was new and beautiful, especially the stars. I felt like I was living a long time ago, in an age without lightbulbs or streetlights or televisions. When the only entertainment at night was the fire and the stars. The stars were much cooler than anything I'd ever seen on TV.

And for a little while, Diana and I had the entire universe to ourselves.

"I should get back to Hollis," I said as I reluctantly got to my feet. "I'm so sorry, but I have to make sure he's doing—"

"It's okay, Leo. Really. We can still hang out tomorrow."

"It's a promise," I said, and walked to my tent, feeling good all over. But before I could slip inside, I heard kissy noises coming from the darkness.

"You have fun with your girlfriend?" Dmitri said, turning on his lantern. "You spent too much time talking, not enough time smooching."

"Dmitri, I'm done talking to you. You need to stop spying on me, and just leave me alone, or there'll be trouble. Got it?"

I snarled and took a menacing step toward him, and in return, he flashed a kung fu pose back at me.

"You don't want trouble from me, Leo. I have two black belts."

"I'm sure you do," I said. "And a Swiss Army knife. But don't ever threaten me again."

"Leo, you have it backward. I'm your friend. I'm just being friendly. Crane wants to see you. He's in a very good mood. He has a present for you."

"Tell him thanks, and I'll get it tomorrow."

"He wants to give it to you now."

"You don't want to test my lion style," I said, making two claws with my hands. It was straight out of *Five Deadly Venoms*, one of thousands of kung fu movies I'd seen with Trevor. "Perhaps you don't know this, Dmitri, but my master is Shifu Shi Yan Ming, 34th generation warrior monk. I doubt your street moves are any match for my Shaolin kung fu. Come, you motherless dog, let's shadowbox."

Dmitri just stared at me like I was crazy. I didn't care. It felt good to harass him.

"I will tell the boss you are coming," he said.

I took my sweet time heading over there, and Crane was waiting for me.

"Leo! There he is! Care for a bottle of soda pop? I've also got some delicious hot cider. It goes splendidly with caviar. Have a blini. "

Crane was jubilant, festive almost. He had placed a table in the center of the room filled with maps and an assortment of luxury food items. Both Klevko and Mr. Singh were also in the tent, Mr. Singh morose and bored as ever, sitting in a chair, cross-legged.

"What's this all about, Crane? Dmitri said you had something for me?"

"I do. But first, have a snack and enjoy yourself. I also have some veal jerky if caviar doesn't suit your tastes. We're celebrating tonight."

"Why?"

"We're less than a day from the fork in the river, Leo. I've just dispatched two of the porters to serve as advance scouts. What are their names, Klevko?"

"Cyril and Kavi, sir."

"Whatever. They will attempt to find Byong Ku, make contact with the villagers, and ask for our permission to enter. They will place orange flags in the ground to lead us there. Are you with me so far, Leo?"

I nodded.

"Once we're rid of our saintly anthropologist and her somewhat annoying daughter, we begin the perilous phase of our mission where I will be calling on you to help me locate the mask we are both so intent on finding. To thank you for your help thus far, and to equip you properly for the challenges ahead, I want to give you a small token of my appreciation. Klevko, you may retire for the night."

"You got it, boss," he said, slithering out of the tent.

Crane produced a small metallic suitcase from the ground and laid it on the table, sweeping aside the foodstuffs and maps. He opened the suitcase and inside it was filled with gray foam. Set into the foam was something that looked like a dagger, but when it caught the light from above, the reflection of its jeweled hilt nearly blinded me. He laid the dagger on the table.

"This is a very special item, Leo. It is a Sikh kirpan, a ceremonial dagger carried by all members of the Sikh faith. But it is no ordinary kirpan. This one is said to have been made for Queen Elizabeth the First's royal astronomer, John Dee. History does not say whether or not John Dee ever received the dagger, but as you can see for yourself, it was surely crafted for a person of nobility and learning. Go on, give it a try."

I was too stunned by this whole thing to know what to do. The dagger was unbelievable. The grip was made of a glowing purple resin, filled with swirls of colors that changed in the light, and on the blade were etchings of scientific men gazing through telescopes. It was an amazing-looking thing.

"I, too, Leo, was stunned to silence by its beauty. But make no mistake, this is not the tool of assassins or thugs, but a symbol of an enlightened mind. With the blade of knowledge, one may shear away the weeds of ignorance and reveal the truth. Go ahead, Leo, try it out."

"I don't know what to say, Crane. Thank you, I guess."

Everything in me wanted to pick up the dagger, maybe slice up the tent a little bit, but I stopped myself short, afraid that I might sound bend it.

"Go ahead," Crane smiled. "Pick it up. It's yours."

Not wanting to offend him, I used my shirt to pick it up, claiming that I didn't want to smudge it. Etched into the other side of the blade, men were gazing into crystal balls. Crane and Mr. Singh exchanged glances, watching me as if I was an actor in a play and they were waiting for my next line.

"Thanks so much, Uncle Crane. I need to get back to Hollis now. In case you hadn't noticed, he's having a rough day."

"Still whining about malaria, is he?"

"Dr. Reed said it can take more than a week for the symptoms to appear," I said, pocketing the blade quickly.

"Dr. Reed," he scoffed. "What isn't she an expert on? Well, she surely isn't an expert on what I have to show you next. In preparation for the final leg of our mission, Mr. Singh and I want to bring you into a recent discovery."

Crane produced another metal suitcase and switched it with the kirpan suitcase. The other suitcase held the mask. Its dark eyes glared at me.

"While examining the mask, Mr. Singh has discovered an element previously hidden to us." Crane picked up the mask and reached his pale white hand into the mouth of alexandrite fangs. He twisted one of them and then pressed something inside the mouth until I heard a click. At once, two slits opened above the empty eye sockets and two glimmering sheets of gold slid down over the eyes. Instead of dark sockets, the face now had convex eyes. The whites of the eyes were fashioned from the gold, while the irises were made of sparkling red gems. The pupils appeared to be clear diamonds.

"Impressive, yes?" Crane smiled.

Crane slid the mask across the table to me.

"Since you are such an integral part of our expedition," he continued, "please feel free to examine the new elements and tell us what you think."

I put my hand to my chin and pretended to think really hard. "Quite a discovery."

"Why don't you touch it, Leo?" Mr. Singh said from his shadowy chair to the side of Crane.

"Oh no, I couldn't," I said. "I wouldn't want to damage it."

"We'd like you to pick it up," Mr. Singh repeated.

I stared into his mysterious eyes, trying to determine what he knew, but I couldn't read them. His face was as solemn and blank as ever.

"Yeah . . . but, um . . . I don't know what more I could tell you. . . ."

I trailed off into silence. Crane and Mr. Singh let the silence develop, then looked at each other. Mr. Singh

236

nodded to Crane from the shadows, then leaned over and whispered something in his ear, after which, Crane spoke.

"You and I, Leo, have fallen into a rather predictable routine," he began. "A routine of mistrust and deception. It is as much my fault as it is yours. But I have no more time for this game. The moment of truth is upon us. It's time we both lay our cards on the table. If we play together, Leo, we both win."

"I'm not following you, Crane."

"Don't be coy. I know you have a gift. A real and true gift. My mother had it. And you have it. There is no reason to hide it from me. Mr. Singh and I recognize you for what you really are."

"And what's that?" I asked. My heart was beating fast, though I tried to show nothing.

"In India, I have studied all manner of supernatural phenomena," Mr. Singh said. "I believe you are a young man with an extraordinary talent, possessing powers beyond the comprehension of ordinary men."

"Listen, you guys," I said. "I'm going to be as honest as I possibly can be. I have no idea what you're talking about. Thank you for the dagger, but I really should go check on my brother."

"Do you really believe, Leo, that I am so blind as you imagine?" Crane said, rising to his feet. "No, I have a thousand eyes and a million cameras and associates everywhere. I have seen everything. I have seen you roaming my warehouse with your gangly friend."

"I really don't know what you mean, Crane. I'm sorry I stole your dolphin helmet—that was a mistake. But—"

"Leo, look into my eyes. Do you see an enemy? Do you see someone out to ruin you? Look at me freshly, and I guarantee you will see a true friend."

Crane leaned forward across the table, and I looked into the dark hollows of his eyes, the whites gleaming like his bald scalp. Then I looked into the strange golden eyes of the mask, its sparkling jewels frozen with hidden secrets from the past. I didn't know which set of eyes was more frightening.

"You're scaring me, Crane," I said.

Crane shook his head, then turned to Mr. Singh.

"What do you make of it, Singh?"

"It is possible," he answered, "that he is unaware of his gift. Perhaps he regards it as a normal child might regard his sense of touch or smell."

"And perhaps, Mr. Singh, he is merely lying to me." Crane started to pace, his hands clasped in a tight hold behind his back.

"Leo," he said, the tension in his voice evident. "Mr. Singh has made it his life's work to study matters of a psychic nature. He was a protégé of my beloved mother, Marie. If you tell us the truth, he will be your teacher, help you to develop your potential."

"I don't need developing."

"That's where you're wrong, Leo," Mr. Singh said. "For instance, I can teach you to exercise your power without needing to touch anything. If your powers were at full strength and properly channeled, touch shouldn't be necessary."

"This is what I'm talking about," Crane added. "A gift like yours cannot be wasted on childish trial-and-error experiments. People like you need a path. Mr. Singh can show you the way, if he chooses to take you on. What do you say, Mr. Singh?"

"My work is guided by your mother's life and writings, Mr. Rathbone, and as such, I would be delighted to have Leo study under me, provided he could give me a demonstration of his gift."

"Are you guys serious?" I said.

"There are no limits to your potential," Mr. Singh said, lowering his voice to a barely audible whisper. "The inner worlds are *real*. The universe is nothing but the Mind. I can teach you the occult arts — bilocation, astral travel, necromancy. All are possible."

"Necromancy?" I mumbled. My head was spinning, and nothing seemed real. It was all I could do to repeat Mr. Singh.

"Yes, necromancy. Communication with the dead. That is very possible, Leo. It was Madam Marie Rathbone's specialty."

"That is how my mother and your grandfather met," Crane chimed in. "She helped your grandfather Tiberius communicate with his dead wife. My beloved mother established a channel between Tiberius and your late grandmother Pearl, who told him to accept my mother's love. So you see, Leo, this is your true family history. This is who you are. You cannot hide the truth of your life from me anymore. I believe in you."

The ground was shaky under my feet, almost nonexistent. I had no idea what was keeping me from falling through the floor. I could barely recognize anything around me. Not the tent, not Crane, not Mr. Singh.

"I feel . . . sick . . . dizzy. . . ."

"Of course you do, Leo. You are unrooted, without footing. You have tried to have it both ways. You have tried to live two lives, and now both are dissolving. It is time to choose a side — either be a normal boy who goes to school and accepts the normal rules or become so much more than that. You will know the secrets and be able to hold Truth in your hand. The choice is yours. Now, pick up the mask, Leo, and show us what you can do."

Crane picked up the twin mask and held it out to me. I stayed perfectly still for a long time, looking at it, at Crane, at Mr. Singh, trying to find something real, something solid to hang on to. Finally, I took a deep breath and looked Crane in the eye.

"Maybe I do have a power, Crane," I said, feeling a smile not my own spread across my face. "And maybe I don't. But if I did, it'd take a lot more than a Sikh knife to get me to perform for you."

Crane threw his head back and let out a belly laugh. Then he put the mask back into the suitcase and slid it off the desk. Mr. Singh nodded at Crane. "Have it your way, Leo. The time will come. Now run off to bed. You'll need your sleep for tomorrow."

As soon as I left Crane's tent, my mind began reeling and swarming with questions. Was it a bluff, or did he and Mr. Singh really know about my power? And what about everything Mr. Singh was saying about the occult arts, like necromancy? And what about my father's warning, the words he wrote me in the letter I opened on my thirteenth birthday, only a month before, when he told me of my birth on an uncharted island and left me that blue disc that awakened my power? His words rang in my mind: *Always keep this a secret. Tell no one about your history. It is for you and you alone.*

Was he warning me, telling me how deal with men like Crane? Or had he somehow foreseen that Crane, with his scheming ways, would bribe me into his service and then trap me into revealing what I'd been warned never to reveal? Had I revealed too much? Was this all a test? I had no answers.

I staggered around the campsite in a daze. Nothing was as it seemed. Everything around me seemed alive and moving, thinking and plotting. The trees swaying in the wind weren't really trees, and the wind was like the breath of an alien. At one point, I drew my kirpan, the metal swooshing as I held the blade in the air and growled at the dark wall of jungle, "Who's there? Show yourself!"

CHAPTER 20

Far before sunrise, the entire camp was awakened by a horrible shrieking. Everyone rushed out of their tents, bleary-eyed and in varying stages of undress, to find Crane's driver, Lim Sum, wailing and trembling on the jungle floor by the river. Some of the other porters tried to calm him, but it was no use. Dr. Haga interpreted.

"Lim Sum has had a terrible nightmare," he said, leaning over his shaking and sobbing body. "He claims an evil mountain *toh* is following our party. The mission is cursed."

The sun was still an hour from rising, but all of the stars were blocked by thick, dark clouds. A warm wind was blowing from the northeast, rattling all the thousands of leaves in the jungle.

"Well, Lim Sum," Crane said. "That was a rather rude awakening, but now that we are all up, I suggest we depart at once. We are within twenty miles of the fork, and if we leave now, we could arrive by early afternoon."

"Mr. Rathbone," Dr. Haga said, still tending to Lim Sum. "Have you looked to the skies? It seems the weather will be most extreme today. I'm certain many of the porters would agree we should not break camp."

"What do you suggest we do, Leo?" Crane said, gazing across everyone at me. "The expedition will follow your lead."

I felt everyone looking at me, especially Diana and Dr. Reed, but I didn't return their gazes or ponder the question for a second. "We should leave now," I said.

"Are you certain, Leo?" Dr. Reed asked. "We're still in the tail-end of monsoon season, and—"

"And why are you in such a hurry, Leo?" Diana asked, stunned and deflated.

"Come now, everyone, what's a little weather?" Crane said. "We're human beings, not animals. We tame nature, we tower over it. We don't run from a little rain."

"But, Mr. Rathbone—" Dr. Haga started.

"I'll hear no more of it," Crane said. "Leo is my voice in this matter, so if you wish to question his judgment, realize that you are also questioning mine. We leave in twenty minutes."

"You heard the boss," Klevko said, clapping his hands. "Let's go now. Move."

"Wait a moment," Dr. Haga said. "We are missing two of the porters, Kavi and Cyril. And a boat is missing, as well."

"I sent them downriver last night, to search for . . ." Crane said, trailing off.

"Why wasn't I informed?" Dr. Haga asked.

"Because *I* am their boss, Haga. Now back to work, everyone, and no more questions."

As Hollis and I went to our tent to pack up our gear, he let out a long sigh.

"I'm sick of that longboat. I'm sick of talking about *tohs* and evil spirits. And why are you in such a rush, when we could just take a day off and hang out here with Diana and Dr. Reed? I really like them."

"I like them, too," I said. "They'll be back in New York in six months."

"I just hate to say good-bye, that's all."

"Me too. But the faster we say good-bye, the faster we find the mask and go home. And then, we'll be back at the same school. If you want, Hollis, I'll call everybody from Mom's old quartet to help you find a new music teacher." I didn't mention that I was also planning to ask them as many questions about Antarctica as I could, to help prepare for my fact-finding mission. They'd been with my parents on the trip, and were the last ones to see them before they took a small plane out to look at glaciers . . . and never returned.

"I'm still deciding about that," Hollis said. "I'm not really sure what to do."

"Well, get packed up for now, and we can talk about it on the river."

I put *The Immortal Underground* in my bag, zipped it up, and moved on to Hollis's bag, shoving everything of his in as fast as possible.

"Hey, Leo, last night I was reading that Borneo book you're so obsessed with," Hollis said.

"Really?" I said, avoiding his eyes and pretending that it took all my concentration to pack his bag, as I tried to figure out exactly what he knew and how to respond. The truth? Partial truth? Lies? My mind raced through all of them, but I took the easiest way: stony silence.

"Yeah, it was really weird," he continued. "Just a bunch of boring stuff about glaciers and rock layers."

I laughed. "I have to admit, it was pretty boring at first, but the author was just providing a very thorough history . . . of Borneo. She has some interesting ideas."

Dr. Reed stuck her head in our tent.

"Leo, can I steal you for a moment? I *need* to talk to you."

"I'm not finished packing yet, Dr. Reed. Can it wait?"

"Till when, Leo? We'll go our different ways in a matter of hours."

She was upset, and I couldn't blame her. I'd been avoiding just this conversation the whole trip. She had to know by now that this was not merely a pleasure cruise. She was too smart not to figure out something was off. I didn't know what she knew, but I didn't want to find out. Cornered as I was in my tent with my web of deceit, I stayed silent.

Thankfully, I was saved when Klevko trotted up to the tent.

"You look very beautiful this morning," he said to Dr. Reed, who had pulled her head out to face him. "Come with me. Crane waits for the lovely lady."

"For what?" she said.

"To talk to you. You must. It concerns your transportation to the Kayan village after we drop you at the fork. There is some problem."

Dr. Reed sighed loudly and stomped away, saying she'd be right back. Klevko popped his head inside the tent.

"We leave, five minutes," he said, and gave me a knowing nod. Klevko to the rescue!

I'd dodged that bullet, but I didn't know how much more of this I could take. I just wanted to get on the boat as fast as possible and get our mission done, without having to explain myself to anyone. So as soon as I had Hollis's bag packed, I left the tent and found a hidden spot on the riverbank to wait it out until we were ready to go. I watched as all the tents were taken down, the bags packed and loaded, and the campfire buried. I saw Dmitri stuff his duffel of stolen goods under another larger bag of supplies. I also watched Diana wander around the campsite without a course, as if she were lost. Maybe she was just looking for me. At least, that's what I hoped.

When the expedition was ready, I abandoned my hiding spot and crept through the dusky shadows to Hollis, Tamon Dong, and our waiting boat. As I approached the embankment, Diana and I made eye contact. She looked at me with a puzzled expression, almost identical to the face Hollis had made when I told him about my power. She opened her mouth to say something but then stopped and looked over my shoulder.

"Would you mind, Hollis, if I rode with your brother today?" I spun around to find Mr. Singh standing there, cane in hand. "Leo and I have important things to discuss."

Hollis was already in the back of the boat with his gedang between his knees. "Yeah, I do mind, Mr. Sting. I mind a lot."

"The name is *Singh*," he said. "There is no *t*."

"Actually, Hollis," I said. "Um . . . Mr. Singh and I have some plans to go over. Could you maybe ride with —"

"Are you kidding me, Leo?" he said much too loud. And at that, Dr. Reed headed over to check out the problem.

Quickly, I huddled with Hollis and whispered to him.

"Chief, it's about the . . . you know . . . thing we're going to find. It's really important. Can you just play along? Just for today. And not a word to anyone, right?"

He rolled his eyes, but I could trust him not to talk.

"What's going on, Leo?" Diana asked, and by the look in her eyes, I knew it was a question with about four different meanings. I chose to answer it as superficially as possible.

"We're just switching up boat assignments," I said. "Can Hollis ride with one of you today?"

"Of course," Dr. Reed said. "You want to come with me, sweetie?"

He nodded.

"Hurry up, you laggards," Crane screamed from his boat, which had just pushed out onto the river. He was riding with Klevko today. "Let's move at once!"

Dr. Reed took Hollis to her boat, and that left Diana alone.

"Hey, babe," Dmitri said, walking up to her and stretching his arms over his head, showing her a touch of his ever-present armpit. "I guess there's only my boat left. You're a lucky girl."

Diana stared right at me and snarled, so angry she couldn't even speak.

"I'll explain it all—" I began.

"You're a jerk, Leo," she snapped. She stomped her feet and turned away. "A real jerk."

"Come on, babe," Dmitri said, and tried to grab her arm.

"Get away from me, you creep."

"I'm just being friendly. I'm just like Leo, only more fun."

"If I catch you staring at me with those little beady eyes, I'll poke 'em out with my . . ." she said, her voice fading as they walked away.

I glanced over at Dr. Reed's boat and caught Hollis's eye for a moment. I put my finger up to my lips. He nodded. Turning to my own boat, I found Mr. Singh in the back, legs crossed, hand in his chin, his dark eyes studying me.

"Quite a bit of excitement," he said.

Except for the grinding motor and Hollis's thumping drum from far ahead of us, Mr. Singh and I rode in silence until long after the sun rose. I kept waiting for him to talk. I knew he would try to find out more about my power. When I couldn't wait any longer, I broke the silence.

"How come you wanted to ride with me, Mr. Singh, even though I refused to give you a demonstration last night?"

"That did not concern me, Leo. In fact I was impressed with your fortitude. Had you tried to touch the mask, I am certain nothing would have happened."

"Why?"

"Without training, psionic powers such as yours only operate when they are needed, when normal forms of communication are unavailable. For instance, those who are isolated, imprisoned, or nearing death—those in great pain—are often able to transmit a psychic message or gain psionic powers."

I kind of understood what he was talking about. Trevor and I had tried to really study how my power worked, but anytime we set up an experiment, it never activated.

"Let's say I had this so-called power," I asked him. "Why do you think that touching isn't necessary?"

"Leo," he said, and paused, letting river sounds into the conversation. "The hand grasps, but only the Mind touches."

"I don't get it. You mean I can touch things with my brain. I'm—"

"You are too eager for answers, Leo. Have patience. When I say *Mind*, I do not mean the miniscule chunk of brain inside your skull."

"Hey, my brain isn't *miniscule*."

"Compared to *Mind*, which is infinite, it is. Soon, you will understand that *there is only Mind*. Tell me, Leo, where do you suppose you are right now?"

"I'm in a boat with you. We're in Borneo."

Mr. Singh sighed loudly. "You are certain?"

"Sure."

"What makes you so certain?"

"Because I'm in a boat with you," I said, and knocked my knuckle against the side. "Is this a trick question?"

"Your senses tell you that you are here, yes? You can see the water, hear the motor and my voice, knock your knuckle against the hull, and so on. Now I want you to concentrate on what I have to tell you. Listen only to the sound of my voice. If you concentrate and relax, you will begin to understand."

Mr. Singh's voice seemed to get louder and closer, or were my ears playing tricks on me? But I wanted to hear what he had to say. I was positive he knew about many mysterious things and that he could help me with my own mystery.

"You have no doubt heard many frogs on this expedition," he continued, his voice drowning out the motor, filling my mind. "Now, consider the eye of the frog. A frog's eye is only sensitive to four attributes: to light and darkness, to sudden moving outlines, to sudden decreases in light, and finally, to small moving objects. A frog sees just enough so that it may sleep safely, avoid predators, and catch flies. So you see, a frog is quite blind. And we are not so different from frogs."

My mind flashed to that little frog that lived in the pitcher plant, and I tried to imagine what it saw. Things were getting a little woozy. The river and the jungle were blurry, without hard edges.

"Are you still certain you are in the boat?" Mr. Singh asked.

"No . . ."

"You are starting to understand the concepts, Leo. Our senses do not give us the whole picture. Your training will be entirely mental. We will begin by breaking down many of your old beliefs, about what is real and what is not. This will take years. When you truly believe that there is only Mind and that Mind is infinite, you will discover that your potential is also infinite. You will no longer need to touch."

"When do I begin my training?"

"You already have. Are you ready for your first lesson?"

I confess, I had little idea what he was talking about. But he seemed to know, so I decided to give it a shot. "I am."

"Very well. Now take a good look at your surroundings, Leo. Examine everything. And when you are done, place this blindfold over your eyes." Mr. Singh handed me one of the eye masks from the Sultan's plane.

I looked all around, then put on the blindfold and listened to the jungle soundscape. Back in New York, I'd often close my eyes and just listen. It was amazing to discover all the sounds you could hear when you weren't looking at things. This was no different. While previously I'd only heard Mr. Singh talking and the engine grinding, now I could hear my Windbreaker rustling, Tamon Dong sniffling, the high buzz of insects in the jungle, the leaves and branches rattling in the wind, and far upriver, Hollis's gedang drum.

"Now, Leo, try to recreate what you saw a moment ago. Create it all in your mind's eye."

Amazingly, I could. I could see everything in my imagination. It was easy, really easy. I could see my legs in front of me, even the folds in my cargo shorts. I saw my shoes—one of them was untied—and I made a mental note to tie it later. Then it dawned on me that I was looking at my shoe from only inches away. I had gotten smaller. "I" was no longer inside of my head—I had moved down near my feet. And with this thought, I realized that I could control where I moved in my imagination. I saw myself from the side, saw the blindfold and my body sitting still. Then I went behind me and looked at Mr. Singh, even honing into little details of his knotted old cane.

"It is quite easy, yes?" Mr. Singh said, and I could see his lips moving. "You can see my mouth moving now, yes? Do you believe this is real?"

I moved my hand in front of my blindfold . . . and saw it moving in front of my face from in back of my body! But all these visions were not like normal vision. The light was different. Everything seemed to glow with a soft yellowish light—a light from my mind. I recognized it as the light of the figure who visited me in my dreams. It was all imaginary, but it was also real at the same time.

"Very good," Mr. Singh said. "Now travel up the river, around the bend. Do not feel fear. It is perfectly safe. You will find it is quite easy."

And it was. I could do it. I really could. All I had to do was believe I could. I floated ahead past all the boats in front of us, then sped ahead of our procession, rounding the bend to a deserted stretch of river, traveling faster and faster, almost out of control, skimming along the brown murky water like a bird.

But something else was happening at the same time. With each bend, the light of my inner vision grew dimmer, darker, until it was almost pitch-black. Suddenly, the vision was windy and thundering, and I started to feel very afraid. Then I felt a heavy drop of rain on my arm.

I tore off the mask, panting. "Whoa."

"A very good first try, Leo. I have a feeling you've done this before. We will try again tomorrow."

The hot winds had picked up. Thunder rumbled in the distance, moving closer with each successive roll. We were in a narrow valley of the river with solid and steep rock walls on both sides of us. They soared almost a hundred feet above us.

"Rain comes now," Tamon Dong said from the back of the boat.

As we rounded the next bend, the sky got much darker, and the thunder closer still. A hard wind was blowing, and the green-brown water was swirling with white caps. Big heavy drops of rain began to fall in a steady rhythm. Tamon Dong gunned the motor to catch up with the rest of the party, pulling alongside three of the luggage boats and talking with the other porters. There was panic in their voices, and for good reason.

With one gigantic bolt of lightning, the sky opened up, and rain poured down on us in sheets. It was the hardest, heaviest rain I'd ever seen. Thunder roared right overhead, followed by another massive bolt of lightning that hit the water just ahead of us. Everyone screamed. The porters, shouting to one another, began making crazy maneuvers. I saw Dmitri scramble to secure his precious duffel while others tried to lash down the supplies that were rocking in the boats. Crane screamed, boats shook in the suddenly turbulent waters. The sound of the flooding upriver was deafening.

The rain only fell harder as lightning continued to criss-cross the sky. A few of the porters tried to paddle, but there was nowhere to land, no safe harbors, no sand banks — only the steep rock walls on either side. I looked up and saw torrents of brown foamy water pouring over the cliffs into the river. And the river was suddenly almost white, churning rapids filled with sticks and rocks. Visibility plummeted.

"Get us out of here!" Crane screamed. "It's flooding!"

"We've got to push on," Dr. Haga replied, his voice hoarse and shredded by the wind and rain. "We must get out of the valley."

"Do whatever it takes, Haga!"

"Everyone, full speed!" Haga cried against the storm.

All the porters stood up straight and gunned their motors, the tails of their boats sliding out diagonally. We were in heavy rapids. Waves of brown foamy water were pouring over the sides of our boat, and we bobbed up and down like toys in a bathtub, now catching air as we cata-pulted over a wave, now sinking down into the trough with water pouring over the bow. Two supply boats in front slammed into the rock wall and snagged, only to get freed in time to tumble straight into a swirling rapid. I heard heavy logs and rocks bouncing off our hull. Clutching the sides of the boat, I hid my head under the bow as water poured over me. I heard Diana screaming and glanced up to see her hanging halfway off her boat.

"Diana!" I started to scream, but a torrent of water filled my mouth, and when I came up for air, I saw that she had righted herself.

We battled through the heavy rapids in the rock valley for what felt like hours, though I think it was only a few minutes. Finally, our boat cleared the rock walls, but we were cast into a section of the river that seemed to split off in fifteen different directions. There was nowhere safe to land with the rapids still coursing, and the rain and thun-der still booming.

"That way!" I cried, and pointed left to an estuary that seemed the calmest.

Tamon Dong gunned the engine and went full speed in the direction I was pointing. Everyone followed. We plowed full through more dangerous rapids and more heavy rain, trying to find a safe spot to land, but finding none. I was soaked, head to toe.

As we catapulted down the estuary, Tamon Dong tried to steer but without much success. We were at the mercy of the storm. Gradually, the thunder died down, and in another few minutes, the rain began to abate until it became just another unthreatening drizzle. And then it stopped altogether.

Tamon Dong killed the engines, and we drifted, waiting for the other boats to arrive. I looked back at Mr. Singh. His eyes were closed and his lips were moving, and although he was speaking a different language, I could tell he was saying the same phrase over and over again. Beyond us, the river was still churning with the echoes of the storm. Mud and debris were strewn everywhere. The jungle was all around us. From a distance, I heard birds chirping from the interior and looked up to see the slightest sliver of blue sky. All of our party's boats gathered together in the center of the river. Everyone was safe, although we had lost most of the supplies in the river.

I searched for Hollis in Dr. Reed's boat. She looked a little green, but he was fine, actually smiling. He had always been a roller-coaster nut, sneaking on the big ones even before he reached the height limit. Diana seemed totally fine, too. She was busy fending off Dmitri, who was trying to put his arms around her for protection. I wanted to slug him. I couldn't see if his duffel had made it through the storm, but I hoped it hadn't.

It was Crane who was green with fright, hunching over and holding his guts, rocking back and forth.

"We have missed the turnoff," Dr. Haga said, pulling out a laminated map from his bag. "We passed the fork miles ago."

"Can we go back?" Dr. Reed asked.

"And battle these currents?" Haga answered. "It is not safe now. We must accept the fact that we are off course."

All of the porters were talking among themselves, their voices agitated and shrill.

"What are they saying, Haga?" Crane asked.

"They believe the evil *tohs* are following us and have thrown us off course. They are not familiar with the area."

"I thought your men knew this river like the back of their hands?" Crane said. Now that he was safe, he was returning to his usual obnoxious self.

"They are not my men, Mr. Rathbone, they are their own men. And no one could possibly know everything. They believe we are on a backwater estuary."

"That tells me nothing, Haga."

Dr. Haga huddled over his map.

"I cannot place us," he said. "I do not see this estuary on my map."

"Pathetic," Crane said. "You're all pathetic! I hate the water, and no one is getting paid today. Now let's concentrate, Dr. Haga, and find our place."

Crane was hiding most of his face in his parka, but I could see that it was all broken out in red splotches.

The boats remained in a tight circle in the middle of the river while Dr. Haga and Crane studied the map and tried to determine our location. Everyone seemed very tense.

"How about a little music, people?" Hollis said, pulling out his gedang and nose flute. "Lighten the mood."

Holding the drum between his knees, he played a steady beat with one hand and, with the other hand, brought one of his little nose flutes up to his face. Sticking it in his nostril, he played a sweet birdlike note over the plodding drum beat. And then another note, and another, until he was playing a simple melody, almost like a children's song, over the steady beat. I watched his face and noticed, as I often had, how much he looked like our mother when she played music. The way the corners of his mouth arched upward, his eyebrows raised. The way his eyes stayed open, but weren't really present. That simple melody grew more and more complex, until it transformed into the song he played on the sape in our tent, the one he'd thought he wrote. I saw his look of concentration grow as he played both instruments at once, realizing a goal that maybe he didn't even remember he'd set.

"Yeah, Hollis," I chanted. "Yeah!"

Even the porters smiled. But not Crane.

"What is that racket?!" he shrieked. "I hate that terrible music!"

He turned sharply toward Hollis, his splotchy red face clear for all to see, his shining white teeth bared.

"Let me see that," he croaked from the back of his throat, reaching out to Hollis's boat. He snatched the nose flute from his hand. The drumming stopped. Crane cracked the little bamboo flute in his hand and tossed the broken pieces into the river.

"Crane, how could you?" Dr. Reed gasped. "How could you?"

"Just shut up! Everyone just shut up. Give me silence.

I'm trying to get us to shore. So just shut up and let me think."

Dr. Reed was furious and told Crane so, but I wasn't watching her — I was looking at Hollis. He hadn't moved since Crane had snatched his flute, just stayed in exactly the same position, except for his face. I saw his expression change — saw his mouth grow into a thin line, his cheeks tighten, his brow lines thicken, his eyes squint. It was that face, the one he made when I lied about him being adopted, and when he learned about the plane crash. I couldn't even look at him; I didn't want to see the tears. All I could do was look past him to the dense trees and the jungle.

Suddenly, four of the boats, the ones with our gear, gunned their engines and made dramatic 180-degree turns. Their wakes splashed the rest of us, and they took off and sped back up the river from the way we'd just come.

"Come back, you fools," Crane called after them. "You can't leave us here."

Apparently, they couldn't take it anymore, and I didn't blame them. Crane had shown his true colors with Hollis, how cruel he could be. To them, no amount of money he could pay them was worth it.

"Go ahead and leave," he shouted at them. "You're all fired anyway. And, Haga, I'm holding you personally responsible for the belongings your men just stole."

Dr. Haga defended himself vigorously, but I tuned him out, just staring off into the trees and the dark jungle. And then I saw it, a tiny orange flag on top of a bamboo pole ten feet off the shore.

"Hey, Crane," I called. "Look. There's the sign. The orange flag. About two hundred feet up."

Crane's eyes grew wide, and he actually let out what sounded like a high-pitched giggle. "They found it," he said. "Kavi and Cyril, they did it." Then, looking at me with a smile on his face and dollar signs in his eyes, he held out his hand to shake mine.

"Leo, my boy," he whispered. "I can always count on you."

CHAPTER 21

We made it safely to land, carrying only our backpacks and the few supplies we were able to salvage, and found a clearing by the river to set up camp, bare bones as it was. Crane was the first to disembark, and I noticed he was clutching the metal suitcase with the mask against his chest. Of course he was.

We had no tents and only three bags of supplies had made it safely onshore. Four, if you count the duffel that I saw Dmitri sneak off the boat and stash behind a cluster of ferns. We opened up all the bags and spread the contents out on the still muddy ground. One contained mostly food provisions—dry packages of soup, nuts and raisins, protein bars—enough to sustain us until we reached our destination. The other two were stuffed with clothes, bedding, and assorted necessities for camp. Crane rummaged through and pulled out two tarps for himself, and a dry sleeping bag, moaning about the fact that two bottles of vintage champagne and his feather pillow had not survived the flood.

We all changed into dry clothes and hung our wet ones on tree branches and vines. Luckily, the weather was humid and warm. While Dr. Haga sat with Crane going over the map, Diana and her mother went behind a stand of trees to change. Hollis and I grabbed whatever had been left in the bottom of the bags. For me, it turned out to be white linen pants from Mr. Singh and a plaid safari shirt of Crane's. For Hollis, it was pink sweat pants from Diana and a tank top of Dmitri's that said I AM THE MAN on the back.

With only two hours of daylight left, Dr. Reed decided that she and Diana had no choice but to stay the night. In the morning, she and Diana would take two of the remaining porters and hike downstream along the river until they came to the fork, where we had originally planned to drop them off. By land, she figured it was no more than two miles. She hoped their guides would be waiting to take them to the village where they were staying, but even if they weren't there, she knew the way, having been there many times before.

We all helped gather wood for the fire, everyone but Crane, that is. He was hunched over the metal suitcase, his back to the rest of us, no doubt inspecting the mask to make sure it was undamaged. Dr. Reed took Hollis to pick some mangoes she had seen growing several hundred yards downriver, and I followed Diana into a grove of trees to gather fallen branches.

"That was pretty exciting," I said to her back. She didn't answer.

"Okay," I went on. "So you're mad at me for sticking you with Dmitri. I'm really sorry about that, but we can still hang out tonight."

She pushed past me and stooped to snap off some twigs from a larger branch.

"Those will be good for kindling," I tried again. "If you need help cutting anything, I've got a knife."

Still nothing.

"Listen, Diana, I'm really sorry. I . . . I'm just not good at that—"

Suddenly, she wheeled around and glared at me, her green eyes angry and hurt.

"Why didn't you tell me what you're really doing here?" she hissed. "You lied to me. I had to learn it from Dmitri."

"What did he tell you?"

"That you're on a secret mission for Crane. That you guys are going to steal something from a village that's not even on the map. I thought I knew you, Leo, but obviously I don't."

She turned back toward camp. I saw her mother and Hollis returning, Dr. Reed carrying dozens of mangoes in the fold of her shirt.

"Diana, wait," I said, chasing after her. "You know Dmitri, he just makes up stories to seem important. You don't actually believe him?"

She threw up her arms. "I don't know, Leo. I know that I don't believe you. So just stay away from me until tomorrow morning, and I won't have to see you again."

I trailed after her, saying, "Diana, please wait."

"Leave me alone, Leo," she said, breaking into a full run. I jogged after her for a few steps, then stopped and watched her go. By the time I got back to camp, she was with Hollis and Dr. Reed, and none of them wanted much to do with me. After the sun went down, she spread out her tarp next to her mom, rolled over on her stomach, and went to sleep.

There wouldn't have been time for a long heart-to-heart with Diana anyway, because I had my hands full with Hollis. As excited and happy as he was to run the rapids on the river, that's how scared he was when it was time to go to sleep. The kid was like an emotional Ping-Pong ball. I put his tarp down next to mine, gave him my backpack to use as a pillow, and tried to offer him soothing words. It didn't work.

"I wish I had a tent," he said. "I feel like snakes are crawling on me."

"There's nothing on you, bro. Look up at the stars and admire the sky."

"I don't want to. I want to go home. I think I'm getting malaria."

"I think you're fine. Look, there's my constellation. Leo the Lion."

"Your constellation sucks. So do you. I wish you had never brought me here. I'm not kidding, I feel a snake."

I checked his tarp for snakes, not once, but twenty times. Finally, he fell into a troubled sleep. Every now and then, he'd let out a little whimper. I stayed by his side for hours, looking up at the stars, remembering how great it was to watch the night sky with Diana. I craned my neck to see if she was up, but she was still lying there on her stomach, her face turned away from the beautiful sparkling sky.

The night was filled with sounds, not just the sounds of the frogs in the jungle but the sounds of our human animals, too. Klevko snored like a grizzly bear, and Dmitri like a baby grizzly. They both smacked their lips in between snores in perfect rhythm with each other. Mr. Singh made a kind of humming noise, like he was chanting a single sustained note. Crane clicked his teeth like he was chewing on walnut shells, and every now and then I'd hear him mutter something incoherent. I tried to get lost and travel in the pristine night sky, but the stars above felt so cold and distant.

It was clear I was never going to fall asleep. After hours of lying there, I couldn't stand it another minute. Very carefully, I rolled Hollis over and unzipped the pocket of my backpack, pulling out my headphones. And just like I had done on the plane, I slipped them on and listened to the Byong Ku death dance, and my dad narrating his travels in his reassuring steady voice. It seemed impossible to believe that within just a few hours, I would be there, tracing his footsteps, traveling his path.

There was no melody to follow and no singing, just drum sounds, metallic and echoing like the steel drums in the subway. And like the steel drums, there were several differently tuned drums. They played slowly, one after the other, as if communicating. It was accompanied by a chorus of gongs and bells and chimes. It reminded me of when I used to go to Chinatown for dumplings with my dad. He'd always stop and listen to the wind chimes they sold in all the street stands next to the paper lanterns and ceramic pagodas. Some were made of copper tubes, some bamboo, some glass, and when the breeze blew, their sound filled the air with a harsh persistent ringing in all different pitches and tones. That's what the Byong Ku death song sounded like, but the sound of shuffling feet in the background, and every now and then a mournful human wail.

There's only so long you can listen to chimes, and eventually, I fell asleep and dreamed I was in another world filled with jagged bolts of green lightning. A dark shadowy figure with a knobby cane was stooped over me, trying to get me to walk along the lightning bolts. In my dream, I felt someone coming for me from the waking world. And before I felt his hand touch my shoulder, I opened my eyes.

"No," I said.

"Yes," Dmitri whispered, his hand on my shoulder, kneeling on the jungle floor right next to me. "Time to wake up, Leo. You too, Hollis. The others are waiting."

It was still dark out and I was wet from the heavy mist in the air. The fire had gone out hours before. I rolled across the damp ground and touched Hollis's shoulder.

"You ready?" I whispered to him. His eyes were closed, but I knew he was awake.

"I'm not going, Leo. No way."

Quietly, I rose, brushed myself off, and scratched at about forty-three new mosquito bites. I looked across the campsite to Diana and Dr. Reed, still fast asleep.

"Leo, Hollis must get up," Dmitri said.

"I can hear you, Dmitri," he said. "And I'm not going. I just want to go home."

"Ojciec," Dmitri whispered sharply. "Come carry Hollis." Klevko came trotting over.

"Fine, I'll get up," Hollis snapped. "No one carries me."

"Keep it down, chief," I whispered.

"I'll talk as loud as I want."

"Come boys," Klevko said.

"I know, I know . . . the boss waits," I said.

"All of you guys have lost your minds," Hollis said. "Dmitri, you're not my friend anymore. And you, Leo, you're the biggest liar I know. You made it seem like we were going on a fun trip with yachts and stuff. Why'd you bring me all the way down here? I just want to go home."

"I know, Hollis. We'll be home in no time. I know you're pissed at me, but just trust me, everything I've done, I've done for you."

"No you didn't. You did this all for yourself. I'm just your kid brother you dragged along."

"You boys can argue on the way," Klevko said. "We have five-hour hike. Come, Crane waits."

"Five hours?" Hollis sighed.

"Come on, chief. This is what it's like in the field. Make the best of it."

We tiptoed across the campsite toward a clearing a few hundred yards inland where Crane and the rest of our shadowy crew would be waiting. We passed within a hundred feet of Diana and Dr. Reed. Their fire was still going.

"Wait," Hollis said. "I have to say good-bye to them."

"No time, buddy," I said, grabbing his arm, just as Klevko did the same. "I have their e-mails, and we can all meet up when they get back from Borneo."

"In six months?" Hollis said. "We're just going to sneak off like a bunch of creeps?"

"That's the plan," I said.

Klevko took a step in front of him, blocking the fire light with his massive body.

"Fine," Hollis said. "But I'm not talking to you, and don't try to talk to me, either."

In silence, we trekked to the clearing and out of the jungle canopy, where Crane, Mr. Singh, Dr. Haga, and two of the remaining porters were waiting in the starlight. Behind them were the charcoal outlines of a great mountain ridge, the same one my dad had mentioned in the journal. I knew that if Kavi and Cyril were correct, beyond it was the village of Byong Ku. I turned back toward our campsite, just to sneak one last peek at Diana, but I couldn't even see their fire through the trees.

"Morning, gents," Crane said. "I feel light as a feather now that we're free of the deadweight." He fished into one of the pockets of his khaki adventure suit and pulled out two candy bars, handing one to each of us. "Hollis, I'm sorry about my outburst yesterday. I shouldn't have destroyed your little instrument. That was uncalled for. When we get back, and if you play along, I plan to book some time for you in a professional recording studio, so you can nurture your considerable gifts."

Hollis took the candy bar and dug into it.

"Thanks, Crane," I said. "Hollis isn't talking, but I'm sure he—"

"I'm talking," he said. "Just not to you."

"Ah, the silent treatment," Crane said. "Just like Kirk and me. Now, silent or not, we must begin. Mr. Singh is not physically a hundred percent, so we must get under way if we hope to arrive in the village before it's too late."

"I apologize for my condition," Mr. Singh said. "I should stay behind."

"I'll hear no more of it, Mr. Singh. If need be, Klevko will be happy to carry you."

On cue, Klevko puffed out his chest and cracked his neck.

We set off for the dark mountain looming in the distance, bringing only what we'd need for a day and a night. The two porters sprinted out ahead of us. They were taking the lead, going up the path to find the next orange flag marker left by Kavi and Cyril. The land ahead of us was completely barren. My dad had described how he'd hiked over a steep mountain range with steam or smoke rising off it, and into a valley where the village was located.

We hiked single file at a very easy pace. Within twenty minutes, we started walking uphill, and that was when Crane sat down on a rock and began complaining that his new boots were defective.

"These worthless boots. Twenty minutes of hiking and I have a blister the size of a fist. It's eating my poor foot alive."

I paused and looked back. Mr. Singh was already trailing far behind, taking slow halting steps and laboring with his cane. From my vantage point, I could see the river and the immense walls of jungle surrounding it. I wondered how this mountain had become so desolate. By our old campsite, I could just make out a faint wisp of smoke rising through the jungle canopy. In front of us, steam was already rising from the brown rocks, obscuring the top of the mountain ridge.

We continued for over an hour, the porters sprinting ahead to the next flag and waiting impatiently while our party followed behind slowly. Crane was a very poor hiker and a pathetic outdoorsman. Hollis and I had no trouble keeping up.

The sun rose behind us as we marched single file up the hill toward the bleak mountain ridge in the clouds. We had spent days surrounded by nothing but green stuff, and I didn't like the look of the rocky mountain ahead. It seemed out of place, and maybe a little haunted.

Despite our ridiculously slow pace and frequent water stops, the trek gradually grew more taxing. The sun had burned away all the clouds in the sky, and without any trees, the heat was stifling. The trail grew much steeper, too. I was behind Dmitri, and with each step he took, he kicked up dozens of loose rocks and mud clods that tumbled downhill in thick yellow dust. As hot as it was, I had no choice but to cover my face with a bandana, which I sweated through in five minutes.

"Klevko," Crane said, sitting down on a rock and dabbing his face with his handkerchief. "Run downhill and fetch Mr. Singh. I don't want anyone following us."

"You got it, boss," Klevko said. He ripped off his elastic shirt, his hairy chest gleaming in the morning sun, and sprinted downhill in a cloud of dust. From our vantage point, Mr. Singh, with his cane and stooped posture, resembled some sort of ancient shepherd.

"Almost to the top, boys," Crane said to us. "After that, it's all downhill. You must be excited, Leo, to be so close to the mask that will enable your fact-finding mission to —"

"I'm really excited, Crane," I said, cutting him off. I put my finger to my mouth out of Hollis's line of sight. "I can't wait."

"Oh, I see, Leo," Crane said, picking up on my signal. "And you, Hollis, still silent as a stone?"

"To Leo, yeah."

"Mmm-hmm. Has Leo told you anything about the object we seek? Has he mentioned it might be worth millions?"

"Leo hasn't told me anything. Just that you want some mask. But I just want to go home."

"As do I, little Hollis. Here's a trick my mother taught me. When you find yourself in dreadful surroundings, such as this mountain — such as all of Borneo, for that matter — just disconnect your senses, and all will be well. It takes discipline and willpower, but anyone who can play two instruments at the same time surely has those qualities in spades."

Klevko came sprinting toward us, holding Mr. Singh in his arms like a puppy. It was quite a sight. Klevko, shirtless, hairy chest dripping sweat, huffing and puffing up the hill in a cloud of dust, carrying a tall, skinny man dressed in a fine white suit with Singh's legs and cane bouncing with each bumpy step.

It was a difficult climb. At times, we had to make our way up the loose brown rocks on all fours. And the rocks were scalding to the touch. But by high noon, we'd made it to the top and paused briefly to survey the terrain on the other side. It was a narrow valley, maybe five miles across to where more brown mountain ridges rose, barricading the far edge. The valley was barren and lifeless, colored mostly brown and yellow. Against such empty, colorless land, and from our vantage point, the next orange flag was easy to spot, as was the next one and the one after that. Our path ran downhill, swerving toward the right, eventually reaching a small pocket of green trees.

"And now, everyone, follow me down," Crane said, "as we go to seek our fortune."

With much fanfare, he lifted one foot regally, and with great aplomb, put it down on the brown sloping rocks. His boot sunk into the ground and slid a few inches before he caught himself. Hollis couldn't stop himself from chuckling.

Embarrassed, Crane tried again, taking an even more exaggerated step down the mountain. But this time his foot *completely* slid out from under him, and he skidded downhill, dust rising, doing a very painful-looking version of the splits. He flailed his arms wildly but that didn't help. In a flurry of desperate grunts, he fell flat on his stomach and slid down the hill feetfirst, his white hands in front of him trying to grasp on to anything solid.

Our whole party stared dumbly at him, too amused and stupefied to do anything.

"Help, you fools!" he croaked.

"I'm coming, boss," Klevko called, and ran downhill at full speed, until he also tumbled and followed Crane down in a cloud of dust, hollering, "Olga!" When the dust settled, Klevko was sitting almost directly on Crane's chest. The porters looked at each other and shrugged.

"And now, everyone, follow me," I said, imitating Crane's pompous first step down the ridge. Hollis cracked up. And at his laughter, I intentionally flailed my arms, did the splits, then threw myself down the hill, screaming, "Help me, Mama, help me, Mama."

"Wait up," I heard Hollis scream, as he flung himself down after me, followed shortly by Dmitri.

Hollis, Dmitri, and I made it down the mountain in no time. We mostly tumbled down, rolling in the loose rocks, or running and skidding, and sometimes tackling one another. When we reached level ground, we were covered in yellow dust, wheezing, and laughing.

"No girls is much better," Dmitri said. "You can play

much more fun games without them. When the girls are around, Leo just wants to make kissy faces."

"Knock it off, Dmitri," I said, and pushed him.

"Yeah, is Diana your new girlfriend, bro?" Hollis asked.

"No," I said, turning red. Not after what I did to her, I thought. I had been a real jerk. Oh well, I thought, keep your eyes on the prize, Leo.

But before we could start for the prize, we had to wait for the laggers, who barely seemed to be moving. Every few minutes, Crane would yell at someone, either to ask for help or to berate them, and his voice would echo down the mountain, hollow and disembodied. While Dmitri and Hollis played a rock-throwing game, I just watched them with my hands on my hips, tapping my foot.

I was getting nervous. I wanted to do what I needed to do, see my powers work when they were supposed to, and get the heck out of Borneo. I felt like I was waiting to take a final exam and I hadn't studied for the test.

When they finally made it downhill, Mr. Singh seemed to be in considerable pain. After a very quick standing lunch, we got back to hiking, single file and in silence. I glanced back at the mountain, covered in steam or possibly smoke. It towered over us and was so foreboding it almost seemed volcanic.

Within forty-five minutes, we spotted two small figures approaching us.

"Are those the villagers?" Hollis asked, looking back at Crane nervously.

"Ah, my scout team," Crane said. "Wonderful, wonderful. I see no reason to meet them halfway. Let's wait for them here. Klevko, my chair."

Klevko snapped his fingers at one of the porters, who produced a canvas bag from the load he carried on his back. Klevko unzipped it, pulled out a little collapsible stool, and set it out for Crane.

"Any more chairs in there?" Hollis asked.

"Just the one, Hollis," Crane said.

With a satisfied grin, he sat down, cracked open a fresh water bottle, and took a long sip. Beside him, Mr. Singh leaned heavily on his cane.

CHAPTER 22

Although Kavi and Cyril were out of breath as they scurried up the steep hill to meet us, Crane did allow them a few minutes to rest while they relayed the story of their contact with the villagers of Byong Ku. Dr. Haga translated.

In order to find the village, they had traveled to many of the surrounding villages, asking questions and doing detective work, which had also produced a good deal of folklore about the village. Dr. Haga explained that Byong Ku was spoken of only in whispers among the villages in the area. It was said to be cursed, filled with fierce warriors. Those who dared to enter their sacred valley were swiftly killed. It was thought that the villagers still practiced head-hunting.

After hearing these tales, Kavi and Cyril had approached Byong Ku quite gingerly, playing a daylong game of cat and mouse. First, they stood in a clearing in the valley, making themselves highly visible to the villagers, and then placed three metal pots and pans in the spot, before leaving and hiding out. When they returned to the clearing an hour later, the pots and pans had been taken, and in return, the villagers had left a parcel of dried rice and a spear tip. That was the go-ahead for the scouts to approach the village. They were brought to the chief, where they offered him more western goods: candy bars, jugs, and beef jerky. Kavi had grown up in the neighboring village of Tryong Loa, so he shared some words with the villagers and, using those words and many signs and gestures, he thought he had gotten permission for Crane and us to enter the village. Upon further questioning by Dr. Haga, it appeared that he wasn't entirely certain that he and the chief had actually come to that understanding at all.

"That's good enough for me," Crane said. "Let's get going. At the very least, we'll get out of this midday sun."

"Mr. Rathbone," Dr. Haga said meekly. "I hate to bring up such a delicate matter, but since Kavi and Cyril went beyond their call of duty and helped you to locate the village, they feel they deserve a bonus."

"Tell them they'll get a substantial bonus, Dr. Haga, once my stolen luggage is recovered," Crane said, putting on his sun hat and heading toward the village.

"Dr. Haga," Hollis said, "do you think the villagers are watching us, right now?"

"Of course," he said, glaring at Crane. I thought Dr. Haga deserved a substantial bonus as well.

"Oh," Hollis said, furrowing his brow. "I think I'm going to stay here, if that's okay."

"Nonsense, Hollis," Crane said. "I've been in this position countless times. There's nothing to fear from a bunch of tribal hocus-pocus, not after I show them real magic."

"I will also be staying here," Mr. Singh said, sitting down stiffly on a boulder and stretching out his gimpy leg. "I will watch the boy. Would you like to examine my cane, Hollis? It does many surprising things."

"You bet," Hollis said.

"Watch yourself, chief," I whispered to Hollis. "Mr. Singh is very crafty."

The rest of our party walked for another hour toward the patch of green in the distance. As we approached, the scouts had us walk in zigzags. This was a sign of peace to the villagers, to show them that we weren't trying to hide anyone or obscure our numbers, so they wouldn't mistake us for a war party. I couldn't escape the feeling that we were being watched.

Eventually, the barren brown earth gave way to grasslands, and in the distance I saw a small, stagnant-looking river. Across the river, there were more trees and a thicker jungle. That's when I saw the first signs of human construction. Spanning the narrow river was a thin suspension bridge, made entirely of bamboo. It was a complicated contraption, with hundreds of bamboo poles woven in an elaborate lattice. Even the walkway was bamboo, just two bamboo poles pressed together, its width no more than six inches.

The sight of it got my blood pumping. At the entrance to the bridge, there were two poles, and about twenty-five skulls were suspended across them, stitched with twine and yellowed palm leaves. I was glad Hollis hadn't come to see that. I jumped ahead of the rest of the group to cross the bridge first, but Dr. Haga stopped me.

"Let the porters go first, Leo," he said. "You are unfamiliar to the villagers."

"Okay, but do you think we should make some noise or rustle some branches, so we don't catch them off guard?"

"No need, Leo. They are well aware of us."

I didn't see or hear anyone. Kavi crossed the bridge first, and when he'd made it to the other side, Cyril started. Crane decided that Klevko and Dmitri would remain behind, so as not to overwhelm the villagers with too many people. Klevko shoved his backpack at me to carry. It was heavy and cumbersome and seemed to be filled almost entirely by small items with jagged edges.

After Cyril made it across, I started. The bridge was surprisingly steady, especially since I had two handrails to balance myself on either side. When Dr. Haga had made it across, we all turned to watch Crane.

"Turn around, people," he said. "I'm not a spectacle for your amusement."

Crane took almost five minutes to cross the tiny bridge. I closed my eyes and tried to use some of the visualization skills Mr. Singh had taught me, but all that came to mind was an image of Crane flat on his belly and clutching the bamboo walkway for dear life. When I opened my eyes, I was not far from wrong.

We continued along a wider walkway, suspended ten feet above the ground, which weaved through a thick canopy of trees until it reached a stairwell leading up to a dark wooden house. It was built on stilts and partially hidden in the trees. The house was spectacular, with a covered front porch that ran all the way up and down the longhouse, at least two hundred feet in length. Along the covered porch, there were dozens and dozens of poles, some supporting wooden figurines, others supporting skulls.

The front door to the house was open, but I saw no evidence of people. Kavi and Cyril made for the entrance.

"We just go in?" I asked Dr. Haga.

"Yes, but bearing gifts. I believe you have the gifts. Give some to the porters."

I opened the bag, and it was filled with candy bars and sweets and bags of jerky. I grabbed a few bags of jerky and handed them to the porters. They went in, and we quickly followed.

Inside, it was immaculate and bright. Dozens of windows let plenty of light in, which shined on the polished wood floors. The longhouse appeared empty. Two rows of beautifully carved support beams stretched down the middle with a long bamboo mat in between them almost resembling a red carpet. The ceilings were also expertly built with hand-painted wood planks. Leafy, colorful contraptions resembling cheerleaders' pom-poms hung from the ceiling at intervals, and lining the walls was an assortment of wicker baskets, bamboo mats, spears, jugs, and tools I couldn't place, all neatly arranged on shelves.

"Are all longhouses this well built, Dr. Haga?" I asked.

"Yes, of course, Leo."

"But, Haga," Crane whispered, "there's no one here. I sense a trap. This place is abandoned."

"Not entirely, Mr. Rathbone," he said, and with a sweep of the hand, he gestured far down the longhouse, all the way to the end of the bamboo mat, where there were some splashes of indistinct color. "This way," he said. "Follow the scouts."

We walked down the hallway on the bamboo mat toward the splashes of color, which I soon realized were people. There were about five of them, all sitting on the ground, relaxed and leaning back with their legs outstretched. Many ornate ceramic jars lined the walls. As we drew close, I saw that there were four men and one woman, all of them gathered around one man in a red hat with several giant feathers sticking out of it. He was skinny and nearly naked, his body covered in black ink tattoos. He was smiling at us — they all were, even though on the wall behind them, several skulls were placed atop their precious jars. He wore a necklace made of claws. That was the chief.

When we were within thirty feet of him, one of his men rose and struck an ancient-looking gong. Its vibrating metallic clang filled the longhouse. The chief raised his hands slightly, smiled, and said several words.

"This is a traditional greeting across many parts of Borneo," Dr. Haga said. "His words mean, 'flow, flow, the current flows.' It is polite to reply by saying, 'Harus,' three times."

We all replied with our Haruses, except for Crane. Our response pleased the chief, and he smiled warmly at me, almost as if he recognized me. He seemed friendly, not at all like the fierce warrior and headhunter.

Kavi approached the chief with a bag of jerky and, eating a piece on the way, presented it to the chief. He dipped his nose in, took a whiff, and then passed the pouch off to his entourage, each of them sniffing, taking a bite, and smiling. When the pouch got to the old woman, whose earlobes stretched to her shoulders and supported several heavy wooden earrings, she dumped the jerky into a wicker basket and examined the plastic bag, holding it up to the light and puzzling over it.

The chief smiled at us and then held up a palm-leaf platter. At once, several women materialized and placed other palm-leaf platters on the floor in front of us, motioning us to sit down. One carried a baby in a colorfully beaded sling on her back, a fat, happy baby who smiled at everyone. My platter was filled with rice and steaming chunks of brown meat. Before the chief motioned for us to eat, I grinned and rubbed my belly. The chief slapped his leg and laughed, then said a few words, pointing to himself.

We were going to have a hard time getting across our ideas, as Kavi understood only a little of their language, and Dr. Haga had to translate for him. So anytime we tried to talk, there was a long pause while the double translation was going on. While I was waiting, I played peek-a-boo with the baby, hiding my hands behind my face, then taking them down and making a funny face. The baby seemed to think I was a riot, and every time he laughed, his mother smiled at me.

"The chief of Byong Ku, Laki Jau, meaning Grandfather Jau, welcomes you to his house," Dr. Haga said after the first of these long waits.

I smiled and said, "Thank you," and the chief didn't need that translated. Crane was putting me front and center in this contact. He had positioned himself behind me and off to the side, and only reluctantly even sat down. The chief spoke again.

"Laki Jau is happy to have foreign friends in his house," Dr. Haga interpreted haltingly. "No one comes to visit them. Outsiders fear them, and they are lonely. The chief is happy the boy has come back and fulfilled his promise."

"Does he mean me, Dr. Haga?" I asked.

"He must, Leo."

The chief and I exchanged a smile, and he put his hands to his chest, laughing. I did the same, and then he did it again. He was trying to tell me something, but I wasn't getting it. He said something to one of his men, who got up and brought him one of the ceramic jars. It was very similar to the broken ones Hollis and I had seen in the cave. The chief reached in and pulled out a photograph and had his man bring it to me.

I couldn't believe my eyes. It was a Polaroid picture,

yellow and faded, but you could clearly see two men staring at the camera and smiling. One was the chief, Laki Jau. And the other was my father!

It was something I had seen my dad do the few times I was able to travel with him. He would take a Polaroid camera and snap some pictures of the people he visited, especially the children. They'd gather around him, laughing and pointing as the picture developed in front of their eyes, marveling at the magic box he had brought with him. And he always left the pictures behind as a souvenir of his visit.

Tears burned at the corners of my eyes as I held that picture and studied it — not sad tears but glad ones — just seeing my dad so happy doing the work that he loved. He looked much younger then, and I saw my face in his. When I looked up, Laki Jau was watching me carefully. Again, he put his hands on his chest and laughed, and I knew that he had recognized me as my father's son. My dad must have sat on this very same spot and had the same halting but friendly conversation with the chief.

"I am Leo," I said, patting my chest. "The son of Kirk."

I pointed to the baby and the mother. The chief seemed to understand and pointed quizzically at Crane.

"Tamon Dong," I said, remembering the name meant something like stepfather. "Stepuncle." I didn't expect him to understand my words, but he nodded as if he did.

"This is all very touching," Crane said, moving from the back row to face the chief. "But enough of the pleasantries. Let's get down to business."

At the sound of his voice, the baby started to cry. Quickly, the mother covered his eyes, put her arms around him, and left the room. Crane didn't seem to notice, or if he did, he didn't care. He grabbed the backpack from the floor and unzipped it.

"We are happy to visit your village," he said, his words being transformed twice before they would reach the chief's mind. "We have traveled from far away, and as a token of my friendship, I have brought precious goods from my village, as gifts to honor you, Chief Laki Jau."

He riffled through the bag and pulled out at least fifty candy bars. "Delicious sweets," he said, and mimed eating them, rubbing his belly. "Mmm," he said, laying them before the chief. "We have brought cooking utensils and drinking vessels," he said, taking out pots and thermoses, miming how to use each. "We have brought instruments for clothes making," he said, taking out twenty sewing kits, then threading one of the needles and making a few fake stitches in his khaki.

Three of the men gasped and clapped their hands.

"I bring magic boxes, which hold the spark of life," Crane said, pulling out five metal lighters and snapping one to make a flame. This was met with gasps not only from the men in front us, but also behind. I looked back and saw many shadowy heads and eyes staring through the windows — adults, grandparents, even a few kids. "And I bring the warrior's steel," he said, and pulled out eight machetes. He unsheathed one to gasps, held his spare sun hat in his hands, and sliced it clean in two. "I also bring a magic eye," he said, pulling out a telescope and holding it to his eye. He handed it to the man to the right of the chief, who examined it for a moment, put it up to his eye, and dropped it with a shriek. Then he smashed it against the ground.

"Can't please everyone," Crane said, and shrugged.

The pile of goods in front of the chief was heaping. The chief made a signal to one of his men in waiting, and he trotted away, quickly returning with two other men, both of their arms filled with tribal goodies. They placed them on the floor in front of Crane. They'd brought wicker baskets, bags of dried rice, spears, and hand axes, pumpkin storage jugs, wooden carving knives, fishing buckets, necklaces of beads, bamboo mats, earrings, wooden figurines, and an assortment of old artifacts, everything glowing and covered with a thick patina from years of use. One of the men even placed a hat similar to the chief's on my head.

Crane examined the pile deliberately, picking up certain things and showing modest approval.

"Yes, yes. Tell the chief these are all fine examples, and I am grateful for them. But I am a man of discerning taste."

"I cannot possibly translate 'discerning,'" Dr. Haga said.

"Do your best. Tell him I am looking for one specimen in particular, for which I will trade them many more magical secrets."

"Crane, I must protest," Dr. Haga said. "That is a completely unethical —"

"Quiet, Haga, now translate. In particular, I am looking for an object much like this one," Crane said. Then he reached into the backpack and pulled out half of the conjoined-twin mask that he had carefully wrapped in banana leaves.

The chief smiled and laughed.

"He recognizes it?" Crane asked Dr. Haga.

"He does."

The chief then spoke with animation, making happy and vibrant gestures.

"The chief would like to see the mask, Mr. Rathbone. May he?"

"Only for a minute," Crane said, handing the mask to Dr. Haga, but holding on to it for too long.

Dr. Haga gave the mask to the chief, who turned it around in his hands and smiled, then handed it to one of his men who took off with it and disappeared into the longhouse.

"What the devil just happened?" Crane exclaimed. "Haga, tell him to give it back."

An animated exchange followed between the chief and Dr. Haga, after which he turned to Crane and said, "The chief thanks you for returning the mask, and he has something for you." The chief's right-hand man returned with a square black object. "The chief says when this object is returned to the boy, the circle is complete."

The chief looked at me and held out his hand, offering me the object. I stepped toward him and took it. On contact, I immediately heard my dad's voice in my mind, speaking in halting sentences, just like Dr. Haga.

"In return . . . for the mask . . ." I heard him say, "I give you this object . . . that will let you hear your music. I will hold on to your mask and guard it, and let it serve as a symbol of our friendship. And let our trade serve as a promise . . . that one day . . . I will return and feast with you in your home."

It was the clearest sound-bending experience I'd had in a long time. My dad's voice was unmistakable, each word crisp and clean. I snapped back and in my hand I saw a mini-cassette recorder, one of those old tape recorders they used to make in the '90s. I always loved those things. I even bought one once from Stinky Steve. The cassettes they used were so little!

I looked at the cassette recorder and understood why the chief thought I had returned to fulfill a promise. My dad and the chief made a trade, with the promise that one day my dad would return to claim his mini-tape recorder and return their mask.

The chief was talking again, looking specifically at me.

"The chief says," Dr. Haga was saying, "that your father claimed this object had amazing properties. But they did not understand its use, so they sealed it within a sacred jar to await his return."

"No, no, no!" Crane snapped. "This is all wrong. Just tell him I want my mask back. He can have the worthless tape recorder. That's the deal. I want my mask back or else."

"Or else what?" Dr. Haga asked.

"Tell him that I possess strong magic powers, and I will be quite angry if my mask is not returned."

While Dr. Haga did his best to translate for the fuming Crane and the oblivious chief, the row house was becoming louder. Many of the tribal people had gathered outside, and the chief's men were picking up the machetes and examining them in the light. Suddenly, the old woman with the long earlobes shrieked bloody murder, terrible fear in her eyes. She jumped to her feet and came rushing for me, grasping my wrist hard. She pulled one of the men's machetes near, gazed at it, gazed at me, then back to the machete, shaking her head and speaking a mile a minute at me.

"What's she saying?" I croaked.

"I don't know," Dr. Haga said, asking Kavi to tell her to slow down. Kavi listened to her and translated as best he could while Dr. Haga nodded.

"Kavi says she is the dayak of the tribe, the medicine woman and soul catcher. She says she saw your shade in the metal. She says . . . you are missing your soul, it is adrift in the . . . netherworld. . . . I am unsure of the translation. She insists on performing a 'soul-catching' ritual, as soon as possible, to restore your soul to your body."

"What?" I gasped as she let go of my wrist and ran off to get her soul-catching instruments.

Could that have been the old woman from my father's tape? The one who tended to the dying man? As amazing as that might have been, I didn't want to wait around to find out. I wanted to keep my soul just where it was. All the villagers stared at me blankly as if they didn't seem to recognize me anymore.

"No, no, no," Crane cried. "Tell them it is just a reflection. There will be no soul-catching rituals. Repeat to the chief that I demand my mask back immediately. Or else."

But the chief had risen to his feet and was looking out the window. All the villagers outside were stirring and whispering. One of them put his hands to his mouth and made a piercing whistle that sounded like a siren. The chief gave a signal and all his men rose to their feet, grabbed their long axes and spears from the wall, and ran out of the house, whooping and making what sounded like war cries. Two of the men stayed behind, pointing their weapons at us.

"What's going on?" I shouted at Dr. Haga.

"Where is my mask?" Crane shouted in an even louder voice.

"They believe the village is under attack," Dr. Haga said. "There are invaders approaching."

"No! Stop! It's all a misunderstanding," I yelled, but no one understood me.

I hoped it was a simple mix-up. I hoped that the invaders they saw were just Klevko and Dmitri, wandering in over the bridge. But most of all, I hoped with every breath I had, every cell and molecule in my body, that Hollis hadn't left the clearing with Mr. Singh.

CHAPTER 23

We were held for what felt like hours at ax-point, our guards never taking their eyes off us. Crane tried to protest, but shut up quickly when one of the men waved his new machete in his face. From outside, we heard people approaching, men whooping and laughing. They were the sounds of a successful battle, I thought morosely. I craned my neck to catch a glimpse outside, to see if Hollis was there, but one of my guards stepped in front of me to obscure my view. But then I heard children's voices in the mix, laughing and shouting joyously. And in the background was a booming operatic laugh I thought I'd never hear again.

"No!" Crane growled, and ground his teeth. *"No."*

Our captors lowered their weapons. Dr. Reed strode into the longhouse. She was jubilant, surrounded by almost all sixty villagers. I almost dropped to the ground when I saw who was with her.

"Hollis!" I shrieked, and sprinted for him, making it across the longhouse in half a second. I gave him a huge bear hug, crushing his arms against his chest. "You're alive, chief!"

"Of course I am," he shrugged. "Why wouldn't I be?"

Then I saw Diana following after Dr. Reed, surrounded by all the young girls in the village, who were fawning over her hair and her earrings and her green eyes, which didn't even glance at me.

"You were supposed to have gone in another direction, Margaret," Crane seethed. "What are you doing here? Dr. Haga, Margaret's porters will receive absolutely no pay, got it? Your men have disobeyed my orders for the last time."

The man who was guarding Crane waved his machete again, but Dr. Reed smiled warmly at him and indicated that there was no need.

"A little birdie told me that you were heading to an uncharted village," Dr. Reed said to Crane. "And I see from this horrific pile of gifts that you are completely out of your depth. In one move, Crane, you have irrevocably altered this village's natural development."

"What happened, Hollis?" I whispered to him as Dr. Reed made for the pile of bribes.

"Pretty much what you'd think. Diana told her mom about you, she got furious, and they followed your trail. When they came across me and Singh, Dr. Reed asked if I wanted to go with them to the village. And since it turns out Old Man Singh isn't such great company, and all his cane does is just help him limp around, I said, 'Sure.'"

"What about the guys with the weapons?"

"I'm getting to that. After we crossed the bridge, we were swarmed by guys with axes and spears, but Dr. Reed played it so cool. I think she even speaks some of their language!"

"Where are Klevko and Dmitri?"

"Didn't see them — I thought they were with you."

"What is this, Crane?" Dr. Reed was saying to him, practically screaming, as she picked through the pile. "You gave them processed sugar?! Are you out of your mind? Some trinkets as gifts are one thing, but this pile of bribery is grotesque, Crane. Processed sugar? Really? Get out of here at once. I'm taking over this expedition."

"No, Margaret, this is *my* expedition. You miserable woman, you're nothing but a moocher. If it wasn't for men like me, you'd be a bum. A bum! I generate the wealth in this world, and that gives pointy-headed snobs like you the luxury to spend their lives studying worthless nonsense. This is *my* mission."

"Crane, really," Dr. Reed said, her face turning almost purple and veins popping out in her forehead. "Just like your mother, you know nothing about the field of anthropology. You're an amateur." She looked like she was about to erupt, but suddenly she became aware that the villagers were watching her. She checked herself and smiled at them, giving an elegant curtsy to the chief, who had resumed his place at the head of the longhouse.

"How'd Diana do with all this?" I asked Hollis. "Was she scared?"

"She's totally fine, except she hates your guts, bro."

"Oh well, can't win 'em all," I said, and gave Diana a wave. She acknowledged me by raising her eyebrows, but didn't wave back.

"Looks like it's Diana's turn to give you the silent treatment," Hollis said. "You're on a roll today, Leo."

I sauntered over to Diana, approaching her and her group of admirers sideways, until I had managed to become part of the group. Diana gave me another one of those eyebrow-raising non-smiles and turned away.

"Diana, listen . . ." I started, and tugged at my hair. "Everything . . . it all just spiraled out of control, and —"

"Stop, Leo," she interrupted, finally turning to me. I saw there was something gone from her eyes. She wasn't the same person I'd gotten to know over the past few days, and I knew she wasn't going to show me that person anymore.

"Can I just talk to you, Diana?"

"*No*, you can't. I thought it was such an amazing stroke of luck that we wound up here together," she said. "Almost written in the stars. I'd get to see this kid from my childhood who had grown up into an awesome person, someone I wanted to get to know. Someone who broke into warehouses, stole military experiments, and traveled around the world rescuing dolphins."

"But I am that guy."

"Oh really? Then why are you working for a bald creep who bribes these innocent people with candy bars and knives? *Who are you, Leo?* Wait — I don't want to know, so just leave me alone, okay? Will you do me that one favor?"

"Okay," I said, and walked back toward Hollis, my head hanging down on my chest.

"Didn't look like it went well," he said.

"Not at all, chief," I said, feeling my chest start to really hurt.

"Probably went better than them," he said, pointing to Dr. Reed and Crane, who were arguing nose to nose in hushed tones.

"So we're at a stalemate, Margaret," he said. "You're not leaving, and I'm not leaving."

"Fine," she answered. "I've already accepted an invitation from the chief to stay for dinner and spend the night, so you won't be getting rid of me any time soon."

"Nor you I," Crane said.

Suddenly, I felt someone grab my wrist, fingernails digging into my skin. The old medicine woman was back, but this time she held a long tube of bamboo to her lips and pointed it right at my head. She chanted a few words, made a spitting sound, and blew a huge puff of smoke right into my mouth.

"Hey! Stop it."

But she was in another world. Her eyes were rolled almost all the way back in her head, and she was chanting, trembling, and rubbing her other hand vigorously against my scalp, all the while covering my chest with spit. It felt like there was a little pebble or hard piece of rock in her hand, because it hurt.

I tore myself free. By then, the longhouse had grown completely chaotic. Crane and Dr. Reed were arguing; Diana was surrounded by her gang of little kids; adults were eating all the candy bars and freaking out on sugar; Dr. Haga was standing there stunned and cleaning his glasses. Squawking chickens had even barged in and were being chased by gangs of kids.

The chief was sitting at the head of the longhouse, as relaxed as ever. Just when I felt like my head was about to explode, he made several *tst, tst, tst* whispering noises, and everyone froze. One of his men hit the gong, and when it faded out, there was silence.

The chief motioned with his arms for everyone to calm down, then spoke in his steady voice. Dr. Reed started to translate for Diana.

"You speak their language?" Crane said, suddenly Dr. Reed's new best friend.

"I speak a similar dialect. They've transposed many of the vowel sounds and have a peculiar accent."

"I don't care about your linguistic gibberish," he said. "I just want to know what he's saying."

"Shut up and let me listen, Crane."

Hollis and I sidled up to Dr. Reed as well.

"The chief says he apologizes for the commotion," she translated. "His village is not used to guests, and his people are very excitable."

Then Dr. Reed began speaking directly to the chief in his language. Crane called over Dr. Haga and Kavi to translate her.

"She says she is happy to be here in Byong Ku," Dr. Haga told us. "She says she is a wise woman from far away, and she traveled here because she loves to meet and learn from other people. She does not bring gifts or other such items to disrupt the harmony, but brings friendship and smooth water. She says the hairless man has brought poisonous food. She asks permission to take the poisonous food and destroy it."

"That two-faced pig . . ." Crane muttered.

The chief paused and thought for a long time, tapping his lip and watching Dr. Reed's face. She didn't look him directly in the eye, just stood quietly and waited for him to speak. When he answered her in his steady voice, I asked Dr. Reed to translate — she was better than the two-man team of Kavi and Haga.

"The chief knows that the hairless man has brought rotten foodstuffs," she said. "He sees how his people tremble and act crazy after they have eaten it."

She paused and waited for the chief to go on. He was looking at Crane now and seemed to be addressing him.

"The chief thanks the hairless man for bringing the son of an old friend," she said, "and for returning a special . . . some kind of item . . . I'm not familiar with the word. For this, he is grateful. But the hairless man has also brought many gifts with black magic." At this point, she turned to Crane. "He is considering whether or not he will allow you to stay here until the river waters are less turbulent."

"Well, tell him this from me," Crane said. "I'm staying whether he invites me or not. I'm staying until he gives me what he owes me."

"I'll tell him no such thing."

The chief sat silently for several minutes, deep in thought. At last, he spoke again.

"The chief says it is getting dark and is almost time to eat the evening meal," she translated. "He has decided that we will have no more fighting but will all eat together, drink rice wine, tell stories, and enjoy our new friends. Tomorrow, our new friends will go back to their lands. The foreign woman will take the rotten food with her. To destroy."

He stopped talking, got up, and left. Just like that, he was done.

After that, the villagers went back to their normal routines — the women prepared rice and sweet potatoes and other food over open fires in the longhouse. The men went to the river to bathe and catch a few fish. The kids just chased the chickens around. Crane sat down with Dr. Haga by his pile of bribes and showed some of the villagers how to work the tools. Diana and Dr. Reed went on a tour of the longhouse and the surrounding area with one of the women. And Hollis and I threw on our backpacks and went out to explore on our own.

"So what happened to Mr. Singh?" I asked Hollis as we balanced on the amazing bamboo bridge over the stagnant river. Twilight was approaching, and the bugs were coming out.

"I left him back there with the stool," he said, slapping at a mosquito on his forearm.

"Think he's still there?"

"He said he'd be fine," Hollis shrugged. "He said he was going to meditate and then boom, he just started chanting. He's an odd dude." Hollis shrugged and slapped another bug. "We should go back now, bro. Too many mosquitoes out here . . ."

"You go," I said to Hollis. "I'll meet you back there in five."

"Make it three, Leo."

After Hollis left, I pulled out the mini-cassette recorder from my pocket. It was an odd thing for my dad to leave behind. I tried to play it, but the batteries had been dead for years. Luckily, I had a few spare ones in my backpack. I was really excited when I put them in, hoping to hear something, some sort of special message from my dad, but the tape was completely blank—it had never even moved one rotation on its reel. Not to waste two perfectly good batteries, I made a quick recording of the frogs as they started to croak out their twilight songs, then hightailed back to the longhouse.

The whole house smelled of fresh chicken and pork, and rich aromatic spices. Along the central bamboo mat, the women had laid out dozens and dozens of bowls in a line on the ground, along with cloth napkins and jugs of juice. The villagers streamed in, sitting down in rows, as if the bamboo mat were a long dining-room table. They dug in as soon as bowls of food were brought to the table.

I found Hollis quickly.

"Better find a seat before there's none left," I said.

But the chief had other plans for us. He'd already reserved a bunch of seats surrounding him for all the foreigners. There was no arguing. Hollis, Crane, Dr. Haga, and I sat on one side of him. Dr. Reed, Diana, Kavi, and Cyril sat on the other.

"Allow me, Dr. Reed," Crane said, taking her cup and pouring some rice wine into it. "No reason why we can't be civil for one night, eh? If two enemies can't enjoy a good meal and a strong drink after a hard-fought battle, who can?"

"I don't like military metaphors, Crane," she said. "But I'll toast to a night of peace."

They clinked glasses and each took a sip.

"Blech," Crane grunted, and spit it out. "I could brew better rotgut in a toilet."

Dr. Reed drained her glass in one swig, and Crane quickly refilled it. Hollis reached for the rice wine and started to pour some in his glass.

"I like your nerve, Hollis," Crane said. "But this juice is for grown-ups. Can I top you off, Margaret?"

"Oh no, two's my limit," she said.

While the villagers chattered and had a great time, we ate in silence. The food was tasty, but my stomach was killing me. Diana was polite, ate with good manners, smiled at everyone, but didn't even look at me.

After the meal, the women cleared the plates, set up their beds on the far side of the longhouse, and put their children to sleep. The chief invited us to gather in a circle around him, and one of his men brought him a huge ceramic jug. He took a big swig, poured a little out into a crevice in the floor, and then handed the jug around the circle, asking each of us to taste it. Crane made an exception for Hollis and me this time, as Dr. Reed did for Diana. The jug then circled back to the chief who took many more drinks and rose to his feet to speak, very talkative. Dr. Reed translated.

"It gives me great pleasure to have you in my house. I am a wise and just chief. I am a father to four, a grandfather to nine, and a great-grandfather to three. I am an expert hunter, and have killed many bears and wild cats. I am the fiercest warrior in my village; grown men tremble before me. I am Laki Jau. I have been chief for thirty-four years."

The chief walked to the skulls on top of the ceremonial jars, rubbing the scalp of one, then after another sip of the rice wine, continued talking.

"Before me, my father was the chief, Urip Lao. Before him, Urip Liko. Before him, Urip Kila. Before him . . ."

The chief listed off about forty chiefs who had come before him, touching all the skulls atop the jars.

". . . and before him, was the beginning of time. So you see, I am a proud chief."

Dr. Reed spoke to him in his tongue, then reported to us what she'd said.

"I told the chief that where we come from, we have forgotten our story of how the world was made. I've asked him to share his, and he agrees."

"Tell him to make it short," Crane yawned. "I've had a long day."

The chief took another tremendous swig from the jug, then Dr. Reed translated more.

"Before he begins the story, the chief apologizes for its telling. In long ago times, he says, the story used to be told in a more . . . pleasing voice . . . like birds. I think he means they used to sing the story. But many years ago, they forgot the melody to their story."

"What a loss," Crane snickered, but Dr. Reed ignored him.

"In the beginning of the world," she translated from the chief, "when there was only water, there were two gods, Laki Tenangan and Doh Tenangan. They were twins, twins of one flesh. Conjoined. The twins created all the lands, the trees, the winds, the animals. They also created humans."

At the mention of the conjoined-twin gods, I saw Crane's eyes light up. He shot me a knowing glance, raising his eyebrow as if to say, *See, what'd I tell you, that mask is worth a fortune.* Dr. Reed didn't notice. She was too busy concentrating on telling the chief's story.

"The twins saw that the world was good, but that it was also filled with monsters, evil beings and subhumans who spread chaos and violence and destruction. So they roamed the lands, taming the chaos and destroying every subhuman their four eyes beheld. They brought order and harmony to the world, and the men and women lived in peace and knew immortality.

"Over time, the twins grew restless and longed for blood. They were too powerful and warlike for the peaceful world, so using a blade of gold, they split themselves in two. Laki Tenangan rose above the clouds, to dwell on the highest mountaintops, and Doh Tenangan went below the Earth, to rule the netherworld. They left the middle Earth for humans to rule, and soon the humans no longer knew immortality, and death came to our land.

"And so it was that after their vital spark went out, all humans of middle Earth had to travel to Doh Tenangan's underworld, to the Land of the Dead. But they were unruly and would escape to disturb middle Earth's peace. To punish them, Doh Tenangan forced them to dig tunnels underground. My great-grandfather told me that in his day, if a man stayed out too late hunting, he might chance to hear the dead in their underworld, hear the rumbling from beneath the ground, as the dead built their tunnels and toiled away for all of eternity."

The chief paused and took another sip from the cup. From the other side of the longhouse, I heard the kids crying and settling into bed, and from outside, the croaking frogs and the shriek of insects.

"Will you ask him, Dr. Reed, where the Land of the Dead is?" I said. It had occurred to me that the other half of the mask just might reside there, if there was such a place.

Dr. Reed gave me a puzzled look.

"Excellent question, Leo," Crane said. "I like a boy with curiosity."

Dr. Reed put my question to the chief and translated his answer.

"Byong Ku is near the center of the world, so it is near the Land of the Dead. After they split, each of the twins felt that he should be the one to rule middle Earth, and they have been fighting, like two brothers, for ten thousand years. The dead want to rule. The warriors of Byong Ku have sworn to keep the dead underground, and for that we are cursed."

"And will you ask him, Dr. Reed," Crane said, "if he would lead us to the Land of the Dead?"

"I most certainly will not."

"Dr. Haga and Kavi, please step in."

Kavi put the question to the chief, and immediately the chief's face turned stern, and he waved his arms, saying no with all the force of his body.

"It is absolutely taboo," Dr. Reed interpreted. "Under no circumstances is any foreigner allowed to visit the Land of the Dead. I won't let you break their taboos, Crane, absolutely not. You cannot come here and simply —"

Suddenly, Dr. Reed stopped speaking and grabbed her throat. The color drained from her face, but she tried to go on.

"That's not for me to decide. They have their rules . . . and . . . oh . . ."

She rubbed her forearm across her brow. Beads of sweat

had suddenly broken out on her forehead. She put her head down and seemed to be struggling for breath.

"Mom, are you okay?" Diana said, taking her hand.

"I'm all right, sweetie . . . just a little . . ."

"Margaret, you're pale as a ghost," Crane observed, his voice detached and calm.

"I'm okay. . . ." She swallowed hard. "Must have been that river fish . . . I think I'm gonna be sick."

She bolted to her feet and clutching her stomach, dashed for the window, throwing up everything she'd eaten and then some.

"Charming," Crane said. "That's always a lovely way to impress your hosts."

CHAPTER 24

know where the Land of the Dead is," I whispered to Crane as we all waited in the longhouse for Dr. Reed's attack of nausea to subside. Diana was at her mother's side, trying to help by putting a cold cloth on her forehead.

"Do you think the mask is hidden there?" he whispered back.

I nodded. "You heard the chief. That was Doh Tenangan's realm."

"And he was the other half of the conjoined twin." He grinned. Crane's eyes glowed with excitement. "It stands to reason they would hide his mask in his realm where it could safeguard his kingdom."

"I'll bet you something else, too, Crane. I bet when we find the Land of the Dead, we'll find underground tunnels there."

"I agree, Leo. Myth and truth have a way of intersecting. I can't wait to see those tunnels. Some of the more *open-minded* scientists believe that underground tunnels lead to the hollow center of the Earth."

"Oh yeah, where those alien guys lived, the ones your mom wrote about."

I didn't mean to make him angry, but apparently I did. His lips got really tight and his left eye twitched.

"For your information, nephew, my beloved mother, Marie, did not write about 'guys,' as you so clumsily call them," he snapped. "She was a scientist conducting advanced research."

Dr. Reed groaned as another intense wave of nausea attacked her. Diana helped her crawl to her feet and get to the window. Crane didn't flinch.

"Poor, poor Margaret," he said. "However, her unexpected illness does give us a rare opportunity to leave here and take a midnight stroll. Do you think you can lead us there, Leo?"

I nodded again. "We cross over another mountain ridge and then cross a small river."

Of course, I didn't mention to him that I had read the directions to the Land of the Dead in my father's journal.

"The mountain ridge you refer to —" Crane was musing. "That has to be the one that towers above the village. I have formed an alliance with several of the villagers who can escort us."

Wow, Crane was good. I hadn't even noticed him talking

to anyone. He certainly was a person who knew how to get what he wanted.

"Now I just have to get us out of here," he whispered. "At my sign, Leo, you must play along and convince Hollis to come without incident."

"But what about Dr. Reed? We can't leave her. She seems really sick."

"Don't worry about her," Crane said much too quickly. "I have a feeling these stomach events have a way of passing quickly."

Dr. Reed was still hunched over the window, retching and barfing, with Diana at her side trying to comfort her. The whole longhouse was deadly silent except for her groans. Many of the children had awakened and were peering at the commotion. When Dr. Reed finally picked her head up, her face was ashen and sweaty and covered with red splotches. Two of the villagers gasped.

"Why isn't anyone helping?" Diana cried. "Why are they all just staring?"

"Kavi says they believe she is cursed," Dr. Haga explained. "The chief believes that the foreigners have attracted the attention of an evil *toh* who is inhabiting Dr. Reed and causing her illness. He has asked the medicine woman to cleanse her demons, but wishes the other foreigners to leave at once."

"No way. I'm not leaving her," Diana said.

Kavi conferred with the chief then whispered in Dr. Haga's ear.

"The chief says the daughter may stay," he translated. "The others must leave immediately."

The medicine woman entered carrying a basket filled with small eggs and gray stones. She wore her bamboo tube on a cord around her neck, and when she caught sight of me, she pointed it at me and screeched. The chief shooed her away, guiding her over to Dr. Reed. Then on his signal, five of his men raised their weapons and took a step toward us.

"Tell the chief we're leaving at once," Crane said to Dr. Haga. "Diana, we'll send one of our party back with proper medicine."

"Can you hurry?" she asked.

"Margaret," Crane said, bending down so Dr. Reed could hear him. "Klevko has my ditty case. Fortunately, I always carry something for nausea and vomiting, plus nutrient pouches. I'll fetch it now and send someone back with it right away."

Dr. Reed nodded weakly. "Thank you," she mouthed, holding the medicine woman's hand as she laid her down on a mat on the floor.

"She doesn't have malaria, does she?" Hollis asked as our group was hurriedly shown out of the longhouse.

"No doubt it was something she ate," Crane said.

"But none of us got sick," I said.

"That's enough, Leo," he snapped. "You're not helping."

We left the village and walked down to the bamboo bridge, all six of us — Dr. Haga, Cyril, Kavi, Crane, Hollis, and me. It was hot and sticky out. The frogs were croaking and the mosquitoes biting.

"Klevko," Crane muttered into the night.

"I'm here, boss," Klevko echoed, and at once, he and Dmitri seemed to emerge from the vines.

"And Mr. Singh?"

Klevko pointed to a large dark tree. It took a second for my eyes to adjust, but when they did, I saw a tall charcoal figure standing perfectly still and silent by the trunk.

"And the villagers?" Crane asked.

"This way, boss. There are five waiting."

"Excellent, Klevko. I hope we brought enough knives."

We followed Klevko, who led us into a thicket where five male villagers from Byong Ku were waiting. All of them were teenagers — one even appeared no older than me.

"Ask them if they were able to recover it," Crane snapped at Dr. Haga. One of the boys nodded and produced a wicker basket. He reached in and pulled out Crane's mask.

"There you are, my sweet," he murmured, taking the mask in his hands. "I think it's time to go find your other half." He carefully wrapped the mask in a banana leaf before putting it into his backpack. Klevko was smiling.

"What are grinning at, you donkey?" Crane barked at him. "Give them their pay."

I was expecting Klevko to reach into his pocket and pull out a roll of rupiahs, but instead, he unzipped a pouch in his backpack and took out five small blades. He gave each of the villagers one, and they received them with great joy. The boy my age seemed especially delighted and waved his new prized possession in the air with glee. Dr. Reed's far-away wails echoed through the night as another wave of nausea started.

Crane hurried about, rearranging his pack and making the final preparations for our expedition. I looked up at the cloudless sky. The stars were out and glimmering. Just over the mountain ridge, I could see a sliver of a crescent moon. I thought about Diana. I'd been so awful to her. And now I was leaving her again, with no good-bye, no explanation. I wondered if I'd ever be able to look at the moon again without feeling terrible.

"Be right back, Hollis," I said. "Tell Crane I had to take a pee."

I dashed off and found a sheltered spot a hundred yards away from the group. I reached into my pocket and took out my dad's mini-cassette player and pushed record.

"Diana. It's Leo," I whispered into the little speaker. "I know you won't forgive me, but I have to at least try to explain myself. Please listen. I came here with Crane to help him find something, a mask that he said was worth a fortune. But I didn't come for the money. I came here because . . . because . . . Crane promised to fund a mission to investigate my parents' deaths. I think it's possible that my parents might still be alive. Crane was my only hope to help me find them."

I paused. I hadn't expected to tell her all that, but now that the truth was out, it felt right.

"I made a deal with him because he's all I have, except for Hollis," I went on. "But then I met you, and I know this sounds corny . . . but I didn't feel quite so alone. Now all I can think about is how I treated you and how I'd give anything to take it all back. Things are out of my control, Diana. I . . . I don't know who to trust. And I don't know who I am anymore. Maybe one day I can become the person you thought I was. But as I stand alone and look at the moon, I just feel so lost."

I pushed stop.

"Leo, are you a camel?" Crane shouted. "How long can it possibly take to urinate?"

"Coming, Uncle Crane!"

I stuffed the recorder back in my pocket and ran back. Crane was impatiently tapping his toe. When he saw me, he picked up his gear and started to walk in the direction of the mountains.

"Wait a minute," Hollis said. "Aren't we going to send back some medicine to Dr. Reed? She's really sick."

Crane stopped dead in his tracks. "Oh, of course, I almost forgot. Klevko, bring my ditty case."

Klevko brought out a ditty case filled with about twenty different pill bottles. Crane searched them all, found one, dumped out the pills, and quickly placed two new ones in the empty bottle. I could barely see his hands, but I noticed the pills looked a lot like Tic Tacs.

"Dmitri," Crane said, "Run up to the longhouse and deliver these pills to Dr. Reed. Make it snappy."

"Right away, boss," Dmitri said, and took off. I jogged after him.

"Wait up, Dmitri," I called. When I caught up to him, I slipped the mini-cassette recorder into his hands.

"Give this to Diana," I told him, "and tell her it's from the lion. I'd consider it a personal favor, Dmitri."

"What if I don't want to?"

"I'd hate to have to tell Crane about what's in that special duffel you keep hiding from him," I answered. "You know how *annoyed* he gets when people double-cross him."

Dmitri nodded. Like all crooks, he knew when to fold.

"No problem, Leo," he said. "I'll see that she gets it. You can trust me."

Dmitri took off for the longhouse, and I returned to our rendezvous point where Crane was giving Hollis a pep talk on our midnight stroll.

"We're going to use this opportunity to do some real archeology, Hollis. Leo, how long do you suppose the hike will be?"

"Close to seven hours," I said, remembering that in my dad's travel journal, the villagers had started their death ceremony at 8:45, and didn't finish till nearly four in the morning.

"Seven hours?! We're going to the Land of the Dead, aren't we? That underground place the chief talked about? Well, I don't want to go there. I'm not going."

"Hollis, we are no longer wanted back in the longhouse," Crane said. "And you cannot stay here alone. There's no choice but to come with us, Hollis, with your family."

"It'll be okay, Hollis," I said. "We're just trying to find a cave, that's all. A regular, normal underground cave."

"I heard the chief describing those underground tunnels. They didn't seem normal to me."

"This is going to be fine, chief."

"Stop calling me that, Leo! I'm sick of it. Just call me Hollis. I'm sick of all your dumb nicknames, trying to calm me down so you can drag me around on this pointless trip. Just call me Hollis."

"Keep it down, boys," Crane said. "I see Dmitri on the way back. As soon as he returns, we set off. While we walk, Hollis, I'll tell you all about this mask and the precious jewels that were hidden inside it."

"Jewels?" Hollis raised his eyebrows.

"Diamonds. And more. Now, I've gotten two of the villagers to come with us and serve as guides, while the other three stay behind us and cover our trail. Dr. Haga, introduce them, if you will."

"This is Aru and Dosa."

Both of them had their new knives tucked in their belts. Aru was the kid, probably about my age, though up close, I saw how muscular he was.

"Leo, would you take the lead?" Crane asked. "Perhaps you'd like to just hold the mask before we set out? Do you think that's a good idea, Mr. Singh?"

"I don't think it's necessary," Mr. Singh said. "I believe Leo knows the way."

When Dmitri returned, we began our expedition. I turned to the craggy mountain ridge above us and put one foot in front of the other. I really had no clue where I was going. I just knew that we needed to get over the steep mountain ridge ahead of us, which was at least four thousand feet high, and find the river on the other side. And maybe once we crossed that river, the Land of the Dead's location would seem obvious to me. I could always sound bend the mask to see if it would provide me any clues, but now that I knew its history, I was afraid of messing with its power.

I was surprised that Mr. Singh was able to keep up with us as we started the uphill climb. The terrain was gray and bleak, and steam rose off the rocky ground. The stars overhead were bright and pristine, but I didn't feel like looking at them. We kept an easy pace, though Hollis trailed toward the back with his head down, and I noticed that he'd found some black soot to rub on his forehead. I felt good walking. It was hard to believe that I had made it all the way across the world, and that we were finally on our way. The path narrowed ahead of us.

We entered a faint zigzagging path through towering boulders. The trail was steep. I fell in step next to Mr. Singh.

"So can you see ahead?" I asked him.

"A dim picture, perhaps," he said. "Though I seek the mask, I am less entangled with it than you. For you, it is personal. For me, well, I have my reasons. Your display of blind sight powers on the river was impressive, Leo. But my eyes are old. I no longer have the vision of a young person."

"What kind of special powers do you have?"

"You would not believe me if I told you."

"Maybe not, but you can tell me anyway."

He nodded. "No doubt you noticed I have developed an injury to my leg while we have been on the river. And yet if you were to examine my leg, you would find nothing wrong with it."

"So that's your power. You can heal yourself?"

"No. I received the injury in Mumbai, more than two thousand miles away. My mother is quite ill, and I paid her a visit the other night."

"Are you saying you can be in two places at once?"

"Yes," he whispered. "I can bilocate."

"Unbelievable! Why don't you bilocate over the mountain and wait for us there?"

"As I said before," his voice barely audible and weak, "I am not personally entangled with the mask. Further, I am expending all of my mental energy on keeping up. Now, no more questions. I must preserve my strength for later."

I couldn't wait to tell Trevor all about Mr. Singh. He would have a million questions for him. I had a million more questions as well. He was a real master of psychic powers. If there was a whole universe outside of our five senses, then I would have no better guide. As I gazed at the cloud-covered summit above us, I knew we were going the right way. I knew that on the other side, we'd find the Land of the Dead and the lost half of the twin mask. I felt it in my bones: I'd been there before.

CHAPTER 25

After several hours, we made it to the summit and looked down into the bleak moonlit valley on the other side. From our ridge, I could see the small river ahead of us running horizontally across the gorge, but I didn't hear any moving water.

"There's the river, Leo," Crane said, gripping my shoulder. "You've led us right to it. And on the other side, the object of our obsession. A truly remarkable gift. And it's all mine."

"Huh?"

"The mask, Leo, the mask. Soon it will be mine."

We started downhill, making steady progress. On the walk up, Hollis had befriended Aru — the villager just older than me — and I heard him trying to teach Aru to sing as they sidestepped down the loose rocks. He was having no luck. I remembered how my dad had written that the villagers of Byong Ku never sang, their only music was the grisly death dance, which they claimed not even to remember. Hollis was trying to teach Aru to sing "You Are My Sunshine." He'd sing a line, then wait for Aru to mimic it, but he couldn't do it.

Eventually Hollis switched to just the melody, humming it. I heard my mom in his voice. She had sung us that song every night, but she never sang the lyrics to the second verse, the one where the guy wakes up to find his sunshine is gone so he hangs his head and cries. She always just hummed that verse. It was funny—both she and Hollis were born with the same amazing musical gift, but neither of them could sing on key. As I listened to Hollis humming the notes exactly as my mom had, I wished that she had taught us the lyrics to that second verse. It might have prepared us better for the challenges we had to face.

We reached the river within an hour. It appeared stagnant, muddy, and sickly green in the dim moonlight. Mr. Singh stuck his cane into it, claiming it to be rather shallow, but when he pulled the cane out, the bottom two feet were caked in gooey mustard-colored ooze. There was no bamboo bridge crossing this river, no signs of human life at all. Crane sent Aru and Dosa to try to find a passable stretch. We waited, breathing in its putrid rotten-egg smell.

"Once we cross the river, Hollis," Crane said to him, "I'll tell you more about the mask and why it might very well change our whole view of history."

Hollis was more concerned about the immediate future.

"We're walking through that mung?" he said. "Count me out."

"I've sent who's-it and what's-his-name to locate a suitable shallow spot to wade across," Crane answered. "But trust me, Hollis. If you truly understood what awaits us on the other side, you'd put your head under and swim across this instant."

"No way. The mud on Mr. Singh's cane looked like baby poop, and the water smells like a hospital Dumpster. And what if there're snakes in there or blood-sucking leeches or some sort of jungle parasite no one even knows about?"

"You are going to have to work on your negativity, Hollis," Crane sighed. "Your brother will go first."

"Me?" I didn't like the look of that foul water any more than Hollis did.

"Who else, Leo? I believe you signed a contract saying you would 'prove instrumental in recovering the missing half of the mask.' Wasn't that the phrase?"

Man, Crane knew the contract by heart.

Aru and Dosa returned and reported to have found one spot that they predicted would only rise to the knees. We followed them to the shallow part of the river where billows of steam were belching up from the stinking, foamy water. The river smelled absolutely putrid — it didn't seem like the water had moved for years. I secured my gear in my backpack, tightening the straps all the way until it was hugging my shoulders, stuffed two shreds of old napkin up my nostrils, and wrapped my bandana around my face, skintight. Then I picked up a walking stick, dipped it into the water until it reached the mushy ground, and limped like Mr. Singh into the river.

The warm water instantly seeped through my safari pants, and when my foot hit the ground, it sunk several inches deep into the squishy mud. Leaning heavily on my staff, I brought my other foot in and started across. I could feel the river bottom sucking against my shoe as I tried to lift my leg. It was about forty feet to the other side, and though each step brought a feeling of utter disgust, I eventually made it without getting bitten by a snake or falling into the slimy liquid.

I took off my mud-caked, stinking shoes and socks, and waited. Everyone followed, one at a time, each groaning and complaining and gagging from the hideous stench—everyone except Dmitri and Klevko, who thought it was funny to splash each other. As Hollis came across, he took off his shoes, plopped down next to me, and wallowed in the misery of having forded the most disgusting body of water on Earth.

Klevko opened Crane's collapsible stool, and Crane took a seat while Klevko cleaned his shoes and socks. With his legs spread wide and pants rolled up, his bare disgusting feet and hairless white calves almost glowed in the moonlight. Hollis and I sat with him as he spread out some packets of veal jerky and exotic nuts, and poured us some hot cider from his thermos. The rest of the crew was still wallowing, but Mr. Singh was up and walking haphazardly across the almost Martian terrain. He was limping again with his cane, but every few seconds he would stop, tap the cane on the ground a few times, pause, and then continue on. He was a white speck in the distance, the steam between us making him seem to go in and out of focus.

"What's Mr. Singh doing?" I asked Crane.

"He's tapping the ground with his cane, trying to detect any cavernous regions beneath our feet. Go catch up with him while Klevko tends to my shoes and feet."

"Come on, chief—I mean, Hollis, let's see what Mr. Singh's up to."

I got up and headed over to Mr. Singh. Hollis followed me for just a little bit, then stopped in his tracks.

"I don't want to, Leo," he said. "I'm really worried about Dr. Reed. Maybe we should head back and see if she's okay. Maybe she has some exotic stomach virus or something— she could be dying, Leo."

"She's not dying, she just ate something rotten. Bad river fish or something."

"But maybe we should check on her anyway—I think it'd be easy to find our way back."

"There's no going back."

"I don't want to go any nearer to the Land of the Dead. What if it's like that cave? Or worse? I should never have gone in there. A *toh* followed me from that cave, and it's cursing us. What if I didn't make the black sooty mark right? What if—"

"Hollis, stop."

"No. What if the *toh* follows me home? What if we go to the Land of the Dead, and even worse *tohs* are there? Mom and Dad are just *tohs* now. They don't have bones or a coffin. What if they've just transformed into evil *tohs* and are going to follow us our whole lives? What if you get hurt—"

"There's no going back," I said as Hollis's forehead scrunched up.

"Why?" he said.

"Because," I blurted out, "because if I go back then there's no fact-finding mission to Antarctica."

"Leo? What are you talking about?"

"Mom and Dad aren't *tohs*, Hollis. I have to get that mask to prove it to you."

"Then where are they? Where are their bones?"

"I don't know where they are, but I think they're alive. I heard something on that card in Jeremy's record shop, the one from the Belgian diplomat. None of it makes sense yet, but if I help Crane find the mask, then he's going to fund a fact-finding mission to Antarctica. A hundred-thousand-dollar fact-finding mission. And then maybe we can learn what really happened to Mom and Dad and get to the bottom of this, once and for all."

"What?"

"You heard me, Hollis. Now pull it together."

"I don't believe you, Leo."

"Ask Crane. Go ahead, he'll confirm I'm telling the truth. I have a signed contract with him. Hollis, listen to me, I think there's a chance Mom and Dad might still be alive.

You can come with me or not, but I'm going after Mr. Singh. I'm going to the Land of the Dead. I'm going to find that mask, and I'm going to bring our parents back."

My heart was beating out of my chest, about to explode as I sprinted after Mr. Singh's blurry silhouette in the distance, without even putting my shoes back on. The soles of my feet stung on the rocks, but I didn't care. I just wanted to run. Run anywhere. Run away. Run away from it all. Sweat was pouring down my face.

Right before I reached Mr. Singh, he hoisted his knotted old cane into the air and twirled it.

"Mr. Singh!" I cried. "Have you found something? You've found it? I know you did!"

I ran all the way over to him, and when I stopped, pain seared across my chest and I bent over, coughing hoarsely until I caught my breath.

"Leo, your feet!" Mr. Singh gasped, the first hint of emotion I'd ever heard in his voice.

My bare feet were streaked in blood. That's when it started to hurt. I sat down on the hard rocky ground and stared at my soles. They were grated with hundreds of cuts. Some were minor scratches, but some were worse looking.

"Your feet are badly damaged," Mr. Singh said, taking off his thin outer jacket and handing it to me. "Are you in pain?"

"Yeah, but I don't care," I said. I took my kirpan dagger out of my backpack and sliced up the coat into shreds, then wrapped the bandages around my feet, adding more and more layers to soak up the blood.

"Apply pressure," he said, removing his laces from his shoes. "Wrap them tight."

"You found the entrance?"

"Leo concentrate on —"

"On what, the pain? No. Did you find the entrance to the underground?"

"Much of the surrounding area appears to be cavernous, hollow. There is a crevice over by those shrubs," he said. "If you listen, you can hear the water trickling down."

"I hear it," I said. I bounced to my feet and gasped in pain. "I need to get down there, now."

I walked to the shrubs and saw a small crevice in the earth, a thin black crescent in the brown rocks. It was a narrow fissure — only a kid could fit. I took a few pebbles and chucked them in. They took much longer than I expected to reach the ground, and their echoes were deep and hollow.

"This is it," I said to Mr. Singh.

He nodded.

"Okay, I'm going in," I said, sitting on the edge of the crevice and dangling my legs inside. I couldn't see the bottom.

"Leo, even if you had blind sight, you'd be foolish not to prepare for the darkness," Mr. Singh said. He scooped a huge handful of gravel and placed it in my hand. "Leave a trail so you may find your way back." I shoved the gravel in my pockets as Mr. Singh placed his flashlight in my bag and extra water.

I slid myself down even farther, my legs fully below ground, my feet searching for a ledge. As I began to lower my torso in, I stopped and looked at Mr. Singh. "You'll tell them I went in already?"

"Yes. Now remember, Leo. All is Mind," he said, and placed his finger to my forehead, between my eyes. "I'll be watching you."

Before I could lower myself in, though, a booming voice echoed in the darkness.

"You've found it!" Crane's voice filled the air. I pivoted to see Crane and the rest of his shadow crew jogging up to us. "I knew it, I knew it. What a remarkable team we make, eh? They'll never doubt me again."

I didn't want to talk with Crane. I just wanted to get down there and find the mask. I lowered my feet farther in, searching for a ledge.

"Now wait a minute, Leo," Crane gasped. "Don't be rash."

"Don't tell me what to do, Crane," I barked, pivoting aggressively, but my weight shifted, and I lost my grip on the ledge. I started to slide, losing traction with the stone, my hands scraping against rough edges. My trembling arms were the only things holding me above ground.

"Leo," Crane cried as I scrambled madly for a ledge in the darkness. There was none. My muscles were burning; my elbows felt about to rupture. I stared into the depths below, and felt its pull.

I let go of the surface of the world and slipped into the darkness.

CHAPTER 26

fell down the narrow shaft, my hands and legs skidding and scraping along the rocky cavern walls, until my backpack broke my fall. As I landed, I heard something crunch. I thought I'd broken my tailbone. In the darkness, I patted my body checking for damage. There were a few scrapes on my hands and forearms, but nothing major. No fresh gaping wounds. I could move all of my appendages. Above me, I heard everyone screaming into the dark hole.

"I'm okay," I called up. "I'm not hurt."

"Just stay where you are, Leo," Crane said. "We'll get you out."

"I will."

I groped through my backpack for my flashlights. The first one I found rattled when I pulled it out. As I clutched it, I felt pointy broken plastic. I tried the power switch, but it was busted to pieces. The other flashlight, my Mini

Maglite, was undamaged and functional. I turned it on and shined it up the shaft to let them know I had light. But looking up the shaft was a depressing sight. In the light, I could see that there was no way to get up on my own — no ledges or footholds, only smooth rock. It was at least twenty feet up.

"Tell Hollis I'm okay," I shouted, my voice echoing wildly.

"He's not here, Leo," Dr. Haga shouted down. "He was with us only a few minutes ago. He couldn't have gotten far."

"What? You've got to find him!" I shouted.

"I'll have Kavi and Cyril track him," Dr. Haga answered. "They'll have no problem finding him."

"Leo!" This time the voice was Crane's. "You just worry about your own neck. We'll take care of Hollis. Now, Dr. Haga, which of your men has the rope?"

"The rope? No one. I did not know we would be spelunking."

"Excuses, excuses. A rope is an essential tool in adventuring. And don't your men know how to make all sorts of items out of plants and trees? They can certainly fashion a rope in no time."

"I do not see any trees, do you, Mr. Rathbone?"

"Irrelevant! Irreleva—"

"Just find Hollis," I shouted. "You can get the rope later."

Tired of listening to the surface folk argue, I shined the light on my surroundings. I was in a large cavern, a real cave like you'd see in a National Geographic special. Long, fang-shaped stalactites hung from an arching ceiling with equally impressive stalagmites reaching up from the ground to meet them. The cave must have been around for thousands, if not millions, of years to produce such immense structures from just dripping water. I was in a big chamber, but I guessed there were many other chambers in the cave, because I could hear air flowing through them.

"I'm going to have a look around," I called up. "Maybe there's another way out."

I followed my ears toward the sound of slight hissing. At one point, I stopped and reached out to grasp several different stalagmites to try to channel them, but with no luck. All I heard was silence and the distant *whoosh* of air circulating in the underground rooms. The rock walls were light and beige, possibly limestone, I thought.

As I reached the far end of the chamber, the ceiling got lower until it was just a few inches higher than my head. The great room narrowed into a tunnel that appeared no wider than a one-yard fissure in the rock. I poked my head inside and shined my flashlight down the corridor, which became narrower. Right by the entrance to the corridor, I was surprised to see some drawings on the walls of the tunnel. They weren't elaborate murals of bison or anything, just some black geometrical shapes and patterns that looked like the tribal tattoos I'd seen throughout my stay. People had been in this cave.

"There's some paintings on one of the walls," I shouted up. "Basic shapes and designs."

"I'm impressed with your fieldwork, Leo," Crane shouted down. "But please stay put. We're working on a solution."

"You find Hollis?"

"Not yet."

I could still hear the faint hissing of air coming from the fissure ahead. I took a sniff and shined my light down the narrow sliver. The air smelled fresh, and the tunnel appeared to extend for quite a while.

"I'm going to press farther in," I shouted up. "This looks promising."

I squeezed myself into the narrow tunnel, walking lightly on uneven ground. After I had gone about twenty feet, I realized that I hadn't laid down a gravel trail. That was no problem. I would start once I got to the next chamber. As the corridor narrowed considerably, I had to turn sideways to go forward. I held my arms winglike along the walls, nudging my backpack forward on the ground with each step. I was starting to sweat, both from the heat and my nerves. I'd never been claustrophobic before, but suddenly I found myself considering such thoughts as, *What if the ceiling collapses?* or *What if I get wedged in and am unable to free myself?* I was finding it difficult to breathe, afraid I might black out at any minute.

Just when it felt like the corridor would keep narrowing until it squeezed me into a sheet of paper, it widened slightly and opened up into another chamber, and I tumbled out and into a big empty room. As I looked around, I realized this chamber was not normal. There were no stalactites or stalagmites, nor were the walls uneven. No, this room had been carved out—the brown rock walls were covered with little notches, the evidence of tools and human hands. Human hands made this room, there was no doubt about it.

On the opposite side of the room, on the far wall, there was a wide opening with an arched ceiling, opening onto a tunnel that extended into the distance, until it split in two. And right by that opening there was a giant stone disc leaning against the stone wall, some sort of barricade or door that had been rolled aside. I ran my hands along the rough textured walls but heard nothing. That didn't matter. People had actually made this. Maybe there was something to crazy Marie's ideas? Maybe the tunnel led to the center of the Earth? Could this be evidence of the immortal Boskops?

"I've made an amazing discovery!" I called into the narrow crevice, my voice wildly distorted and echoing. My voice sounded older, deeper, bigger. "I'm going farther inside."

"Come back," I heard faintly from the crevice, just an echoing whisper of Crane's voice.

But I didn't listen. How could I? I headed down the brown rock tunnel, its arched ceiling only six inches taller than me. Maybe, I thought, maybe if I kept going and went deep enough, I'd find some of those immortal Boskops people, or maybe even the dead souls hammering away for eternity. Who really knew?

I took the left-hand tunnel and began laying down my gravel trail as I crept ahead. This tunnel sloped downward and led to successively narrower tunnels that veered left, then veered right, then sloped down again. To my surprise, the end of the tunnel opened up into a small room, a kind of hub, and from there, at least ten more tunnels radiated outward like bicycle spokes. I couldn't believe it. This place was immense.

Immense and completely empty. There was nothing on the ground, no art on the walls, no signs of humans at all—except that this tunnel system was clearly built by humans . . . or humanlike beings. In one of the later chapters of Marie's book, she'd channeled a Boskops named Pastor, who told her that the interior of the Earth was like a honeycomb, filled with numerous empty chambers, home to the immortal Boskops, who created their surroundings through mind power. Maybe there were invisible Boskops all around me, and while I just saw empty tunnels, they saw beautiful forest trails.

"It's absolutely amazing down here," I screamed, but only heard my faint voice echo back to me from twelve different tunnels.

I chose a tunnel that sloped downward the sharpest and followed it. It led steeply downhill past more branching tunnels. I knew I was at least fifty, if not a hundred feet below the surface, but the air was still somewhat fresh, and the heat manageable. But I wanted to get deeper. Every time I saw a steep downward tunnel, I took it. I lost count of how many times I'd veered. Somewhere along the path I ran out of gravel, but I didn't care. Something else had attracted my attention—little circular stone knobs, ranging from the size of a small fist to a big dinner plate—that were carved from the rock and lined up every fifty feet or so along the tunnel. Maybe they were some sort of language or code? I tried to channel them, but got nothing. They were puzzling, but intriguing. Another thing puzzled me, too. None of the tunnels were more than four or five inches higher than the top of my head, and I'm only four feet, eleven-and-a-half inches.

The next tunnel opened up into an underground room about fifteen feet high and twenty feet wide, a room much different than the others. As I looked around, I immediately noticed that the ceiling was covered with large patches of a tarry black substance, indistinct and blending into the rocks, almost caked on. Exploring the chamber, I soon discovered that there were also about ten patches of that same tarry substance on the ground, all of them right underneath the ones on the ceiling. Was it some sort of mold? Or weird bacteria colonies? I touched one on the ground. It felt a lot like soot, really old soot, but definitely soot. Those were spots of old fire hearths! Next to one of them I found a small stone shaped like a triangle, with edges so sharp they nearly cut my skin. It appeared to be a spear tip, and it looked straight out of the Stone Age.

Going around to all the ancient hearths, I found six more stone spear tips, dozens of other strangely carved rocks that were clearly tools of some kind, bone fragments from small animals, and three teeth. The teeth were molars — human molars. It didn't make sense. Were these the remains of this underground city's builders? Or were those the remains of squatters who had chanced upon this underground Boskops city one day and decided to make it their home?

I didn't like this—the air was beginning to feel close and stifling. I realized I had reached the lowest level of the cave. There were no more tunnels branching off from this chamber. At the far end, there was another giant stone disc.

I stood and looked around this room that had once been the living room of another civilization. Why was it here? Who had built it? Had its inhabitants been evil *tohs* or Doh Tenangan's slaves or alien Boskops? Was I really in the Land of the Dead?

As I looked at the giant stone disc that guarded the final leg of my journey, I knew that behind that barrier, I'd find the truth.

CHAPTER 27

couldn't imagine how much the stone disc weighed, but there was no way I would be able to budge it with just my arms. I set my backpack and flashlight down and pushed with my whole body into it, but it didn't move. I leaned my back against it and pushed until my muscles trembled and stung.

"Come on you worthless rock, move!" I cried, and smacked it with my fist. "Get out of my way!"

I growled, put my head down, and charged, lunging at it with my shoulder. My feet slid back against the wall, and I anchored them — bloody and bandaged as they were — trying to lift myself off the ground with my knees bent, ready to fly open like a spring. I screamed with all my power, in pain, in anger, in fear. With rage — no stone was going to stop me. I pushed and screamed until my world shook. I felt the rock budge and heard it creak on the floor and slide a few inches until it wobbled. Then, with a slow-motion eeriness, it tipped over and slammed onto the rocky ground with a crack so booming it vibrated my skull.

Dust from the rock floor rose into the ray of light from my flashlight. A dark chamber awaited me. I grabbed my flashlight and went in.

The room smelled of an ancient decay, musty and stale. My thin beam of light bounced around, illuminating snatches of rock walls and the ceilings. It was another chamber, much smaller than the one before it, and it was a dead end.

As I shined my light toward the floor, I saw a thin curving form as wide as a stick, with a yellowish hue and a jagged edge. I moved the beam along it, until I realized it was emerging from a rib cage. The rib cage connected to a shattered skull. A skeleton! I waved the flashlight around and saw that skeletons covered the entire chamber in a complex lattice of bones three feet high. A shattered femur here, a mangled hand there, a fragment of a skull with its hollow eye cavity staring at me. They were human bones.

It didn't take an archeologist to know that I had stumbled onto a huge find, an amazing site that would require years of tedious digging, sorting, and cataloging, and that I should leave it exactly as it was to let the professionals do their work. But I had to know more. Stepping carefully through the web of bones, I inched my way to the complete skull nearest to me and examined it carefully.

It was a human skull, certainly, but it was strange. For one thing, it seemed way too small. And its shape was weird, too. It had really wide teeth and a brow that was thick and ridged. Its forehead was nearly nonexistent. It was human, but not. It seemed old, very old. Primitive. Were these the subhumans of the chief's story? I kept trying to find a place for these skulls in my brain, a name to call them. But they were completely unknown, and that was terrifying.

I tiptoed toward another skull with half its forehead shattered, but as I bent to pick it up, I stepped on a sharp edge and fell back on the bones, dropping my flashlight. It landed in a shattered rib cage, and the beam of light shined to a point high up the far wall. As I followed its beam to a spot near the cave ceiling, I noticed dozens of little specks of light, glittering red and green and blue.

I picked up the flashlight and shined it directly onto them. There, staring down at me from high up the cave wall, was the lost half of the conjoined-twin mask. It was solidly lodged into a crevice in the rocks.

The mask watched over this room from upside down. Even so, I recognized it instantly. It matched Crane's in almost every way. It had the same alexandrite teeth that reflected rainbow-colored rays of light. The same glowing wood and batlike ears. The same golden eyes and diamond pupils.

I fell back against the bones and started to laugh — uncontrollable laughter, ringing off the walls.

"I found it!" I screamed, and clapped my hands. "Hollis, I found it! You hear me, Hollis, I did it. I really did it. I'm going to bring them home, you'll see. You'll see!"

The mask was at least ten feet off the ground, watching over the bones as if it really were Doh Tenangan, guardian of the Land of the Dead. I gazed at it and wondered how I could get it down. There were a few ledges and craggy holds where I might be able to climb and get within arms' reach of it.

"Now you're mine, god of death. I own you," I proclaimed to the silence.

And when I would hold it in my hands, maybe I wouldn't let it go. Maybe I would tell Crane that I hadn't found it, and keep it for myself, then sell it for millions. After all, he'd stolen the other half from Dad. It had belonged to my dad, and now this one would belong to me.

I'd have more than enough money to launch my own mission and find Mom and Dad, wherever they might be . . . even if they were beyond the grave. I had a gift, and I could use my gift to build a real Spiricom device, not like that phony one on the record. And if Trevor didn't want to help me build it, I'd do it myself, even if it took years. If I ran out of money, I could use my power to find other precious artifacts . . . and sell them.

I pushed a heap of the bones into a pile against the wall, put my Maglite in my pants pocket and the Sikh kirpan in my belt. Balancing on the pile, I climbed toward the mask, holding on to jagged pieces of rock. With one foot and one hand wedged into a thin seam in the rock, the other foot dangling seven feet above the ground, I leaned toward the mask and tried to grab it. It was just out of my reach.

I slipped the kirpan from my belt, thinking I could pry the mask loose with the edge of the blade. I reached out with the dagger, but the mask was fixed solidly to its spot. It seemed to be jammed into a natural fissure in the rock layer. If I could drive the blade into the sliver between the mask and the rock wall, perhaps I could jimmy it out. I held the dagger with my chin pressed against my chest and put the flashlight in my mouth. This was going to be an awkward procedure, trying to jimmy the mask out while suspended in the air.

I started in, using the beautiful Sikh kirpan as a crow-bar. My jaw was tight from holding the flashlight, and I was already feeling my leg begin to cramp up. Only a little tip of the blade had worked its way behind the mask so I jammed it in farther, making throaty grunting sounds. As I drove more of the knife in, I leaned farther over the cave floor, my left arm shaking, my calf seizing up in spasms.

Come out already, you stupid jungle mask, I thought. I came halfway around the world for you. Left my kid brother out there alone, roaming the Land of the Dead, who knows where. I pushed away Trevor and Jeremy, my two best friends, and even the new friend I'd made, just for you. Because you called me here. You wanted me to find you. I'm going to hold you in my hands.

I tightened my grip on the hilt of the dagger and pried hard, but the mask felt like it was never going to come loose. I was filled with rage, realizing all I had given up just to come to this moment of frustration and failure. I needed to focus. Hadn't Singh told me it's all in the Mind?

I took several deep trembling breaths and rolled all my hate and rage into one convulsive spasm, screaming so hard my throat burned. Pivoting with everything I had, I felt the mask pop out, the dagger fly from my hand, and my feet slip from their hold. I was falling to the floor. I heard the blade and the flashlight hit the ground. With magnetic force, my hands grasped the mask as it tumbled through the darkness, and I held on with a dead man's grip.

I fell into an instant trance. The world melted away and I felt myself falling, falling through the center of the world, sinking away into nothing. Swallowed whole into a blackness that was infinitely deep. The darkness without shadow. The drums blared around me. I recognized them from that night in Crane's office. Pulsing, the metal clangs echoed through the darkness, the souls of the dead toiling away for all eternity as they hammered their walls and built their tunnels. I felt the drumming worm its way inside me, burning away all of my memories, all sense of who I had once been until I was no longer a person, and I knew a silence worse than eternal toil. I wasn't even an animal. There was no I . . . I was nothing.

I opened my eyes just as I saw the dark floor approaching. I let go of the mask and broke my fall with my hand, feeling it bend backward as I crashed down on top of it until I heard a nauseating pop. A wave of sparks flared in my eyes — but this was no sound-bending trance, this was the real world again, and this was pain. A searing white-hot pain.

I was in complete darkness — the flashlight had shattered. The pain in my hand and wrist was immense, so sharp I couldn't even breathe. I tried to hold my hand in front of my face to see the damage. But I had no sight, just pain and blackness and the sounds of my screaming.

I felt tears streaming down my cheeks.

"Help me!" I cried. "Please someone help me!"

But there was no one to hear me but Doh Tenangan, the silent mask of death.

I lay on my back and cried my eyes out. All I felt was pain and confusion and fear. Maybe if I kept crying someone from up above would hear me and help. Or maybe one of the Boskops would materialize. No, even in my pain I knew there were no immortal Boskops beneath the earth . . . only bones.

I concentrated on the pain and tried to use it to call out to Mr. Singh, so he'd bilocate down here and rescue me. But he didn't hear me; there was no one on the receiving end. I yelled for help until my throat was on fire. No one up there would ever hear me. In that complete darkness, I hardly believed there was a world up there. I hardly even believed I was real.

I was absolutely alone.

When the pain became a step below excruciating, I got to my knees and groveled around the bone-filled floor for my possessions, holding my injured arm motionless against my chest. I found my flashlight, but it was worthless. The glass had shattered, and the batteries had popped out. I found the kirpan and the mask and put them in my backpack, along with the remnants of my flashlight.

Hearing nothing but my trembling breathing, I groped my way out of the bone room. Every time I even grazed my hand along the wall, the pain was so intense that I would shriek and hear my gravelly voice come echoing back to me. My hand was throbbing. It felt as if it were the size of my head. At least two of my fingers were broken, maybe more. I'd done real damage.

I found my way to the room with the fire pits, then squeezed through the small arching tunnel, hugging the wall, until I entered one of the hub rooms. I leaned back against one of the smooth walls and held my wrist close to my chest. I could find no trace of my gravel trail, and I knew I'd never get out of this underground maze. I couldn't even see. It was all so unreal.

How did I get here? My thoughts raced to that morning when Hollis came bursting into my room, and the terrible news story that had started everything. The split between Hollis and me, that fifty-cent piece from Crane, the emergence of a darker form of my sound-bending power. I felt a surge of anger — at Crane, at my parents, at Mr. Dickerson and those punk kids at school, at everyone trying to push me around. It had all overwhelmed me until I found a shred of hope in the note I channeled from the Belgian diplomat. And from that moment, I became driven. So driven that I'd signed a shady deal with Crane, traveled halfway across the world to find the mask . . . and that had led me here, to this moment — to pain, to darkness, to isolation.

I'd been certain that finding this mask would make everything better, but now that I had it in my possession, I felt nothing but emptiness. I'd lost everything to hold it. I'd signed away my life to Crane, to someone who stole and bribed and did anything to get what he wanted. I'd put my faith in Mr. Singh, hoping he could guide me through the mysteries, but he was a complete fraud. Nothing that reincarnation of crazy Marie had whispered was true. What was real? Who had I become?

I was the person who'd signed that shady midnight deal with Crane, the signature on that blank page next to my blood. Just to chase after nothing. I was like that Belgian diplomat Bertrand Veirhelst, hollow as a drum. I'd brought a blank journal to Borneo, so when I re-created my dad's trip down the Kayan River, I could record every thought I had, just like him. But I'd been so busy reading crazy Marie's book of lies that I hadn't written a single word. I was a big nothing.

I touched my backpack and felt the mask inside my bag, and I couldn't help laughing. I'd searched so hard for that stupid thing, when I'd hardly even looked for that blue Audograph disc from my dad with my naming ceremony on it. That unbelievably special record that opened my ears and told me who I really was, I'd just glanced around my room for it like it was a missing dollar bill. It was special beyond meaning. There was only one record like it, the only one in the entire universe.

Two days before, I'd made a real connection with a real friend. With this amazingly sweet person, this lonely, weird girl, and together we'd watched the stars and had the whole universe to ourselves. I'd met someone who really saw me, who I could be completely myself with. Someone who I even told about that figure of light, my true sound-bender self. The figure who appeared in that dark dream and told me:

In the darkness there is more than enough light, but it is hidden deep within Mother Night.

As the words echoed over and over in my mind I longed to relive that night under the stars. I laid down on my back, closed my eyes, and imagined she were right next to me. The stars glittered on my inner eyelids, vivid and alive. And I knew then that my real guide was that figure of light — he was the light in the darkness. I promised myself that once I got back to Brooklyn, *if* I got back to Brooklyn, I would tear through Crane's warehouse until I found that blue disc. If it wasn't in the warehouse, then I'd search everywhere for it. I'd never stop searching for it.

I could see the light now. The universe was so real in my imagination that when I opened my eyes, starlike pinpricks floated above me, like a tiny patch of night sky out of the corner of my eye.

I sat upright and looked again. It wasn't imaginary. There really was an opening in the surface of the ceiling, and through it, I could see a small square of faint starlight. I got up and stood directly underneath it.

I could touch it. It was a thin shaft that stretched all the way up to the surface, and I smelled the air wafting down. It was a ventilation shaft. It stretched fifty feet up, and from underneath it, I had a window to the night sky.

Even in the Land of the Dead, I could still see the stars.

I held my hand under the shaft to check the damage, and to my surprise, it cast a faint shadow on the cave floor. I fished out my flashlight, hoping that I could see well enough now to put it back together, but when I opened my bag, the ray of starlight fell on the mask. I took it out. Its alexandrite teeth changed from red to green to blue to indigo with the slightest movement. The colors sparkled and lit the cave. All it took was just the tiniest sliver of starlight to illuminate the world again.

Unafraid, I touched the mask, letting my fingers fall on the jeweled teeth. Immediately, I was whisked away to the space. But it wasn't the same trance I'd had while I fell. Somehow, miraculously, I felt at peace. I heard the tide and felt myself drifting. Everything was okay. I heard the drums again, but not the pulsing drums of terror. I heard the sounds in a new light. The sounds came soft and steady, each beat bringing with it the sound of chimes and a splash of alexandrite color, reds and blues and indigoes as vivid as the stars I saw that night with Diana. Each drum would sound, followed by another one, and they would echo and reverberate. But there was a melody in it, like blacksmiths beating on different metals, or like hammers striking rock walls in a cave. And I could almost swear that what I heard was a type of language, communication.

A terrible shooting pain in my wrist pulled me from my trance — the mask had grazed my broken hand. I screamed but I was okay. It was just pain. It meant that I was alive, that I could feel. I'd let myself be led down here because I'd been so afraid of the pain. I would have done anything to drive that pain away, the knowledge that our parents were gone. But I knew that I could handle it now. Hollis and I would deal with it together.

I no longer believed anything Mr. Singh had told me, but if there were ever a time when normal communication was blocked and I could send a psychic message, this was it. I sent one to Diana. The message was simple: *thank you.*

My vision was beginning to adjust. I could see shapes in the starlight.

As I gazed through the ventilation shaft at the patch of stars, I could see just the slightest little halo of the moon's light. Then, I heard a rumbling overhead, the vibrations of people walking on the surface near me.

And then I heard the unmistakable voices of Dr. Reed and Diana.

"Mom, I think Leo's around here," Diana said softly. "He is! I can feel it."

They'd come!

CHAPTER 28

"Keep it down, Diana," Dr. Reed said. "Crane's people are all over here."

I called up sharply through the ventilation shaft. "Diana. Hey, Diana. Dr. Reed. Hey. Can you hear me?"

But they didn't hear me, and from their overhead rumblings, I knew they were about to pass by. I took out my Sikh blade and banged it against the inside of the shaft.

Bing . . . Bing . . . Bing . . . Bing . . .

It made a sound similar to the hammering sounds I'd heard in my sound-bending trance. Maybe what I had heard was those people communicating, using the sound of their swinging hammers to talk to one another across the underground city? Maybe, but I needed to communicate now. I wished I knew some Morse code.

I tapped louder, faster. It had to work. Come on, Diana, I thought, please listen.

Bing . . . Bing . . . Bing . . . Bing . . .

"Do you hear that, Mom? That weird ringing sound?"

Bing . . . Bing . . . Bing . . . Bing . . .

"I *do* hear something," Dr. Reed said. "I can feel it in my legs, too. It's coming from underground. How can that be?"

"I think we're right on top of it," Diana said.

"Diana! Dr. Reed!" I whispered sharply again. "Margaret!"

"Leo?" Diana said.

"Yes! It's me. I'm down here. Way below ground. Follow the ringing sound."

I kept tapping the kirpan, hearing their footsteps growing louder, until when I looked up, I saw Diana's face filling the opening.

"Leo?!"

"You came!" I hollered. "Is your mom okay? I think Crane poisoned her."

Diana's face disappeared and was replaced by Dr. Reed's.

"I'm fine," she called down. "I'm fine now. I wasn't, but I walked it off. But what are you doing down there, Leo?"

"I went to find the mask. And I found it. But I also discovered a whole underground city down here. Tunnels and tunnels. A whole labyrinth. And bones, too, ancient human bones."

"What?"

"I think they're skulls of really early humans. Is Hollis with you?"

"No, we haven't seen him," Dr. Reed said. "Did you say skulls? Not skull?"

"Yes, there's hundreds of skeletons down here."

"Hundreds?" she echoed in astonishment. "Why don't you come out of there, then?"

"Listen, I lost my flashlight, and I think I broke my wrist. I've got the mask, but I'm not giving it to Crane. I can't let him see me. Find Hollis, and I'll figure out a way out of here. Do you see Crane?"

"You broke your wrist?" Dr. Reed gasped. Then she modulated her voice into a whisper. "Wait. He's coming. Diana, stand up and move away. Pretend you were tying your shoe. We'll find Hollis, Leo."

Then Dr. Reed pulled her face away, and I heard them jogging away. I could hear some scuffling, then the far-away sound of Crane's lizardy voice.

"Well, if it isn't Diana and Dr. Reed," I heard him say. "What are you doing out here, ladies? Come here to steal my prize, eh? Well I won't let you. Meet your new best friends."

"Hey, babe," I heard Dmitri say, right above of me.

"Get off me!" Diana shrieked.

"Margaret, for the sake of my boys, I've given you a great deal of rope during this expedition," Crane said. "Now, Klevko, tie them up."

"No rope, boss."

"Use your shoelaces, then, you donkey."

"Get your hands off me!" Dr. Reed screamed.

I heard the sounds of a struggle, and Diana and her mother were led off. It took a minute for their cries and protests to stop, but they eventually did. My heart sank. I wouldn't put it past Crane to abandon them or even hurt them. He'd already poisoned Dr. Reed. I had to get to the surface and help.

Tucking my dagger into my belt and slinging on my backpack, I tried to retrace my steps. With my eyes adjusted to the darkness, I saw that every fifty to a hundred feet or so, there was a ventilation shaft that let in the faint star- and moonlight. It was just enough light to see shapes and the slope of the ground. I jogged ahead in the darkness, kicking my foot along the ground searching for my gravel trail, and sliding my hand along the wall until it bumped into a few of those knobs I'd seen earlier. Perhaps, I thought, those knobs were like little rock drums. I tapped the kirpan blade against one of the knobs, and the sound it produced was entirely like those sounds I heard when I touched the mask and not too different from the chimes from the Byong Ku death dance. I tried one of the bigger knobs.

Each differently sized knob made a beautiful ringing sound, and each note bounced off the rock walls, back and forth. And though I can't be certain, immediately after I'd tap a knob, I could see a brief flash of alexandrite color ricochet against the walls. And if I listened really deeply, I could almost feel the shape of the tunnels, like a type of radar. Between listening as deeply as I could to the reverberating tones and the faint light from the ventilation shafts, I had enough information to navigate. I could find my way out. I'm on my way, Diana.

I jogged uphill, tapping knobs and searching for starlight, and in almost no time, I picked up my gravel trail. It would lead me to the entrance. But Crane would be there. He'd be waiting. And he'd take the mask. I wasn't going to give it to him. It wasn't his, just like the other half. That wasn't his, either. It was mine. It had been my father's, and when he died, it became mine. Crane had stolen it from me, claimed it as his own, and when somehow, through a twist of fate, the mask had found its way back to its rightful owners, he'd stolen it again. That was his way.

But he wouldn't get his way this time. I had to defeat him. But he was smart, and tough. Not even Mike Hazel could get the best of him, and I'd been watching Mike Hazel take down slumlords and New York conmen for years.

The solution was suddenly simple. I had to think like Crane. What would Crane do if he were in my position? Crane used lies, deception, and misdirection. And his most effective trick was to find what you really loved and take it away from you, use it as bait against you. Make it rotten. And what did Crane love? Money . . . but above all else, his beloved mother, Marie.

The secret password to my escape, my key to the surface.

I took out my H4n from my bag, the one I'd traded Trevor and Jeremy for. I turned it on and pressed *record*, the red light steady. I spent the next few minutes leaving Crane a personal message I was sure he'd love. Then I hurried to the entrance to the underground city, the chamber just after that tiny crevice of a corridor.

"Crane! Crane! Can you hear me, Crane?!"

I heard his voice a moment later, thin and hollow.

"Leo? Where have you been? We're still working on the rope — Cyril jogged back to the village an hour —"

"Never mind the rope! I've been exploring and I've found a whole underground city down here. I've never seen anything like it. The farther down you go, the lighter it gets. You've got to get down here, now! Your mother, she was right about everything, Crane. Everything!"

His voice no longer sounded thin, but excited and intense.

"Tell me what you saw, Leo!"

"A path to the hollow Earth!" I said. "Boskops artifacts, amazing technology from the future. Just come down right now, Crane. It's so dark you're going to have to follow my voice. But the deeper you go, the lighter it gets — you won't need a flashlight. I'm serious! I can't believe it myself!"

"Did you say Boskops, Leo?"

"Yes. Just like your mother wrote. They were here."

"I'm coming right now," he panted. "Right away. And the mask? Did you find it?"

"It took me a while, but I got it. I'm holding it now, but forget the mask! This is the real deal down here. The discovery of the century, maybe of all time. Your mom got it all right. Everything. Come down now. Just follow my voice!"

"I'll be right down. Klevko, you wait here for the rope. We'll need it to pull me out. Don't stray or I'll have your hide. Okay, Leo, I'm heading down now!"

"Don't worry," I called. "The shaft will break your fall!"

I heard something big sliding down, then a hoarse groan.

"I'm on my way, Leo. I'm down. A bit rough, but no bother. No bother. No pain, no gain."

"Just follow my voice, Crane," I said, and continued saying things like that, egging him on, as I made my way into the underground city, through one labyrinth after another, until I came to a dead end. There I took out my H4n, turned up the volume all the way, and placed it in a small crevice near the ceiling. Then I pressed *play*, and set it to play an infinite loop.

"Follow my voice," the H4n blared.

I dashed back the way I'd come, following the knobs and the starlight and kicking apart my gravel trail. I made it all the way to that first tunnel, where I'd taken the first fork to the left. This time I ran the opposite way and there I waited.

"I can barely squeeze through this tunnel. Leo? Where are the artifacts?"

"You're almost there," I said. "You have to be patient. Go left at the first fork. Just follow my voice. You'll be there soon."

"Oh my goodness," Crane said, his voice really near me. "This is man-made. What treasures I'm going to find here."

He felt his way down the tunnel.

"Oh my. Oh my. Mother, you did it, Mother. I knew you were right, Mother," his voice rang out, and trailed off as Crane sprinted into the deep.

After he'd passed, I ran for the exit. When I got there, I looked up to see Klevko's puffy face staring down at me.

"Where is the boss?" he called down to me.

"He's heading to the room with all the treasures," I said. "He wants you to come down with the bags so he can carry everything. Dmitri, too. There's more than enough for everyone."

"But how will we get back up?" Klevko said. "We still have no rope. Dmitri, he is small and strong, and perhaps he can climb through. But I am a large man."

"Don't worry about it, Klevko. I'll get the rope from Cyril and we'll pull you up. Come on, you'd better hurry. I can hear him yelling now. There's a ton of gold and stuff down here."

"One minute, Leo. I will just put on my jacket."

I heard him whispering frantically to Dmitri in the same voice I'd heard in the Pomantong Cave.

"Put on your jacket like me," he whispered. "It has pockets, so we can take many things for ourselves. He must not see."

The grave robbers were at it again.

"I'm coming, Leo," Klevko called. I looked up and saw his feet dangling above me. The shaft was narrow, and it was all he could do to wedge his big belly through it. He fell the last five feet on his padded behind. Dmitri followed him down, looking like he was ready to do business.

"Which way?" he asked.

"Straight ahead," I said. "Turn left. You can't miss it. Help me out before you leave."

Klevko hoisted me up and I climbed on top of his massive shoulders. I saw an outcropping near the top that I thought I could use to pull myself to the surface. But with my broken hand, I didn't think I could do it. The pain would be unbearable.

Then I thought of Diana and Dr. Reed, tied up somewhere outside. And Hollis . . . who even knew where he might be? I took a breath and put my broken hand on the ledge, and the good one on the rocks across from it. Then I pulled the entire weight of my body up. I pulled and screamed at the same time. The pain was indescribable — like an electric shock traveling through my body. But it was brief, and in a matter of seconds, my head was poking out of the crevice. The sky to the east was slightly blue. I scrambled with my feet to get some traction against the shaft wall, kicking Klevko in the head in the process. And then I was up, stomach on the ground, slithering away from the opening.

"Go," I called down to Klevko and Dmitri. "I'll wait here."

I watched them take off down the labyrinth of tunnels, knowing that they were in for a wild goose chase.

Dr. Haga was there, staring at me. Mr. Singh was nowhere to be seen. Our villager guides were just watching. They didn't seem to know about the secret crevice, and their eyes were wide in amazement.

"Dr. Haga, can you help me find something to cover this up?" I said, pointing to the crevice.

"If you cover it up, it will be difficult for those inside to find the opening," he said.

"I know."

He smiled. "We'll use my jacket," he said, laying it down over the crevice. "Would you like my shirt, too? My pants?"

"Nah," I laughed, breathing deeply.

He said something to Kavi, and all of them burst into hysterics. Then they used their knives to slice up Crane's bag, and splayed it over the hole, tucking dirt around it so no light could get in. The sky was getting lighter blue to the east, a hint of faint purple bleeding into the night.

Beneath the still unseen sun, I saw Dr. Reed and Diana sitting back to back on the ground, their hands tied together. They were blindfolded. I recognized the eye masks from the Sultan's plane. Maybe Mr. Singh had taken a few extra.

I ran over to them, reaching them just as the first rays of the sun streaked down into the valley from behind the mountain.

"It's me," I said.

"Leo!" Diana cried.

"It's okay, now," I said, taking off their blindfolds. "You're okay."

I cut their shoelace binds with my kirpan, then hurled it away as far as I could throw with my left hand.

"I knew you could do it," Diana gasped, bounding to her feet and throwing her arms around me. And she gave me a kiss on the cheek, then turned red and rushed over to her mom to help her up.

"Sorry," Diana said, embarrassed her mom had seen everything.

"That's all right, honey," Dr. Reed said as she rubbed her wrists. "I believe anyone who finds his way out of the labyrinth and saves the girl deserves a little bit of love for his heroism."

"Are you guys okay?" I said, blushing. "Did he hurt you?"

"We're just fine, Leo," Dr. Reed said. "But what about you? Let me see that hand."

She reached out, but I recoiled, holding it against my chest.

"Don't touch it," I snapped. "I'm sorry, it just hurts a little. I have to find Hollis now."

"Hollis is back at the village," Diana said. "Aru found him and took him back. He was scared."

"But how did you know where to find me?" I asked Dr. Reed.

"It helps when you speak the language," she said. "I figured you were all heading to the Land of the Dead, and Diana here has learned a thing or two about tracking from her time in Borneo. So I guess it hasn't all been a waste, huh, sweetie?"

"Can we see Hollis now?" I asked. I needed to see him with my own eyes, to know for sure that he was unharmed.

Diana and I ran all the way there — with Dr. Reed, Dr. Haga, and the villagers following behind. On the way, we met Cyril, who was returning with the rope. Dr. Haga said something to him in their language, and Cyril just nodded and turned to follow us, bringing the rope back with him.

When we got to the village, we found Hollis sitting on the steps of the longhouse, playing a song on a nose flute with Aru and some of the village elders gathered around him. The chief was there, too, and the amazing thing was, he was singing along as Hollis played. Not in any kind of tone we might recognize. It sounded almost like those hollow chimes I had heard in my visions or on the knobs from the Land of the Dead. It wasn't Mozart or anything, but it was definitely a melody. When he saw us, he stopped singing and spoke to Dr. Reed. She smiled at him, nodded, and turned to Hollis and me.

"Laki Jau says the sons of Kirk have shown him the music," she said. "Perhaps now he can sing his ancestral songs. He thanks you."

I loosened the straps of my backpack and approached the chief.

"This is for you," I said. "I brought it back from the Land of the Dead, to replace the one my uncle has stolen from you."

I bowed and laid the backpack down at his feet. Laki Jau took it and held it up, turning it around in his hands. He didn't know what to do with it, so Hollis reached over and helped him unzip the pouch. Then he reached inside and pulled out the mask.

"You found it!" Hollis cried. "Way to go, Leo."

When Laki Jau saw the mask, he gasped. Turning it over and over in his hands, he ran his fingers over the face, touching it like the sacred object it was. He didn't linger over the diamonds and gold—they seemed no more interesting to him than the batlike ears or the carved wood.

All the villagers had gathered around by now, and he

held the mask up for them to see. Dr. Haga, who had been watching the chief from his position behind me, stepped forward. From out of his backpack, he produced a leather pouch with the initials CR embroidered in red silk thread.

"Your uncle gave this to me for safekeeping," he said to me.

Then he walked up to the chief and handed the pouch to him.

"If you would, Dr. Reed, please tell the chief this is from me, with apologies for bringing Crane Rathbone to disturb the harmony of his village," he said.

The chief looked at the leather pouch and touched the soft calfskin.

"Here, let me help you with that," Hollis said, again reaching out to unzip it so the chief could see what was inside. Hollis held the pouch open for the chief, who reached inside and pulled out the other half of the Siamese twin mask, the one Crane had stolen from them. Dr. Haga looked over at me and smiled.

"The circle is complete," he said simply.

The chief picked up the familiar mask in his free hand. It was more faded than its twin half, but in all other respects, it was completely identical. The jagged edges where the masks had once been connected seemed to match perfectly.

Laki Jau rose and held both masks over his head in the morning sun. As if drawn by a magnetic force, the two halves of the mask fused together in a perfect fit. When the chief saw this, he let out a high-pitched scream that echoed through the village. He held the conjoined masks and sang some words, in a halting and unpracticed melody.

"What's he saying?" I asked Dr. Reed.

"He says that now at last Laki Tenangan and Doh Tenangan are reunited. The twin gods can rule together, and all will be good for our people. The sons of Kirk have brought peace to our village."

The chief walked over to me and held the mask out. The eyes, all four of them, no longer seemed hollow and dark but hopeful and full of promise. I reached out and touched the sacred object, and heard its song in my secret ears — the lapping waves, the beautiful chimes, the birdsongs of Borneo. And underneath it all, I heard my father's voice repeating my name.

"Sound Bender, Sound Bender," he called.

Yes, Dad, I thought. *I'm here.*

EPILOGUE

Crane didn't die down there in the Land of the Dead. But they let him stew for a full day. When at last, Dr. Reed and a few of the villagers took pity on him and went back the next day, they found him delirious, ranting and raving in broken sentences. In a rather satisfying turn of events, Crane had contracted malaria at some point in the expedition, and the fever finally hit as he roamed the underground city, looking for the path to the center of the world. For all his bluster and power, it was a lowly mosquito that took him down.

While we waited at the village to arrange for transportation back to Samarinda, the villagers kept him in a wooden cage just outside the longhouse. He spent three days in there shivering, curled up, and yelling at everyone who passed by him. It cost Crane his watch and his diamond pinkie ring, but Klevko eventually found a longboat to take them to a town backriver, where he was airlifted to the hospital in Samarinda.

Hollis and I stayed with Dr. Reed and Diana at Byong Ku for a few more days, learning about the people and their ways, feasting and singing with them. Dr. Reed was going to stay in the area for quite a while, at least until a delegation from the local university could arrive to investigate the tunnels and the bones, which raised more questions than they answered. There are no shortcuts to knowledge, she said, and no easy answers to difficult questions. It was possible that the underground city and its bones would be a mystery for many years to come. Perhaps forever.

Diana was going to stay with her mom and help her with the investigation. But she would be back in New York in six months, though that might as well have been forever.

Dr. Reed helped Hollis and me find transportation back to Samarinda, and Dr. Haga volunteered to ride with us back to the city. We went with him to Crane's hospital, where he tried to collect the money owed to him and I had my hand checked out and put in a cast. Since it took me more than a week to get my hand treated, the doctor told me that it might never totally heal. The last time I saw Crane, he was screaming at the doctors about their pathetic lack of private rooms. Klevko was giving him a sponge bath, and Dmitri was rubbing powder on his feet. I guess that's the reward for grave robbers — that and a few gold beads.

Though he wasn't able to collect from Crane, Dr. Haga helped Hollis and me get a commercial flight back to New York. I promised to pay him back someday, somehow.

Jeremy met us at JFK Airport, waving papers he'd just received from the court that give me the right to choose my own school. We still have to live with Crane, but at least he's not back for another week. And I plan to use that time to search for my disc and to root through the crates for any more of Crane's questionable artifacts. Trevor's coming over tomorrow, and he's ready to dig in.

Hollis and I were so relieved to be back and malaria-free. The first thing he did was call all of his buddies from Secret Stairwell to set up their next band rehearsal. And the second thing he did was call Arturo from Mom's old quartet, for a lesson on the violin. Me, I went to my room, got out the blank travel journal, and wrote Diana a letter. Then I started to record my experiences from my adventure. If I am ever going to understand my power, then I've got to do a better job understanding myself.

As I sat down to write, using green ink in honor of my dad, Kirk Lomax, I noticed that my phone had four messages. Two were from Mr. Dickerson to make sure Crane hadn't called the school board, and one was from my dentist to schedule an extraction of one of my baby incisors.

But the last one, that was different. The voice was electronic, a ringing, distorted sound not unlike Dr. Bill's mechanical voice from the Spiricom record. That made it difficult to understand, as did the speaker's foreign accent. Here's what it said:

"Hello, Mr. Lomax. Do not be alarmed by my voice filter. It is a necessary precaution. As was the absurd story about my fall from a balcony some months back, but I assure you, rumors of my death were greatly exaggerated.

"I hear that you have taken up quite an interest in me. Yes? Then we have something in common, Mr. Lomax, as I would very much like to speak to you. I have pressing matters to discuss, which I cannot mention over the phone. Make no efforts to contact me, for I shall be in touch."